Sirocco Wind from the East

SIROCCO WIND

FROM THE EAST

The Keys to the Kingdom Series

Virginia Ann Work

ISBN:1-40677-779x
ISBN-13:978-1-40677-77-6 (Xulon Press)

Other Books Written by Virginia Ann Work

KEYS TO THE KINGDOM SERIES:

Sirocco Wind from the East
Mistral Wind from the North
Coming spring of 2012: Zephyr Wind from the West

***

Jodi Fischer Mystery Series for Young Adults:

The Mystery of the Missing Message (updated 2011)
The Secret of the Silver Box (updated 2011)

***

GINA LINDSEY MYSTERY SERIES FOR ADULTS:

Deadlocked (2011)

ACKNOWLEDGMENTS

I wish to thank all those who helped me in so many ways with the writing, editing and publishing of this book, and for all those who prayed for me, wept with me, and cheered me on toward publication.

I thank my wonderful husband for his help in reading this manuscript and commenting on it, for being patient when I disappeared for long periods of time in my study. Thank you, Dan, for believing in me and encouraging me to use my God-given talents. Without you I could not have done this.

I thank my children, Brian, Sherry and Vicki who also read the manuscript, believed in me, and prayed for me. Thank you, Vicki, for your help in the initial plotting stages and for your many critiques and readings.

I thank my mother for believing in me and praying for me. Mom, if you can see from Glory, I know you will be pleased.

Mostly I thank my Savior, Jesus Christ, to whom all glory and praise belong.

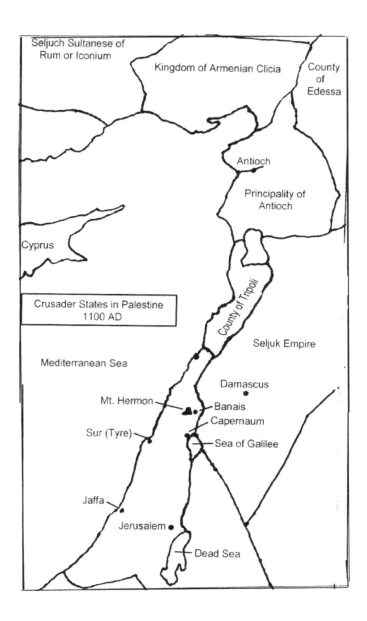

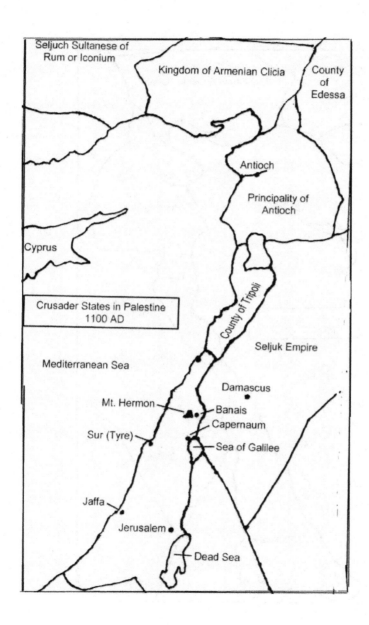

BOOK ONE

A KINGDOM LOST

The road goes ever on and on
Down from the road where it began
And I must follow if I can.
Pursuing it with eager feet
Until it joins some larger way
Where many paths and errand meet
And whither then? I cannot say. J.R.R. Tolkien,
The Fellowship of the Ring

CHAPTER ONE

Trees are not known by their leaves, nor even by their blossoms, but by their fruit. Eleanor of Aquitaine

Brittany, February 1194

A troop of armored men and horses perched atop a hill. The men raised their visors as the horses blew and stamped on the rocky ground. A smear of red, low on the horizon, heralded the coming day. Slowly, the light grew into a pale red band, spreading upward as the sun climbed the heavens.

The lord halted on the very edge of the cliff and turned his black eyes to a young knight. "Where did you say he was going, Sir Reynold?"

"I … I think they said north, my lord. He usually rides north. Along the river." Reynold shifted in the saddle, his mouth a taut line.

"Think!" The baron's roar startled the horses; some of them reared—all of them jumped. "That is not good enough, Sir Knight! If we miss the prince, you shall pay." He studied the rolling fields below and gazed at the castle spires on the horizon. "We shall angle north, and intercept his troop on the loop of the river. If he comes not, you shall pay in blood. I vow it upon my sword."

He kicked his gray roan into a startled leap down the side of the hill. Black was the pennant that flew from his lance—black with a fierce red bull upon it.

***

A boy clattered across the cobblestones of the courtyard of the ducal castle Mordelias, darting like a hare to his saddled and bridled destrier. He was tall for his age, and crowned with yellow hair that fell unhindered to his shoulders.

Grabbing a fistful of long white mane, he planted his left foot on the knee of his stallion, and vaulted into the high-backed saddle. After allowing his squire to place his feet in the stirrups, he took the reins, wondering how many other boys his age could mount alone. Kazimer, his white Andalusian stallion, had snorted and side-stepped the first time he tried his flying mount, but now he only shook his head, impatient to be off.

"That will be all," he said to the squire who bowed and backed away. The boy smoothed the bright red saddle blanket that bore a Plantagenet emblem, and pushed back his thick brocaded cape that was lined with white fur.

A low mist, like ghost shrouds, swirled along the river and a cock crowed in the lower bailey. He glanced at the sky. It was the color of robins' eggs, speckled with the flight of birds near the tree line. Not a cloud in sight; it would be a fine day, for certes.

Thirteen knights stomped from the barracks, leaped to saddle and gathered the reins their squires held without a glance in his direction. Jean, a younger man, nodded to him and smiled. The boy returned the smile, noting that he would favor Jean with a small reward when they returned.

It was an odd hour for a run, but he wanted to go and return before his lady mother discovered his intent, before she sent a command that would halt his expedition. He waited until Lord DeArmond, his teacher and mentor, appeared and mounted. DeArmond did not smile or greet him; he only grunted as he settled himself in the saddle.

The boy, Prince Arthur, son of Lord Geoffrey, lifted his right hand and led the way across the castle drawbridge. He was in a keen mood this new day and his spirited steed knew it. Kazimer raced down a small hill and thundered across a bridge spanning the river. Arthur directed him north, following a well-worn road along the river. He reined to the right, entering a dim path that led east into the forests of Brittany. Kazimer took the hills without pause, his gait never slacking.

The white mane whipping his face, Arthur lifted his free hand and laughed, feeling the surge of power and the sheer pleasure of the ride, his small body as one with the great horse beneath him.

He had planned this ride for months, cajoling DeArmond into secrecy, for he was not allowed to ride far afield. Brittany was not secure, nor were her borders watched that the eight-year-old prince could ride at will in her lands. Indeed, he had never been allowed more than ten furlongs from the castle. That was a pity. What of the wide, wide world out there, waiting to be discovered?

He glanced back and laughed again, for his knights could not keep up. Mother will have a fit of ten wet kittens when she hears I am gone. Ah, well. He would bear her indignation for the joy of the moment. Who would harm him anyway? He could think of no enemy, besides the English. But the English? Was not Uncle Richard the High King of England and half the world? He would not harm a freckle on Arthur's cheek. The French? The French would not harm him, either, for his mother was second cousin to King Philip Augustus.

The morning flew as swiftly as Kazimer's heels and after a time Arthur tired of the pace and pulled back on the reins. He looked about, realizing he had ridden farther than he thought. Aye, it was strange country. He rode in a wide valley that was ribboned with a slender river—to the right, a fen, its pools of stagnant water glittered seductively in the mud. To the north, the mountains loomed closer, their rocky sides catching the morning sunlight. A desolate country, no sign of road or path or village.

Where were his knights? He slowed to a walk and stopped altogether.

It was dark here under the eaves of giant oaks with the gentle *drip, drip, plop!* of water from the hanging boughs. He sniffed the pungent scents of moss and decaying vegetation and pine. Cocking his ear, he heard no sound of hooves approaching from behind. His neck prickled. It felt as if a wad of cotton was stuffed in his throat as stories of murders, rapes and tortures filled his mind.

"Come, friend, perchance we should go looking for my knights." He reined Kazimer around and indeed, the horse seemed anxious to depart. Suddenly he heard a noise, a crackling of a tree bough. *What if a band of brigands exploded from those trees just over there?* Wait. Was that the trod of a hoof? The jingle of a bridle? He laid a hand on Kazimer's neck, staring toward the sound, willing it to be his knights.

With a crash, a troop of knights, the leader sitting upon a gray roan, exploded into the clearing, their eyes set upon him in fierce concentration, lances in hand.

"Come along, prince," the large man called in a hoarse voice. "We have you surrounded. Come peacefully and we shall ..."

Arthur heard no more. With a savage yell, he dug his spurs into Kazimer's flanks. The horse leaped to action. From the corner of his eye, he saw more knights erupt from cover. How many? A dozen?

He drew sword, the sword given him by DeArmond just yesterday. Screaming and slashing with all his might, he drove straight into the right flank of the encircling knights. Surprise flitted in their eyes as their mounts gave ground. An opening appeared where one horse stumbled. Kicking Kazimer, Arthur broke through the circle and thundered down the lane.

He was not free of them. They came in a close pack and there were more than he thought. He glanced back. Two dozen? His only chance was to throw them off. He reined sharply to the left, leaped a creek and mounted a bank. Under the low-hung limbs of old oaks and young maples, he rode like one possessed.

Yet it was not good enough. He tried doubling back on his tracks, he tried speed, he tried agility, he tried riding on solid rocks, to no avail. He burst into a small meadow where a dolmen protruded from the rich, black soil, and an ancient oak spread its thick limbs. He turned and drew sword as his pursuers surrounded him.

Hoof beats sounded on the path. He lifted his head. To his relief, DeArmond and his familiar bay charged into the meadow, breaking through the line of enemy knights with a yell. Behind him, his knights skidded to a halt.

Prince Arthur swung his horse closer to DeArmond. "Where did you ... ?"

"They decoyed us. We did not know where you were." DeArmond's face was pale and wet with sweat.

The strange riders drew the circle tighter and lowered their lances.

Arthur lifted his chin, forcing himself to stare at them fiercely regardless of his heart's pounding. He was dismayed that his voice sounded high and boyish, yet he spoke with the voice of command that no man could ignore. "Who are you and what do you want? I do not recognize the red bull and the black banner. Are you so cowardly that you do not show your faces? Come now, speak out, if you are men."

There was no response, only guttural laughter and lifting of lances in derision.

Across the clearing Arthur noted a young knight who held himself straight and rode a fine, black horse. His pale gray eyes bored into Arthur's with hatred—a hatred that seethed with the fires of hell. He held Arthur's gaze; their eyes locked.

The prince tried to break away but found himself captive. It was as if a branding iron had touched his soul. *Who is he? Why should he hate me so?* He did not recognize the face. The knight dropped his visor.

An emotion Arthur seldom felt clutched at his stomach; bile crawled up his throat. He swallowed. It was like the time a bear charged him from the forest when he picnicked with his mother. But this was worse—far worse. He scorned it, tried to push it aside, told himself he must be brave. Yet his hands shook and his stomach twisted. The sun disappeared under a bank of dark clouds—*where had they come from?*

The horses were restive, pawing the ground, tossing their manes, mawing their bits. What was once a quiet meadow now crackled with high tension as if lightning was about to strike. A crow gave voice from the boughs of the old oak. The sun broke through a rift in the clouds and Arthur lifted a hand to shield his eyes.

"Take the boy and the old man. Kill the others." The hoarse voice of the leader rang out to the accompaniment of visors being lowered, lances readied, horses snorting and swords screaming from their scabbards.

DeArmond grasped Arthur's elbow, his voice grave. "Flee, my lord! We shall cover your retreat."

"Nay!" Arthur held his sword with white-knuckled fingers, fighting the sick feeling in his gut, praying he would not do anything stupid, hoping he had the courage of his father and Uncle Richard.

The strange knights kicked their chargers.

Adrenaline pulsed through Arthur's veins and time stood still. The beauty of the meadow smote his senses—cheery-faced daisies bobbed in the lush grass, dappled white bark of alders gleamed against dark green firs, a brook rattled over small stones in its bed. He smelled damp moss and oak and horse and mint.

'Tis a good place to die.

He shook his head. His mouth formed a thin line. He would not die today.

DeArmond grabbed for Arthur's reins in a futile attempt to steer him from the path of the oncoming horses but Arthur pulled away. He raked his spurs against his mount's sides and with a yell, entered the fight.

The quiet air exploded into a blur of slashing, whirling, yelling, the shriek of steel on steel, the screams of horses, dust and desperate fury. Arthur defended himself as blows fell upon him like rain, but was at a disadvantage with his height and weight and lack of armor. Blood flowed from his wounds, but he scarcely felt them and fought on. Time and again, when a sword descended, Kazimer reared or dodged sideways or lunged forward, and the blow missed by a breath.

From the corner of his eye, Arthur saw men crashing to the ground. Was that Rene? *Oh, God!* Blood spurted from wounds; bodies lay like sacks of grain. The knight with the pale, soulless eyes attacked, his monster of a horse shouldering into Kazimer and forcing him, pace by pace, plunging and skidding, toward a ditch.

Arthur's sword arm wearied, yet he parried the blows and managed to stay in the saddle. His enemy's horse tripped and sent the knight reeling. Arthur followed closely, aiming for the opening of the mail in the armpit. He sank in his blade; the young knight shrieked but then he turned, his attack doubled, his eyes blazing with hatred and purpose. Arthur saw his own death in those eyes and in the weapon aimed for his heart.

He could have turned, could have fled. But he yelled and, Kazimer, sensing his intent, lunged forward. Arthur ducked, felt the blade brush his hair. The two horses met with bone-shattering force, yet the knight held his seat and, with a roar, swung back his arm to deliver another blow.

Arthur parried, feeling his arm would break, yet he hung on, his steel engaged, deadlocked, face to face with his enemy, dragging air into starved lungs in a grin of effort. The blades broke free, and the black knight swerved away, parrying an attack from the other side. Then, sinking his spurs into the flanks of the black, he rode out of the circle of warfare into the forest.

Arthur followed, filled with blood lust, an unholy fervor, a boiling rage. Dodging low limbs that threatened to unseat him, he clung to the saddle, having no need to direct Kazimer, for the horse was as fully engaged in the battle as he.

They came to another small meadow where the knight waited, sword aloft. Arthur noted again the cold rage in the man's eyes and fear swallowed him whole. He had difficulty breathing, his hands shook, his stomach heaved. Yet he shouldered it aside, shoved it down, blinked and brought himself back to the fight. The heavy weapon fell; he parried and was caught again in a dance of death.

Arthur held on with both hands, but sweat blinded him, caused his fingers to slip. His blade slipped off his opponent's—with a grunt, he fell forward. Kazimer reared, his forelegs pawing toward the black, his teeth gashing the glossy neck. The horse screamed and reared; the knight was thrown off balance, yet he recovered in an instant and, with a bellow of hate, lifted his sword.

Aided by Kazimer's quick forward lunge, Arthur dodged under the deadly weapon but the knight wielded it again, this time a stab, and this time it found its mark—Arthur's side. The blade bit deep, a serious wound, yet Arthur did not drop his eyes. He raised his blade to parry again.

The knight drew back. Motions and sounds slowed to a crawl. There was sweat on the man's brow, a rent in his armor, rust on his helmet just below the visor; a fly buzzed his head.

Arthur tried to raise his arm, but it was heavy … too heavy. He screamed, yet his voice was a wavering wail. Mist drifted into his vision, the world seemed to spin in a lazy circle. He strove to bring himself back, knew his enemy's weapon cut the air, this time on target, saw himself lying on the turf, dead.

It seemed a strange thing to die. Sadness swept through his soul. He mourned the boy who lay bloodied and dead. His thoughts flicked to his mother, saw her crushed, heard her keening cries, knew she would perish in her lamentations. The two of them would find their way to heaven or hell, he knew not which. For himself, he would go into the pit of hell, for certes, for he had not confessed to the priest for many weeks.

A man's shout brought him back. A bay jostled against the black, a jolt against his leg. He clung to the saddle with all his strength and knew vaguely that someone fought for him. He heard the clash of steel on steel, lifted his eyes in time to see his enemy's weapon struck from his hand, a sword pierce his shoulder.

Dimly, as if from a far distance, a man's voice cried, "Frederick!"

The clearing was silent, save for labored breath. Arthur looked down at his side where he clutched his wound. Blood gushed around his hand.

"M'lord! You are wounded!" DeArmond's voice seemed far away as Arthur swayed in the saddle. Hands pulled him from his horse and laid him on the ground. Pain ricocheted through his body as someone tore his clothes. They bound up his wounds and carried him, lifted him to saddle. Someone mounted behind, arms wrapped around him, holding him erect.

After a time, he awoke. It was dark. He lay on a cot, a small lamp fluttered above his head, the walls were wattle and daub. He moaned, tried to move.

A woman's voice, sharp and clear, said, "Here! Let me treat the prince, you great oaf!"

He knew no more.

***

DeArmond entered the Great Hall and glanced toward a knot of people, at whose center stood the queen. He was on familiar ground here. He did not need to look at the walls to see the faded tapestries, or the brass cressets that held the torches, or the queen's grand throne—a throne gilded with gold and padded with velvet. What arrogance the woman possessed. She was no queen at all, only a duchess. Yet he owed his allegiance to her.

He met the queen's eyes, saw her lips press into a white line, her small hands clutch her staff. His heart sank. She knew. With a wave of her hand she dismissed the courtiers and strode down the hall.

He dropped to his knees. "My lady, we were on a morning run, an exercise, and went too far. The prince would not heed my calls. He rode furiously, as he is wont to do, and we were diverted from his side by strange knights. They carried a black pennant with an emblem of a bull. I know not who it was, my lady. When we got free of them, we rode like hellfire and found the prince in a meadow. They had us surrounded. There were many of them, my queen, maybe thirty or forty. I urged the prince to flee, but he disobeyed me. He was wounded. I am sorry, I could not—"

"I do not want to hear your excuses, you ... you dolt! You lackwit! I shall have you whipped within an inch of your life."

He bowed his head, but had no serious qualms concerning her threats. She would not horsewhip him.

She lifted her arms heavenward. "Alas! Am I to be bereft of my son? Oh, my God and sweet Virgin Mother!" She dropped her arms and turned to him, boring him through with her blue-eyed stare. "My son is without fault, DeArmond. Your task is to protect him and you failed. Do you hear me? Failed! Who were these knights who desired to kidnap my son for a ransom?"

"As I said, I do not know. One seemed familiar but I cannot lay a name to him. They came upon us—"

"Be still! I should have you beheaded. I will have no one touch my son for harm. He is all I have ... and now, he may die ... and I ..." She raised her head. "How many did we lose?"

"One. Dominque, my favorite. It is a miracle that any survived. All have serious wounds." He lumbered to his feet, his face drawn and weary. "May I go?"

She rose and faced him with a mad glare in her eyes. "Yea. Go. I would not see thy face for a time. Mayhap you shall find favor with me again, but now, get out of my sight!"

Arthur recovered with the speed of youth, and it was not long before he missed his mentor and teacher, Lord DeArmond. So it was that in a short time, DeArmond again resided at Mordelias and was seen in the company of the queen's knights.

The people of Brittany, from the villein in the field to the lord of the manor, called the incident in the clearing the Battle of Bille, for the village of Bille was where Arthur had been taken after his injury. The story had been told and retold, sung about, laughed about, and exaggerated to such an extent that he was almost ashamed to show his face in the countryside.

Two months later a ceremony graced the lawns of the castle. The night before, Arthur kept a vigil in the chapel, purifying his soul in prayers. Actually, he dozed more than he prayed, but no one minded that from a boy of eight. As the morning light glazed the colored glass windows, a priest celebrated mass.

Arthur was stiff from the kneeling position he had maintained most of the night and he was ravenously hungry. He joined his mother, his stepfather Lord Ranulf, Lord DeArmond, his sister Eleanor and others of the family in the Great Hall, where he broke his fast on a meal of roasted duck, strips of venison, boiled eggs, cheese, fresh bread, pears and apple fritters.

Afterward, he was bathed and dressed in clothes made especially for the occasion—a white silk robe, a white surcoat, and a pure white ermine robe. The silk material felt good against his skin as it slid down over his shoulders and reached his feet, and he stroked the ermine fur, pleasuring in its softness. Over all, he wore a red cape on which was embroidered the crest of the house of Plantagenet—two black lions facing each other, rearing in fierce combat.

A platform had been constructed in the open square before the castle, and around it stood minstrels and trumpeters. The knights of Brittany stood to attention, their eyes smiling, their armor shining in the blinding glare of the sun. When Arthur stepped from the castle gate, the trumpeters sounded a blast that set his ears ringing and the crowd broke forth in applause and cheers.

"Kneel!" Lord Ranulf said, raising a sword close to Arthur's head.

A bandage encased his side, and Arthur's wound still pained him at times, but he knelt without hesitation before his stepfather, bending his head and receiving the *colee*, or *buffet*. It was not a gentle tap, but a strong *whack!* on his shoulder that sent him sprawling amid laughter and cheers. It hurt. It hurt like the dickens, but he did not wince. He regained his position on the stool and listened as Lord Ranulf intoned the oath.

"I dub thee Sir Arthur of the House of Plantagenet; Knight of the Realm of Brittany; Lord of the lands of Lord Geoffrey, son of King Henry II; Vassal of King Richard, the Lionhearted, King of England. Be thou a true knight and courageous in the face of your enemies. Be thou brave and upright, that God may love thee, and remember that thou springest from a race that can never be false." Lord Ranulf paused. "Do you pledge your life, your honor, and your loyalty to His Royal Highness, King Richard?"

"I do." Arthur did not know where the words came from; his throat was so dry.

"Rise, Sir Arthur, Knight of the Realm!"

Scenes burned themselves on his mind—his new armor, his knights bending before him to help him into it, Lord Ranulf and DeArmond strapping on the sword of his father, a sword gloriously wrought with silver and gold. He kissed the hilt in which, it was rumored, contained a bone shard of the Apostle John.

Yet Arthur's lady mother, Queen Constance, stood at the center of everything. In that first moment of being knighted, he looked up into her eyes. The blue of them today was not muted sea-green, but dark, almost black, sparkling with unshed tears, gleaming with fierce pride. She nodded and smiled.

Kazimer, his white coat gleaming with an ethereal light, was brought to him, dressed in ornaments of gold. Arthur took the reins and, because of his armor, was aided in mounting. Once on his destrier, he lifted his shield.

On it he had taken the emblems of the lion, the unicorn, and the griffin, emblems of King Arthur of Camelot, after whom he was named and to whom he was distantly related. Indeed, it was rumored among the common folk that he was the great king returned in the flesh.

The men roared, banging their swords on their shields, and the crowd picked up the cheer, raising another great shout. It seemed that Prince Arthur was now their king and would soon take his rightful place on the throne of England.

The duchess watched her son with a smile on her delicate lips. He was tall for his years and possessed clear blue eyes, a strong nose and golden hair—the heritage of the Plantagenets—that flowed to his shoulders. Every move he made, every word of his mouth, every thought in his head she had planted there.

Tears stung her eyes when a loud shout from the throats of thousands was raised. She laughed and clapped her hands, tears coursing down her cheeks unheeded. *Oh, sweet Virgin Mother, if only Geoffrey could see him now.* She lifted a black lace handkerchief and dabbed at her eyes.

The sun disappeared behind a cloud and her eyes slid sideways to her would-be husband, the detestable Norman that her father-in-law, King Henry II, had chosen for her. Lord Ranulf did not join in the jubilation, for he was Prince John's man. She knew of the messages he sent to John; she knew he spied into the matters of the land of Brittany, that he harbored no love for Bretons, nor for Arthur, least of all for herself.

She swung her head to watch the progress of the newly knighted prince as he rode jauntily through his men, smiling and waving at their cheers, as he led the way to the tables loaded with food and wine. Arthur deserved this triumph. He was proven in battle, a true son of kings, a sweet and courageous young prince. Why should they not rejoice?

She lifted her scarlet mantle over her head, swirled her black silk skirts and made her way back to her apartment in the castle where servants brought mulled wine, cold chicken and a wheaten roll. While she ate, she allowed her mind to wander down paths well trodden, taking her to the court of King Henry II and his beautiful wife, Eleanor.

Eleanor! She laid her food aside and paced to the window to look unseeingly down upon the festivities. Eleanor possessed everything Constance had always wanted: beauty, wealth and power. On the few occasions when Constance found herself in the presence of the Queen Eleanor, she fought against the urge to reach for a knife and plunge it into that handsome breast.

Constance returned to her chair and sighed. If only Geoffrey had been king. When she first wed Prince Geoffrey, she thought she was a step away from the highest throne in the world. True, Geoffrey was younger than Richard, but accidents happened and people died.

When Little King Henry, the eldest of Henry's brood, died at an early age, her hopes rose again. But Richard stood forever in Geoffrey's way, and Geoffrey lacked the ambition to contest his older brother for the throne, despite her urgings, despite the animosity she instilled in her husband against his family. Yet Richard remained childless, so Geoffrey had hopes for his own children.

Their first child was a girl he named Eleanor to please his mother—certainly not to please Constance. Then she was with child a second time, but before she gave birth, Geoffrey was killed in a tournament. With his death, her hopes died, too.

There had been no question as to who would rule the kingdom when Henry died. No one seriously considered John, who had thoroughly botched the job of ruling Ireland. No, the golden boy, Richard, was chosen. Richard the Lionhearted. Richard the heirless.

She bit down on the crusty roll, her teeth crushing, destroying. She must bide her time. No one would deny her son's right to the throne when Richard was dead. And through her son, she would rule the greatest kingdom in the world.

CHAPTER TWO

You ought to go quietly, and you ought to go soon. J.R.R.
Tolkien, Fellowship of the Ring

Troyes, France, May 1194

"Judith, bring me my reading stone, please." Moshe ben Itzchaki unrolled a scroll as he sat in a swing that was shaded by a giant date palm. "Be careful, child."

"Yea, Gran-abba." Small feet pattered away.

A few moments later he heard the soft slap of sandals on the sandstone pavement and raised his eyes. She carried the precious stone with both hands and laid it on his knee. Smiling, he covered her tiny hands with his large ones. Reading stones had been around since the days of Nineveh, but this particular one had been created in Venice. Moshe's son, Elias, purchased it from one of the great caravans that traveled the Salt Trail and came at last to France. It was a treasure, to be sure, but nothing compared to the child who stood before him.

"I was careful." She climbed up on the swing, adjusted her green gown, and looked up at him with dark brown eyes that sparkled like jewels. "Please, will you read me, Gran-abba?"

He chuckled and rested a hand on her glossy black hair. Ah, what a child. Was there ever one like her? It was past time for her parents to begin marriage pledges, but they delayed. No one in the household could bear the thought of losing her.

"See my flowers?" She touched the ring of bluebells and lilies of the field that crowned her head. "Aren't they pretty? Anna holped me."

"I see. They are very nice. Would you like to read? The scroll is open to Isaias."

Her bright face was full of innocent joy and smudged with a bit of dirt. "Nay, I love hearing you read." She settled herself and folded her hands in her lap.

He smiled at her intent expression. Even though she was only six years old, he taught her to read Hebrew, count her numbers and study the names, and forms of the stars. He noted that often she lingered inhis library, her face glowing as she gently touched the scrolls and books lining the walls.

He cleared his throat. "'The Spirit of Yahweh is upon me, because Yahweh has anointed me to bring good tidings to the afflicted; He has sent me to bind up the brokenhearted, to proclaim liberty to captives, and freedom—"

"Oh, Gran-abba!" She tugged at his sleeve. "Read about the Messias who comes from Bozrah with glowing robes! Please, oh joy of my heart!"

He laughed. "Where did you get that? Ah, yes. I remember. Your aunt called you that the other day, didn't she? Well, let me see … " He unrolled the scroll.

"Who is this who comes from Edom, with garments of flowing colors from Bozrah, this One who is majestic in His apparel, marching in the greatness of His strength? It is I who speak in righteousness, mighty to save. Why is Your apparel red, and Your garments like the one who treads in the winepress? I have trodden the wine trough alone, and from the peoples there was no man with Me. I also trod them in My anger, and trampled them in My wrath, and … "

"So, this is where you have gotten to."

Judith opened her eyes, lifted her head from Gran-abba's shoulder, and smiled up at her mother, Sarah. Amma stood with her hands on her hips, a frown puckering her brow.

"We were reading from the prophet Isaias," Judith said. "It was about when the Messias comes, right, Gran-abba?" She reached up and combed her fingers through his long white beard.

"Many apologies for disturbing you, Abba," Sarah said with a slight bow, her breath thin and gasping. "I looked everywhere for the child and could not find her. I was so afraid that … that she had wandered off, or that … Did you not hear the gong for dinner?"

Judith heard the sharp tone in mother's voice and scrambled down from the swing, catching her dress on the corner. It ripped. "Oh! I am sorry, Amma!" She glanced up, saw her mother's frown, and tried to press the gown together between her fingers. Tears stung her eyes. "I will fix it, truly I will!"

Sarah smiled and patted Judith's hand. "Oh, child! Whatever shall I do with you? Hannah will fix your gown, dear. Come along now."

Grandfather lumbered to his feet. "I must have nodded off, too. Is Elias home?"

"Elias sent word he would be late, that we should begin without him. He will join us soon." Sarah led the way to the dining room where a whole wall was taken with large windows revealing a view of the busy city below and farther out, the green, rolling hills of France.

Judith folded her legs and sat upon a cushion at the low table while Amma lit two candles in silver holders. She must not pick up the clear glass plate that had come all the way from a country called Cathay, but she leaned over and looked at her reflection in it. Her big, round eyes stared back at her, and above them, her braided hair held the ring of posies, now a little askew and wilted.

Amma set a bouquet of roses and lilies in the center of the table and sat down.

Gran-abba entered the room and lowered himself to sit on the cushion, moaning a little as he folded his legs. Just as he was about to say the blessing, Abba entered the room. He wore a white tunic and a blue robe, edged with gold trim. His dark eyes lit when he looked at Sarah.

Judith rose to her feet and bowed. "Good even, Abba."

He smiled, warmth creeping into the worried lines of his face. "Good even, child." He sat at the table next to Grandfather.

Sarah did not trust his service to Hannah or to Nero, their elderly black servant. She leaped gracefully to her feet, her green silk robe whispering on the tiles, and brought a laver of warm water and towels to him. It was only after he had washed and she poured his wine that she sat again.

After Gran-abba prayed, Hannah brought in roasted lamb, rice and lentils, and a dish of stewed figs. Nero served a platter of two fish that swam in a sauce of wine.

Judith nibbled at her food and gazed through the candlelight at her mother. She noticed how her hair shone, how her eyes glowed, how she laughed at Abba's story of a man and his wife who came to look at the jewelry he sold in his stall in the marketplace. The woman, he said, was fatter than any cow he had ever seen, and she leaned so far forward to look that she rolled into the street. His tale of the ensuing uproar brought laughter to everyone—even to Gran-abba's stern face.

Judith watched the lamplight reflect from Amma's beautiful eyes, how her laughter brought up the dimples in her cheeks. If only she could be like her someday. Amma could do so many things like arrange flowers, create lovely rugs and blankets on her loom, sing, and dance. Judith remembered times when Hannah played a lute and Joseph, her son, strummed a tambourine. Mother danced in the soft light of the setting sun, her thin voice singing a song of David. Judith kept time, clapping to the music until the song ended and Amma collapsed on a cushion nearby, drawing Judith into her arms.

"I canna sing, and can barely dance," Amma had said, between panting breaths, "but it was a good effort, na?" They laughed until they cried, and even Hannah joined in the laughter.

Judith brought her mind back to the conversation, for Abba's tone was grave.

"They burned everything, and killed the men and raped the women and spitted the child ... " He glanced at Judith, choked on his food and took a sip of wine.

Judith knew he spoke of the Christian knights from the north, knights who marched across the German Empire and then south, raiding cities on their way to Palestine. She heard whispers from the servants, bloodcurdling stories of atrocities the knights committed in other places. But she knew nothing of the stark terror that rode with the armored knights, of horrors that made grown men kill themselves, of rape and blood and violence in the streets.

Sarah cleared her throat. "Judith, dear, when you are finished, you may play with Hiram for a while before your bedtime. Would you like that?"

"Yes, Amma." Judith pushed away her plate, her appetite gone. She pulled on Grandfather's sleeve. "Gran-abba, will the horrid knights come here?"

"Na, child." He patted her arm and leaned closer. "Our king will not allow them to come here. We are safe. But you must pray for others who are not so blessed as we. Will you pray, child?"

"Yea, sir." She rose, for she had heard enough. The fear she tried to keep at bay loomed large and terrible in her mind. Her knees shook with the strength of it. "Thank you, Amma, for the meal. Good even, Abba."

"Good even, dear," he said. "I shall see you before your bedtime."

She ran to the soft evening sunlight filtering through the palm branches in the courtyard and played with little Hiram, Hannah's grandchild. For a few precious moments she forgot the nameless fear that stalked her days and nights, reassured that Amma and Abba and Gran-abba seemed at peace.

Elias watched her go, then arose and paced to the window.

Sarah followed him. "Are you sure we will be spared?"

He gazed unseeingly upon the city below. What would they do if Frankish armies entered that gate over there? He gazed at Sarah. How he loved the slender lines of her body, the soft shine of her eyes, the tender touch of her hands, the sweet smell of her luxuriant hair. Who could ever replace her? How would he manage without her? What if she was like those women who ... he stopped. He could not envision Sarah brutalized, murdered.

He turned to the window, tears stinging his eyes. "Who can tell what will happen?" His words were sharper than he intended; he modulated his tone. "Jews in other places have lost their homes, their wealth, and even their lives. I hope King Philip will protect us, that our barons and lords will buy our peace. Perchance the Franks will not come here. Troyes is a small plum compared to Lyon or Marseilles." He turned to cast a troubled glance at his father.

The old man nodded. "I believe the king will stand with us against the Franks. If not, we must flee." His words brought a deathly hush to the room.

"Flee?" Sarah stared at him, her face blanching. "Where shall we go? This ... this is the only home I know. My family is here. How can we flee?"

Elias touched her shoulder. "Sarah, listen to me. We may have to leave Troyes. Many Jews are going to other places. Our business is such that we may pick it up in a satchel and be gone in the morning, if need be. But we will not leave until we are forced to. I know you love it here, that your family is here." He sighed and shook his head. "Please, go to bed now. You are tired. I will join you in a little while, but Father and I must discuss this thing."

Eyes downcast, Sarah nodded. After apologizing to Moshe, she slipped from the room.

"Let us go down to the courtyard," Moshe said, struggling to his feet. Elias hurried to help him stand. "I always think better under the date palm and the stars."

Moshe picked up a warm woolen cover and allowed Elias to help him down the steps to the courtyard where they sat near the fountain. Elias tucked the robe around his father's knees. They sat in silence while mourning doves cooed and the day faded away in soft colors of pink and purple over the mountains to the west.

Elias glanced at his father. "There is snow still on the mountains. We shall have a late spring."

"Aye. But early or late, our fortunes may be turning."

Elias chuckled. "That sounds grim, Abba. What shall we do?"

"When luck enters, give him a seat, it is said. We shall give good luck a seat."

"We are leaving, then. You have decided."

The old man stroked his beard. "What are the options, my son? There is talk of another crusade. The armies may be on the march again and this time they may go through Troyes. Who knows?"

Elias sighed. Silence descended and fear was palatable, a millstone on his chest.

Moshe continued in a low voice. "We have other options—yes. We could appeal to the baron for help. But one must ask oneself, is he dependable?"

Elias turned away as nightmare scenes filled his mind—Jewish men, women and children slaughtered like animals in Mainz, in Italy, England, Palestine—wherever the crusaders took their holy war. When they conquered Jerusalem in 1099 it was said the blood ran in the streets up to the stirrups of the riders, and nearly every Jew in the city was massacred, most of them butchered in the Temple. No wonder the Jews preferred Muslim rule.

"He may protect us," Elias said, shifting to pull his robe closer. "Or he may betray us like Bishop Rothard did in Mainz. It is the always the same. Whatever amount the Jews may raise for protection, the Christians will offer more. When money speaks the truth keeps silent, it is said. And even though our king hates them, he loves gold more. No, I do not trust him."

"Nor do I."

Elias noted that the moon was new, that Mars was unusually bright. "When are we going?"

"The question is where. The Caliph in Tunis has offered refuge for the Jews. He likes the trade they bring. He has even declared he would provide land and housing. It is a fair offer. What do you think?"

"I do not know, Father. Either way seems fraught with difficulties. I hate the thought of wrenching Sarah from her family, yet we cannot take them all." He paced to the fountain, then back. "Tell me what is on your mind. Do not play games as if I were a child."

Moshe straightened. "I was born here in Troyes. We are a noble family, having descended from the great Rashi."

Elias sighed and closed his eyes, for he knew the family lines better than his father. Yet he allowed the old man to continue as if he were a stranger.

"We raised our families, lived in peace, and prospered. We have been given respect and honor in the eyes of the heathen, and I have sat in counsel with the great Caliph Salah uh Din Ayyubi, he who is called Saladin, when I traveled to Alexandria last year."

Elias sat down beside him. "I know."

"But that does not mean our good life here will continue." Moshe sighed heavily. "It is a violent world, and all hearts seemed turned against God's people. We are beset on every hand, driven from our homes, our properties and wealth stolen, our women violated in the streets." He snatched a moth from the air, considered it for a few seconds, then opened his hand and released it.

He looked up and a light sparkled in his solemn eyes. "What shall we do, then? I will tell you. We shall go to our Holy Land." He held up a hand and smiled when Elias gasped. "Yet in stages, my son. First we will travel south to Dijon. I hear it is a lovely city and we can participate in the fair held this spring. From there we can travel on to Lyon, and then perhaps to Marseille."

"Then to Jerusalem?"

He shook his head. "Nay, not Jerusalem. Where does your uncle live, son? In Antioch of Asia Minor. There is much commerce in that city. We would have a fine business there from the caravans that travel from the East. The Caliph who rules it alongside the Frankish king is disposed toward our people."

"Antioch." Elias rolled the name of the city on his tongue and smiled at Moshe. "You have spoken of Antioch ever since I can remember. It is like the Golden Horn to you, is it not? The land of riches and fortune, where the streets are paved with gold?"

Moshe laughed, hefting himself up. "I care not for fortunes, only for Yahweh's will. We should try to be ready to move in a few weeks. Do you like my idea of Dijon?"

Elias nodded and allowed the old man to grasp his elbow. He looked up at the stars that twinkled like diamonds in the black sky. The breeze that was so gentle and warm during the day had now turned chilly, bringing with it the scent of the mountains and freshly fallen snow. "Aye, Abba. Dijon it will be, but it will be hard for Sarah."

Moshe nodded. "Aye, I know. We have grown like ... like our date palm." He glanced overhead where the palm bent to the wind. "We are well established here, but it could be swept away in a moment. We will find friends and beauty wherever we go. You must tell Sarah."

"Yes, Abba. Sarah will do whatever we say, but it will be hard. It will be very hard."

CHAPTER THREE

Grief teaches the steadiest minds to waver. Soplocles Antigone
(495-406 B.C.)

St. Jacques, Brittany, June 1194

Brother Louis stooped over his writing, quill in hand, a parchment spread before him on a crude wooden desk. Sweat beaded his clean brow and his shaven head like droplets of blood. He wished he was one of the village children he could hear splashing in the mill pond just beyond the walls of the monastery.

He lifted his head. The light patter of sandaled feet on the stone floor of the scriptorium heralded the arrival of a young novice, Samson John, as unlike the Samson of the Bible as anyone could possibly be.

Louis smiled at the wide, blue eyes and rosy cheeks of the boy who stood and waited to be recognized. "Yes, Samson John? You want me for something?"

The boy nodded.

"Something urgent?"

The boy motioned to the open courtyard. He strutted across the hall with head held high, then knelt, then stood again and swung a sword toward a point below his waist. These motions he accompanied with a leap in the air and frantic waving of his arms.

Louis set down his pen and rose. "I know. Give me a few moments. I will meet you at the gate."

The boy leaped and dashed from the room.

Louis smiled again and set aside the illustration he was drawing, wrapping the parchment in thin vellum sheets and storing it in a box by the side of the desk. Poor Samson John, deaf from birth. Yet he could read lips, if one spoke slowly and distinctly, and he seemed happy inside the walls of the monastery. Outside them, Louis shuddered to think what his fate would be.

He rose, paced down the hall to his cell and refreshed himself with a drink from the pitcher that sat on the stand, the only piece of furniture in the room besides the cot by the wall.

Slowly he made his way to the gate where he motioned to Samson John and three other boys. Together they walked two miles to the castle at Mordelias, arriving just in time to hear a clash of cymbals and a blast of trumpets. The boys were soon lost in the crowd, squirming their way to the front, but Louis found a vantage point on a large rock. He clambered to the top of it and stood, waiting.

It was much as he expected. The prince looked pale and drawn, yet showed no signs of pain when he received the buffet. Surely that hurt. Louis had treated the prince when he arrived in Mordelias after the incident at Bille, and so he knew the wound could not be healed yet.

Ah, well. The prince was making a good show. Louis joined the crowd in the applause and cheers, then gathered his little troop and walked back to the monastery, listening to the chatter of the boys, warning them of the dangers of pride, wealth and power. Yet his warnings fell upon deaf ears. He smiled, seeing himself as a young lad, fourteen summers ago.

He must have been around six when Father was brought into their little wattle and daub cottage, gravely injured. Someone whispered that he had been gored by a bull. They laid Papa on his bed and heaped over him a mound of coverlets. His face was the color of gray mud, his hair disheveled. That evening, Louis went with Mama to St. Jacques to pray for Papa, but it did no good.

He died in the night while Louis slept.

The next night, sleep would not come. He tossed on his bed, terrors filling his childish mind, terrors of hell and damnation, of demons and evil spirits, of a fearful, vengeful God.

He heard a muffled choking sound, almost like an animal snuffling in the darkness, and realized it was his little sister, Bethy. Creeping on silent feet, he padded across the floor and found her trundle bed. Bethy was only three, but she knew, she sensed, she grieved. Lifting the thin coverlet, he crawled into her bed and wrapped his arms around her, smoothed her tangled blonde hair from his mouth, whispered in her ear.

"Sh! Don't cry, Bethy. Papa's in heaven, they say. He's not hurting anymore, Bethy. Sh!" Slowly the sobs that shook the little girl's body stopped. Warmth enveloped him. He slept.

The work was too much for Mama. Her slight frame dwindled as day by day she rose at sunrise, went to do the work required by the baron, and then returned home, staggering to the croft to tend their cow and chickens. Louis learned how to take care of the animals and the garden, to prepare the meals and to watch Thomas and Bethy.

The summer he was ten, things began to improve. Mama's smile came more often. There was real meat on the table now and then, and they wore clothes made by the seamster. Mama whistled about the house and paid her rent and her due to the Baron. Indeed, she told Louis once that she was excused from work, for she paid to be let off.

He never asked where she got the money. And then, she was gone. He stopped in the road as the boys ran ahead. He did not know how Mama died.

He remembered the day he was taken to St. Jacques' monastery along with his brother and sister, how he hushed Bethy and held Thomas' hand while they sat on a hard wooden bench and waited for a monk to take them to their rooms. How his breath came in gasps and his hands were cold and yet sweaty, how he wondered what would happen to them.

Bethy and Thomas were soon taken in by two separate families in the parish, yet Louis stayed on at St. Jacques.

He lifted his head, for the boys were belting down the lane, far in advance of Louis' more sedate pace. "Hey, Elton! Guilliame! Walter! Wait up!"

The boys glanced back and slackened their pace, but Samson John disappeared around bend in the road, not hearing his call.

How did she die? Somehow the question took on mammoth proportions. He must know, yet he had no answer. Had she taken ill? He knew she was often sick with a cough. But, no. It was not illness.

The grey stone monastery came into view. He nodded to the three boys and they dashed ahead, entered the gate, and were promptly lost to sight. Louis sat on a bench in the herb garden where he grew plants to ease the pains and wounds of those he treated.

From the depths of his soul, pain shot across his consciousness with the intensity of a sword thrust, rocking him to his core. It was familiar, something he struggled with almost daily, but he now knew its face and could name it. Guilt. Guilt associated with Mama's death. He groaned and cradled his head in his hands. Why did he feel this way? Had he poisoned her unintentionally?

He shook himself and straightened. Slowly, he stood and pulled desultorily at a weed. Why did it matter if he knew why she died? What was this evil spirit that troubled him?

He thought back over the long days and nights since her death. Even though it had been difficult at first, he loved the monastery, for it was an ordered life, a secure life. His days were filled from the dark of early morning to the last lingering rays of sunset with services in the chapel, prayers (both private and collective) and his studies. He learned to read Latin, Greek, and English and he learned to write. His only textbook was the Bible. Gradually he advanced in the order and became a monk himself. He was free to travel about the countryside, to help the sick and bring comfort to the dying.

Now, shaking off his torment, he filled a leather purse with herbs and salves and started out on one of his walks. In the village of Guichen he paused to help an old basket weaver whose eyes were infected and runny. After examining them, he straightened and saw a book that was almost covered amid a pile of rubble on a crude wooden shelf. He picked it up and wiped the dust from the cracked leather cover. "Where did you get this?"

"I dunno, Brother Louis." The old man peered up at him. "I cannot see it, and even if I cud, I cannot read." He chuckled at his joke.

Louis smiled and was about to replace it on the shelf, when he stopped. There, in Latin, were the words, "By Fulk of Chartres, Historian, Year of Our Lord, 1099." It was the great historian who traveled to the Holy Lands and wrote of the early Crusades! His pulses quickening, he opened it slowly, but the great age of the parchment caused it to crack. "I cannot pay you money for this, but may I borrow it?"

The man shrugged. "Give me someit for my old eyes and you cun keep it, Brother."

Eagerly, Louis reached into his pouch and drew out a salve. "This will help you. It is all I have at the present but I will bring you more. Spread it on your eyes twice a day, sir. It will bring relief and I hope better sight."

Back at the monastery, Louis chaffed for the first time in his life during evening vespers, joining his voice in the songs with the other brothers of his order, praying, standing, sitting and listening. Time moved slowly. He found himself itching to be in his room, reading his precious book. Where had the old man acquired such a treasure?

At last the last prayer was chanted and the last song died on the cool evening air. Quietly the monks filed from the vast room with its domed ceiling so far overhead that it could scarcely be seen. Curbing his steps, Louis paced slowly to his room and opened the door. He pulled the book from the large pocket inside his black woolen cloak, laid it on the table and lit the lamp. He had little time to read, for his lamp oil was doled out in small amounts and was expected to last a long time. This night he would read until the oil was low indeed.

The ancient pages crackled under his careful fingers as he turned the pages. He gloried in the rich texture of the parchment, the age of the document and the flowing Latin words. His trembling fingers traced them and his lips moved silently. It was a story beyond calculation, beyond imagination, beyond belief. It captured his heart and soul.

It told of bloodshed, bravery, death and great deeds of honor and courage. When darkness forbade him read any longer, he crawled onto his humble cot and wept for the joy of it. The next morning he rose long before dawn and leaned so close his nose touched the parchment and his eyes ached as he read on.

The bell in the chapel sounded for prime, the hour of morning prayers, but his head was full of battles. Only when the bell sounded the second time did he rouse himself and hustle to the cathedral, to be last in line as the brothers filed in. He caught the eye of Father Adolph, whose look included reproof and surprise. Usually he was the first in line.

He often wondered later why he did not share his wonderful treasure with the other monks. Perhaps it was because for the first time in his life he had something that was his, his alone. It was something he did not want to share, something that so inflamed his mind and soul that he could think of little else. It was as if he had fallen in love.

Thoughts of the Holy Lands crept into his every waking moment, and he walked the long dusty road to Palestine many times during the weeks that followed. What joy it would be to worship in the Church of the Holy Sepulcher. What a divine blessing it would be to die for the cause of Christ, to free the Holy Lands from the Muslims and Turks.

He copied the magnificent words of the ancient historian and hollowed out a place under his bed to hide the work in progress. And so it was that the words of Fulk of Chartres became engraved on his heart and mind, and there was born in him an aching desire to be a pilgrim to the Holy Lands, whatever the cost.

When it was finished, he took the original to Father Adolph. Wonder and amazement lightened the wizened features of Father Adolph and he spent hours pouring over it. Then the father carried it in solemn procession to the bishop, who took it to Rome, where it resided permanently. Louis was forgotten as the instrument of the wonderful discovery.

Yet Louis did not forget.

Another crusade had failed, for King Richard, while winning glory and honor on the Third Crusade, returned home as empty handed as a maid who gathered eggs from molting hens. The Church of the Holy Sepulcher remained in heathen hands, and Richard had been captured by the Austrian king and held hostage. Only recently had he been freed, due to the intervention of his mother and a high ransom price. Now the king resided at Chinon in Eleanor's beloved Aquitaine.

Occasionally Louis sighted Prince Arthur as the boy ventured from the castle on hunting trips, well guarded. Each time he marveled at the steely nerve of the boy and the fierceness of his countenance, as if a small sun burned inside his body, fueling his passion and resolve. *I am looking at the next king or my name is not Louis*, he thought with a grim smile. He could only hope and pray that Arthur would be a good king, that he would ease the tax burden of the common people, that he would be fair and just.

King Richard was not evil, but he did not care for the common people of the land who groaned in oppression and injustice under the heavy taxes. Richard spent most of his time raising money for his wars with the French. Louis shook his head and sighed, thinking of the old adage—when elephants made love or war, it was the grass that died.

A full moon looked down upon a chaotic scene several weeks later. The square in front of St. Jacques seethed with crowds of commoners who rubbed shoulders with men in silk tunics and purple velvety robes and shoes with curled toes.

A year after Louis' discovery of the book, an itinerant preacher, a priest from a monastery in Nevilly arrived in the district preaching about a pilgrimage to the Holy Land. Louis followed his superiors from the abbey, standing a discreet distance from the man who had taken the name of John.

The priest wore a tattered robe and a rope belt; his feet were shod in sturdy sandals, his hair long and uncombed. He was so dirty there were visible layers of filth on his skin, for some considered it a sacrifice to give up cleansing oneself. It was rumored that he was Peter the Hermit come back to life, but Louis did not believe it. He had seen the man consume a whole chicken, a loaf of bread, a great wedge of cheese, and two large mugs of ale. He was flesh and blood, for certes.

Father John's voice echoed off the stone walls of the cathedral, and from the first syllable Louis was entranced. The priest spoke of the indignities to which the Muslim heathens subjected the holy sites, of the torture and slaying of noble Christian rulers, knights and pilgrims. He told the story of a man who was flayed and then roasted and still remained enough alive to shout out that he saw Jesus and the great apostle Peter at God's right hand.

"Oh, my brothers! Can we stand by and watch this happen? This is only one instance of many thousands who have died in shame and great pain for the cause of Christ! Rouse! Rouse! We must fight them until the sand is red before the mighty city of Jerusalem, and the Holy Sepulcher is once again in the hands of Christians!"

The crowd wept and cheered, and then a tall, broad-shouldered youth with flaxen hair stepped out, knelt before the preacher, and cried, "I will go! I will take the cross!" A knight came next, drew his sword, and laid it at the feet of the prophet.

Many men came forward after him, men who knelt, lifted their hands toward heaven and shouted out their vows. Brother John laid his hands upon each one and gave them a red cloth cross to sew front and center upon their robes.

Louis stood rooted to the spot, his eyes fixed on the sword of the young man as it lay on the ground not two feet from where he stood. Terror blinded him; he shook as if a strong wind, like a blast from hell, struck. He fell forward and the moonlit scene disappeared.

It was gloaming, early twilight, and low sunlight filtered through thinly scattered clouds. A light, misty rain pattered on the mulberry leaves in the hedge, and the earth gave up a damp, mossy scent. He led Juneberry from the pasture, and when the rain increased, he picked up his pace. But the cow would not be hurried. She stretched her neck and lowed with bovine sufferance.

He tugged on the rope. "Come along, you stupid old cow." Suddenly he saw something that made him drop the rope and fall to his knees behind the hedge. Wetness soaked through his hose, but he took no notice and pushed aside the damp leaves to get a better look.

Mama was coming home. He saw her red scarf tied around her auburn hair, a mattock over her shoulder. But this was not what caused his alarm. Two knights, mounted on fine steeds, halted near and called out to her. She lifted her face and replied to their greeting. One knight stayed in the saddle, but the other dismounted and began talking to her. Louis could not hear what was said, but the horses and the armor took his eye—the horses were a black and a bay. What he wouldn't give for a ride on one of them.

He almost rose from his knees, almost called out, but something happened. The knight on the ground made a grab for Mama. She shook her head, first with a laugh and a wave of her hand, then anger laced her tone. Why did she talk with them? What did they want of her?

He trembled like a leaf blown upon the wind, struggling to understand, wondering and worrying, willing his mother to leave these men and run to the safety of home.

Now the knight grabbed for her but she dodged away. She seemed small and frail next to his bulk. The knight grabbed a handful of hair, yanked her toward him. She screamed and did something that Louis could only imagine was a bite to his arm. The man yelped. She danced away.

Louis ground his teeth and gripped handfuls of damp earth. He longed to cry out, but his throat was too tight. Besides, what he could do against two armed knights? Mama, flee! Don't speak with those men. They are evil, and—

"God bless you, my son!"

He opened his eyes. He was kneeling, the damp earth soaking his hose, just as in his dream. A coarsely woven cross was in his hands. Tears washed his cheeks. He kissed the cross and bent his head to the ground. *I could not save Mama when she needed me. Has God given me the vision to show how I can redeem himself?* He lifted his hands and cried, *"Deus lo Volt!"* God wills it!

His words were taken up, until all those who gathered in the square shouted it, their voices echoing off the walls of the cathedral. *Deus lo Volt! Deus lo Volt! Deus lo Volt!*

CHAPTER FOUR

Let not the one who girds on his armor boast like him who takes it off. II Kings 20:11

Tours, France, April 1198

Sir Frederick FitzRauf pulled back on the reins of his destrier on the verge of the hill and surveyed the softly folding fields, the greens and yellows of spring that spread out before him like a huge palette. From the top of his lance, a banner whipped in the wind. It was a black banner with a charging bull in its center. On the horizon, smoke hung from his raid last night of several small villages on the French-Brittany border.

"It was a fair day's work, my lord." He tipped his chin to indicate the line of palfreys and wagons bearing the loot they had stolen last night.

Lord Ahab FitzRauf grunted. "I would say that, my son. You have won the right to ride by my side in honor. We have conquered this little part of the world while King Richard is busy fighting his father and the French. How many women did we capture last night?"

Frederick did not smile, but sat straighter in his saddle. "Forty-two, m'lord. Ten fine wenches. All of them good to look upon."

FitzRauf threw his head back and roared with laughter. "Leave it to you to pick the lovely ones! And what of gold?"

"Five sacks from the castle of Langeais. We killed the lord and his family and servants, except for a fair maiden that took my eye. For certes, m'lord. It t'was a profitable night!"

Sir Frederick bobbed his head when his adopted father burst into another peal of laughter. They rode through a village, raising dust, chickens, and even a peasant or two that fluttered from their path. A young boy beside the road shook his scraggily head and lifted his dirty face in awe as they passed. Frederick's mind flew back over the years.

He had not always been Sir Frederick, the son of Baron Ahab FitzRauf. Long ago he had been as that boy at the well. One evening he went to fetch water at the well, and soldiers thundered into the village, uttering yells and brandishing their swords. They lighted the straw-roofed homes with fire and killed all who tried to protect themselves.

He ran home screaming only to witness his mother's rape and murder. When he dashed into the street, sick with shock and terror, his father was being hacked to pieces in front of his eyes. He sank down beside the well to heave up his small dinner and weep. Several hours later, another band of soldiers descended on the village and captured all those who survived the raid. The soldiers rounded up the survivors and they trekked through the long night.

The next morning, Frederick found himself at FitzRauf's castle Renault north of Tours and was told it was King Richard's men who attacked their village, that the baron had saved the village and drove the Brabacons away.

FitzRauf brought the boy into his study the next morning—dirty, untaught and ignorant—noted that he had the look of royalty, adopted him as a son, and cleped him a grand name in honor of his hero, Frederick Barabossa.

He was trained first as a page, then he advanced to squire and then was knighted. His most important lesson was in the field of hatred, for he was taught day and night to hate the English, to hate King Richard, to hate all his kin. To hate in particular the young Prince Arthur of Brittany.

"Why should I hate him, Father?" he asked once.

FitzRauf chose his words carefully but they came with the force of an earthquake, so passionately did he speak. Frederick never forgot a single word. "Because the English destroyed your village and your family. Because they are set on destroying all that is good on God's green earth. Because we are better than they and some day we will till their lands and tend their shops and rule from their thrones. That is why, my son. I have chosen you because you are a fine, intelligent boy. You must believe me when I say the English, and especially this brood of King Henry's, the Plantagenets, are evil above all creatures on earth. They are spawned in hell, for certes, and it is our duty to root them out and kill them to our dying day."

If Frederick had been a little older or a little wiser, he might have seen through the thin guise of righteous indignation and named it something else—perhaps greed, perhaps jealousy, most certainly evil—but he was only a very young boy who had been rescued by a powerful and wealthy man. So he swallowed the lies whole and they became the very fabric of his life.

Now he pulled back on the reins at the top of a ridge. His father reined in beside him to survey the Loire Valley spread out before them. Frederick sighed. "I wish we had taken Prince Arthur at Bille. It was my fault, father. To think I would be bested by a boy of eight years. I shall go to my grave in shame."

FitzRauf shrugged. "Think not of it, son. That was four years ago. Now we are in a good position. I build my fief and you shall share in it, for I have no other son. And someday you shall marry Aubrey and rule in my stead. Then you shall know that the path to success is paved by aggressive warfare, not by hanging your head in sorrow over a failure past. That you recovered from your injuries was an answer to prayer."

Frederick nodded, but his face was solemn. "Yea. I know you are right, but it cuts to the heart of the matter. I shall practice harder than ever, Father."

FitzRauf laughed. "Come! Let us ride. I feel in fine fettle this morn."

At the castle, FitzRauf leaped to the ground in the outer bailey while servants came scurrying to tend the horses. He yelled commands as he strode into the main hall, kicking aside dogs and children. Frederick followed at a more leisurely pace, seeing to the well-being of his horse, taking messages from his page, and drinking a mug of wine. He found his father in the dungeons in company with Egbert, his seneschal.

"I want to see the women," FitzRauf said, rubbing his hands in delight.

A creaky door opened and in a room smelling of musty rushes and manure, ten women sat, stood, or lay on the straw. Most of them were young, some mere girls, and all were dirty. The younger girls regarded him with lively eyes and lovely faces.

"This one and this one." FitzRauf indicated a young girl in her early teens and another older woman who was very comely. "They will do." He ignored the questions, wails, tears and screams. He turned to go. "Which one do you want?"

"I have already chosen, Father, and she is now in my quarters being scrubbed."

The baron barked a laugh and cast him an appreciative glance.

At the table that night, sitting beside his father on the raised dais, looking down the Great Hall at their hundred or so retainers, knights, servants, and slaves, those above the salt and below it, Frederick allowed himself a sigh of content, for he knew his future was secure. Yet he could not remove from his mind the picture of that young boy on a white stallion who showed such courage and mettle on his first field of battle.

He glanced over at his father. "When shall we fight again?"

FitzRauf sat alone, drinking steadily from his wine cup. "Eh?" He set the mug down, sloshing some wine on the table. "Speak up, boy! I canna' hear thee for the noise in this place!"

Frederick raised his voice, leaned forward. "When shall I fight Prince Arthur? I am itching to duel with him, for I am much improved in my skills with the sword."

FitzRauf eased back in his chair and studied him as if he were a horse in his stable. "Aye, I see you have grown, filled out, and they tell me you are clever and quick with the sword. But be at ease. Your time will come, and your enemy will be within your reach. Aye, my son. You shall be ready and you shall destroy him as you would stomp out the life of a rat!" He belched a laugh, called for more wine.

Frederick allowed himself a small sip of wine and pushed away from the table. In his room he lit the lamp and leaned over his books. Pictures of warfare filled the pages. He studied each drawing as if it were life itself to him. His desire to sink his sword deep into the heart of Prince Arthur brought sweat to his brow, the shakes to his hands. After awhile he walked in the castle gardens to ease his mind. It was only then that he sought rest, but even in his dreams, he fought the Prince. And he won.

That evening a lone rider approached the barbican gate of the castle. A guard moved into the lamplight. "Halt! Who goes there?"

"A friend. Come and see, my good man." He held out his right hand on which resided a large ring.

The guard approached warily, backed by two burly men. Their faces changed when they saw the insignia on the ring.

The young man on the tired horse drew his hand back and nodded. "Open the gate."

The guards sprang back to the gate, pulled at the chains, and lowered the drawbridge. The rider proceeded to the outer bailey where grooms came to take his horse and a page accompanied him into the waiting room of the Great Hall.

"Baron FitzRauf is at his ease," a servant said, bowing low. "He left word that he was not to be disturbed."

The young man shook his head. He was weary from long days in the saddle and longed for a bath, a meal, and a bed. But he had business to do first. "I must see your master immediately, alone, and in private. Here. Take this ring to him."

The servant bowed again and left on quiet feet.

Fifteen minutes later, the young man was ushered into a bare cold room. FitzRauf sat in the only chair. His hair was wet and his face was red, but he stood when the young man entered. "I am sorry for the delay. Can we not talk in the morning? I am in the middle of … something important."

The young man nodded and smothered a smile with the back of his hand. "Yea, my lord. It is only this missal from my lord Prince John." He untied a leather pouch at his side and withdrew a rolled parchment that was sealed with wax and the prince's seal. This he handed over to the baron with a bow.

FitzRauf took the roll as if holding a live coal, but he did not untie the purple ribbon or break the seal. "Very well." He cleared his throat and pulled his silk robe closer around his naked body. "I shall see that you are housed and fed. If you desire a young maiden…"

The messenger smiled but shook his head. "All I desire is a warm meal and a bed, my lord. I shall see thee in the morning. There are things my lord bade me tell you that he would not dare to commit to writing. And I am sure you will have messages for me to take back to him."

"Yea. In the morning, then." FitzRauf caught himself in the act of bowing. Calling a servant, he gave brief instructions and watched as the young man departed down the hall. He wanted to return to the young girl who lay in his bed, yet his curiosity was even greater to read the message from the prince. Carefully he untied the ribbon, broke the seal and unrolled the parchment.

Skipping down through the lengthy introductions, he stopped at the first paragraph of note. He read it with bated breath, racing through the lines to the end of the letter. The veins on his forehead turned purple, stood out like miniature rivers. He raised his arms, crying aloud, a cry that resounded throughout the castle. "Yes!"

***

May 1198

Spring was in evidence throughout all the land—one could hear it in the whir of bumble bees, the song of the meadowlark, the chuckle of the brook. Yet the heat in the stables that day rivaled that of summer as Prince Arthur applied a brush to Kazimer's belly. The white stallion snorted and shifted his feet. Arthur poured a mixture of linseed oil and bear's lard onto a soft cloth, then lifted each hoof and polished it. At last he set the last hoof down and admired his work. Kazimer seemed to understand that he was beautiful, for he nuzzled his master's hand for an apple.

"Aye, my friend, now you are fit for a king to ride." Arthur smiled, producing the apple and scratching the arched neck. "And tonight you shall carry me on my—"

"Hard at work?" DeArmond strode into the stall. He ran his hand over the smooth withers and rump of the stallion, his eyes twinkling. "You have done a good job. Are you ready?"

Arthur set aside the brush and nodded. "I am ready, save for donning my clothes. Do you think the service will take long, DeArmond? I would love to go for a run this evening, if my lady mother does not talk too long a time." He grinned because he knew how unlikely that event would be.

DeArmond shook his head. "I know not how long the queen will speak, lad. But I know you will face her displeasure if you are late. Look! The lords of Brittany arrive."

Arthur stepped outside the stable and watched as baron and lord and earl followed in procession across the drawbridge of the castle, followed by their standard bearers, their men at arms, their servants, pages and squires. A few even brought their dogs. To DeArmond's repeated warning, Arthur sprinted up the back stairway into the castle proper, ran down a series of hallways and burst into his quarters where half a dozen young men waited to dress him.

He dressed in white hose, a blue silk tunic held at the waist with a gold chain, a white velvet doublet that was padded on the shoulders and embroidered with gold thread, and a dark blue cape lined with white fox fur and embroidered with the Planatagenet emblem. A thin circlet of gold rested on his fair hair. He strutted in front of the full-length bronze mirror, twirling his beautiful cape, admiring his reflection until they hustled him out. Servants paced before and after him—those forward cleared the way and announced his arrival, those after guarded his back and kept the crowds at bay. A little servant girl threw flower petals before him as he entered the Great Hall.

He never lacked for attention, and this occasion was no different. When he entered the Great Hall, smiles of welcome were on the faces of the courtiers, the barons and lords, his knights and squires and a small group of French nobility. They all wanted a word with him, crowded around to pat his back, to congratulate him, to curry his favor. He spoke a word here and there, then allowed Dominque to lead him to the table on the dais where his mother, sister, stepfather and DeArmond waited.

After the meal, Constance rose to her feet. A hush fell upon the bedlam of the hall. After a lengthy speech during which Arthur stifled more than one yawn in his sleeve, she picked up her glass. "And so today I present to you my son, Prince Arthur."

He stood and bowed to the spatter of cheers and light applause. He felt suddenly embarrassed, unsure. Constance looped her arm through his and flashed him a smile.

"He has come of age, being twelve years this month, and so is able to rule this kingdom. I thereby proclaim that Prince Arthur will rule beside me until his fifteenth birthday, when I shall step aside, and he shall rule alone!"

The prince bowed while the barons and knights made much of the occasion, calling out toasts in his name, standing to declare a deed the prince had performed, calling for more wine, feasting until they could hold no more. He accepted this adulation with the air of one long accustomed to much praise, nodding his head politely to each man, but silently wishing the affair were over.

"I raise my glass to the new king!" DeArmond called out, lifting his cup, a grin lurking beneath his beard. The uproar in the room lasted a full five minutes.

Arthur saw Lord Ranulf stiffen and cast a doleful glance at DeArmond. He wondered if Ranulf would challenge the statement, but then shrugged, caring little for what his stepfather thought or to whom he sent messages.

It seemed that the kingdom truly was his—his for the taking. Richard himself had already declared Arthur as heir apparent. Yet he had scarcely met his royal uncle. Richard was busy at his castle Chinon in Poitou, marshaling his forces for a war with the French. At times, Arthur fretted over the lack of contact he had with Richard. Why hadn't the king asked him to come to be trained for the throne? Was that not the custom? Did Richard still hold out hope for a son?

DeArmond signaled to Arthur with raised brows when the affair was finished. Arthur rose, bowed to the assembled guests, gave his arm to his mother, and began the procession to the outer bailey. The barons and their ladies followed, cheering as they went.

He mounted Kazimer while his audience, augmented by several hundred from the nearby village, roared their approval. Riding a tight circle around the outer bailey, knowing he made a fine sight, he galloped across the drawbridge, under the barbican gate and out into the forest.

***

"What are we going to do about the upstart in Brittany?"

Prince John sprawled in opulent grandeur in the rose garden at the royal castle at Rouen. Two girls, one at each elbow, nestled close to him on the cushioned bench. He wore soiled robes of silk and velvet with ermine at the neck and wrists. A circlet of gold nestled on his dark head.

John glanced up at the questioner, his dark eyes sharp with intelligence. Lord FitzRauf had proved to be loyal to his personage, an able spy in the court of Constance. Sighing, John dismissed the two girls with the air of one burdened with the affairs of the world.

"I have a suspicion that you have an answer to your own question, my friend." John adjusted his robes, but did not bother to cover his pudgy legs. The jewels on his fingers twinkled in the light of the late afternoon sun.

The baron bowed. His clothes were impeccable, from the curled toes of his shoes to his fur-lined cape. "The boy has been named co-regent, Your Majesty." He shifted his weight and eyed the couch beside John. "He begins to think he will one day rule the English throne."

John snorted. "Don't we all?" He glanced up at the man, despising him. "By God's ears, man, sit down." He motioned to a hard wooden bench not far away. "What do you propose I should do about Prince Arthur? Assassinate him?" He laid back his head and chortled with laughter, ending with a snort. He wiped his eyes with his sleeve.

The baron lowered his bulk to the bench, but remained ramrod straight, a frown playing upon his stern features. "Hardly, Your Majesty. But you must know that Richard is favoring the young lad as an heir."

"I know, you fool!" John leaped to his feet, pressing his face close to FitzRauf's. John whirled to stride the length of the small garden, then returned. "We need to discredit the boy in Richard's mind and we must insinuate fear and distrust in Constance's mind toward Richard and the English. Also, we must not allow Richard to train the young boy in his court. A man in both courts, English and French. Can you manage such a thing?"

FitzRauf chuckled. "I shall be the man in the duchess' court, my liege. It will be an easy task, for certes. The queen is half mad as it is because of her hatred for Richard and the English. She likes you, though." His eyes glinted as he slanted a glance at the prince.

John grinned. "Yes. We are kindred spirits. Get someone in Richard's court, FitzRauf. His mission is to discredit the prince in the king's eyes. But we need someone placed close to the most influential man in the kingdom, Sir William Marshall. He must believe that I am the better choice for England when my illustrious brother dies."

He stopped pacing and pierced the baron with a bright gaze. "I shall take that task upon myself. I know the Marshall and I think he likes me." John smiled and cast a glance at the doorway through which the girls had disappeared. "Now, if you will excuse me, I have other matters to attend to. Send me regular reports."

"Very well, my liege."

"FitzRauf." John's voice was low, so low the baron had to turn back and cock his ear.

"Yes?"

"On occasion, you may find yourself in a position to cause ... what shall we say? An unfortunate accident to the prince. I should be appreciative if the prince did not to recover. Very appreciative. Do you understand?" John's black eyes, like tiny rapiers, met the baron's with deadly intent.

The baron nodded. "I understand, my lord. I shall send you reports. Good day."

Two months later, Prince Arthur answered a summons to his mother's private chambers. In her audience room, Lord Ranulf sat at the foot of the long table with his arms crossed over his chest and a frown on his face. To his right sat his staunchest ally, Baron FitzRauf. Also in attendance were DeArmond, two other barons and five knights.

Princess Eleanor graced a window embrasure, keeping busy with her embroidery.

Arthur perched beside her, jostling her elbow and grinning impudently when she lost her place. "A letter from Richard," he whispered. "Listen, Eleanor. My wager is that the king wishes me to go to him at Chinon. How much will you raise?"

"Sh!" The Pearl of Brittany frowned, ruining the perfect brow of which so many jongleurs sang. "I don't know. How about my ring?" She displayed a ring Mother had given her for Christ's Mass last year, one of exceeding beauty, a large emerald encircled by small diamonds.

"But what shall you give me?" Dimples played beside her mouth, her blue eyes twinkled.

"My dog, Gawain!" Hearing his name, the dog loped up to him and lay down beside his feet. He scratched an ear. "I swear. Sh! Listen, now!"

"But I don't want—"

"Sh!"

The seneschal read the letter. Salutations and formalities aside, it was as Arthur surmised— an invitation for Constance to bring her son to Chinon.

"Your ring!" Arthur whispered, nudging her elbow. "Come, Sister. You promised."

"It is not fair. You knew. You had to know." She flushed, but she drew it from her finger. With a grin he pocketed it, and then turned back to the conversation, for something was amiss.

Constance was pacing nervously. "Nay, I do not think we should go. I have forebodings about it."

"Ma Mere." Eleanor rose. "I would like to meet Queen Eleanor, for I am named for Her Highness! I have heard she is very beautiful." Heavy silence descended. "Though not as beautiful as you."

Constance shook her head. "There are many things to consider, child, not the least of which is the safety of the prince."

"Safety, Ma Mere?" Arthur stood, annoyed that his voice cracked as he spoke. He swallowed, spoke in a lower tone. "Uncle Richard said he would send his soldiers to protect us on our journey. We can take some of our own knights. Why do you say I will be in danger? Mere, are you well?"

He took a step toward her, for she was frozen in place, a glazed look in her eyes. He had seen her other times when she looked like this and it worried him.

She snapped from her reverie, paced nervously to the window and back again.

Arthur reached for her arm. "I beseech you. I shall be safe and well tended. We all need a holiday." He drew himself up to his full height. "I am the prince of Brittany. We shall go!" But he might as well have been talking to the wind, so much did she heed his words.

She looked at the quiet man at the end of the table. "My lord Ranulf, what say you of this? FitzRauf? You are a man of wisdom. Shall we go to Chinon? So my son can be trained in warfare, in courtly ways, in the ways of royalty, as Richard wrote? As if I could not train him! As if we are destitute of manners." She folded her arms under her breasts. "Speak, or I shall die."

Ranulf stared with open hostility at his wife.

To Arthur, it seemed time itself stood still, only his heart proceeded with loud knockings in his chest. "I already said that we should—"

"Be still and sit down, thou puppy!" Ranulf turned to him with hatred gleaming from his small eyes. "This is not a matter for you to decide. FitzRauf? What do you say?"

Arthur fell back on the bench as if he had been slapped. He thought surely DeArmond would spring up, challenge the cursed Norman lord to a duel...do something. DeArmond shifted his weight, cracked his knuckles, sat back and sighed.

FitzRauf raised his large head and stood. "My lady queen, I am against this expedition. I can say nothing but good of King Richard, for I have given him my allegiance, but neither can I encourage you to throw your life away, and the life of this fair young prince."

The queen gasped and threw her hand to her breast. The others in the room stirred uneasily, for his words were close to treason. There was the sound of the clank of swords in hilts and the rustle of booted feet in the rushes.

FitzRauf lifted a hand, his face the color of rust. "Nay! Hear me out. By God's ears!" He used an epithet common to John. "Do you imagine that the king wishes to prosper the prince? What dreamers you are. Tell me this. Who is the most likely candidate to depose him and seize the throne? Even though Arthur is a boy of tender years, yet it has reached the King that he now commands Brittany."

He took a step nearer to the queen and lowered his voice. "I have heard by trusted means that the King has become morose and is given to fits of ill temper. He rants in his delusions of eliminating all other contenders for the throne. And who is the next in line? Is it not Prince Arthur?"

His voice rose. He paced the hall, flinging his arms about as if he were fighting off a horde of demons. "What then, my queen? Would you put the Prince in the way of danger? Nay! I plead with you, in the name of all decency, common sense, and caution to desist in this ill-avowed plan. Go not to Chinon, nor even near to it. And let not Richard so much as set his eyes upon the boy. Thus all of Brittany will applaud your courage and great wisdom. I plead with you. I beg you!" He ended the speech upon bended knee before the queen's chair, tears streaming down his cheeks.

The words struck like the deadly poison of a snake. Arthur saw his mother's face turn from red to a pasty gray, her hand clutch her throat. He heard DeArmond mutter under his breath, saw the blood race to his face, his hand inch toward his sword hilt. With the clarity of youthful eyes, he knew the deception for what it was.

FitzRauf was a good actor and could have carried his weight with any traveling troupe of thespians, yet Constance swallowed the lies whole.

Arthur rose, paced to the front of the room, his hand on his sword. He addressed his stepfather. "My lord, I must say a word in behalf of my uncle and liege lord, King Richard. Is it not the custom for a youth to be trained in the court of the king, or lord, or baron if he would be the heir of the fief? There is nothing more sinister in this than that. What means FitzRauf to accuse the king under whose banner we serve and live?"

"Sit down!" Constance stood beside him, glaring with her sea-green cat eyes, her fists balled at her sides as if she were about to strike him. He sat, his face burning with shame, his heart drumming loudly, his knees suddenly turned to water. Who could stand before his mother when she was like this? How could he get her to see the truth?

"You must forgive my son." She paced the long hall and returned. "What does a lad of his years know of the affairs of the kingdom? Lord FitzRauf, your words have struck my heart like a thrown lance. I thank you for them, for I see my way clear at last. We will not respond to the king. Come what may, we will protect the prince from King Richard! We will not go to Chinon!"

DeArmond shuffled his feet, looked at the floor. "My lady," he said in his deep, rough voice. "I seek permission to ask a question."

She turned her glittery eyes upon him. "Ask."

"What shall we do in case King Richard takes the matter … seriously? Shall I muster men for war, madam?"

"War! It will not come to that, DeArmond," FitzRauf said hurriedly. "Richard will not push the issue that far."

DeArmond turned to look the man square in the eye. "Are you sure of that? Can you stake your life on it? Are you aware of what it means to disobey the king?"

"You are a man of war, DeArmond. I am for peace. I am a servant of Their Majesties."

And also Prince John, Arthur thought bitterly.

"Above all, we must protect the Prince." FitzRauf bowed to the duchess.

"Peace! That is rich from a man like you." DeArmond turned away.

Constance lifted her hand. "He is right. We will face whatever consequences lie ahead. My mind is made up. The prince will never be sent to King Richard as long as I draw breath in my body!"

DeArmond bowed. "As you wish, m'lady."

It did not take long for another message to arrive at the castle Mordelias from King Richard. This missal was more pointed. Prince Arthur must come or measures would be taken. When that, too, was ignored, Richard sent yet another message to Constance.

In this letter he invited the queen to meet him at a point on their borders to discuss the matter openly and frankly. Once again, Constance and FitzRauf objected strenuously. And so, for the last time, Richard sent a message, addressed to Lord Ranulf.

Prince Arthur, flanked by DeArmond and his friend, Lord Pierre de Gironde, sat on the dais in the Great Hall at the close of dinner with his family, FitzRauf, half a dozen barons, knights, a bishop and two dozen servants who sat below the salt. The noise in the room had reached mammoth proportions when a messenger appeared in the doorway.

Lord Ranulf beckoned to him. The room fell silent as he stepped to the front and began reading. The tone was harsh. Either comply with the king's command or face imprisonment. Furthermore, it placed Brittany on notice of war. Richard's Brabacons would march within a fortnight and take the prince by force.

Prince Arthur sat stiffly, eyeing his mother, cold fear squeezing his heart. Silence reigned in the hall; all eyes stayed upon the duchess and her Norman husband. No one, save Arthur, noticed the pleased smile that FitzRauf hid behind his hand.

"Now what say you, Constance?" Lord Ranulf asked in his high, almost feminine voice that could be heard above a dogfight for a bone. "Will you send the boy or not?"

Arthur noted his mother's clenched jaw, how she gripped the armrests on her chair fiercely and he knew her answer before she spoke. "I will never send Arthur to him as long as I have breath in my body!"

"Aye, Constance. So you have said many times." Lord Ranulf leaned closer, his narrow, pinched mouth almost smiling. "As a loyal subject to my king, I must do as he says. I must have you imprisoned. Is that what you wish? Your royal brother-in-law is determined to have his way. He means what he says. He will have the boy one way or another. The Lionhearted will overcome you. Nothing will stand in his way."

Arthur wanted to shout out that it was FitzRauf who had urged them to defy the king. It should have been him who was imprisoned—him and Lord Ranulf, that blackguard of a Norman. He reached his hand under the table and felt the cool metal of his sword. How he longed to plunge its length into his step-father's heart. But he held himself stiff and sat silent beside DeArmond. The others in the hall maintained their frozen postures; no one dared hardly to breathe.

The queen folded her arms inside the red velvet sleeves of her robe. "Prepare for war, DeArmond. I will go pack. It seems my husband must obey his king." She turned and swung dramatically through the door.

Arthur wanted to call her back, to demand that she give in to Richard. He sat silent and cold, his anger turning to the ice of bitterness. The men around the table looked at one another with raised brows. The Queen's footsteps faded away. The moment was gone.

The prince sat while the Great Hall erupted into sound and motion—DeArmond shouting orders, knights leaping to their feet, dogs barking, captains issuing orders, squires running with urgent messages. He stared at a faded tapestry on the wall: the betrayal of Jesus by His friend and companion, Judas. He blinked several times against a strange stinging in his eyes and hoped no one noticed when he sniffed and rubbed his nose on his sleeve.

Rising slowly, he made his way off the dais, through the corridors and down the long stairways to the stables. Kazimer whinnied low as he approached the stall. Feeding him an apple stolen from the table, Arthur stroked the warm, soft flanks of his horse and wept silently into the flowing white mane.

Father, I hope you cannot see from heaven. I have failed thee. God knows I tried to change their minds, but they would not listen. And now...now the kingdom is lost. And so am I.

That evening, cloaked in secrecy, Arthur made his way down the corridors of the great castle, through the Hall, and out into the inner bailey. There he mounted a sturdy little Welsh pony that had been his favorite as a child. A groom held the reins. Arthur pressed a coin into the man's hand, heard his murmur of thanks, then kicked the horse and made for the barbican gate. It, too, had been raised, and the prince proffered more gold coins into the hands of those who stood silently, waiting for him to pass.

"I shall return when the moon is high," he whispered to Gallaent, the head guardsman on duty that evening. "I will give the call of the owl, my good man. Can you keep a still tongue in your head?"

Gallaent nodded, but his mouth was a straight, thin line and Arthur knew he disapproved. "Take care, my lord. It will mean my head if anything—"

"I know." Arthur patted his shoulder. "I shall return. Watch for me."

Then he was out and away, riding down a forest path that he knew so well he could close his eyes and ride it safely. The little pony knew it, too, and desired to return speedily to his warm stall and half-full feed bag, for his feet beat double-time on the pine-needled path.

After a while, Arthur noted a large dolmen and slowed the pony to a walk, turning after a few steps into a dim track that led deeper into the forest. Suddenly he pulled back on the reins. Had that been the stomp of a horse's hoof on the path behind him? He listened. A mist rose from the ground and gathered in the trees like a soft veil. Something moved in the underbrush. Fear brushed his heart, sent shivers down his arms.

He tried to shrug it off but his stomach knotted and his mouth was dry. Who would follow? Who knew of his plans? Would a black knight come bursting from the fringe of fir trees just over there?

"Come on, Thunder, thinking about things won't help." He kicked the pony and continued, but stopped again. There was someone coming. Directing his horse behind a bush, he slipped off, drew sword and crept back where he could see the dim trail.

The moon that had been under a bank of clouds now burst into the clear evening sky with a brilliance that lit the forest. Green-silver fir needles framed his view of the meadow; the old oak tree down the trail shimmered in the moonlight; the shadow of a large stone loomed nearby.

After what seemed an interminable wait, a horse and rider emerged around the bend, the rider bent almost double, studying the ground. He seemed a large man. Something of his build stirred a memory. Who was it? Why did he follow?

He decided on the bold approach and stepped out, drawing his sword. "Are you looking for someone, sir?"

The man jolted upright. Arthur sensed rather than saw his hand reach for his sword hilt. The horse stepped closer and the moon played fully on the man's face.

Arthur let out a sigh. FitzRauf.

"I find your actions a little strange, Prince," the baron said in his gruff voice. "I saw you leave the castle furtively and thought to ride behind and keep you from harm. Is that a crime?" His friendly words belied the tight way in which he spoke and the spark of anger flashing from his eyes.

Arthur laughed. "It seems we are both upon a mission of secrecy. I assure you that I am in no harm, save for strange knights who ride with their sword easy to their hands. But since no damage has been done, I suggest you go your way and I shall go mine. Agreed, my friend?"

FitzRauf shook his head. "I cannot let you go alone. If anything happened—"

"Nothing will happen." Arthur deepened his voice, made it ring with authority. "I am not a child. I am your liege lord and I command you to stop following me and return to the warmth of your bed. Do I make myself clear?"

"Abundantly, Your Majesty." He swung his mount around and was gone.

Arthur wondered if he should set out upon his errand on another night, but with a shake of his head, he mounted and continued down the path. It seemed to deteriorate with each step and soon he wondered if he had lost his way. He could have sworn he knew this path from the old days. He had come here so often as a child ... and yet, he couldn't remember that blackened pine, or that stream.

He broke out into a small meadow. In its very center stood a hut. The door was open and inside he saw the dim flicker of a single candle. Dismounting, he tied Thunder to a bush and stepped up to the door. An old woman sat beside a plain table. Near her hand was a wooden cup and a crumb or two of stale bread. The hut was poorly appointed, only a bed along the wall, a wash basin, a cupboard and an altar.

"Come in. Heard you half a mile away. So you had an encounter, did you? Come in. Why do you stand on my doorstep like a discomfited child?"

"So you are here. I thought—"

"That I would be dead? It has not been so long, Prince, since you came to me."

He glanced at the altar and her eyes followed his gaze.

She nodded. "Yes, I still worship my little gods. Is that what you were hoping? That I could pray for you? Work some kind of a miracle for you?" She cackled and drained the ale from her cup.

He nodded. "A miracle would be fine, Mother D'engle. Here. Let me show you what I brought." From a pouch at his side, he withdrew a loaf of bread, a chunk of cheese, an apple and a small flask of wine. "I can pay you for your services."

She laughed again. "You always brought me rich gifts. Ah. Real wine. Since when have I tasted real wine? And an apple! Oh, my lord. You have outdone yourself this time." She took a sip of the wine, then stoppered the flask and laid it aside.

"What is it you want, Arthur? Name it to the highest heaven and I shall do it for thee. You are a valiant and brave prince, but you have many enemies. Some of whom you do not know."

She carried the flickering candle to her altar. It was a crude wooden affair, draped with a gold cloth that was tattered, but clean. She bent low and touched the flame to a candle on the altar. Then she reached into a flask that lay on the table and sprinkled some fine powder on the flame. It flared up, crackling and popping, blazing with all the colors of the rainbow. Her eyes slid to his face as if to measure his reaction. "Come, then, son. The gods are awakened. You must pray beside me."

He hesitated. His knees quaked and his sweaty hands shook. He wiped them on his tunic, but his feet refused to move. Why this strange feeling? He thought of his mother's Catholic faith and wondered if the Lord God would strike him dead and send his soul to hell if he prayed to the old gods of the druids.

"Come." She moved over so there was room in front of the altar and reached up a hand for him. He noticed the wrinkles on her face, that there was a twinkle in her faded eyes. She was a kindly soul; she had been a confidant and friend to him when he was young. Now she mocked him for his fears. He saw it in the sideways glance she gave him.

Silently he knelt beside her, his heart thudding in his ears, a voice in his mind telling him to flee and never return.

She murmured something so low he could not hear, then said, "What is it you want, Prince?"

"My kingdom. It is being stolen from me. I am…afraid. Afraid to flee the castle, yet afraid to stay. I feel…I feel so helpless and without power. Can the gods help me, mother?" Tears trickled down his cheeks.

"Why do you want the kingdom?"

"Because … " It was obvious, was it not? Yet, why *did* he want the kingdom? He plumbed the depths of his heart, but words failed him. "I … do not know, Mother. It is something I have always wanted. From my first breath."

She shifted and a brief smile lightened her wizened features. "Did you bring the blood, my son?"

He retrieved a tiny flask from his pouch and laid it on the altar. "This morning. A chicken."

"Very good." She pulled the plug from the flask and poured the blood on a plate. This she lay carefully on the altar and dipped her fingers in it. While she dribbled the blood over tiny clay figures that were shaped in hideous forms, she said her prayers in a strange language. Then she turned to him. "Dip your finger in the blood."

He could not extend his finger. Something hindered him. He thought of the rosary his mother wore with a cross and the figure of Christ on it.

"Prince?" The woman was waiting. "Do you truly want this prayer answered?"

He gulped, then dipped his finger in the blood and flicked it on the figure of the god, feeling a little foolish for it, yet nonetheless determined to see it through. He must win the kingdom. He must. For father.

The prayers were soon finished. Mother D'engle kissed his forehead. They rose to their feet. He pressed a gold coin in her hand and thanked her.

Her eyes shone. "Ah. You have done my old heart good. Come to see me more often, Arthur." She allowed her hand to linger on his arm. He wanted to shrug it off, for her touch burned.

She withdrew her hand and pulled from her finger a large ring. On it was the face of the same god whose little clay representative they had anointed with blood. She pressed it into his hand.

"Here. This is the Dagda—the All Father, the excellent god. He carries a double-ended club and will kill your enemies. Take him. He is thy god. He will watch over thee, Arthur, in all your ways. He will give you courage in battle, strength against your enemies, prowess in your bed, success in all your endeavors. Pray to him, Arthur. He wants your prayers."

Arthur's flesh shrank from the ring with the ugly face on it. He longed to refuse it, but he did not dare. Slipping it on his small finger, he bowed to her and made his departure.

As he rode home through the moonlit night, he wondered. Would he have success? Was this god real, or was it a sham? He shook his head and with a finger rubbed the face of the god.

"Whoever you are, Dagda, the god with the ugly face, I pray you give me the kingdom."

CHAPTER FIVE

It is not because things are difficult that we do not dare; it is because we do not dare that they are difficult. Seneca

Dijon, France, May, 1198

Dijon was a lovely city situated in a broad valley with the Cote d' Or Mountains to the west and farther away, like a snowy fringe on the horizon, the rugged peaks of the Alps. Trade here was busy, for all the caravans passed through regularly. Twice a year a fair was held in which thousands of people attended and hundreds of vendors sold wares from all over the world.

Moshe ben Itzchaki and Elias set up their stall and entertained a lively business, alluring the ladies and the wealthy lords and barons with their display of jewels and gold.

They found a home perched on a hill that closely resembled the home they left in Troyes, and the family was soon swallowed into the larger Jewish enclave. Sarah's sister and her husband accompanied them, so she was content. It took Judith many months to accept her new home, for she longed for Troyes and spoke often of it and of her friends there.

That spring trouble brewed in the country, disturbing the trade routes and caravans. Strange knights, unattached to any lord or baron, prowled the countryside and preyed upon the people, stealing, burning and raping. A ship that Elias invested in was raided by pirates and sunk. He rarely smiled and the servants seemed to tiptoe about the place.

"Amma, I would like to return to Troyes," Judith said one day as they sewed together in the cool shade of the courtyard.

Sarah glanced up and smiled. "I know. You've said it often. I would like to return, too. I miss my mother and father and my brothers very much."

Judith heard pain in her voice and glanced her way. But Amma sighed and completed her stitch, turning the garment over, smoothing the silk through her fingers.

"Why don't we go back?" Judith leaned forward, hope blooming in her heart like the primroses bloomed at her feet. "I have heard the Jews fare better there. They are protected from the heathens, the Franks. Could you talk to father? Perchance just you and I could return. For a short while."

"Daughter, I will never leave your father, so you may as well find some new friends and stop pining for something you cannot have." Sarah's tone was gentle, yet her look was stern.

Judith sat back, fighting tears. "I know, yet I was hoping that—"

"Come quickly! Mistress! Come!" A serving girl ran into the courtyard, panting.

Amma looked up. "What is it, Tabitha?"

"It is ... it is the master, my lady. He fell, and ... you must come quickly."

Sarah stood so suddenly that her embroidery fell to the stones. Judith gathered it up and placed it on the bench. With her heart beating itself out her chest, she followed the sharp slap of Sarah's anxious steps into the wide hallway, through the solarium, across the inner courtyard and into the apartments where Grandfather lived.

"In here," Tabitha said, leading the way into the library.

Judith cried out when she entered. The old man lay on the floor, his legs twisted beneath his body, his eyes closed, his face as white as the rabbi's robes. Sarah knelt beside him. Judith flew to his side. The servants had covered him with a blanket but were afraid to move him.

"Call Hiram!" Sarah shouted. Hannah, Tabitha, Hiram and Nero hurried into the room. "We must get him to his room. Help me straighten his legs."

Judith watched as they worked over Grandfather, her head dizzy and her stomach queasy. Grandfather moaned once, but at last they had him safely in his own bed, the covers pulled up around his neck, and his white beard neatly placed on his chest. His breathing seemed easier, yet he did not open his eyes. One lone lamp spread a soft yellow glow from its niche in the wall.

"Fetch the doctor," Sarah said to Nero. "Tell him it is urgent!" She turned to Tabitha. "Bring some water. We shall bathe his face and keep him comfortable."

"What happened?" Judith cried out, unable to stand at the side any longer. She knelt beside him, grasped his hand. It was icy cold.

Hannah shook her head. "I heard a noise, like something falling. He must have climbed on the stool and it moved beneath him. I found him just like he was and covered him with a blanket before I sent Tabitha."

Judith turned back to the still form. "Gran-abba!"

He opened his eyes, smiled wanly. "Judith. You have come."

"Yes, Gran-abba. How are you feeling?"

He tried to smile but was unsuccessful. "It comforts me to … know you are … here."

"You will get better, I know it! And we can take walks in the sunshine, and I can read the scrolls to you, like you love. Right, Gran-abba?"

He closed his eyes. "Yes, child. I must rest now."

"Can I bring you something? Perhaps warm milk? Perhaps some wine?"

"Nay. I care for nothing, but only your presence. Do not leave me."

She patted his arm. "Of course not. I will sleep right here beside you, if that is your wish."

He sighed, but made no reply.

"Come, child." Sarah lifted her, led her to the courtyard. "I believe our noon meal is prepared. Would you like to eat something?" She glanced back. "Tabitha, stay with him."

Judith shook her head. "No, Amma. I can't even think of eating. I'm going to move my bed to his room. I will lie on the floor to be near him."

Sarah nodded. "Yea, child. He loves you more than life itself."

When the doctor came, he examined the old man and then met with the anxious family. "He has broken a hip, and his mind is … something has happened to it, which is why he fell. We do not know what this is, but it affects older people. It is very serious, but sometimes they do recover. I am afraid that there is very little we can do for it." He rummaged in his bag. "Here is something you may give him to aid with the pain. Be sure he drinks water. Most of all, he needs rest. I will come to see him again tomorrow."

"Is he ... will he ... live?" Judith's throat tightened. Tears flooded her eyes.

"I know not. We can only watch and pray." With a bow, the man left and Judith returned to her silent vigil.

Her world became Grandfather's room. If he murmured in his sleep, she was there to fetch water, to fluff his pillow, or to rub his aching muscles. Some days they had hope he would recover. On those days the servants would carry his pallet to the courtyard and he would lie in the shade while Judith read to him, or he would watch while she stitched her needlework. His low voice, mumbling disjointed words, did not disturb her.

He lingered through the hot days of summer and into the fall. He lay unmoving, eating little, his mind wandering. It was nearing Hanukkah when Grandfather took a turn for the better. Judith joined in the celebration of the Feast of Lights, purchasing gifts for the children in the neighborhood.

Grandfather sat up on the first night of Hanukkah, while Judith, as the only child, lit the first of the seven candles. He drank some pomegranate wine and quoted some of the old prophecies. But the day after the last of Hanukkah he fell ill again, very ill. A chill wind howled down through the valley with the hint of snow in it. They brought coverlets for Grandfather, but nothing would stop his shivering. Judith, too, shook with cold that seemed to seep into her very bones.

For six days Grandfather alternated between chill and fever. For six days Judith nursed him tirelessly while her own body grew frail and her hopes died before they were born.

One morning, Father left to tend his stall, for a caravan approached the city, and Mother went to the marketplace with Nero and another servant to replenish their supplies.

Judith sat in the darkened room, unable to stop shivering even under several layers of blankets. She listened to Grandfather's raspy breath, willing him to live. Dear, dear Gran-abba, how could she survive without him?

His breathing stopped.

She reached over, shaking him, terror piercing her through. "Gran-abba! Breathe. Please breathe. Don't die!"

He took a deep breath and opened his eyes. "No, child. Not yet." His voice was clear and strong. "There is something I must give you before I go."

"I, Gran-abba? What is it that you would give me?"

He motioned that he would like to sit. She helped him, propping the pillows behind his back. He gasped from the effort, then motioned to the cypress chest in the corner. "It is time, child, and you are the one. Open the chest. Here is the key." From around his neck he lifted a golden key on a golden chain.

Wide-eyed, incredulous, wondering if his mind still wandered, Judith took the key and with trembling fingers opened the chest. Inside were his keepsakes—papers, the most precious of his scrolls, Gran-amma's wedding dress. Lovely scents wafted to her—jasmine, myrrh, cloves. It reminded her of Troyes. She wept.

"Yes, it brings back happy memories for me, too. But we have little time. At the very bottom of the chest .... " He gasped. " ... is a small box. Gold. Inlaid with jewels. Get it out, child."

Judith did as she was told. She had never seen the golden box. She held it in shaking hands. It was heavy and the sheen of dull gold, the beautiful chased work, and the jewels embedded on the lid told her it was precious. With timid fingers, she carried it across the room, much like the stone she brought to him that day so long ago.

"You must learn the secret ... while there is time." He took the box.

With quivering hands, he showed her a secret lock in the very heart of the olive tree engraved on the lid, where a large emerald resided. When he pressed the emerald and a spot on the bottom of the box, the lid sprang open. "Now you do it." He shut the lid.

She tried several times but was unsuccessful. To her satisfaction, she hit upon the right pressure at the right time and the lid opened. Inside were several large jewels—two beautiful diamonds that took her breath away and several smaller emeralds, rubies and sapphires. Her mind was so taken with the jewels that she did not see a roll of cloth at the very bottom.

Grandfather lifted the cloth and slowly unrolled the material. Inside was a tiny scroll, made of brittle parchment, of great antiquity. He showed her spidery writings on the scroll. "It is Hebrew ... ancient Hebrew." His voice was weakening. He handed her the scroll and leaned back on the pillows. "It is over one thousand years old. It has been passed ... to me through all the generations."

"What does it mean, Gran-abba?" Judith held the scroll with her fingertips as if Yahweh inscribed it Himself. She could not read the faint lettering. "What does it say? Why are you giving this to me?"

"One question at a time, Judith." Now his voice was so faint she had to lean forward to hear. His breath stirred her hair and brushed her cheek. "Someday you will study the scroll. You will understand what it says."

"Why, Gran-abba? What does it say?"

He shook his head. "You will know when the time comes. For now, you must only know that it is very precious. It is a secret of our people."

He looked at her with such intensity that it sent her pulses racing, and if she had not already been kneeling, she would have fallen on the floor beside the bed. Her throat constricted and fear closed in on her. She expelled her breath and replaced the scroll in the box.

Gran-abba's thin voice continued. "Four families were entrusted with a great secret. I was the keeper of the scroll in our family. The scrolls must be read together to unravel the secret. The names of the other families are written in the scroll." He paused. "Do you understand what I am saying, child?"

"No, Gran-abba. I do not know, cannot know. What great secret are you talking about? I am frightened. I don't want this terrible thing! Why me? Shouldn't this be passed to ... a man?" She thrust the golden casket and the scroll toward him, but he shook his head.

"You are the one, child. You care for the return of our Messiah. You are intelligent and have learned to read the Hebrew. There are no male children who live nearby. Nay, it is yours."

"But what am I to do with it? It is too much!" She clenched a handful of the coverlet, fighting against a trembling of soul and body, so much in dread that she felt she was sinking into a black pit.

"You must have courage, Judith," he said, reaching a frail hand to her head. "You care for the ancient ways. Yahweh has His hand on you. You will know what to do when the time comes." He raised her chin. "Keep the scroll as you would keep your own soul. You are now the guardian of the Secret. Pledge to me now. Pledge to me that you will keep it."

"I cannot …" She gasped. "I … don't want you to die! I don't want to be the keeper of this fearful thing!"

He lay back on the pillow. His breathing became very shallow and then stopped. Judith shook him, called his name.

He opened his eyes, too tired to speak. But she saw in the depths of his eyes the love and admiration he held for her. She knew what she must do. She knelt beside him and while the aged man's life ebbed from his body and the light flickered above her head, she laid one hand under his thigh, the ancient pledge of her people, and the other on her heart.

"By the Name of our great and holy Yahweh, maker of all things, I do vow before Him and before you that I will keep the Secret forever. That I will perform my duty for you … " Sobs choked her throat. "For my people, and for Yahweh, our God. May I be cursed forever if I fail at this task."

He opened his eyes and whispered, "I love you. May Yahweh bless you and keep you and make His face to shine upon you forever. Judith, my darling, the joy of my heart."

Judith knelt beside his bed for a long time while tears fell on the marble floor. Death rattled in his throat. The cask she held in her hands seemed heavy indeed, too heavy for a girl. She ran her fingers slowly over it and sighed deeply.

But a ray of the morning sun touched her head. Her heart filled with inexplicable peace. It was as if strong and gentle arms enclosed and drew her to a place of sanctuary. The words from a psalm of David came to mind. *In the day of my trouble, I will trust in Thee.* A bird, she supposed it was the goldfinch who had built a nest on the wall, sang a lilting melody. She smiled.

"Judith?" Mother's quick step on the tiles and her soft voice roused Judith from her reverie.

"Coming, Amma." Quickly, she replaced the small box in the chest, locked it, and put the key around Gran-abba's neck. She would leave the box hidden in the chest now, and perhaps later she could hide it in a better place.

***

Mordelias, Brittany, July 1198

56

Prince Arthur rode from the castle, across the drawbridge and into a dim forest track. A large party of his personal servants, squires and knights followed close behind. All were quiet, even glum. No joy-riding tonight, no sense of adventure or the thrill of high spirits he felt on the ride he took when he was eight.

He heard the thump of horses' hooves on the pine-needled path, the creak of leather, the jingle of a bridle, and an owl on its nightly scavange for a meal. A quarter moon hung just behind the north tower of the castle.

The Sieur de Vitre rode opposite him. Further back in the column, Princess Eleanor rode with her women, her golden hair closely confined beneath a warm woolen scarf.

At the turning of the lane, Arthur pulled on the reins and looked back for one last glimpse of Mordelias, almost expecting to see his mother's red silk scarf waving from the lower windows of the keep. But, of course, she was not there. She had been taken prisoner to one of Ranulf's castles in Normandy. Now he must leave home.

He did not think of the moon, or the damp forest smells he loved so dearly, or the feel of the fine steed he rode. No, his mood was dark as if a curse had been laid on his future. They must go stealthily, as thieves in the night. No one knew their destination save his guardian, de Vitre.

Arthur reflected bitterly on his plight, how he must flee as a fugitive from the law, a renegade in his rightful domain. How had it come to this? He knew why his mother had been taken, for she defied a direct order of the king. But why must he cringe like a dog with tail between his legs? Couldn't Brittany muster enough men to stand against King Richard? Or, if they could not, was he in such great peril from his uncle?

He rubbed a thumb across the face of his ring. The old god had not done much yet. Would he help him now? Around his neck he wore the Crown Jewel, a treasure his mother entrusted to his care should he ever have to prove his identity. It was a prize, truly. An emerald the size of which he had never seen equaled, surrounded by thirteen diamonds. The feel of it beneath his tunic filled him with comfort.

As dawn etched the sky with an array of pastels, and a lark announced the coming day, the column halted at a small inn on the outskirts of the village Piesse. At the forking of the road grew a gigantic oak which gave shade and shelter to all the creatures of the wood, both large and small. The innkeeper, a round-stomached man with a white beard and twinkly eyes, greeted de Vitre and showed them into his establishment with pride.

The princess dismounted stiffly. Weariness slumped her shoulders. Adrian took her elbow and led her into the inn. The common room contained only an old man in the corner who was rousing from either a late sleep or an early nap. The innkeeper called his wife from the kitchen.

She was as thin as her husband was round, her hair bound tightly in a scarf. She wiped her hands on her apron but failed to erase the flour from her cheeks. She bowed. "We welcomes you to our humble establishment, m'dears. It be a pleasure to have you, e'n though we mayn't speak of it. Not yet, anyhow. Annie will show you to your rooms. Hot water's acomin' and food and drink." She patted Eleanor's arm. "Ah, m'dear! I am pleased to see you safe and sound. You look tired near to death."

"Aye, madam." Eleanor lifted her chin and pulled her arm from the touch of a commoner. "We have come a long way. All I require is what you mentioned. Please do not disturb us."

Arthur hid his smile as he followed de Vitre up a flight of stairs. How could they keep their location a secret with his sister in attendance?

It was a small inn, but the food was nourishing and hot. After a meal, he sat in the croft behind the inn and strummed on a viola that a troubadour had left behind for payment of a debt. He was not a minstrel, but singing and playing came naturally and often relieved his stress.

Eleanor sat beside him and kept time with her foot as he sang. The early morning sunlight touched her golden hair and brightened the deep blue of her eyes.

Arthur stopped and laid aside the instrument.

"No, do not stop." She laid an imploring hand on his sleeve. "Your singing makes me remember ... or, helps me to forget, I should say." She laughed and looked down in her lap where her fingers intertwined with each other. "I hope Ma Mere is well."

"If anyone can manage, it be Ma Mere, Eleanor." He dug in his pocket and pressed something into her hand. "Here. You may have it back."

"Oh!" She jumped and slowly opened her hand. Her emerald ring lay there. "What? Oh, my ring! Arthur, you won it fairly. No, I do not want it. Keep it. It will remind you of me." She tried to return it but he refused and enclosed her hand within his larger one.

"Eleanor, we may be separated, for this is a crazy life. They are not after you as much as they are me. I want you to have it back. Remember to pray for me when you see it on your finger. Promise me."

She bowed her head; he caught the glimmer of tears on her cheeks. She swiped at them, then lifted her chin, her Plantagenet spirit rising. "Aye, my brother, I promise to pray for you." She slipped the ring on her finger and sighed. "But I hope we are not separated. You are the only family I have."

He kissed her cheek. "God will protect you. Now I think we should get our rest, for we shall ride far this evening. Are you well? Can you do this? Or should I send you to Ma Mere?"

"I am fine." She stood. "I can ride better than you, for I taught you how to ride, little brother. Don't forget that." Her eyes flashed and she held her back ramrod straight.

Arthur laughed and mounted the steps to his room, looking forward to a long day of sleep. Yet it seemed he had barely closed his eyes when de Vitre shook him awake. It was late evening, already dark.

"Prince! Prince!"

Arthur sat up, wide awake in an instant.

deVitre was lacing on his boots. "You must dress immediately! My lookout has spotted a contingent of the king's Brabacons, not two leagues away."

Arthur sprang from bed and noticed his valet was already hastily jerking Arthur's clothes from the bench. "Dress yourself, Paddy. I shall manage … somehow." He pulled on his own clothes for the first time in his life. "How about the princess, deVitre? Is she up?"

"She is downstairs packing food."

Arthur fumbled with his points and had to have Paddy tie the knots that held his hose to the tunic and thought about deVitre. He was an able man in the Cabinet, but how was he with a sword? Could Arthur count on his aid in a pitched battle? Or was his arm too weakened with age?

As if reading his thoughts, deVitre unsheathed his sword. It was beautifully wrought and he obviously took great pride in it. His eyes glittered as he shoved it back into its sheath. "I keep it sharpened. I'm not too old to fight, if it comes to it, but we are small in number, and I would rather avoid trouble. If we do fight, we must kill them all. Just one escapes, and he will run back to his master and we will have the whole army down upon us."

The prince smiled as he led the way out the door and down the steps into the common room. "Come, let us see what this day has for us, then. I am not afraid to fight, as you well know. Bring them on. They shall see how a Breton fights."

Several folk from the village gathered in the courtyard to watch the squires ready the horses, their murmured comments rising to applause when Arthur and Eleanor made their appearance. Arthur took the time to smile and acknowledge his admirers before they hoisted him into the saddle.

He tarried overlong, for he heard the hoof beats of the soldier's horses approaching as they clattered over the cobblestones and flew from the village. The Brabacons spotted them and gave chase. Arthur loved the dead run of a good chase, but he sorely missed Kazimer. Since his beautiful stallion was as easily recognized as himself, he had left him in his stall at Mordelias.

They followed deVitre's lead through the forest lanes, up steep embankments, across streams and through villages, scattering chickens and children alike in a thundering pace. The soldiers behind steadily gained. Arthur glanced back and noted that his sister rode well and seemed to be enjoying the chase as much as he.

deVitre allowed Arthur to ride up beside him. "Take the right fork here. I will take the princess to the left. We will meet at the castle Fontaine."

Arthur nodded, caught the eye of his sister for a brief instant and nodded to her. "I will see you in the morning."

Her eyes widened, then she smiled, nodded and reined her horse away. He spurred his horse, motioning to Paddy and five others to follow his lead. There was little time for thought, but a premonition darted through his head like a thrown spear. *You will never see Eleanor again.* He spat his disbelief. Of course he would see her again, in the morning at the castle.

His horse plunged through a frothy creek. He spurred it up a steep incline. The pack behind closed in. On the clear morning air, he heard a yell.

"The prince! Prince Arthur!"

Arthur glanced back and saw several hard-faced soldiers were in the van of the chase, closing now with great speed. He couldn't help but notice Paddy's pale face. Arthur must soon stop and fight, or completely elude the enemy. He knew they would be seriously outnumbered and that some of them, namely his valet, who was not trained to fight, would be killed outright. "Stay with me!"

They urged their horses closer, then at a turning of the road where overhanging oaks shielded his passage, Arthur swung off the road and straight up an embankment. It was hard going, but his horse scrambled up, up. The grunts of the other horses, the scraping of their hooves on rock and the rattle of stones followed him as the others urged on their mounts.

Halfway up, in a copse of alders, he pulled up on the reins. The others arrived. He held his hand for silence while he listened, a slight breeze carrying away the dust. The sound of hoof beats thudded below. Soldiers passed the point where he left the trail. He waited a few more seconds and then looked at his men.

"This won't keep them puzzled for long," he said. "We will go back the way we came, but now we have a few minutes reprieve. We will split up. My valet and I will ride south, where there is a forest I know. Lord Pierre, take the others and ride to the castle and join deVitre. If you are overtaken by the king's soldiers, you will rightly say you do not know where I am."

"But, sire," Pierre said, "we have all avowed our lives to protect you. We must not leave your side."

Arthur gathered the reins. "There is no time for discussion. We will find each other again. Brittany is not that large, nor am I a child that I should lose my way. Now! Ride like the devil!"

He followed his plan, riding with his valet to the forest he had in mind, hiding through the long night and emerging at dawn. Yet when he cautiously motioned for his valet to follow and rode out into the misty morning, a lone rider appeared, a dark man with a hood over his head. Arthur drew his sword and waited with breath held.

The rider threw back his hood and called out, "Sire. It is I, Pierre. Is all well?"

"Aye, friend Pierre. All is well. Now we shall go on to Fontaine castle."

Pierre shook his head. "Trouble befell the Sieur deVitre. He had to stop and fight. The princess got clean away. We know not where she is, but I found deVitre. He said he suspects there were spies who knew where we stayed. He wants you to proceed to St. Brieuc on the sea. He has a castle there." He sighed and kicked his mount to a trot. "It will be a long journey. We will not reach it today, nor even tomorrow."

Arthur adjusted the gait of his horse to match the young lord's. "I would like word of the princess."

Pierre nodded. "So would I. She had several men with her and her servant, so she will be well looked after. Let us pray we don't meet up with highwaymen. It is a lonely stretch we travel, known for miscreants."

"They will face two disgruntled knights. I am itching to put my sword to some good use. How about you, friend?" Arthur patted the rapier at his side.

Pierre urged his horse to a lope. "For certes. Even a whole troop of them would not stand before us. For God and Brittany, prince!"

"For God and Brittany!"

***

Chateau Briant, February 1199

Arthur's occupancy of the Sieur deVitre's castle at St. Brieuc was of short duration, for his location became known, and deVitre did not wish the Brabacons to lay siege to his castle. So the young prince rode by night to another, more remote castle, and then on, and on, and on. Now he was taller by an inch, less of a boy, more of a king. His mother and sister were together, lodged securely in the Castle Romeneuf, Lord Ranulf's castle in Normandy.

One night a page announced the arrival of a guest. Arthur straightened from the game of chess he played with his squire, rather annoyed, for he was about to check his opponent's queen.

"Lord DeArmond has arrived and wishes to meet with you, my lord," the page said, bowing low.

Arthur leaped to his feet. "DeArmond! Yes. Show him in." He dismissed Jacques with a wave. In a few moments, his old friend strode into the room. Arthur met him with open arms. He blinked hard against his tears.

When released, he motioned to the chair by the fire. "Warm yourself, my friend. What a boon to my soul. You look like an angel of heaven to me. You have no idea how lonely I have become and cut off from news of the world. Have you eaten?"

DeArmond laughed, his voice a throaty roar, and stretched his hands to the blaze. "Ah. This feels good. I am not getting any younger, you know. No, I have not eaten, and a morsel or two would be good. I bring one piece of good news for you. I brought Kazimer."

"No! Kazimer? You jest!"

"I jest not, my prince. He is even now in your stable eating a bag of grain like a common work horse, the greedy little bugger."

Arthur's joy erupted in a high peal of laughter. He danced in front of the fire and called DeArmond every endearment he could think of. DeArmond laughed with him and then motioned to his stomach.

Arthur nodded and ordered a meal. He poured DeArmond a cup of wine and sat back to look at the man. "So. Tell me all there is to know. Most of which I wager I will not want to hear."

As DeArmond told his stories and the food came and the fire sank and the castle went to bed, Arthur realized the truth of his statement. A sick feeling worked its way from his stomach to his heart.

After he'd eaten, DeArmond pushed his plate back and stretched out his legs. He shot a rueful glance at the prince and sighed. "Even though Richard keeps a battalion of his forces here in Brittany, he is tiring of the war, and has said quite openly that … that, well…"

"That Prince Arthur can go rot, I suppose, or something like that. Am I right?" Arthur's voice squeaked on the last word and he squirmed. Why did it always change just when he wanted to sound most grown up?

DeArmond looked away. "Aye, lad. His mind is on warfare and this time it is with France. But he will not withdraw his soldiers from Brittany, for he feels bested by a woman."

Arthur leaped to his feet and flung his cup across the room; the clang of it echoed off the stone walls. "Pah! This is for naught! These fine clothes, this wine, this food—they are nothing to me, DeArmond. My life is forfeit because of my stepfather's interventions, because Prince John wants me dead, because my own mother is blinded by her suspicions and jealousies. I am forever hunted. I am as a rabbit who hides itself from the fox. And Richard makes other plans for the one who will sit on the throne of England when he dies."

He paced the room. "Must I abide forever in hiding, my lord? Tell me now. I am not a child and my heart is breaking for lack of purpose."

DeArmond stood and turned his back to the fire. "Am I a sage that I should see your future, Your Highness? Perchance your fortunes will change. Perchance Richard will name you as his heir and you will occupy your rightful place as the next King of England. He has little liking for his own brother, Jack Lackland, the spawn of the devil if there ever was one." He spat.

DeArmond crossed his arms. "But it may not be the will of God that you occupy the throne of England, my prince. Is there nothing else you desire? Can you not see beyond the Kingdom of England; to be content perhaps with a more lowly title and position?"

His stare was one Arthur knew well. It meant, think, boy! Think! Prince Arthur turned away, not wanting to play schoolroom games. "Do you have something in mind?"

"Nay. I do not." DeArmond sighed, stirred the fire, then faced Arthur, his voice ringing with certainty. "You must find your own way in the world. Perchance you will leave Brittany. You will need to make your way without counsel. Can you do that, or will you forever wallow in self-pity and bitterness? Do you want to be like your mother?"

Arthur froze and stared at the man, his breath coming in gasps as if he had run a mile. "You overstep your familiarity with me, DeArmond."

The baron said nothing, merely rocked back and forth on his heels.

Arthur's fury drove him to the length of the hall and back again. Twice. Then he stopped in front of DeArmond. "I see your meaning. You are saying that I will probably never occupy the throne of

England. That I must settle for a lower position and content myself with that. But how can I attain contentment when injustice stalks my path? Tell me that."

DeArmond laughed, his throaty voice echoing down the hall. "Injustice. It is a way of life, my son. But you. You are strong and good. I see that in you despite your tempers." He lowered his voice and stepped close to Arthur, gripping his arm. "Keep strong, sire. Never let anything get you down. Life is strange. Your biggest opportunity may arrive at the very moment you are most cast down. Remember that."

Arthur gazed at him and their eyes locked. He nodded. "Aye, sir," he said, his voice husky. "I will be faithful, and moreover, I will never forget what you have taught me this day."

CHAPTER SIX

The real hero is always a hero by mistake; he dreams of being an honest coward like everybody else. Umberta Eco

St. Jacques, near Mordelias, June 1198

"One more load, Samson John." Louis straightened his aching back and wiped off the sweat dripping into his eyes. He gripped the handles of the crude wagon and began to push. Samson John, taller by three inches and of handsome face and bright eyes, nodded and bent his back to the rope, pulling the wagon while Louis pushed.

They maneuvered the wagon, which was full of stones, until they reached the building site, an addition onto the cathedral of St. Jacques.

Louis lowered the handles and glanced at the skilled workmen who took the stones and laid them in neat rows. "Someday people will come and stand in awe and wonder at the beauty of our new cathedral." He lifted the handles of the wagon. "And you and I will have been part of its construction. Can you not see how important this work is, my son?" Samson John nodded, but Louis noticed his sweat-stained tunic, the blood on his hands, how his shoulders sagged. "This will be our last load. It is nearly time for vespers."

It had been almost three years since Louis had taken up the Cross, while he waited and prayed for a sign from God that he could leave the abbey and begin his journey. It seemed eons of time had passed since that night with the full moon and the words of the monk ringing in his ears. How many had died at the hands of the heathen in that time? How had the cause of Christ suffered while he tarried?

But he had not given up on his dream and had been preparing himself for service in Palestine. On one of his walks about the parish he met a Greek man who taught fighting with hands and feet—an ancient discipline from the East. After watching a demonstration, he studied with Alexander for six months, the most rigorous training he had ever endured. Yet at the end of it, his teacher declared him able to defend himself in hand-to-hand combat.

This evening, he determined to seek an audience with Father Adolph after vespers and plead for his release. The problem was support—each man was expected to raise money to support himself for two years. Even if Louis had been free to leave, he had not more than two farthings laid by.

I am willing to go, even as I am, he thought as he pushed the wagon to the abbey. He would be willing to go crawling on his knees, if his feet became too weary.

He sent Samson John to his quarters, then went to his own room where he washed and prepared for vespers. First the monks gathered for prayers, then they paced silently to the common dining room. Speech was forbidden after vespers, so he had plenty of time with his thoughts, composing his plea to the father.

Father Adolph was a spare man in his late sixties with a thin face and sharp, bright eyes. He nodded to Louis when he entered the abbot's office and continued his meditation. Louis waited with eyes downcast.

The father lifted his eyes. "Yes, my son? You wanted a word with me?"

Louis nodded and took a deep breath, gathering his thoughts as if they were sheep gone astray on the hill, aware of the intelligent gleam in the eyes of his superior. "Father, I have served you faithfully since the day I set foot in this abbey, some eleven years ago. I have delighted in the service of God and have learned many things. This abbey has become my family. For that, I humbly thank you." He took another deep breath and saw the slightly amused glint in the Reverend Father's eyes.

"Do you remember that I took the cross three full years ago and vowed to journey to the Holy Land? Alas, time and circumstance has hindered me in fulfilling my vow. Now I am pleading with you. If there is any bit of compassion in your heart toward your son, I beg of you, give me permission to leave!" In his eagerness he departed from his rehearsed speech and found himself kneeling before the Father Abbot.

Father Adolph leaned back and steepled his fingertips.

Louis kept his head lowered. "My life is in this venture. I have vowed to worship at the Church of the Holy Sepulcher, to fight the infidels. I must fulfill my vows."

"And if I say nay?"

Louis shuddered. "I will come to your door morning, noon, and night to petition you, Father. So great is my desire to go that I will perish if it be denied me."

"My son, my son!" Father Adolph stood. "I have not seen such ardor for many a day! I remember well the day you came to us, and the day you took your oaths. But, my son, consider. What do you have laid by to live on? Will you depart from here only to starve on some lonely road? And what do you know of warfare? Do you have any weapon to fight with? How will you defend yourself?"

Louis looked up with a light of joy in his hazel eyes. "Fear not, Father. The Good Lord, Jesus Christ our Savior, will provide me with the tools of warfare."

In the moment of hushed silence, the song of the choir floated softly on the air and one last beam of sunshine pierced the clouds and shot through the window to rest upon the crucifix on the wall.

Father Adolph smiled and patted Louis' shoulder. "You shall go. I knew this day would come, but I hated the thought of your departure. You hear a higher calling and so you shall go."

Louis leaped in the air, shouting for joy.

"Stay a moment." Father Adolph lifted a hand. "You shall not go from here a beggar, to die on the road to the Holy City. You are the ambassador of the Abbey of St. Jacques. You shall be properly provided for."

He stepped to a safe in the wall, extracting from it a small leather scrip. "This contains something you gave the abbey many years ago, and I return it to you now to use as the Lord directs. But you must be cautious, my son. Do not trust anyone. There are many you will meet who would cheerfully slit your throat for just one gold coin, nay, for the robe you wear or the sandals on your feet."

Louis received the leather purse with wonder, for he was unaware that he had brought anything with him to the abbey. He longed to ask, but forbore, knowing he could discover later what the purse contained. "I should trust no one?"

The father shook his head. "No one, my son. Keep to yourself, mind your own business, do what you can to relieve the suffering you will find." He went to the safe again and extracted a leather pouch, long and narrow, and carefully brought it to the desk.

"This pouch contains a book that the monks in our abbey have worked on for many years, a copy of our Holy Scriptures illustrated with beautiful drawings. I see you know which book I speak of, for you did some work on it yourself. It is our desire to present this book to our Holy Father, Pope Innocent the Third as a gift. I lay this burden upon you, that you shall be our ambassador and take this pouch to the Holy See." He peered at Louis. "Do you need help? Shall I send someone with you?"

Louis shook his head. "No, Father. I only need your prayers and the blessed Virgin's mercies. It is a great honor to carry the Blessed Book to the Holy Father." He bowed, tears falling again on the wooden floor. Then he lifted his eyes. "But if I may petition you for one companion, I would ask for Samson John. I have found him an apt young man. I could use his service and his company."

"Nay, it is not too much, son. You have chosen well. I am sure the young lad will be delighted to accompany you. You shall proceed to Mont St. Michel's where the order there desires a courier to carry a similar book to the Holy See. At prime tomorrow we shall have a commissioning mass for you, Brother. Go now in peace. Tomorrow you will begin your long journey."

Louis bowed, kissed the hand proffered to him and backed from the room.

Alone in his cell, he opened the scrip Father Adolph had given him and emptied into his hand a diamond—a jewel that dazzled the eye and weighed solidly in his hand. He stared at it for many moments as if it were a star dropped from heaven. "I canna believe me eyes!" he murmured, dropping into his Welsh accent, for his mother was Welsh.

He remembered Father Adolph's words. *It contains something you gave the abbey years ago.* Closing his fingers over the jewel, he quested back into his memory. How could he have given this to the abbey? Where would he have gotten such a thing? Could it be that Father Adolph was mistaken? But, no, he had been very definite.

Louis placed the jewel in the scrip and tied up the strings. Tomorrow he would ask Father Adolph about it, and when he got to a city, he would see about selling it. He knelt beside the cot and recited his prayers, saying his *Hail Marys* a hundred and fifty times with the aid of his rosary beads, and thirteen *Our Fathers*.

After his prayers, he read again his manuscript and then stretched out on the bed, but he did not sleep. The bell tolled for prime.

He found Samson John at his door, a sack slung over his shoulder, his eyes brimming with tears. The boy mimed his thanks and eagerness. Louis nodded and patted him on the shoulder. The two of them walked to the great cathedral where the priests, the monks, a bishop and Father Adolph waited.

The service was grand, one Louis would remember many times on the long, hot trails of the East. He felt as if he was floating far above the ground, somewhere near the vaulted ceiling, just where the angels of God touched the earth. Side by side with the lad, he knelt at the altar as the priests chanted, prayed and gave them communion. Father Adolph solemnly laid a hand on their heads and prayed earnestly for God's blessings, for good fortune and for a safe return.

They stood and turned. First this brother and then another one brought gifts forward—a fine leather belt and sturdy shoes, a staff and a pouch for water. He received these gifts humbly and pledged to the assembled brothers that he would return to them. "I will pray for each of you upon the very steps that lead to the most holy of all places, the Church of the Holy Sepulcher. I vow this to you today."

A few moments later, he and Samson John stepped out into the sunshine and started down the road. *Ah!* Such lightness of heart swept over him that he had to look down to make sure his feet tread the earth. He wanted to shout to each person he passed, "I am on my way to the Holy Land. Look! I, Brother Louis of St. Jacques. I have been chosen."

It was only after journeying for ten miles or so that he remembered the jewel. He had forgotten to ask Father Adolph about it. *I shall let it lie. Perchance one day I shall have the opportunity to ask him, but for now, I am on my way!*

***

Dijon, France, July 1198

Elias left soon after Grandfather's funeral to travel to Marseilles, for it was Moshe's dying wish that the family move to that city, and from there, to Antioch in Syria. He traveled in a company of wealthy Jewish businessmen, partners who owned a fleet of ships. In Marseilles, they were to receive their share of profits from a newly returned vessel.

Judith would always remember waving him good-bye on that day as he gathered the reins of his horse. He smiled and blew a kiss. "I will be back in a month," he called to them. "Say a prayer for me."

But the time for his return came and went and he did not come home.

Dread seemed to settle over the household and Sarah haunted the marketplace for any word. The wives and families of the other men were just as frantic, but it seemed the party had fallen off the end of the world.

News came two months later in the shape of a ragged, starved Spanish boy.

"I must speak to Sarah, the wife of Elias," he gasped as he swayed from exhaustion and hunger.

Fear pounded hard in Judith's heart and tightened her throat as she ran to find Amma.

When Mother and the servants gathered in the courtyard, the young boy told his story. Nero, their elderly black servant, translated from Spanish to Hebrew.

"We were south of Lyon, returning from Marseilles, where a forest makes it dark and there is a narrow passage between two mountains."

"*Un momento!*" Nero laid a hand on the boy's shoulder and translated. He motioned for him to continue.

"We made camp and the next morning, very early, I was saddling the horses when they came from the trees, riding like devils, killing everything in their path. We had no warning." He listed wearily to one side like a sail suddenly gone limp. Nero repeated to them what he said.

"They struck like lightning. I hid in some bushes, but I saw with my eyes the killing! Blood was everywhere … in puddles on the ground … I alone escaped with my life. I am very sorry to bring you this ill news." The boy swayed uncertainly as Nero told them what he said.

Silence, like a heavy curtain, descended on the room. Judith stared at the boy, her grip tightening on the folds of her robe, the world shaking beneath her feet.

"Who was it?" Nero asked in Spanish, a husky question betraying his deep distress.

The boy shook his head and spread out his hands. "I know not. They were Christian, to be sure. Franks, I suppose. The leader was on a great gray horse and carried a black banner with a red bull on it. I shall never forget the bull."

Hearing a sigh, Judith turned to look at her mother. Sarah stood with staring dark eyes in a frozen face. Then, without a sound, she collapsed on the floor. Nero reached her first.

Judith patted her mother's hand and called to her. "Amma! Amma!"

Her eyes opened, but they were wide, full of shock. She sat up. Her voice was a whisper. "What of my husband, boy? Of the others with him?"

Nero translated the question to the boy who spread in hands in distress.

"I know not, my lady. The last I saw, the raiders captured the animals and there were many dead lying around. It was a fearsome thing." He reached for something to steady himself and fell into a heap on the floor.

Hannah wept loudly. Judith sagged against her comforting plumpness while sobs tore at her throat.

"There were no captives taken?" Sarah whispered. Nero asked the question.

The ragged boy seemed to consider for a few moments. "Yea, there may have been some taken." He struggled to his feet. Nero held his hand. "The Franks like to sell men and boys. This I know. But all is lost. I alone escaped." Nero translated swiftly.

"Then there is hope." Sarah stood with the aid of Hannah and Tabitha. "Elias may have been taken as a slave. He may escape and return home. We must wait...and pray."

Judith gripped her mother's arm. "Let us send a party of men to search for them, Amma. I would like to go."

"No, child. It has been too long. They would have been taken far away by now, and all trace of them gone." She waved a hand towards the boy. "See that he is given a bath and a meal. He is not to blame."

Darkness descended upon Judith as surely as if a blanket had been tossed over her head. Blindly, she stumbled from the room, flung herself upon a low couch and gave herself up to weeping as if her heart had been torn from her body. She felt hands lifting her; mother's voice implored her to be still.

Nero carried Judith to her room and laid her on the bed. Slowly her sobs subsided. Amma had gone for some wine, Hannah for her cat. A butterfly flittered in and out of the room; the jasmine bush by the door wafted its sweet scent to Judith on a quiet breeze; out in the courtyard, one of the servants played the harp, perhaps, she thought, at Amma's suggestion.

But nothing helped. The darkness did not lift and fear crept in with it.

Later that evening, a full moon shone its pale light in the courtyard. She roused from her stupor and tiptoed to Grandfather's room. There she wrapped a blanket around her shoulders and sat on his bed, deep in thought.

Where was Abba right now? What was he enduring? How could she find him? How could they live without the business? How much did Amma have laid by? What was going to happen? No answers came on the still night air. She curled into a ball and sobbed herself to sleep.

The next morning the sun spread golden light across the sky, as if apologizing for the events of the previous day. News spread quickly. Friends came to weep and pray and eat. The wives of the other four men came, sobbing on Sarah's shoulders, wailing their grief, then they quietly left. The men said they would send out search parties, but everyone knew they would come back empty-handed.

That evening Judith sat again on Grandfather's bed and held the key he had given her. Lamplight cast flickering shadows as she scrambled off the bed, knelt beside the chest and opened it. Withdrawing the golden box, she carried it back to the bed and looked at the gems. *These will feed the household for many days. Praise Yahweh.*

With careful fingers she withdrew the scroll and laid it on the bed. She did not attempt to unroll it or read it. She cast about, looking for a small container. *If we have to leave, perhaps in a great hurry, how can I keep the scroll safe?*

She looked again in Gran-abba's chest and found near the bottom a wooden cylindrical container, only four inches long and smaller than her forefinger. It hung on a golden chain and was sealed with a cork. She withdrew the cork. The sweet smell of lavender ascended—perfume her Grandmother kept. But it was dry now.

She tried the scroll and found it fit perfectly. Sealing the end with the cork, she removed the golden chain and looked again in the chest. A gaudy piece of jewelry hung on a leather thong. Quickly she exchanged it for the golden chain and slipped the leather thong around her neck.

She sank down on Gran-abba's bed, a great urgency flooding her heart, a feeling that there was a mission for her to accomplish. *I must find Abba!* The words beat steadily into her brain and on the heels of that thought came the objections. *You are too young. You are just a girl. You must stay and care for your mother. Where would you start? You would be putting your own life in great peril.*

She stood and paced to the courtyard. *Nevertheless, I must try.* She thought of the jewels in the golden box, but knew they must conserve those carefully.

Back in her own room, she knelt beside the bed, closed her eyes and spoke with deliberation. "Yahweh, great God my people, God of my Gran-abba, I vow this day to find Father. Whatever the cost, whatever the risk, I will do this thing. Amen."

***

Mont St. Michels, Brittany, August 1198

"You canna go farther on horseback, sir." The bearded man, a guide from the village, stopped. Louis nodded and motioned to Samson John who rode behind him to dismount. A brisk breeze brought the smell of salt water and the cry of the gulls to his ears. The sight before him captured his mind and imagination like nothing ever had before.

Almost a mile out to sea a small island reared its head, and atop the island, the most fantastic monastery in all of Christiandom perched. Mont St. Michel's had begun on a grand scale in 1020 A.D. under the guidance of Abbot Hildebert. Nearly two centuries later, the Church had grown to mammoth proportions, a magnificent and arrogant presence overlooking the Gulf of Saint Malo and the English Channel.

The guide nodded at Louis' stunned expression. "Indeed, sir, you be careful as you cross t'sand. It be treacherous. Many quicksand pits lie await for t'unworthy." He shifted his weight from foot to foot and crossed himself. "T'is said, and I believes what I hear, that if you have sinned and incurred t'good Lord's wrath, then you will sink outer sight before you can reach yonder haven. Watch this young lad. See that he does na wander too far away."

Louis picked up his bundles and helped Samson John with his backpack. "But you said it was low tide. I assumed ..."

"Assume no more. I tell ye onct, I tell ye no agin. Watch yer step, and pray like ye've never prayed before. Watch for the high tide. It should stay low long enough for ye to Cross, but ye never know. T'is no picnic crossing the sand to t'Mont. I'd go with ye, but I've got a sick cow at home." He waited patiently while Louis dug in his purse and produced a coin. With a tug on his cap, he turned into the wind and was soon gone over the low hillock of tufted grass.

Louis glanced at Samson John who stood with wide eyes staring at the Mont. "You heard the man. Stay close."

The boy gripped Louis' sleeve and motioned over the hillock of sand toward the village.

Louis shook his head. "Nay, my son. You're coming with me, and you better have said your prayers."

Someone had erected stone markers here and there, a casual indication where the trail might be safest, but the guide's words echoed in Louis' mind. This was no Sunday afternoon stroll. The tide rose and fell fourteen feet along this coast and shifted the sand to such a degree that one could never be sure if his next step would land on sand or sink into the mire. He heard stories of men who had died in the quicksand pits on the way to Mont St. Michel's.

With an eye to the west where the sun was lowering over the ocean, and with another eye to the sand before his feet, he began the

75

walk, his mouth moving more rapidly than his feet. Samson John's grip on Louis' robe communicated his fear.

It was a lonely place, for certes, and the monastery seemed cold and menacing, peering down upon him as if in judgment. *Step. Step. Splash*! He jumped. A small pool yawned beside him. He skirted its edge carefully, then continued.

He glanced again at the lowering sun, was blinded by the sudden rays that shone from under the clouds. Samson John pulled him to a stop. There, in front of Louis' feet, yawned a sand trap, a hole. *Oh, dear Virgin Mary.* He skirted the hole, trying the sand with his foot every step. Suddenly, his foot disappeared up to his ankle; he shrieked and yanked back, over-corrected, toppled to the left.

Samson John fell beside him. They lay on the sand, tangled, boy and man. The sun sank, but rays colored the sky red. Gray, blue-black sky encroached upon the light.

They had to finish the journey before dark. He glanced up and his heart fell. It seemed the monastery was as far off as ever. Had they only come ... he glanced back ... half the way? *Oh, God.*

He tried to hurry, but found he could not. His heart pounded and he thought he heard the maniacal laughter of demons eager for his soul. Surely the Lord was angry with him. *Dear God, forgive my sins, for they are many.* Samson John shuffled along behind him, a gaunt shadow, a silent victim.

Now it was truly dark. He heard a swishing noise, tried to place it, and suddenly felt water up to his ankles. The tide! It was rising. The man said it could rise faster than a horse ran. The gates to the monastery stood twenty yards away. He called out, but no one answered. Why did no one answer? Was it a test of faith? Well, he had little of that, he admitted freely.

He stumbled over a bit of driftwood and fell to his knees. A great wave slammed into him, sending him reeling back, gasping, floundering in the cold water, trying vainly to find a foothold. The water receded, taking him with it, washing him out to sea!

Someone grasped his robe. The water disappeared with a gurgle. Louis rose to his knees, and there in the darkness was Samson John's face, split in a wide grin of effort. Louis grasped the boy's arm, pulled himself up, and as he did so, saw that Samson John was perched on a rock.

"Thank you, thank you, Son." Louis sputtered, shaking the water from his eyes. "You … you have saved my life. But we must hurry before another wave comes."

They grasped hands and dashed across the wet sand together, not heeding the holes, nor the pits, nor the water. Twenty feet. Ten. The water came again with a roar. It tugged at Louis' legs, rose to his waist and threatened to topple him again.

They came stumbling at last to the stone stairs that rose from the sand.

The water receded with a hiss, as if disappointed that it could not carry away its prey. Louis dropped his bundles in a heap about his feet and rang the bell. Desperately.

A monk appeared, but seemed in no hurry to open the gate. "Yes? What do you wish?"

"I wish … I wish to be out of this nightmare." Louis gasped, clinging to the gates as if to life itself. He heard the boy's rasping breath. "Please. I have messages from the Abbey of St. Jacques. Grant us entrance, for we have suffered the terrors of hell itself in the crossing." He gestured back to the sandy path and to his amazement saw whitecaps atop the waves in the faint light cast by the first stars. The ocean had swept in behind him.

The monk smiled and opened the gate. "Most do. Please come in."

***

Dijon, France, May 1199

Sarah lifted her eyes from her embroidery, gazing at her daughter fondly while she played with her cat under the palm tree. Beside Judith knelt Miguel, the slave boy from the caravans, whom they kept.

"Judith is growing so tall and slim," Sarah said with a sigh.

Hannah glanced up from the pile of clean clothes that she folded. "Yes, mistress. But don't you find it disturbing that she spends so much time with that Spanish slave boy? What could they possibly have in common?" She shifted her ample weight from the bench and gathered the folded clothes into her arms.

Sarah cast a quick glance at her servant. "Don't concern yourself, my friend. She has color in her cheeks and her laughter rings out in the courtyard. Her wedding day approaches, Hannah, and I shall miss her so. Yet she must marry. She is so beautiful. I fear that evil men will see her and take her."

It was true. Judith had grown tall and slender, winsome yet womanly. Men turned to look when she passed if she let her veil slip, for they caught the luster in her dark eyes, her smooth skin and the fine molding of her chin and brow.

Judith heard her mother's comments and frowned. Her stomach always turned when Amma mentioned the subject of marriage.

"Come, Miguel. Let's go to our place where they can't see us." She did not turn to see if he followed, but sprinted to the bottom of the garden, through the gate, beyond the courtyard wall, and into a dry creek bed where thick, jungle-like bushes and rocks provided shade and privacy. She spent most of her time there, planning for the time she would leave to find Abba.

Miguel proved to be an excellent source of information, for he knew the exact spot where the caravan was attacked, he knew where the slave markets were, he knew who would buy the slaves and where they would be taken. He told her at great length about the vast slave markets, about the galleys, about the salt mines, about the slaves who labored for their masters all over the world.

Squatting in the shade of an oak tree by a large rock, she whispered her vow to him. "Can you understand, Miguel? It is a holy thing. Yahweh will help me in this. You shall help me, too." She spoke simply, for Miguel was learning French, but was not fluent in it.

His dark eyes widened as he gazed at her. He shook his head. "Who can tell where your *padre* is, *senorita*? Egypt, on the Great Sea in the belly of ship, or in Marseilles, Rome, Askalon or far away to east. Your *padre* may be dead. Who know? No one."

Silence fell between them. Judith moved a pile of dirt with her toes and tried not to let Miguel see the tears falling down her cheeks. She had waited, planned and gathered information, and now it seemed to amount to nothing. A sense of despair settled upon her heart with the immensity of a mountain. She groaned.

Miguel glanced her way and laid a brown hand on her arm. "*Perdon. Lo siento.*" He leaned closer. "*Hasta luego—*"

"Nay! I shall not wait!" She stood, brushing aside his solicitations. "I shall do what I have vowed to do." She left him and hurried to the house, steely determination garrisoning her will.

In the weeks that followed, she gritted her teeth whenever she thought of Miguel's words. She *would* go. It *was* possible. He didn't know everything.

Summer came to Dijon with the song of the sparrow, with bright red poppies and yellow daffodils, with the excitement of a wedding—her wedding, for Mother and Nero had reached an agreement with the Abrams family and Judith would soon be wed to Levi Abrams and live in a sordid little house near the market. But nothing changed her mind. The stack of parchments in the hole below the large rock in the gully grew. With it grew a pile of coins, bits and pieces of clothing, a pack and a flask.

One bright morning Judith sat in the courtyard stroking her cat when Amma joined her, bringing her embroidery. She handed Judith her project—a lovely table covering Judith would use for shabbat when she was married. Judith took the material and sat on a bench in the shade.

"Daughter, we must make plans for your wedding." Sarah sighed and knotted her thread. "I have set aside some money, so we shall be able to hire musicians. I am planning a fine feast for our friends and relatives. Yet I would like to see you more involved. Tell me what you are thinking. What do you want? This is your wedding."

"I don't know," she managed to say, but could not proceed for her throat constricted and tears threatened. It seemed so wrong to plan a wedding with Father gone.

Levi Abrams was an industrious fellow, people said. Yet Judith barely knew him, much less loved him. She sighed. After her marriage, she would see Amma every day and the Abrams family would care for her. But Judith had seen the living quarters behind the pottery shop; she witnessed the mud, dirt, children, dogs and chickens that inhabited the household.

Amma laid aside her needlework and rose. "Come, daughter. There is something I want you to see and now is the time."

Half-heartedly Judith followed her to a secret cache where Sarah opened a box to reveal stunning sight. Judith gasped when she saw the family jewels, ancient gems that had been passed from mother to daughter for centuries. She let the rubies and diamonds and emeralds run through her fingers and picked up one especially large diamond. Holding it in the sunlight, she gasped as it winked at her with a life of its own.

"This one is very beautiful," she said softly. "Is it ... the one from the King?"

Sarah smiled. "Yes, my dear. The story your Grandfather on the distaff side told you. It has been in our family a long time." Sarah then went talking, but Judith's mind stayed with the fabulous jewel that rested in her hand.

With this I could buy an army. I could hire guards. I could travel the world. With this jewel, I could find Father.

Two weeks later Judith found Miguel in the lower garden. "*Psst!* Miguel!" She whispered to a bush that grew near the wall.

A brown face appeared. He peered up at her as he brushed the dirt from his hands. "*Si?* Your Amma told me to weed down here."

"Meet me at our place. I will go first, then you follow. Mother and Nero have gone to the market." She received a nod; the brown face disappeared.

Meandering slowly through the lower garden, where cacti grew amidst beds of bougainvillea and roses, Judith came to the gully, perched on her favorite rock and waited, her heart pounding.

Soon Miguel arrived. He stood respectfully, but Judith sensed he was not pleased, would rather return to his task. He had gained several inches in the last year; his eyes gleamed with intelligence and he held his head as if he belonged to nobility of a desert tribe. Dressed in a fine caftan with silver-studded sandals and a staff in hand, he could pass as the son of a chieftain.

"What is it, Mistress Judith?"

"We must discuss our plans." She folded her arms. "My wedding day approaches. I have decided we will leave before the wedding, as too much attention will be given me that day. That means we shall leave in a fortnight and you are far from ready for the role you must play. You are helping me, aren't you?"

He nodded slowly. "*Es dificil*. It mean my life if we are caught, but that is small thing compared to what you have done for me." He bowed.

She gazed at him searchingly, for she heard misgivings and something else in his voice. *Is he afraid?* "You must learn not to bow, nor to give me so much as a nod, for our stations in life will be reversed. You shall be the son of a chieftain and I shall be your servant. We will rehearse now. You must take care to learn what it is to be the master." She led him deeper into a stand of trees beside a languid trickle of water and for the next hour taught him how he should act.

He was a quick learner and she noted that he seemed to play the role of master with inborn grace. He sat opposite her on the dirt bank and wiped his forehead. "I will help you, Mistress Judith ... yet, I am sad that we leave your *madre* alone." He looked at her and spoke in a low voice. "You know, she will die with grief."

Ah! That was what troubled him. She did not answer immediately, for she struggled with this very issue and had not come to a satisfactory conclusion.

She shook her head. "I will leave *madre* a letter. She must understand that I will return in a short time, whether I have found Father or not. But I must try. I cannot stand by and do nothing. I made a vow to Yahweh, and I must fulfill it. I must do this thing. I shall die if I do not."

He nodded. "So be it. We shall do as you plan. May this God of yours, this Yahweh, give us good success."

The day of her departure dawned bright and cloudless, a good sign, she decided at the breakfast table. Hannah brought hot bread from the ovens as she did every morning, but this morning Judith found she had no appetite. Nero waited on her, bringing hot cloths to wash her hands.

She glanced up at the old servant, tears stinging her eyes. Hannah had been with the family so long. And Nero. How could she leave Nero? His service stretched back to the days when she was a child.

She patted his arm. "I will miss you, Nero, when I am wed. Promise me you will take good care of Amma."

Nero smiled. She noted he walked with a limp these days, that his face was more lined than she had noticed before and his hands shook as he served. "I promise, Mistress." He turned away quickly, but not before she saw tears glistening down his face.

Sarah adjusted her robe. "You will come home often, dear. You will see Nero again. I am keeping Hannah and Nero, but letting the others go. Why are you so long-faced today? You will be wed in just a week and there is so much to do."

Judith averted her eyes and nodded silently, fighting tears that threatened.

"Is it because your father is not here to rejoice with us?"

"Yes, Amma. I miss him so." She sighed. "But I suppose it must be done." She had eaten very little of the sweet bread, only a taste of pomegranate. "I need some time to myself, Amma." She bowed gracefully and rose.

"Very well, child. But I want you to come with me to the market today. We will chose the gowns you will take with you to your new home. If we live long enough to see that day."

There was something in her tone that caught Judith's attention. She glanced at her quickly. Sarah's hand shook as she raised her cup to her mouth to sip her hot milk. She spilled some of it on her robe. Disturbed at her clumsiness, she called for a towel, then sat back as Hannah mopped up the spill.

"Are you well, Amma?"

Sarah nodded and tried to laugh. "I know not what has gotten into me. An evil spirit, for sure. Look at the mess."

Judith kissed her, then went to her room. A brass mirror hung above her dressing table. She sat before it, staring at her reflection. She saw a young girl whose eyes seemed too large for her face. Weariness, pain and grief were written in them as clearly as if in ink. She drew back and turned away.

Birds chirped on the wall just outside her room. It was the robin pair who built a nest. She straightened and looked to see, and smiled, for the female seemed to be scolding the male. She stifled a sob. Home. Family. Everyone needed these things—even birds. She could have a nest; she could have a husband. She didn't have to go

...

"No!" Balling her fists, she steeled herself against thoughts of self-pity and rehearsed her vow to Yahweh to find her father. She forced her mind into the channels she had trained it to follow. But the doubts continued. Was she doing the right thing? Would anyone understand? Would she come back with Abba, or would she come back at all? Was it ... suicide, or worse, to set out alone in such a hostile world?

I must not think of failure.

Her hand shook as she lifted a sharp knife, took a deep breath and sliced through her long glossy black hair. It lay like a murdered child on the floor around her bench. She sighed heavily and adjusted a plain scarf over her head. Picking up a leather pouch, she held it in her hand and felt the heavy weight of gold pieces.

Then she looked at the note she had written. "Dear Amma, I have gone to search for Father. I am sorry for taking the diamond that has been in our family for so many years. It was the only way I could think to pay for my journey. Miguel will look after me. You must forgive me. I shall return soon, whether I find him or not. Love, Judith."

She left the note on the dressing table and rose, her knees shaking, her hands sweaty. Miguel had found a buyer for the jewel. From the amount he brought back, she purchased the clothes he would wear, food and other supplies. He also bought two horses.

She tied the leather pouch securely next to her skin and dressed in the rough clothes of a servant boy—a short brown tunic that reached below her knees, a sash around her waist, sturdy leather sandals. She pulled the scarf lower over her eyes. A jar of black paste waited in the gully that she would smear over her face, hands and arms.

Now she must escape from the house before anyone saw her. A vine grew up the side of the house past her window. She had used the convenient stalk as a ladder when she wanted to disappear for a few moments to the gully. She looked around her room one last time and, touching the container around her neck that held Grandfather's scroll, backed out the window.

A commotion reached her ears, faint at first and then louder. She heard the sound of wood smashing, sword clanging upon sword, voices raised in anger, screams. Even still, she was so focused on her task that the sounds did not penetrate her mind. She reached the ground, ran to the lower garden, then stopped and looked back.

The noise grew louder. Her heart stopped, then thudded again heavily as she crouched low among the bushes. Nero dashed from the house into the courtyard, calling her name. She almost answered when a knight in full armor, his shield bearing a red bull on a black field, appeared behind him and skewered him through the back with a spear. The old slave screamed. His dying word bubbled with blood as the spear was withdrawn and he fell. "Ju ... dith ..."

A scream wrenched her throat, but she clamped a hand over her mouth and gripped the stalk of a bush, faint and sick. Others fled to the courtyard to escape through the lower gate, but knights followed them there, and they were killed with the same dispatch. Her meager breakfast crawled up into her throat; she leaned over, gagging.

Horror took possession of her mind. She clutched handfuls of dirt, squinted through tear-stung eyes, unable to move, unable to spring to the defense, terror and shock holding her immobile as she watched her family and servants butchered, her staring eyes taking in more than her mind could comprehend.

Silence fell upon the household. The knights left. Still Judith knelt, stunned, tears wet on her cheeks and her lower lip bitten till she tasted blood. She vomited into the sand ... again ... and again. Suddenly a hand gripped her shoulder and she jumped and screamed, but it was only Miguel, dressed in his fine costume, his face bleached white, his eyes staring from their sockets.

"We must flee, Mistress," he said in a low, choked voice.

She shook off his hand, ready now to do battle. "No! I must find Amma! I must see if she lives ... if she needs my help!"

"But they will return." He sank down beside her as cries and screams and shouts erupted from the villa next to theirs.

"I care not. I sat here like a coward and now I must know." Even though he tried to restrain her, she dashed up the hill, into the upper courtyard, past bloodied bodies. She stopped and knelt beside Nero, but he was gone. She did the same for Hannah and some of the other servants, but they, too, were dead. Running up the stairs to her mother's room, she found Sarah lying in a puddle of blood, a scream on her lips, her eyes wide and dilated and empty.

She rushed to her side, spoke to her, called her name, tried to mop up the terrible blood, but the beautiful Sarah was gone. A bunch of purple lilies and a crushed vase lay on the floor beside her. Judith bowed beside the body and wept.

Miguel roused her. "We must flee. I hear them coming back. They will go through the houses now with careful hands and steal everything of value. Hear them? They come! Mistress, we must flee!"

Judith knew he was right. She heard the tromp of their boots, knew they would return now to strip the houses. But Miguel was forced to pry her from Mother's body, weeping and moaning, to carry her down the steps, to throw her over his shoulder and run for the lower gate, and just in time, for the Christian knights now swarmed the house.

Rough voices in the Frankish tongue exclaimed in jubilation. "I claim this! This is mine!" Blows and fights erupted over the booty.

In the gully, Judith climbed off Miguel's back. He handed her the paste and she applied it quickly. She followed as he ran ahead of her down the gully. It ended in a city street. Soon they arrived at the place where horses were tied to a rail.

As she mounted, a great flood of hatred washed over her soul, so black and so huge, she gasped from the weight of it. Yet she welcomed it, took it to her breast, gulped it down...for hatred was her salvation.

CHAPTER SEVEN

No one told me grief felt so much like fear. C.S. Lewis,
Surprised by Joy

Chateau Briant, Brittany, April 1199

"Tis for you, m'Lord." A servant held out a travel-worn roll of parchment to the prince.

Arthur received the roll and walked to the window in the drafty old castle. Down below, the villeins tilled the soil with wooden plows and oxen. A bird sang near the window and he remembered how his mother loved the bluebird's song. Slowly he unrolled the parchment and traced Mother's spidery writing with his finger.

Skimming through the lines he read, *Reports reach us that King Richard continues to ravage the countryside of Brittany in his attempt to kidnap you. Many innocent people have been killed. Now I hear he is tiring of his search, and has grown more interested in war with France. Perhaps my long internment will soon be over.*

I have instructed certain trusted men to accompany you to Paris to stay with my cousin, King Philip. You may find sanctuary there, and you may be able to join forces with him against Richard. I am told Philip is willing to help you win the kingdom you so richly deserve.

Keep me in your heart and prayers. My prayers go with you. Your sister sends her fondest greetings. By my own hand, this 14th day of February, 1199.

Your mother, Queen Constance.

Arthur rolled up the parchment and thrust it into his tunic. He sighed heavily and paced to the empty fireplace, the very spot where he and DeArmond had their serious talk several months ago. Now the fire was cold, the table was bare and DeArmond was gone. He grasped his hands behind his back. What lay ahead in France? Was

Philip truly interested in helping him win the throne? Or would he find himself a prisoner?

Heavy footsteps thudded in the hall. Instinctively he stood to attention, his left hand on his sword hilt.

deVitre burst into the room, followed by his men-at-arms. "You must flee at once! The Brabacons are only a few miles away. These men will escort you to France." He smiled. "I have enjoyed your company, Your Highness. My prayers shall go with you. God speed."

"Thank you, deVitre." Prince Arthur bowed. "You have proved a faithful and kind friend to my lady mother and me. We shall not forget. God be with you."

He hastened into his armor, ran down the corridors and received a pack of his belongings and food. As he mounted Kazimer he remembered with a grim smile what a boon it was to have DeArmond deliver him to this same castle a year ago. With his men-at-arms behind him, he galloped toward the French border with heart beating hard and banner flying high.

***

Castle Renault, France, June 1199

"A letter, my lord." A young knight appeared in the Great Hall and approached FitzRauf's throne-like chair that sat upon the dais.

"Give it to me." The seal was Prince John's. FitzRauf's heart did a flip-flop as he broke it and unrolled the parchment. He glanced up. The young man was still kneeling. "You may go. Find Roger, my seneschal, and he will fix you up with a meal and a room." He motioned to a servant. "Send for my son. I think he is in the tilting lists. Tell him to come immediately."

A few moments later, boots pounded on the stone floor. The door flew open and Frederick burst in. "Here I am, father. Edgar said it is urgent." He shifted from foot to foot, waiting ill at ease while the baron carefully unrolled the parchment and adjusted his robes.

FitzRauf looked up. "Edgar, leave us. Close the door. Sit down, Frederick."

Frederick perched on a low stool at his father's feet.

"Now, read me this letter out loud. It is from Prince John."

Frederick complied, stumbling over a word or two, as his skill in reading did not match his skill with a lance. When he finished, he looked in dismay at his father, his face flushed and his eyes dark with loathing. "So he has fled to France. He is beyond our reach."

"Do not be downcast, my son," the baron said, picking his teeth with a fingernail. "There will come a time when we can strike. John's spies in the king's court will report to us. We must be patient and wait. I am sure he will ride out with the king's knights. It will be an easy matter to accost him in the forest. In the meantime, continue your practice in the lists and with the sword. I hear you are exceeding the hopes I had for you, that you are unbeaten with the sword."

The young man beamed with delight at the unaccustomed praise. "They say they have never seen a more apt pupil. I am strong and agile. I could call out the prince on the morrow and best him, for certes."

The baron nodded and smiled, thinking what a tool he had made of this young man for his own plans. If he could remove Prince Arthur from Brittany, his only deterrent to its rich lands and the fat purses of its barons would be the duchess. It would be an easy matter to depose her. And if John attained the throne, he would be in his favor.

"Well, first things first," he said, heaving himself from his chair. "Come, Frederick, I would watch thee at the sword. Perchance you think you could best me?"

Frederick followed behind his father. "Oh, no, sir. You are the best swordsman in all of Europe." And the practice time that followed proved his words.

Three months later, FitzRauf again called for his son, for he had received a missal from John's spies. Together they laid their plans. It was an easy matter to station men in a copse of trees, ready when the prince rode by in company with the king's knights. The baron declined to accompany Frederick, merely instructing him that his first priority was to kill Prince Arthur.

And so it was that on a brisk spring morning in the forest pathway not far from the palace, knights waited with bows ready for the party that was approaching. The spy, a young man with a thatch of blond hair, rode to their hiding place and informed them that the prince was lagging behind the group, riding his famous mount, the white Andalusian stallion. It should be an easy shot.

But the matter went wildly awry from the very first. The prince arrived first to the copse, not last, and this threw the archers off their mark. Frederick kicked his mount, rode after the shadowy white horse, his jaw clenched. He would not fail his father the second time.

He came upon the prince in a small meadow. All around was the clash of swords, the grunt of men in combat. Blood rushed to his face when he saw his enemy on the ground, sword in hand. Pulling up the reins, he dismounted in one flowing motion, drew his sword, and took the stance. "I challenge thee, Prince Arthur, to clean warfare with swords only." His eager voice rang out in a sudden stillness.

The prince bowed. "I accept, sir. I see the man I wounded so gravely two years ago. I am pleased and honored to fight thee." He shrugged off his outer cloak and raised his sword.

Frederick's armor was a hauberk, a chain link mail that covered the upper torso, waist, groin and upper arms. On his legs he wore steel-plated cuisse and greaves, and on his hands heavy leather gauntlets. But these were for heavy fighting with broad swords, not the kind of dueling with the lighter rapiers knights carried and dueled with. Both men laid aside their flat-topped helmets, their heavy gauntlets and greaves, and stood facing each other in the soft summer sunlight.

Frederick knew the moment their swords touched that he had the advantage. He was taller and stronger of arm and much more skilled. He guessed the prince knew it, too, but the young man opposite showed nothing but disdain in his blue eyes and held himself with poise as they exchanged feint and step and thrust and parry, like two dancers.

To Frederick, it was a dream come true. How often he had conjured this picture in his mind during practice, while partaking of a meal, even in his sleep. To have his enemy at the point of his blade, and to know he bested him in every manner was a delight beyond measure.

As the heat increased with the passage of time, both combatants began to suffer. Frederick, being heavier, tried to ignore it, but sweat soon soaked his undergarments and slid into his eyes. He was surprised at the steady persistence and dogged staying power of the young prince, and he realized with sinking heart that his arm was tiring and his guard slipping. The prince, on the other hand, seemed fresh and alert. His sword arm moved with the same precision and energy as it had when they started.

A group of men formed behind Frederick and several of the king's knights gathered behind the prince, cheering and booing in unison for the mistakes or direct hits of their champion.

"Now! Now!" They called to Frederick. "Take him now. He is weakening. You can take him any time you want." This was followed by a loud moan from them, for Arthur had drawn the first blood, a slash to the arm.

Frederick increased the fury of his assaults, but they were of no avail. The prince calmly parried each thrust, and then the prince's sword was inside his guard and pierced his hauberk. Frederick leaped back, swiped at his forehead, but the prince followed tightly, not allowing him a breath or a gasp. Frederick saw the prince's brow glisten with sweat, but he did not show weariness or fear.

Frederick had been taught a trick to disarm his enemy, and he watched for the opening. Suddenly it came, a lowering of the sword, a loosening of the hold. With a lightning thrust, Arthur's sword went flying into the air. Frederick watched it with a chuckle, lifted his eyes for a split second to receive the cheers of his companions. Then he whirled to sink his blade into the throat of his conquered enemy.

While Frederick took his bows, Arthur found it convenient to be elsewhere. He performed a back flip, landed neatly on his feet, and grasped his sword from the turf where it landed.

Frederick slewed his head around.

"I am here, lackwit." Arthur took the stance.

This time Arthur gave no ground, and the swords flew with no finesse, steel clanging on steel, the blades flashing in the hot sun almost faster than the eye could follow. Sweat poured from Frederick's reddened face, his breath came in quick gasps, his eyes showed white. Frederick was strong, yes, Arthur granted him that, but he did not have staying power.

Silently Arthur thanked his teacher who had goaded, prodded and forced him into long hours of practice until his arm screamed with pain and he wanted to quit, but could not. Now anger pricked his courage, sharpened his aim, strengthened his arm. Sweat poured into his eyes, but he fought past the pain, past the heat, past the fear.

His total focus narrowed upon the figure of the man who fought with such deadly purpose, whose eyes bored into his with seething fires of hatred.

Why does he hate me so?

Arthur drew air through clenched teeth, his arm screaming with pain, his brain reeling. He did not rush his blows, for he knew he could not last much longer. He let the other man dance and wave his sword about. "Now, what say … thee … Black Knight?" He slashed at the knight's arm and drew blood. "Am I … a child that you can … defeat me with ease?"

Frederick replied not, but stepped back and tried to mop his brow.

Arthur crowded within his guard, and in a flick on an eyelash, Frederick fell to his knees, no sword in hand. Arthur buried his blade into the knight's shoulder. After a few seconds while he caught his breath and heard as if from a distance the cheers from the king's knights, Arthur drew the blade out and flattened Frederick in the dust with his booted foot. He pressed the tip of his sword against Frederick's throat.

"Kill me quickly, thou blackest of knights and knavest of men," Frederick cried in a hoarse voice. "I have long hated thee for destroying my village and killing my mother seven years agone."

Arthur paused in the act of plunging his sword into the man's neck. "What village was that, may I ask? And when?"

"The village of Brulon. You know it well. T'was the year of '92! Kill me now!"

Arthur shook his head and straightened. He carefully wiped his sword on the grass and sheathed it. Frederick lay where he had fallen.

"I was six years old at the time," Arthur said slowly, trying to remember. "I rode from my mother's court only a furlong, she did not allow me to ride any farther. Why, man, that is almost in France! We had no war with thee or thy village then, or since. How did you come to think such a thing?"

Frederick sat up, brushed himself off, then stood, glowering. "My father, Baron FitzRauf, told me. I was a young boy in the village. He rescued me, adopted me as a son, and trained me as a squire and knighted me. It was he."

The prince shook his head again. "Nay, it could not be."

"If it was not you, it was King Richard. And you and he are the same!"

"Nay, we are not the same. The King is warring with Brittany even as we speak. I fled to King Philip's court to escape him. Besides, King Richard was in Palestine seven years ago. It could not have been him."

A French knight stepped forward. "I can shed some light on this problem. I remember the time and the place. FitzRauf's fief is small. He is building it by attacking defenseless villages on the border. This village I recall, for we came upon it soon after it was destroyed. We followed the tracks of the knights who carried off the plunder and came to FitzRauf's castle."

Arthur turned to Frederick. "Your adopted father is the one who destroyed your village."

"I say nay!" Frederick's eyes started from their sockets, his face reddened in blotchy spots, a white line circled his mouth. "I do not believe this report. You are an enemy of my father, and you would say what you will. But I believe it not. From this day forth, guard yourself well, for I shall fly at thee, knight, and I shall kill thee."

Arthur gathered Kazimer's reins. "Believe what you will, Sir Frederick, but now you have the truth. Ask your father, and if he is honest enough, he will tell thee. If not, perchance we shall meet again. If you continue to seek me out, I shall not spare the blade the second time. I grant you that."

Frederick gave him a dark look and took up his helmet. "If there is a second time, you are the one who shall feel the blade in your neck. Not only for killing my people, but for your lies and treachery. I swear it." He mounted and rode away.

Arthur donned his helmet, leaped to saddle. As they rode away, he shook his head. "I find it sad," he said to his groom. "Sir Frederick would make a brave and honorable knight, but he has been soured and sickened by hate."

The groom nodded. "Aye, Your Majesty. Now you shall have to ride with double the caution, which is not to your liking at all."

"Ah, well," Arthur replied, settling himself into the saddle. "I cannot hide craven and fearful from all who bear me hatred. I shall be careful, but I shall not flee from any man. You have my pledge on that." He kicked Kazimer and thundered down the forest trail.

***

The King's Castle, Paris, October 1199

"King Richard is dead."

The toneless announcement from the lips of the king's seneschal caused a deep hush to fall in the court of King Philip. It was not an entire surprise to those seated around the still-laden tables, for news had spread of Richard's injury at Chaluz and his subsequent illness. Now every tongue was silent and all eyes turned to the seneschal.

"Being wounded at Chaluz, he suffered for two months, and then expired at his castle at Rouen." He read other details in the same monotone. At the end, he rolled up his parchment and waited with bowed head.

The murmur of voices in the Great Hall resumed, along with the clatter of dishes and the occasional outburst of laughter from one too far gone in his wine. Arthur, now thirteen years old, laid down the knife he was bringing to his mouth. The death of the English king was of small matter to the French court.

"Hand me the missal," King Philip said impatiently. The seneschal hurried to obey. Philip read the parchment, running his finger quickly over the words. "I read here nothing about a successor to the throne."

"Nay, Your Majesty. There is nothing."

Arthur was seated at a table to the right and below the dais where the king sat with his nobles and family. He straightened and swung his legs over the bench, his appetite gone.

Philip glared at him, a smirk playing upon the corners of his mouth. "What say you, Prince Arthur? Who will inherit the crown of England? The suckling, Prince John?" He leaned back and gave himself up to a hearty roar of laughter, answered by a spatter of laughter from his courtiers.

Arthur scowled, anger rising red in his eyes. But he spoke carefully. "I know not, Your Majesty. I would like to retire, if I may."

King Philip of France, who took the grand title of Augustus, had the swarthy skin of the French, a trim beard and large intelligent eyes. He had gone to fat these recent years, but there was nothing that escaped his agile mind. His impatient fingers beat upon the table. He nodded curtly. *"Oui.* Go say your prayers, boy, for you shall need them. But I doubt if all the prayers in Christiandom would suffice to grant thee thy heart's desires."

Philip laughed and again the courtiers echoed it.

Do these dolts have no brains? Arthur gritted his teeth. He marveled at how much his status had changed since he first arrived at the French king's court. Then Philip Augustus doted upon him and required his presence throughout most of every day. But in recent months, Arthur had fallen from favor. He suffered the crude comments made in his presence, was banished from the king's audience and was seated below the dais. Arthur knew the king had no intention to aid his cause.

"Yes, my lord." Arthur stood and bowed and strode from the hall. He heard light footsteps and paused to look back. It was Princess Maria. She paused about the same time he did, hanging back, hiding her face in the folds of her silk scarf.

"Do you require me for something, Princess?" He was anxious to be alone in his apartment, to sort out his mixed emotions, to be away from this court. His words were sharp, so he tempered them now. "Would you care to walk with me, rather than behind me, Princess Maria?"

She came forward shyly, slipping her hand into his.

He led her to a small, enclosed garden. "And now, Princess Maria, may I ask why you have sought me out in this fashion? We must not tarry, for you know it is not allowed for us to talk this way. I would be most sad if you were punished because of me."

Her delicate features promised the approach of great beauty and her dark eyes were lively, intelligent and warm. *"Eh bein,* Prince Arthur, I would like to apologize for the unkindness of my father. He … he does not know you. But I see your heart. I see the hurt in your eyes. I know it matters a great deal to you."

He patted her hand, turning from her to stride to the wall surrounding the garden. The smell of lilac and rose was on the air; a mourning dove cooed in the twilight. The moon rose over the willows and a purple tint of the last rays of the sun colored the western sky. Brittany! How I wish to be home!

He glanced back at Maria, who was tucking a lily into her hair. How could this mere slip of a girl know his pain? How could she know of the wasted days and months he spent in this accursed place, currying favor as a courtier, his heart truly in the sweet forests of Brittany? For too long a time he had walked the halls, looked in empty faces, endured the sneering comments behind his back. And waited.

He bowed. "I am flattered that Princess Maria takes notice of me, a servant to the king. I came to find shelter and help here in France, and I have found it. I have learned much while here in his court and I am grateful to him for his kindness."

She rose to stand beside him. "But ... I sense that is not all, Arthur. You may speak freely with me. I am only a girl, of no consequence."

"*Oui,* you have been a faithful friend to this ... this outcast prince from Brittany. Once upon a time my teacher, a man named DeArmond, told me that I must someday find my own way in the world, and that I must rely upon the strengths I could find within myself. I think I have come to that place, *ma cherie.* And now ..." He glanced toward the west.

"Oh, please don't say you are leaving," she said. "I shall be most disconsolate."

"I didn't say that, did I?" He summoned his smile again. "Now, you have comforted me most thoroughly and I thank you for that. But I am weary from riding the trails of France today and I find myself in need of rest. Will you excuse me?" He took her hand and kissed it.

She laughed. "You do not need to flatter me with courtly speech. I know I am only a child, but I feel with a woman's heart." She looked up at him and sighed. "Do you know that my father is planning to give me to you in marriage?" Her hand flew to her mouth. "Oh! I was not to speak of it, yet it is true. Would that please you?"

He paced away from her, trying not to show his emotions, for the news brought a surge of old hope. If he were to wed Maria, he would be aligned with France, and with France at his side, he could take on John. He turned back, knelt before her and took her hand in his. "I find it most pleasing, *ma cherie,*" he said, kneeling before her.

She smiled, tipped his face with her hand, and gazed into his eyes. "Pledge to me your undying favor, sir knight. Then you shall go, and I shall know you will return for me some day."

He stood and bowed to her. "I do so pledge thee, Princess Maria. You shall always be with me in my heart, and I shall find a way to help thee in thy direst need. You only need to call and I shall be riding to thy side. I pledge thee my allegiance and my devotion."

As he returned to his apartment, he remembered the tears glistening on her cheeks. He shook his head. *Philip, for all his bluster, has determined to wed her to me.* He entered his room, threw off his cloak and lifted his feet for his personal servant, a young lad named Gascon, to pull off his boots. Sipping the mead that was brought to him on a platter, he strode to the window.

Now he knew what he should do. He would escape the French court and flee to Brittany, where he would take the reins of his kingdom firmly in his hands.

Yet he discovered in the ensuing days that it was not an easy matter to flee. Knights of the court accompanied him on his frequent rides into the countryside and soldiers of the castle followed his every step, even to the *necessaire* behind the stairs.

To make matters worse, the death of King Richard began to embroil England and France in a long, bloody war. In a fast succession of raids, Philip descended upon the provinces of Anjou, Maine and Touraine, wresting them from English hands before the succession to the throne was firmly established. Rumor had it that he also had his eyes on Brittany. Arthur would be nothing but a vassal to France.

One evening over a late supper, disquieting news reached his ears. The soldiers who ate nearby gloated over the victory they had that day in razing a small village in Brittany. *So now Philip invades my country!* His throat closed with anger and he pushed away from the table. In the courtyard, he witnessed the men quarreling over their bloody booty.

Arthur kept to himself in fear that his outbursts of anger could be construed as treason, but he could contain it no longer when a small child from Brittany was brought into the Great Hall during a feast several days later, still splattered with his mother's blood. With much laughter, they awarded Arthur as the child's guardian.

He stood slowly, a red tide rising before his eyes, his hand finding his sword hilt, his mouth dry. He glanced down at the child who wailed on the floor. "Take him and clean him up. Give him some food and take him to my apartment."

He lifted his eyes to the king's seat on the dais. Philip was enjoying the spectacle, wiping his eyes where tears of laughter ran, drinking a mock toast. Arthur strode forward, aware that the room fell silent, that swords were unsheathed, that guards positioned themselves beside Philip's chair.

Philip raised his hand to the guards and turned a sardonic grin upon the young prince. "Come forward, cousin," he said in his precise way. "I see you have come to quarrel with us. Say it, boy. It will cause you discomfort if you hold it within." The courtiers snickered.

"Your Majesty, word has reached my ears that your troops are attacking undefended villages in Brittany. These are my subjects and I pledge upon my sword and the Word of God to avenge those who destroy my people."

"You pledge, do you?" The king carelessly waved a bejeweled hand. "Is what I am hearing treason?" The silence deepened.

"This is not treason, O King," Arthur said in a clear, strong voice. He took a step closer and the guards blocked his progress. He raised his hands. "It is not my intention to harm His Majesty." He looked at the king and lifted his voice. "I swore allegiance to you, O King, but that allegiance ends where your sword touches my kingdom."

Not a whisper or a rustle greeted this announcement.

Philip glared at him fiercely. "Am I not at liberty to do what I want in my own territories? Begone now, thou puppy who yaps at my heels. I am tiring of thy speech and would have peace at my table."

"Does this mean that I am free to leave your court and return to Brittany?" Arthur knew as soon as he spoke that he should have kept silent.

Philip leaned forward, his hands gripping the armrests of his chair, his eyes bulging with a piercing stare. Then he sighed as if tiring of the game. "*Eh bein.* Stay by my side. There are things I must teach you before you make your way in the world." He turned his attention to his wine.

Arthur strode from the hall, shouting out commands concerning the child. A woman nursed it, but the little boy died within the week.

Each day Arthur rose with a mounting tension to return home, to escape, to fly. Yet the watchers dogged his every step with open disdain.

His chance came quite unexpectedly. He carried on his person all that he desired to take with him—his letters, a bag of coins, the crown jewel and a crumpled banner of Brittany. That day he was riding with a group of soldiers. As they entered a dense wood, Arthur purposefully hung back, as if to adjust his stirrups. As the last of the soldiers disappeared down the track, he spurred Kazimer into the forest. It did not take long before a hue and cry erupted behind him.

He remembered this forest. He had come here several times and knew there was a small hamlet deep within. Keeping low to the bushes, stopping now and then when the pursuers came near, he emerged at last on the village green. The blacksmith's shop was the most obvious retreat, but he shunned that and led his horse to the inn, up the wooden steps and into the common room. A woman screamed. Kazimer snorted as he cleared the low doorpost.

The innkeeper rushed in. "Here! What are you doing? You may not…" He stared and bowed low. "My lord, Prince Arthur. How may I serve you, and your … horse?"

Arthur nodded curtly. "I am in need of shelter. If you could direct us to your stable, my horse and I would be most grateful. Did not a king from long ago find sanctuary in a stable?"

The innkeeper laughed. "*Eh, bein!* You are in trouble. But fear not, we shall aid thee. Bring your steed through here, sire, through the kitchen. I shall show thee a place to hide that not even the angels can find."

Arthur followed the man's broad back through the hot steamy kitchen, winked at the scullery maids who nearly swooned with delight, then hurried out the back, under the ancient oaks, through a small clearing, to the mouth of a cave that was hidden behind a bank of brambles.

"Tis said to be the cave of Merlin," the man said in a whisper. "We store our goods in here that need to be kept cool. Rest here as long as you like. None of us will betray you."

Arthur loosened Kazimer's girth and settled himself on the sandy ground. He told himself he must listen for footsteps, but he closed his eyes.

The innkeeper shook him awake. He leaped to his feet.

"They have come and gone. Come inside and refresh yourself with a bite to eat and our good wine. It will be our pleasure to serve you, Prince Arthur."

Arthur dusted himself off. "Is my horse welcome at your board also?"

The man laughed. "Aye. Bring him along."

Arthur winked as he tightened the girth. "Nay, I was only jesting. I thank you for your kindness. My lady mother will thank you, too."

As he started out a short while later, a crescent moon hung low in the sky, flanked by a bright Venus. Suddenly the truth hit him. He was free.

"Ah, for certes, it is fine to be away from Philip's court. By morning, we shall be in Brittany." He patted Kazimer's neck and noted the white ears tipped back to hear his voice. "We shall be home."

CHAPTER EIGHT

Courage is fear that has said its prayers. Karl Barth

Mont St. Michels, Brittany, January 1200

"The abbot requires your presence in his chambers."

Louis lifted his eyes from the book he was inscribing and glanced at the young acolyte who stood quietly beside his desk. He laid his pen down. What could Father Frances want of him?

The abbot was a tall man, soft spoken, with a prominent brow and dark, piercing eyes. He received Louis in his private quarters. As Louis entered and glanced about, he was gratified to see that the abbot dwelt in the same kind of living appointments that characterized his priests and monks—a small room containing a cot, a wardrobe and a stand that held a pitcher of water. A crucifix hung on the wall over the bed. The only piece of furniture that bespoke his office was an oak desk, a large affair that sat off to one corner with a chair behind it. A lone candle sputtered in its holder on the desk.

The abbot handed Louis a mug of wine and motioned him to the chair. He himself sat on the cot. "We are conspirators this even, Brother." A smile broke the solemn features. "I cajoled the cook to bring me a bottle of the good wine. I do not usually partake so late. Are you well, Brother Louis? Do you find your life on our Mont a thing of purpose?"

Louis sipped his wine and noted its flavor—full, tangy with the full flavor of the southern slopes in it. He nodded. "My Father, I have found this island a veritable sanctuary of peace and employment."

"I am glad to hear you say that. You are a blessing to our house. What is your desire, my son?"

"I am avowed to present an illustrated book to the Holy Father in Rome. Then I must travel to Palestine to help free the holy sites from the paynim. After that, I would like to visit Alexandria to continue my studies in medicine. If you have a further request to make of me, please name the task and I shall be pleased to attempt it."

Father Frances stood and paced to the window where he gazed out into the dark garden for some time. He turned and pierced Louis with a bright, stern gaze. "Can I trust you?"

Louis was dumbfounded. What a thing to ask. Surely the abbot knew he could be trusted.

He lowered his eyes, glanced up. "Aye, Father. To my last breath."

Father Frances paced to his desk and rummaged through a pile of papers. "It concerns the book you brought to us. We, too, have a book inscribed as a gift for the Holy Father. We also have messages for his eyes alone."

"Messages?"

Father Frances withdrew a package that was wrapped with leather, sealed and tied with a gold cord. He returned to the cot, still holding the parcel as he would a newborn child. "This contains papers that must reach the pope in the shortest time possible. You are not to know what they concern. You will be carrying a box in which resides a fragment of the bones of Saint George, a gift to the Holy See that we received from a crusader."

His voice descended to a whisper and he leaned forward so steeply he was in danger of falling from the cot, his face only a few inches from Louis'. "This package will be hidden in a false bottom of the box. You will travel with a small contingent of soldiers. Very small, to arouse no suspicions. Under no account are you to open this parcel. You are to hand it in person to no one but the Holy Father himself. Do you understand, my son?"

Louis nodded, staring into the intent brown eyes of the father. He was aware of the candle sputtering, as if a wind blew it from some distant land, of his heart thumping loudly in his chest. His throat was dry and his brow slickened with sweat.

He swallowed. "Yes, Father. I am only a young monk. I am not acquainted with the ways of the world, so should I even by accident read the papers, I would not know what I was reading."

The abbot straightened and smiled, satisfied. "You will leave in a fortnight and journey to Orleans. There you will be refreshed, and they will give you an escort to Marsellies and pay your fare for board on a ship. I am sorry you must travel in this weather—you will encounter snow in the passes, for certes. But there is nothing for it. The letters must be delivered."

He cast a sharp glance at Louis. "I must impress upon you without frightening you the vast importance of this mission. A whole city, thousands of people, even a whole nation hangs in the balance and may be utterly destroyed if you fail. Are you willing to undertake this task?"

Louis' knees wobbled and his heart froze. Yet he stood calmly and bowed. "I am honored. To do your will is my highest goal, Father, even if it means I shall die. But I feel unworthy, untrained to undertake this great task. Could you not find someone ... anyone who ..."

"Nay. No one. And the parcel must travel without delay." Father Francis sat at his desk and steepled his fingers, regarding Louis fondly. "You are as you seem, a common monk, one of thousands, who travels to the Holy See. Our enemies will never suspect you."

"Enemies? Enemies who would combat me over matters of doctrine, tradition, or practice?"

The abbot shook his head. "Enemies who would slit your throat for the papers you carry."

"But who ... and why ..." Louis sat down hard on the cot.

"Aye, you are simple." Father Frances smiled. "I wish to God we were all as you. But in the world, my son, things are different than inside these cloistered walls. When you have ... but, stay. I will not lecture you on politics." He sipped his wine. "Have you heard of the new crusade?"

Louis nodded, glad to have some knowledge of the world. "I was hoping to join it."

Father Frances sighed and glanced down at his desk.

"Why? Is that a problem?"

"Nay. None that I can lay a hand on. Yet there are rumors ... perchance more than rumors. The leaders of the expedition, Count Louis of Blois and Boniface the Marquis of Montferret, have decided to take the sea route to Palestine. They sent a delegation to Venice to negotiate transports, ships and the like, with the Doge of Venice, Enricho Dandolo. There has been an agreement reached and gold has been promised. They formed an alliance with Venice. Yet we ... some of us know, er, suspect the motives of Dandolo. He is jealous of the trade of Zara across the Aegean Sea. I do not trust the man. He hates the Byzantines in Constantinople and hungers for the wealth of that great city, for they once maimed him and he goes about nearly blind." He stood and faced the crucifix, as if to gain strength.

Louis found his cup and took a long draught of wine, not tasting it, his mind scarcely registering the act.

Father Frances sighed again. "I know not why I tell you this. But we are concerned about the direction this new crusade. They say they are bound for Egypt, but there are grave doubts, for they when join themselves with Venice ..." He cradled his head in his hands. "It is more than I ... than we can fathom, but Christian cities are in danger from their own Christian brothers." He leaned forward and whispered, "I am terrified, Brother Louis!"

Louis could barely speak, so taken aback was he at the father's revelations. He knew divisions and hard feelings abounded between the Roman Church and the Greek Orthodox Church, yet nothing like this had ever entered his mind. Christian cities in peril from the crusading army? How could such a thing be? From a dry throat he asked, "What would you have me do?"

"We must warn the Holy Father and he will know the right course of action. I am sure of it."

Silence fell. Louis heard the chapel bell ring out the hour: 2:00am, the hour of Prime. Father Francis lifted his head, all mystery and fear banished from his face as if erased by the hand of God.

"*Eh bien.* Our office calls us." He rose and paced to his desk. "There are other emissaries, of course, official couriers to Rome. Yet this matter ... is very secret." He held out the parcel. "Will you do it, my son? Say now and put my old heart to rest."

Louis found himself kneeling before the father, tears streaming from his eyes. "My answer is yes, Father. I am willing to go." He received the parcel and a blessing and regained his feet. The older man shuffled about the room, preparing for the office of prime, but Louis remained rooted to the spot, watching him.

"You may go, my son. I am sure there are—"

"Excuse me, Father, but there is something I must ask you ere I leave the island."

"What is it, Son?"

"I ... I have with me a jewel that I brought to St. Jacques as a child. I do not remember it, yet Father Adolph said I gave it to the abbey when I arrived as a child. He returned it to me for my expenses on my journey. Do you ... could you help me find a buyer for it? I am not acquainted with such things."

"Ah, my good monk and faithful friend." The abbot's smile lit the small chamber. "Bring me the jewel after prime and we shall see what we can do for you."

"Thank you, Father." He bowed.

The abbot opened the door. "Go with God, my son."

***

Mordelias, Brittany, May 1200

Arthur enjoyed a hero's welcome home and was given a throne beside his mother's in the Great Hall. He entertained the barons and castellans and lords of the land as they came in procession to Mordelias. A grand fete celebrated Arthur's ascension to the throne and the coming of the new year. King Philip, reconciled to Arthur after his escape, knighted him and gave him Maria for a bride. The wedding was held on the castle lawn that spring on his fourteenth birthday.

After that, he watched the road every day for word that he had been chosen to be king of England.

One day when he visited a castle some ten miles from Mordelias, a rider arrived with a message for the baron. Upon hearing the news, Arthur mounted his horse without a farewell to his host, and rode back home, spurring his steed mercilessly. He thundered across the drawbridge, clattered under the tower gate and pulled back on the reins in the outer bailey, scattering chickens and dogs. His lathered horse, a leggy bay he favored recently, stumbled from exhaustion. A groom met him, helped him dismount and looked askance at the horse.

"My lord, you have ridden far and fast," he said. "Your horse is nearly done in. I hope Lord DeArmond does not see him in this condition. Begging your pardon, Your Majesty, but he would have your hide."

"I care not for horses, nor for DeArmond. And if you say another word, I swear you shall feel the taste of the whip on your back!"

The young man merely tugged at his forelock and bent his head, taking the reins to walk the horse and cool him down before giving him water and a rub. All the servants in the great castle of Mordelias bore the anger of the young prince with patience, for it was on their heads that his wrath most usually fell. "He is a Plantagenet, after all," they would say, with a pleased look and a nod of the head, "and his grandfather, old Henry the Secund had a temper none could equal."

The prince strode angrily into the stone keep and, a few minutes later, burst without announcement into his mother's apartment, his boots still muddy from the road, his hands clenched, his heart bursting.

"What is it, my son?" Constance rose with a rustle of silken skirts.

"Have not you heard, Mother?" Arthur strode into the room, flinging off his gloves. "They crowned John Duke of Normandy. He sailed to England to be crowned king there. I have lost the kingdom in one fell stroke."

"When did you hear of it?"

"Just now. I was at Gustave's." He paced to the window and looked down on the lists where several knights practiced for an upcoming tournament. He whirled around. "Why didn't you petition William the Marshal? It was he and the archbishop, Walter of Rouen, who decided. Surely they could have been bought. Look at that bauble you wear on your neck. Those jewels could have won me the kingdom, but nay, you sat here in idleness and did nothing."

Constance approached him and laid a trembling hand on his arm. "All is not lost, son," she said in a low voice. "We have an army. We have gold. We shall fight the English."

He cast her a quizzical glance, for he knew she favored and trusted John. Brushing aside her hand, unwilling to play her games, he paced to the fireplace. "We have been fighting the English for as long as I can remember. Now our kingdom is depleted and the barons are complaining of the cost of war. They want peace. We cannot afford a war. If we go to war, I shall lose what little support I have from them." He stormed from her presence, but could find little consolation.

Several weeks later, a council was held, but the barons were closed-mouthed, stubborn and showed little inclination for a war with the English. As far as the matter of Prince Arthur's disgrace, they could care less. The only one who showed any spirit at all was the baron Hugh of Lusignan.

Arthur looked to him most often during the discussion, for he knew Hugh had a private vendetta against John. John had stolen Hugh's promised bride, the lovely Isabella. But even Baron of Lusignan seemed reluctant to promise funds and men.

The next day Arthur was summoned to the queen's private apartments. He went with sinking heart, for he knew his mother had arranged for him to appear before John in England to pledge his allegiance to him. Bowing perfunctorily over her hand, he argued his case. But against all polity, reason and logic, nothing he said changed Constance's mind.

She folded her arms under her breasts, her eyes glittery and cold. "You will go as planned, Arthur. It is all that is left us."

He gazed at her fully, perhaps for the first time since his return. Even though she had maintained her beauty with the aid of creams and tight under-garments, her age showed in the wrinkles around her eyes, in her frail hands that needed creams to cover the brown spots, in the stoop of her shoulders. She wore a gown of black silk, overlaid with costly jewels, cut low at the bodice, and over her shoulders a black cape lined with white fur.

She stood, swirling her skirts, the pathetic gesture of an old woman wanting to be young and gripped his arm with steel-laced intensity. "Arthur! Must I remind you that John has ever been a friend to us? Now that he is king, you must please him. He will help us in our fight."

"Fight? How may I fight when I have pledged my allegiance?" He turned back to the window. "I thought we were trying to gain the throne, that I would be the King of England. Has that ought importance to you anymore?"

She waved a hand as if all of that was of no consequence. "We must face reality, Arthur. Richard is dead and John was chosen king. We must seek a high position for you in John's realm.

Perchance he will name you his chancellor. Or duke of the Aquaitaine."

Arthur strode to the fireplace. She patted a stool beside her chair, but he was too angry to sit, nearly too angry to speak. He ground his teeth as a red haze settled over his mind. If only he could plunge his sword into the black heart of his uncle. "John will not give me the Aquaitaine." He snorted. "I pledge myself, in truth. I pledge myself from this day forward to hate my uncle and to kill him most expediently whenever I find chance."

She threw a hand over her heart. "Oh, Arthur. You must not say such things. We must make plans, dear son. We must ..."

But he was not listening, nor heeding her dramatics. "Ma Mere, I feared this day. All those months I slunk like a dog at the feet of King Philip in France, hiding from Richard, I feared the day I would pledge myself to John. What a fool I was to listen to you. At least Richard did not steal a bride from one of our own barons. It is shameful what John did to Hugh of Lusignan and I am prepared to fight for his honor. Isabella is the fairest of all women on earth, they say, but her beauty does not give John the right to have her as a wife, especially since he already has one. It is ... it is adultery. It is the talk of all the common people."

Constance sighed. She chose a nut from a bowl and crunched it between her strong teeth. "What do we care for talk of commoners? Our dear Hugh, or le Brun as his people are fond of calling him, must realize that when the king wants a woman, none must stand in his way. John is applying to the pope to have his marriage annulled, anyway. They say that Isabella was not overly disappointed by the honor she received."

He did not speak, for he could not. How could she betray one of her own barons? Was there no honor left in the world?

Constance stood, her eyes flashing. "I have made provision for you to sail to England in a fortnight. You shall be announced to the court of King John, where you shall bow before him and swear your allegiance. It is all we can do. There is no further need for discussion."

Arthur complied with truculence, enduring his trip across the Channel and his visit to London and his appearance in the court of King John with patient anger, as one who merely goes through a ritual, but bides his time. Hope flickered in his heart as he waited in the anteroom, dressed in his finest apparel—black hose that showed off his slender legs, a white silk tunic held to his waist with a scarlet sash, soft up-turned shoes made of the finest leather, a tooled belt from which his silver sword swung, and the scarlet cape embroidered with the Plantagenet emblem.

He stood straight, to attention, his hand on his sword hilt, waiting for the call. Perhaps his rights due him by birth would be acknowledged. Perhaps John would invite him to occupy a high position at his side. Chancellor? Bishop of Canterbury? Who knew?

But John seemed bored and inattentive to his duties and barely nodded when Arthur was announced. He did not smile at the young prince and only extended his hand when Arthur knelt and paid his homage. It was plain that the king wanted little to do with this nephew from Brittany. Perhaps he was thinking more of the raven-haired beauty he had stolen from the baron of Lusignan. "I give thee the duchy of Brittany as Lord and Duke," the king said in an understated tone and a bend of the head.

The ceremony lasted a bare five minutes.

During the next few months, Arthur settled into his position as duke. All the land seemed to sigh with relief for the cessation of war, for the return of their prince to his rightful place, and for good crops that fall.

But the young duke could not forget the great wrong done to him. His anger and hatred grew with each passing month, almost consumed him. He thought continually of John, and the throne that should have been his. He discovered that there were many barons and nobles in Brittany who still held the shining dream in their hearts, and none so fiercely as the baron of Lusignan, Hugh the Brown.

Together they huddled endless hours while fires burned low and dawn slowly slipped over the windowsills.

France gnawed away at English holdings in Anjou and King Philip's army had taken many towns and castles—Lyons, Mortimar, and Boutavant, to name a few.

One evening Arthur and le Brun received word that John had arrived in Normandy but he seemed little inclined to war, lying abed with his wife in LeMans while his troops lusted for blood.

Arthur met Baron le Brun's eyes. The time had come.

Several weeks later, at the top of a wooded ridge, Prince Arthur halted Kazimer and held a gauntleted hand aloft. Columns of soldiers behind him pulled back on their reins and calmed their restive mounts. Baron le Brun drew up beside him on his blood bay charger, Caesar.

Below, a river threaded its way through the valley like a shimmery ribbon. A small village nestled in the curve of the river, its thatched roof huts huddled together in the shadow of a castle. Arthur knew Mirabeau, had been here many times, but never as the leader of an army, never to take a castle. He tried to quell the uneasy feeling in the pit of his stomach, and decided that it was caused not so much by the thought of shedding blood, but by the fear of failure.

He lowered his hand, removed his glove, and rubbed his thumb across the face of the ring the old woman had given him. *Come on, Dagda. You must do your stuff for me now, or all is lost.* The ugly face seemed to leer at him with scorn, with evil. A sudden premonition shivered down Arthur's spine. What did it mean? Should he continue the attack? How could he abandon it now?

Shoving the queasiness away, he turned to le Brun. "There it is, my friend," he said in a low voice. "Our first conquest, an easy target. What say ye? Shall we take it?" He looked again at the castle, noted its small size, that it had poor defenses, no curtain wall nor moat, only an earthern battlement raised some ten feet high around a central keep.

Baron le Brun grunted, like the bear he was nicknamed for. "Do you have doubts, Your Majesty? Do you have misgivings?" He was a large man with wide shoulders and long, brown hair that he kept in immaculate condition, much like Absalom of old. Yet it was his command of half the duchy of Brittany, the power of his personality, his wealth and his personal vendetta against John that was the driving force behind the prince's attack.

Arthur laughed, hefting his lance. "I am more than ready for the challenge. I shall gain back the kingdom that is rightfully mine or die in the effort. Nay, I do not have misgivings. I want this more than life itself." Suddenly he knew it to be true—he could do this. He would do this.

Le Brun smiled grimly. "I want it, too. I want to see John begging for his life while Isabella looks on."

The westering sun lit the valley and set aglow the river with a soft purple light. In the castle Arthur knew his grand-mere, Queen Eleanor, was in residence, probably having her afternoon tea. She was an old woman now, but people still talked of her beauty and vitality.

He calculated the purse he would win from such a prize. It would be rich indeed. He had no qualms about capturing his own grandmother, for he felt no affection for any of the Plantagenets. And he was in little danger of the king's troops. John's army was camped a full three days march away. Arthur would sack the town and capture the queen and shake the dust of Mirabeau before John knew they had arrived.

He nodded again and with a firm shake of his head, addressed Lord Phillip de Vaunderville. "We shall proceed with silence and camp in the valley. Surprise is our greatest weapon. We must not flush the bird from the bush too soon, or Queen Eleanor will be forewarned and escape."

The young man saluted and turned to pass the order on down the lines.

The next day, Arthur rode in the van as they swooped off the hills and thundered across the bridge and into the village. "For God and for Brittany!" he cried aloud.

The battle began immediately, but the village men were poorly armed and trained. Fighting raged up and down the village streets—the Bretons were beating them back, for they had taken the sleepy villagers by surprise. But where were the queen's soldiers? Surely she commanded a battalion for protection.

Arthur glanced up and saw on the battlements of the keep above him the figure of a woman. *Grand-Mere Eleanor!* She did not appear infirm. She strode straight-backed up and down, up and down, surveying the battle, calling out orders.

Then he saw them, the queen's men, dressed in red and gold, the color of Aquitaine. They guarded the entrance to the castle with stern faces, holding their weapons grimly. Somehow the queen had been alerted to his presence in time to gather as many men as she could and flee to the keep while her men guarded the castle gates. Arthur's courage trembled. These men were seasoned soldiers, pledged to their queen; they would protect her or die.

By sundown, Arthur and his Breton soldiers took control of the village. That evening his army camped below the castle's walls. They had made a sortie on the gates, but were driven back. Arthur was surprised at the vehemence with which the castle was defended, and reminded himself that his grandmother was not a doddering fool—she knew how to rally her people and she knew exactly what to do in an emergency.

Not expecting to actually lay siege to a castle, Arthur had not brought with him battering rams or scaling devices or catapults. He sent a squad of men into the nearby forest. On the morrow, they would construct the needed weapons to penetrate the castle and keep.

All the next day, he kept an eye on the narrow window at the top of the stone keep, wondering if he would see a white scarf waving from it, an appeal for mercy from the queen. In this he was disappointed, and so that evening he settled into the mayor's house near the castle, which he commandeered for himself and his officers, and ate a hearty meal of beef stew and bread. His men found sufficient food and ale in the larders of the local inn and they settled down the first night in a jovial mood.

The next day he directed the attack on the gates, pacing nervously between where his men constructed a battering ram to the streets of the village where his men battled the few remaining villagers who were loyal to the queen. He then rode to the top of the hill where he scanned the horizon for movement.

As he gazed out over the wooded, rolling countryside, he recalled a letter he had received from his father-in-law, King Philip, promising him aid in his war against John. At the outset, he did not think he would need France's help in taking Mirabeau, but with each succeeding moment, his anxiety rose. He found himself praying silently for the sight of French soldiers approaching. Who would have ever thought he would pray for help from the French?

"M'lord! Come quickly. They are breaking the gates of the castle!"

Arthur leaped on Kazimer and rode furiously to the gates. For certes, his men had won the castle. With cheers and hoots and fists shaken in the air, they chased the remaining soldiers into the keep where a thick metal door clanged shut and bolts were dropped.

From the battlements above, a rain of deadly arrows fell upon his men. A number were killed outright.

"Yo-ho!" Arthur yelled, calling his men back.

The soldiers nearest the walls retreated, dragging the dead and wounded with them.

Time and time again Arthur commanded an attack on the keep, but the deadly arrows fell, and his men died. At sunset he ordered his troops to find rest and food.

"On the morrow, we shall penetrate the keep," he called out to his dispirited men. "We shall build a bigger battering ram and the door will melt like butter!"

There was a weak cheer.

He wheeled his horse. "Where is Baron le brun?"

A knight nodded toward the smithy. "There, m'lord. His horse was wounded."

Arthur spurred Kazimer and dismounted at the smithy. Inside, he found the baron supervising the treatment of Caesar. Arthur paced the small room. "They shoot at my men unceasingly when we attempt to break the door. It is a metal door, le Brun. What should I do? I cannot allow my men to be slain in this manner. But I see no other way to win the keep. Who would have thought the old woman would hold out this long? Look. The day is nearly gone. We should have captured the queen and shaken the dust of this miserable place. Do you think John will come? Or King Philip? Shall we abandon the prize and flee?"

The baron swiped a dirty hand across his broad sweaty face and grimaced. "I do not know. You are captain and prince. You must make the decisions. If you flee, you must deal with the morale of your men, for they will feel they are fighting a losing cause." He turned back to Caesar, as if that was the only matter that concerned him.

Arthur considered the man's broad back for a brief moment, and turned on his heel.

Evening found a more subdued army within the walls of the castle as the men buried their dead and found help for their wounded. Arthur sat by himself, nursing his wounded feelings, watching the moon rise over the wooded ridge to the east. He imagined he heard the snort of horses and the jingle of armor. Was it the English? Could John march his men eighty miles from LeMans in two days? Can cows fly? He shook his head and accepted a cup of mead from Baron le Brun, who seated himself nearby.

"Thank you, my friend." He took a deep draught of the spiced wine. "How is your horse?"

le Brun shook his head. "Caesar will live, but I must find another to ride, for he cannot be ridden for several weeks. I hear you solved your problem of how to win the door to the keep."

Arthur nodded. "The men are building wooden covers to hold over their heads. Tomorrow morning at dawn, we shall attack. I hope by midmorning the queen will be our prisoner and we shall be riding over that hill."

But again, the prince was disappointed. The door of the keep held solidly and his men stumbled and fell and were killed. As he called them back, a cry of victory rang out from the defenders above their heads. Arthur had been totally absorbed with breaking into the keep and had pulled the guards from the battlements to aid in the final assault. He raised his head and heard a sound that was to him the tolling of the bell of doom.

Horns! Horns! Cries of triumph poured from the throats of countless soldiers! The thunder of a thousand hooves! As Arthur gazed, transfixed, the vanguard of the English army, seasoned knights and barons and lords and King John himself, rode down the hill into the village, holding aloft the banner of England. Behind them, wave upon wave of horsemen and foot soldiers and archers swarmed into the valley.

Cheers erupted from the battlements of the keep. The queen's red scarf saluted the new army with a triumphant flourish.

Arthur had no choice but surrender. He raised a white flag. He and his twenty-two knights were led away as prisoners. Arthur looked only once into the eyes of his friend Baron le Brun and saw hatred burning bright in a maddened glare.

"This is not the end," the baron growled. "I shall live to see the day when John lies dead!"

But the prince knew the reality was grim. John was not known to treat his enemies with mercy.

CHAPTER NINE

Not all who wander are lost. J.R.R. Tolkien

Madrid, Al Andulas, October 1200

Judith stared at the ceiling. Outside the latticed window she heard the drunken songs of men deep in their wine. Miguel slept on a cot across the room. She shivered under a ragged blanket, then rose and tucked her cloak around her thin body. While she now felt a little warmer, there was no comfort for her tortured soul. She thought back over the year and a half—had it truly been that long?

First they traveled to Lyon, then to Marseille, then to Monaco. They visited Genoa in Italy, rode south to Pisa, and at Livorno they boarded a ship and sailed to Spain, stopping in ports such as Valencia, Cartegena and Malaga where a vast slave market yielded no clues. Then, on the strength of a weak hint, they traveled inland to Madrid and found poor lodging in the ancient city.

Judith endured the never-ending blur of slave markets and dealers and camps. How much tea had they drunk? How much money had they given for information that led nowhere? Now their pouch was nearly empty, even though they were careful. The steady dribble of coins for inns, food, care for their horses, information and ship fare was alarming.

One time they narrowly escaped disaster. It happened on the road from Malaga to Madrid. They decided to ride instead of travel by ship around the Rock, for they could ask more questions and hopefully garner information while on land. A band of brigands accosted them at a place where the road dipped into a narrow valley and the forest closed in on both sides, and only their swift mounts and quick thinking saved the day. Miguel purchased a sword when they reached Madrid, but he did not know how to use it, other than what he learned from watching sword fighting.

Now his fine clothes were in tatters, they rode poor mounts and they conserved every coin. Judith felt as if she had seen all the worst parts of the world. Her hopes were as thin and brittle as the cakes they bought from the desert tribes, for they still had no solid leads as to where her father had been taken, or even if he lived.

She grew tired of the ritual of applying black paste to her face and abandoned the practice altogether, stating that she was as brown as the natives and no one looked at her anyway. She hated the long rides, the dirt and sand and searing heat, the lack of comforts, the questions, the filthy inns, the meager food and the constant fear of attack, especially from the Christian knights who patrolled the roads and guarded the forts along the coast. She hated the feeling of insecurity, as one who was without home or country.

When she fell asleep that night, she dreamed of Amma who stood in a meadow of daisies. To the east, the sea twinkled in the sun and gulls cried overhead. Amma was leading the way across the meadow with a basket swinging from her arm. She was singing. Then they danced while someone played a lute and someone strummed a viola. Amma's eyes twinkled and she laughed merrily while her black hair flowed over her shoulders like a shimmering waterfall kissed by the sun. They fell on the grass when the dance was done.

But darkness flew across the great arch of the sky and Amma lay beside her, dead. Judith pled for life to come back into those gentle eyes, but Amma lay still. A pool of blood grew larger with each second, threatening to drown Judith. She ran from it and fell.

Darkness! Terror! She screamed, a shriek that became a howling wail, echoing back and forth around her head like a thousand banshees, filling the whole world. She shrank from the sound and saw herself kneeling, alone, desolate.

She awoke. The room was dark and Miguel snored. Judith sat up, and cradling her face in her hands, rocked back and forth, shaking with the grief that swept her barren soul. Weeping began deep in her heart, erupted in a torrent from her throat, took possession of her whole body. Huge, racking sobs shook her as a large dog shakes a kitten.

When her tears subsided, Miguel snored on, oblivious, and the dice game below in the courtyard erupted into a fight.

She prayed to die, but Yahweh seemed far away and silent. Sweeping her tears away, she rose and opened the lattice on a dark new day. Only a pale yellow streak on the horizon lightened the black clouds.

After a meager breakfast of dry bread and a scrap of cheese, she led the way downstairs and peered out the window in the common room. It was raining, not a gentle pitter-pat, but a downpour of such extent that Judith feared they would be swept off the road.

She donned her woolen cloak, the one she bought in Pisa, Italy, pulling its hood down over her head. As Miguel paid the bill, Judith climbed into the saddle of her old mare, a black horse she had named Jochebed. Miguel mounted his big roan. They started out, but had not passed the gate of the inn when she suddenly pulled back on the reins.

"Miguel, wait." Rain drummed steadily on her head. Jochebed twisted beneath her, anxious to be on the way, or return to the dry stall. "Miguel!"

He turned his mount, his eyes weary and his back bowed with a great burden. His wide-brimmed hat flowed with a fountain of water from every low spot.He said nothing, only studied her face.

"I … I have lost the will to go on like this. I want to go home."

"Home?"

"Well, to Troyes. My father's family, the Izchakis, must live there still. They will take me in. We … I can pick up the empty ends of my life. I am tired of this."

He lowered his eyes and did not respond.

She wondered at his silence. "Miguel? Did you hear me? I want to go home."

"Yea, mistress. But I am on a quest of my own. My family once lived around Madrid. I remember the city, very vaguely. I had hoped … " He straightened and smiled at her. "But I am your servant, mistress, and if you want to return to France, then we shall."

She knew not what to say, so astounded was she over his revelation. He had never spoken before of his family. Strange that she never thought he would seek his own, here in Spain. "We shall stay in Madrid for a few days longer, Miguel. You have served me faithfully and well. I cannot deny your request. Come, let us return to the inn and discuss it out of the rain." She turned Jochebed and headed back to the barn.

He rode beside her and laid a hand on her arm. Tears stood in his eyes. "Thank you, mistress."

They dismounted in the barn. The warm smells of horse and cow and hay and leather poured over her like a blanket; the familiar sounds of creaking timber, scurrying mice feet, stomp of horse hoof were as comforting as her mother's songs.

He pulled a creased map from his tunic. He had gotten it off a dead sailor before his body was tossed overboard. "When I have finished my business, then we shall return to Troyes. Which way do you think we should go? Return to Marseilles and ride up the Rhone? Or ride down to Almeria, here, or to Cadiz and take ship to LaRochelle? That route would land us on the western coast of France."

"Let me see." She shoved back her hood and studied the map carefully, running her finger on the spidery lines. "Why don't we ride back to Valencia and take a ship to Marseilles?"

He nodded and rolled up the map. "Whatever you say, mistress. I hope our horses and our gold holds out long enough."

Stepping outside, she lifted her face to the sky and raised her arms. The clouds were breaking apart; a patch of blue appeared just overhead; a sparrow chirped from its perch in the old oak. She clapped her hands and performed a little dance.

She was going home.

***

Rouen, Normandy, October 1200

Prince Arthur paced his prison—a long, narrow room situated high on the castle wall, fighting his familiar demons of shame and remorse and anger. Again and again he replayed the fateful day when he led his men to the town of Mirabeau.

He halted before the barred window, a perpetual frown creasing his brow, and looked unseeingly at the brown folds of the hills and the bright autumn sunshine. His anger was a sharp-edged sword he carried within his heart, a flame he nursed through the long days as he rehearsed ways in which he could wreak revenge upon John when he was freed.

He had not supposed John would show his knights mercy, but he was sick when he heard that they had been taken to England—chained together, two and two—in oxcarts to Corfe, a castle on the Isle of Purbeck. There, John allowed them to die of starvation, a form of capital punishment he seemed to favor. All save two. Hugh of Lusignan John freed to please his wife. And Savaric de Mauleon managed to escape by making his guards drunk and breaking his bonds.

John imprisoned Arthur at Falaise Castle in Normandy, a famous castle built high on a boat-shaped rock between heavily wooded country and the Cleft of Val d'Ante. His keeper, Hubert de Burgh, was a good man and afforded Arthur a large apartment built into the outer wall of the castle. Arthur had light, food, drink, company and news of the outside world.

A large party appeared over the horizon and rode with haste to the castle gates, flying the banner of King John. Arthur leaned on the sill, watching with interest. Why was the king visiting Falaise? He did not have long to wait, for soon he heard heavy boots on the stone floors, the clanging of doors, echoing voices of men. Baron de Burgh opened the door and cast the prince a glance.

John burst into the room without a herald, swirling his rich, purple cape. He was a short, dark man with stooped shoulders, yet with a high, intelligent forehead and bright, inquisitive eyes. Arthur looked at him with detached interest, almost as if an insect had crawled into the room. *Ah! So my enemy has deigned to visit!* He did not so much as kneel and barely nodded his head in acknowledgment of his guest, not trying to hide his hatred and disdain.

John noted this but spoke with a gentle voice. To those who knew him, this meant the king was in his most dangerous mood. "Prince Arthur, I am grieved to find thee, my nephew, in such a sad strait! I have come to see if there is anything I can do to relieve your mind, your spirits, or your sadness." His quick glance took in the bare stone room, a parchment lying on a wooden table, the bed along the wall.

The prince smoothed the material of his velvet tunic, as if to reassure himself he was not in captivity. "Uncle, I have lived and prayed for the day I may repay thee for the kindness you showed my men." He could not stop the trembling of his hands and clasped them firmly behind his back. "What do you want?"

John's eyes glinted with poorly disguised anger, and he strode to the window, swirling his cloak, as if the room was too small for his towering rage. He spoke again in that quiet voice. "It was you who attacked an English town. Would you have been kinder to my knights? I think not. An apology might be in order."

Arthur drew in his breath, trying hard not to throttle the throat above the purple cape. His words, when they came, were hard. "In searching my heart before my Lord and the Virgin Mother, I find nothing there to repent of, sire. What crime have I committed? Tell me speedily, or I shall die!"

The king fingered his golden jewelry nervously. His face flushed, a bad sign, Arthur knew, and his eyes narrowed to slits. It looked as if he were about to throw one of his famous tantrums. "I find thee unrepentant, Nephew, when I would show thee my friendship."

Arthur could hold his anger no longer. "Better the hatred of the King of France!"

The king recoiled, took a step back. His eyes widened, his face reddened a deeper shade. Arthur noted his clenched fists and wondered with some satisfaction if he would strike.

"I am king." He swept his hand in a grand gesture. "I have all power in my hands. Do you hope to escape me? Can you break through these stone walls? There is no hope for thee. You tried once to overcome me and you failed. Now you must bear the consequences of your actions. You must bow the knee before me, or …"

"Or, what, Uncle?" Arthur faced him. "What can you do to me if I refuse? For certes, neither towers nor swords shall make me coward enough to deny the right I hold from my father and my God!"

Silence fell; a small smile settled on the king's face. "Aye." He held Arthur's eyes for the space of a heartbeat, then nodded curtly as if he reached a decision. Without another word he swirled from the apartment.

Arthur watched the king's party depart later in the day and reported the interview to Baron de Burgh. The baron shook his head, worried, yet nothing was heard from the king until several weeks later when another party arrived flying the king's banner. Arthur braced himself for the worst, but was ill prepared to face what Baron de Burgh told him.

"The king has ordered your eyes put out," he said, not sparing Arthur. "I begged them to have mercy, but they told me they have come under orders of the king and will not leave until they have done their duty."

Arthur had courage enough, but when he heard the news, his knees buckled and his resolution failed. He remembered watching such a procedure when he was a child when hot irons were applied to the eyes of a man who had committed a grave crime. He remembered the man's screams, the bloody holes in the man's face, and the servant who led him outside the castle, never to see again.

Tears streaming down his cheeks, he fell to his knees. "Please not that, my friend! I want to see to lead armies, to fight on a field of honor, to see my children play in the sunshine. I would be left a hideous monster, a poor beggar. I beg of thee, find a way to save me from this treachery and this shame. I ask thee, I plead with thee. I will do anything, anything you ask!" He crumpled in a heap on the floor, clinging to the lord's leather-booted feet.

Hubert lifted him and looked into his eyes. "Prince Arthur, I pledge thee. I will not allow them to do this."

The prince gazed upon him with wonder. "Will not the fury of the King come upon you and upon your house? Rather … let me be killed. Perchance as I joust. It was the way my father died, and so must hold honor and glory for me, as well." Regaining his confidence, the prince paced to the window and motioned to the tilting ground. "You may arrange it. Set a strong and fearless champion against me, and I shall die with a horse between my legs and a lance in my hand."

Hubert shook his head. "All will be well, Arthur. Trust me and lose not thy hopes." He departed the room, carefully locking the door. A short time later, Prince Arthur saw the king's men riding off in great haste, as if deeply offended.

Several days went by with no word from the king, then a week and then two.

When the baron visited his apartments, it was plain he had suffered from the silence of the king, for his eyes revealed he had slept little. "I fear I must attempt a deception. I will have the chapel bells rung and give out that you have died. It is the only plan I can devise."

Arthur, full of doubts, continued to shake his head after the baron left. He listened to the bells—one solemn toll for each year of his life, fifteen tolls, accompanied by cries of grief from those assembled outside the castle gate. He did not know of the furor his death raised all over France, Brittany and England. On every hand angry voices were raised against the king.

But John was suspicious and demanded to see the body. When Hubert failed to produce one, he was forced to admit his deception. Knowing minds put together the rest of the story, and John's reputation suffered throughout England and France almost as much as if he had done the deed. It was said that John was relieved that Hubert had disobeyed him, but he could not afford to be bested by the boy a second time.

***

November 1200

Rouen! Arthur had known from the outset that his destination would be John's castle in Normandy, a forbidding mountain of rock and iron, forfended well against attackers, one from which a person did not escape. He was manacled hand and foot, and rode in a long column of grim-faced soldiers, his horse tied to the one in front, for John would not be pleased if he escaped.

He looked about with the air of one who might never see the familiar countryside again, but he would not weep. Not for his mother, nor for his sister, nor for his lost kingdom, nor even for his horse. To his captors he put on a stony face of disdain aas he hardened his heart with hate.

John's castle rose above the lower hills like the abode of the dead, its curtain walls and battlements bristling with guards, its moat and drawbridge and portcullis defended well. Arthur lifted his head only once was when he heard his name shouted by the bystanders who lined the way.

It was a young boy, perchance his own age. The boy lifted to him a tattered banner—his own banner, but the boy and the banner were quickly removed, for no one would risk raising the king's ire by voicing their support for him. Yet he knew his people loved him, prayed to the saints and the Virgin Mother for him, and would claim him as their rightful ruler, had not the hateful English carried him away. It was small comfort to a man who faced certain death.

His new guardian was a man he barely knew, William de Braose, lord of Bramber. The man was a close friend of John's and that was enough to make certain Arthur's doom. He was thrust into the dankest, darkest, most secure cell in the castle, and his small hope that someone would come to his aid dwindled day by day.

There would be no ransom paid for him.

Arthur waited without hope for the sound of the key in the door, for the silent march up the long flight of stairs, for the sudden draught of fresh air and open sky, for the ride in the skiff, perhaps, where there on the river they would plunge a dagger in his heart, and he would be cast overboard.

This was what the world came to believe, for Prince Arthur was never seen after the heavy metal gates of Rouen Castle clanged shut behind him.

But it was not so.

Days and nights melded into one as he lay alone and cold upon the narrow cot. He knew the times when the guards approached, when they clanged open the small flap at the bottom of the door and shoved in a pan of slop. One time he heard steps approach, but they were not the guard's; this person was lighter and wore leather, not mail. A key turned the lock. The door screeched open on rusty hinges.

Soft feet trod into his cell and gentle hands raised him from his cot. The man's face was hooded. His voice was never raised above a whisper.

"Prince. You must come. Canst thou stand?" The man tugged at him.

Arthur shook himself. "Art thou the blessed angel of death for whom I have prayed and watched?"

"Nay! Thou art saved, Prince, for you have friends. But there is need for haste. Here. I shall carry thee on my back."

Arthur felt himself lifted and carried without strain. Then, like a dream in which he floated above the earth, he was carried silently through the halls, up the stairs, and out of the gates of the great castle. All the gates opened before them. The man did not stop until they reached the shelter of the forest.

Then other hands bore him, but he knew this not, only that the journey continued for several days. He knew they camped and saw glimpses of shadowy forms and heard the murmur of low voices around a campfire. Snow fell and he was cold, but someone covered him with a thick robe. He woke when they laid him on a hard bed and spread a coverlet over him, but he slept again and did not dream.

One day—he knew not how many had passed—he opened his eyes to behold an old man, stooped, with a long white beard and twinkly blue eyes bending over him. He ate a bowl of thin soup, looked around at his strange surroundings and slept again.

The next morning he sat up and tried to stand but found to his dismay that his legs would not work.

"You best take it easy, my son," the old man said, moving to his side. "You have been very ill, but I believe youth will assert itself. You will heal."

"Who are you?" Arthur lay back on the pillow and received water in a clay cup. He was in a small cottage, similar to ones dotting the countryside in Brittany: wattle and daub walls; a rough wooden door held by a peg; a thatched roof that rained down bits of straw, insects and even the occasional lizard. One latticed window allowed dim sunlight to filter into the hut, and a fireplace blazed with cheery warmth. He discovered he was hungry, but curious, too.

The old man smiled and leaned forward. "Old Bric is what they call me. I know not why. I was christened Alfred Buttrey. Perchance a servant to a great house was in my lineage."

Arthur tried to kick off the cover and stand but he fell back, dizzy and exhausted. After a short rest, he tried again. This time he succeeded in sitting up. Frantically, he cast about for his clothes, for he wore only a shift undergarment. His clothes were gone.

He shook his head, frustrated and angry. "You must return me immediately, for I do not wish to be the cause of more deaths. There will be a hue and cry such as you have never seen when I am discovered missing. The villagers and all those who live roundabout will be killed."

"That is being taken care of." The old man patted Arthur's shoulder and pressed him down on the cot. When he saw that Arthur was unconvinced, he sighed. "Very well. You must know. There was a boy in the village who resembled you in every way. He was found to have a disease and is dying even now. We blackened his face, and he now lies on the bed where you once lay. They will find the boy, carry him to river and cast him overboard. Thus, Prince Arthur has ceased to be."

Arthur received a cup that held a fragrant stew of vegetables and spices from the old man. "So I am dead."

Old Bric seated himself near the open fireplace and nodded slowly. "Yes. Prince Arthur has died. You are my grandson from southern France. I am taking care of you because your mother and father died in a plague. Your name is … " He raised his shaggy eyebrows.

Arthur lifted his eyes to the old man. His heart churned and he found it difficult to speak. "I … you mean for me to stay here? As a … servant? A villein?"

Old Bric grunted and nodded, his eyes burning holes in Arthur's head.

Arthur set down the bowl carefully on a crude table that had been pulled up close to the bed. "I shall not. I cannot. It is … below me. I am … do you know who I am? I am the grandson of King Henry the Second, the nephew of Richard the Lionhearted." He shook his head. "Nay, old man. You ask overmuch of me."

Old Bric stood and stirred the fire. It blazed up, revealing the tired droop of his shoulders and his weathered face. "If I asked of thee a difficult task, say, of attacking and conquering a fortress held by thrice the men you commanded, would you refuse, lad?"

"Nay. I would try it. I did try it and look what it brought me. But that has nothing to do with—"

"Let me finish. This be your only hope to change your appearance and live humbly as a serf. I know it will be a hard thing for you … nay, not hard, impossible. Yet you must attempt it. There are those who paid a great price for your release. Have you no thought for them?"

"Who paid for my release?" Arthur managed once more to sit upright. "Tell me! I must know!"

Old Bric chuckled and turned back to the fire. "I cannot, lad, for I know not myself. Now. We come again to your name. What would you chose for yourself?"

124

Arthur sighed and leaned back on the pillows. "This is my only salvation, you say. Yet every day as a villein will be death to me. Worse than death." He sighed again. "Nevertheless ... " He looked out the window where a weak winter's sun brightened the snow. "My teacher, my friend, the man I owe all I am to, had a son whose name is Adrian. In the summer we loved to play together in the sea. I would like to take his name. It is a simple, common name. Do you think I should take another?"

Old Bric smiled. "Not at the present. Adrian will suffice, my son. Now, when you are rested, I will teach you the ways of this place. You are in a village, not far from Orleans. It was the safest place we could think of, and you will find sanctuary here for a time. Someday soon, when you are fully recovered, we will make our way down the river. Think that you can learn to be a commoner, boy?"

Arthur considered this for some moments. He doubled his fists and drew a sharp breath as a fierce resolve settled into his soul. He would not give up his dream to reclaim his kingdom. But for a time it may serve his purpose to submit to this old man and learn what he could. And then, when the time was right, he would make his move for the throne. And the second time he would succeed.

He glanced around. Orleans, the man said. FitzRauf's castle was not far—just down the river at Tours. Perchance God had a hand in his fate after all. It was not the ugly-faced god of the old woman in the forest. Nay, that god had failed him. And not his mother's God, the fierce and angry God of the Roman Catholic Church.

That God had failed him, too. Was there another god?

He looked at the old man. "If you be a good teacher, I shall be a good student." He studied him curiously, for Old Bric was the first commoner he had ever had occasion to converse with. "What is it that you live for, my good man? Do you not wish to rise above your station and make something of yourself?"

Old Bric chuckled. "Nay. My God and King, Jesus Christ, has made something of me, by His grace. I live to honor and please Him."

Ah. So that is the name of the man's God. But did not Jesus die? Arthur remembered the crucifix and how a weak and pathetic form hung on it. How could a dead God help? He smiled, content for the time being. "And to free poor, lost souls."

Old Bric handed him a loaf and a slice of cheese. "Aye. I find God's will in many small tasks. I will teach thee many things you will need to know, but for now, you must rest and heal. And I warn thee. I am a hard task master."

Arthur smiled again. "I can believe that, my friend. But I shall apply myself. I shall be the best commoner the world has ever seen."

***

Lusignan, Poitou, December 1200

Two men, riding hard, entered the forest of a baron and slowed their horses to a walk. Their faces were drawn and haggard, and their horses stumbled often and were lathered with sweat.

"We have arrived," the older, gray-haired man said to his younger companion. "Watch thy tongue and follow my lead, for I know this man."

The younger man brushed a nervous hand over his brow. "Is he as they say he is? Hard and unforgiving?" He wore a coarsely woven peasant's cloak of dark green and a large felt hat of the same color.

The older man retained an air of nobility, but had obviously fallen upon hard times. His fine velvet cloak was stained and patched. His leather boots were cracked and peeling. He pushed back a wide-brimmed hat with a dilapidated purple feather in its brim and shook his head. "I know not. This I know, he has little patience with failure, he has been wronged greatly and suffers still, he is fair and honest and brave."

"And will he reward us for our efforts, Lord Montgomery?"

"Ask nothing, and see what transpires, young fool. Above all, this man demands a still tongue in your head. Let us see if you can commence to have one."

They arrived at the entrance of a formidable castle perched on an outcropping of rock. The entrance wound up a steep incline, forcing any would-be intruders to pass closely beneath the battlements. No one challenged their approach, however, and they came in due time to the great gate, barred not only by iron, lance and steel, but by a moat.

The gate was lowered without a challenge, something that made the brows of Lord Montgomery rise. They trotted across the bridge and entered the inner bailey. Liveried servants took their horses and led the way into the castle.

They waited in the outer court for some twenty minutes, nursing tankards of cold ale. At last they were ushered into the Great Hall where on the far wall a dais was erected. Sitting on the dais, like a feudal king, sat the lord. They bent their knees and for some minutes the only sounds was snuffling of dogs in the rushes and the sputtering of torches on the walls.

The lord spoke. "Have you accomplished your mission, Lord Beregund Montgomery?"

Beregund lifted his eyes. "Yea, my lord."

"Tell me."

"It was as you said, my lord. Gold speaks loudly. There are many in Normandy who are richer this night than they ever thought possible. I have put the fear of God into these servants. They will not speak of what they know."

"And what do they know, man?" The voice thundered from above, driving the boy to fall on his face.

"Nothing more than what they needed to know, my lord." Beregund rose, took off his hat and slapped his dusty robe with it. "There was one man only, the captain of the guard, who knows the secret. He is the father of a large family. I brought with me his name and the names of his children. He loves his children a great deal, but he loves the money more. I believe he is by this time the owner of a large track of land."

The man on the throne nodded his approval. His tone softened. "The lad is free?"

Beregund nodded. "Yea, my lord. As free as the bird that flies the heavens. His keeper is a man by the name of Old Bric, a wandering carpenter and tinker."

Again the great man nodded. "It is as I wished. You have done fine work, Beregund. And what of this young boy with you? Can he keep a still tongue in his head?"

"This is my page. I am training him for knighthood. There is nothing in his head nor on his tongue that does not pass by me first. Am I not correct, Sage?"

The boy trembled visibly. "I know nothing but what you tell me, lord, and I say nothing. I am deaf and blind but for thee." He fell flat on his stomach.

The baron burst into a torrent of laughter, filling the room with echoes. "You have chosen well, Beregund. Now I entrust you with an even greater matter. You must follow the adventures of the young man you aided. You shall have monies from my purse to do so. I expect a report from you as the moon wanes and waxes. Do you understand?"

"Yes, Lord." Beregund nodded. "For how long must I do this?"

"Until I give thee word to stop. We must not lose contact with this lad, for the hopes and dreams of our people rest upon his life. When he returns to take his rightful place in this land, I shall have revenge upon my enemy."

He stood, gathering his long robes around him, pacing down the dais steps to stand before them, piercing them with a keen glance. "Remember your tongues, gentlemen. If I hear you have spoken two words of your work for me this past fortnight, I shall kill you slowly—you and all those whom you love. Do you ken?"

"Yea, lord," they said in unison.

"Very well. Go now." Weariness crept into the lord's face, and the hand that waved them away trembled.

Beregund sighed deeply and turned, snatching up Sage as he would a bag of grain. "Come, my stalwart page. We must be off before the sun sets, or we shall encounter worse than Baron le Brun's ire. Come. I only pray they give us fresh horses."

BOOK TWO

THE LONG ROAD BACK

Still round the corner there may wait
A new road or a secret gate
And though I oft have passed them by
A day will come at last when I
Shall take the paths that run
West of the Moon, East of the Sun.

J.R.R. Tolkien, *Return of the King*

CHAPTER TEN

In the ditch where water flowed, it will flow again. Afghan
Proverb

Orleans, France, January 1201

"Boy, fetch the wood. Bring it along." The old man's shoulders drooped as he stepped over fallen logs and elbowed his way past thick laurel bushes, not bothering to look back.

Adrian blinked sweat from his eyes and bent to pick up the pile of branches and small logs they had chopped for firewood. He swept a dirty hand across his forehead, pushing a lock of blond hair from his eyes. Lifting the green wood into his arms, he followed Grandfather's path. Another drip of sweat found its way into his eye. He mumbled a curse under his breath. On his next step, a thorn pierced his thin sandal. He yelped, danced on one foot and lost some of his wood.

Grandfather did not pause to look back.

Adrian dumped his load on the ground, sat upon it and pulled the thorn from his foot, swatting at the flies buzzing his face and itching the flea bites under his rough woolen tunic. Slowly, every muscle aching, he stood and leaned to pick up the wood. Just at that moment, a raven cawed overhead, a nasty sound that seemed to mock him. He straightened and frowned, anger spouting up hot and vivid like tinder set to the flame.

"Nay! I will not!" His words echoed in the silent wood.

Grandfather stopped, retraced a few steps and peered at him with mild curiosity. He waved a hand and turned toward the cottage.

Adrian followed, but did not carry the wood. Emerging from the trees, he stepped into a small clearing that surrounded the hut and looked about as if he gazed upon it for the first time. How long had he lived here? A fortnight? It seemed a lifetime.

In the beginning he allowed nothing to deter him from his goal of learning to be a servant, but it was very hard. He responded to nothing but boy. Grandfather taught him to lower his head in the presence of his betters, and everyone was better than he, it seemed, to tug at his forelock in deference, to speak only when spoken to, to obey without question or thought. He owned nothing. Even the rough tunic on his back and the tattered sandals on his feet belonged to Grandfather.

He and Old Bric worked from dawn until dark and then they fell asleep with stomachs half full. Pigs snuffled at the door and chickens cackled in their sleep. Adrian's meals at the rough wooden board consisted of bread, a thin vegetable broth and, once in a great while, a chunk of cheese, an egg and a mug of milk.

The work itself was beyond anything he had ever dreamed. His muscles ached, his hands were blistered and then callused, and his skin itched from dirt. He learned to milk a cow, harvest vegetables, cut wood, thatch the roof, cut grass for hay, thresh and grind wheat for bread, prepare a chicken for the table. This was a tall order for a boy who had never dressed himself.

He did not mind his anonymity, the work, or the lack of things as much as being treated as a child. As the prince, he had been regarded as a man, now he was a child, the child he had never been.

Grandfather stood beside the cabin, watching him, a hint of a smile on his lips, but his eyes were sober. "Come here, boy."

Adrian came, but he did not lower his head or pull at his forelock. What was he doing here? Did he not have friends? Friends who were loyal to him? Friends who had influence and money? What of Baron Le Brun? Perhaps it was time he left this place and made his own way in the world. Enough of this scraping and bowing and working.

Looking Grandfather in the eyes, he said, "Sir, I must speak with you. I will not carry your wood. I can no longer be a servant to you or to any other person on earth." His voice rose, laced with the old authority that came so naturally. He rested both fists on his hips. "By God's ears, man! I was once the prince! Now I am no more than a beast of burden! Less!"

Grandfather's blue eyes twinkled. "You are less only because my ass does not speak back to me."

Adrian continued as if he had not heard. "I must speak my mind. I thank you for saving my life, but I am still the prince and I believe I can rise to my former glory. I am weary to death of this life, if you could call it a life. That is plain speech, for certes, but it must be said. I have friends who will aid me in regaining my former position. And if they will not, who is to say that I may not find it on my own?"

Grandfather's gaze held only sorrow. Tears suddenly sprang to his eyes. "Is this truly what you desire? Search thy heart, boy. As the Scriptures saith, "Watch over thine heart, for from it comes the issues of life.""

Adrian was surprised. He expected at the very least a cuff to his ears. He nodded. "This is what I desire, sir. I hope one day to repay you for your trouble. But I cannot abide these conditions. I must find my fate and try my chances. If I die in the trying, then so be it. *Deus lo volt!* as the Crusaders say."

"Aye. And what of your enemies? John is still king." Grandfather led the way into the cottage and began stirring the fire back to life. "You will not last long if you show yourself as Prince Arthur and cast about for those who are faithful to you. If any would believe you are the prince, for folks think Prince Arthur is still in the castle at Rouen--or dead."

Grandfather left the cottage and returned with milk and cheese from their stash in the creek. Carefully, he laid the table, then poured out ale into the rough cups he took down from a cupboard. "Sit. You must share my common fare until we decide what you should do."

Adrian noticed it was no longer boy, and sadness roughed the edges of the man's voice. *Or is it disappointment? Have I failed a test?* In a flash of unusual insight, he saw himself standing just inside the door of the humble hut in his rough dirty tunic, hair askew, filthy, a petulant look on his face. It was not the picture of a prince or even of a man. It was that of a spoiled child.

He sat and received his portion of cheese, bread, ale, and milk.

After their first hunger was abated, Grandfather began to talk. He did not focus on Adrian, but looked more generally toward the ceiling. "I want to tell you about a king ... a king who ruled a vast kingdom. He was a good man who loved his people, but he saw that they hated him and plotted against him. He tried everything to win their love and devotion. Nothing availed and voices were raised in angry revolt against his rule. There was only one way to convince his people of his love. He must leave his throne, lands, home and wealth ... and become as they."

"That is an enormous sacrifice," Adrian said in a low tone.

Grandfather carried his mug of ale to the bench near the fire. "This king walked from his castle as the poorest of the poor, living and working and loving his people. None knew his true identity. Many of the common folk believed what he preached to them about love and forgiveness and loyalty, but many hated and distrusted him. They stirred the masses against him, and in the end, they killed him. He died a lonely and painful death, still trying to tell them of the king's great love."

Adrian joined Grandfather at the fire, his eyes on the dirt floor.

Grandfather paused, then continued in a stronger tone. "That king, my son, is Jesus Christ. He taught us a different way to live than to grasp after power, lands and the things of this world. Do you ken what I am saying?"

Adrian perched on a low stool and gazed into the flickering light. "Aye, sir. You are telling me that this life may be common, but it is the way of love. You are laying out two roads for me to travel, are you not, sir? I can choose. I can choose love or I can choose to follow my desire to become king."

Grandfather smiled. "You may find love and the throne all in the same moment. It is your heart that concerns me. Are you lusting after power? I can see it in your eyes at times. You cannot fool me, nor can you have it both ways. Your heart is what you must give to the King of Kings. You must give up your desires and yield to Jesus. Are you willing to do that?"

The fire sparked. Adrian turned his gaze from the bright, piercing eyes of the old man. He straightened, anger asserting itself once more. *Who is this old man to tell me what I must do?* His voice was sharp as he stood to his feet. "I am a knight of the highest order, sir! My desire is to avenge the great wrong that was done to me. What could be more holy and just than that? I am a Christian. I was baptized into the Catholic faith."

Grandfather sighed and leaned against the wall. "What is a Christian? Do you have any idea what you are talking about? You have much to learn, my son. Sit down. We shall talk, if we can avoid your haughty spirit rising against me. *Sit.*"

He sat, cradling his face in his hands, then said, "Pardon my harsh words, Grandfather. There is something inside me that springs up at the least provocation. Is it the Evil One?"

Grandfather chuckled. "Nay, Adrian. It be only your lineage. I have heard tales of your true Grandfather's temper. You must strive to overcome it. Pride is one of the seven deadly sins, ye know." The fire crackled and glowed on his age-wrinkled face.

"I know." Adrian looked away, for tears stung his eyes. "Tell me what I must do. I am willing this moment to leave your home."

Grandfather stirred the fire and added a log. "If you can be patient, we shall wait out the cold of winter and in the spring we shall take a trip. We shall be tinkers, peddlers. We shall travel this part of the world and learn what has transpired and how the people feel about King John." He stood and looked at Adrian with a sharp glance. "We shall know better then what your chances would be of regaining your fief. What say you?"

Adrian rose and ducked his head. "It is more than I deserve, Grandfather." He held out his hand. "I shall abide with you through the winter. I am obliged for your care and concern."

Grandfather took his hand and shook it firmly.

Their eyes met and Adrian swallowed hard. How could he ever repay this man? But Old Bric would not want payment—nay, if he had learned nothing else, it was that the man who stood so straight before him did what he did for God and for nothing else.

Adrian nodded. "Thank you, sir."

***

Mont St. Michel's, Brittany, March 1201

"Watch your step, lad." Louis' call rang out across the sand. Samson John, ahead of him by twenty feet, did not hear but instinctively checked his step, felt tentatively for a firm foundation and proceeded with his slow pace.

A pillow of white clouds low on the horizon reflected the mauve sunrise and a chill breeze from the sea brought the cries of the gulls as they swooped over the sand to perch and eat a breakfast of crab and sand dollars.

Louis glanced back at Mont St. Michaels that loomed above, remembering the terror he felt when he arrived. Now the monastery seemed to smile as it bid them farewell. They traveled with two other monks who lifted their black robes above the water that swished around their ankles, who knew the sands and led the way confidently.

On the shore, Louis met a small contingent of soldiers, four in all, who accompanied them inland. He and the boy walked, each leading a mule. The abbot had offered them mounts, but Louis declined, saying he would rather use his own two feet. Walking was good for the soul and afforded him time to pray. The soldiers rode, but had to stop every now and then to wait for them to catch up.

Louis glanced over at Samson John as they trudged along, sensing the boy's excitement in the journey. The evening before they left, he had taken the boy aside and tried to convey to him the dangers that lay ahead in the long miles to the Holy See.

When he acted the part of the pope, Samson John's only response was a wide-eyed squeal of joy—nothing else seemed to penetrate. He bobbed his head eagerly every time Louis asked if he wanted to continue with him.

"It may be dangerous, son," Louis said, looking as grave as he could into the boy's bright face, for the boy read lips. "It may mean your life. Do you want to accompany me?"

"Yeh." It was a mere grunt, yet Louis understood—it was his word for "Yes!" Samson John pushed back his mop of dark hair from his brown eyes and grinned, showing white teeth and two dimples. He made the motions for lifting a pack on his back, walking down the road, preparing a meal.

Louis laughed. If nothing else the boy was comic relief. "I know. I know. You do not have to act. Very well. We shall leave in the morning."

That evening they arrived at the monastery of St. Frances near the city of Fouregours where they enjoyed a service in the beautiful cathedral and a meal with the prior.

The next morning Samson John saddled the two mules. Louis supervised, making sure the precious parcels were packed carefully. He felt a tap on his shoulder. It was one of their guard, a young Flemish soldier. His broken French was hard to understand, but Louis leaned closer and caught his whispered words.

"I'se taeken a likin' to yous." The soldier paused and glanced around.

"Yes?" Louis shifted impatiently, for he wanted to be away. He wondered what was coming and how he could shorten the conversation.

"Ther's trouble comin', me heaven beck. When yous sees it comin', grabs this here mule's reins and jump onta the saddle. T'won't be easy ridin', but if you kick her, she will run. This one can run. Get off the path. That's all I kin say."

Louis gripped the guard's arm. "Are you telling me that you've been paid to look the other way when robbers or such fall upon us? Because if that is so, I shall report it and we shall find another guard."

The guard's eyes widened. "Nay, nay. Yous wrong. I am just warnin' you, see?" He shook off Louis' hand. "If we lose this job, I will feel the whip on me back. Forget I'se said anyting, yes? Yes, me heaven-beck? Oterwise, I will run you trough, meself." He glared at Louis.

Louis raised his hands. "I will not report what you said. I swear to God Almighty. But when—"

A trumpet sounded and the young man fled to mount his horse. The moment was gone.

All through that day and evening, Louis tried to get close to the man again and find out more information, but the guard stayed his distance.

Louis sat by the fire the third night, his thoughts in turmoil. What did it mean? Did the guard intend to warn him, but decide it was too risky? What did he know? Were they at the mercy of ruffians, if mercy could be found in such men? The abbot said there would be enemies, ruthless enemies. Well, Louis would be alert for trouble. God allowed him that much, anyway.

But nothing happened. They stayed one night in the monastery at LeMans and Orleans was only three days away, if the weather stayed fine. He was looking forward to Orleans, for there they would find sanctuary behind the walls of Saint Aignan Church.

Two days later they descended into a long, wide valley. The sun sank behind a bank of black clouds and mourning doves cooed in the hedges. A small village nestled in the curve of the river, its lights winking at them as darkness descended.

The mountain peak, Les Avalons, ascended to the southeast, snow adorning its top like white hair on an old man. Louis had watched it all afternoon, admiring its forested flanks and rocky spurs where the westering sun reflected on its golden stones.

Now he glanced around uneasily, for he could not help feeling this would be an ideal place for an ambush, right over there between the thick clumps of bushes that grew alongside the river. If only they could get past this. Louis' nerves were as raw as his body was exhausted, for he had watched every moment for an attack and he worried about the cargo on the mule's back. His hand never left the reins of the bridle for a moment, even though it meant he must walk faster than his custom or liking, and the mean-tempered beast nicked his heels with sharp hooves now and then.

He had warned Samson John of the danger of an attack, but wondered what the boy would do. Pile on behind him? But that would hardly be feasible. Mount the mule he led? But the mule was loaded heavily, how could he ride? Would he run? But they would be separated, and how they could find each other again?

Thinking the young soldier must have been misinformed and they would indeed reach the shelter of the inn, he glanced up, alarmed. Five armed men rode from a nearby fringe of trees. The road bent here to the right and the rest of the party was out of sight. In one moment of inattention, he had allowed himself to be cut off. Had they done it intentionally? But there was no time for speculation; the horsemen approached, and by their visage, what he could see in the dim light, they meant business.

"Run!" Louis glanced back at Samson John and was surprised to see an empty path, save for the mule he had been leading. Where had the boy gone?

He leaped to his mule's back, perched atop the pack, grasped the reins, and dug his heels into her sides with a screech that startled the animal into a dead run. Louis was not a good rider, but he clung to the pack with the tenacity of a snail on a lichen-covered rock.

Behind, he heard a shout, then the pounding of hooves.

He reined into the thick brush. The mule smashed her way through the hedge, then broke out into a forest of pines and firs. Rocks, old logs, gullies, low-hung limbs hindered his way, but he urged the mule on, following no path, uphill and down, relentlessly pursued by men who knew the forest, who were riding horseback and sat firmly in a saddle.

Louis directed the mule across a river, glancing about to see if he could spot Samson John. The light was nearly gone, but the mule could see, and she plunged into the water without hesitation. She splashed out of the river on the farther bank. The moon shone clear and bright, emerging from behind a cloud.

The mule stumbled. Louis pulled back on the reins, hearing shouts and the splash of water as horses hit the water. He heard the sound of an arrow released and cried out as it plunged into his shoulder. He fell forward and narrowly missed two other missiles that whistled overhead. The mule found her feet, scrambled up and over the bank and plunged into the forest.

He had never felt such torture, but he hung onto the pack with dogged persistence, in a fog of pain, praying desperately. He tried to think of what to do. Would the mule go on if he passed out, or would she stop? Would the precious papers fall into the wrong hands? What of those hordes of people who depended on the safe delivery of the papers? How could he fail them?

He could not fail. It was settled, then. Despite the pain, his vision cleared and he lifted his head to take in his surroundings. The mule was quick on her feet and a good climber. Dimly he was aware that she climbed up steep gullies, then descended, to climb again, always rising higher and higher. Cool air brushed his face.

He rode with wild abandon, praying for an end to the torment.

He no longer heard the pursuit. Had they given up? Turned back? Had a mule been able to go where horses could not? And what of Samson John? He prayed the boy was safe. It was so dark now he could not see where he was, and even if he could, it would be for naught, for he was well and truly lost.

He pulled back on the reins and climbed off the pack. The arrow, protruding both back and front, caused little pain at the moment, but he knew if it was jostled, he would feel it, for certes. But it had to come out. He had been a physician long enough to know that. Still, it was not as bad as he thought, for it penetrated the high shoulder muscle, away from his vital organs.

He untied the pack, moving carefully, stopping when the pain was intense, and removed from it a soft linen tunic that the prior at

St. Frances had given him. He tore it into strips, wincing when the pain ricocheted across his chest, shoulder and down his arm.

The mule drank from a stream bubbling out of the hillside a short distance away, then began munching on a clump of stiff, frozen grass. Snow covered the ground, scrunching under Louis' footsteps.

He shuffled to the stream and dipped in the cloth, then made his way back to where an earthern bank rose, providing a little shelter. Sitting down he grasped the shaft of the arrow, nearly swooning from pain that seemed to engulf his whole body. "Oh, God. Give me the strength to do this." Each word he spoke louder, until he was nearly yelling. "By Your mercy. Because of Your Son. In the name of Jesus Christ and the Virgin Mother Mary!"

He pulled. Several moments later he picked himself up from the ground where he had toppled over. The arrow was still embedded in his shoulder. His fingers explored it—it had moved maybe an inch. *Oh, God.*

Another tug sent him reeling again into oblivion, but he gained an inch. Maybe more. Taking a deep breath, bracing his feet against a rock and his back against the bank, he pulled—not a sharp yank, but a steady, smooth motion. He screamed—and fainted.

His tunic was sticky wet with blood when he regained consciousness, but the arrow, all of it, lay beside him on the ground. He crawled to the stream and bathed the wound, then bound it with the clean, dry linen. Taking a long drink of water, he crawled back to the bank and pulled the saddle blanket over him.

The mule woke him long before dawn in the cold nether light of a new day. A brisk wind blew over the snow. A layer of it had fallen during the night, covering the blanket. He shivered and looked about for firewood. But, nay. Fire would send up smoke and his pursuers would be watching for smoke.

His shoulder ached, but not unbearably. He dug out beef jerky, a chunk of cheese and an apple from his pack and after a prayer, broke his fast. Then he prayed in the new day.

When it came, he sucked in his breath in surprise. He was on the mountain—Les Avalons. The growing light revealed a vista of forested hills, valleys with a river looping through them and little hamlets dotting the river. Long wisps of wraith-like mist lay in the valleys below.

How in heaven's name had they ... ? He turned to look at the mule, who returned his gaze with a long-faced look, as if to say, "Don't ask me."

Louis fell to his knees and greeted the rising sun with a hymn of praise. It was only by God's grace that they climbed the mountain. How had the mule found her way to the top?

And how could he find his way back? He looked again at the mule. Let her have her way and she'll find a stable. He started to tighten the cinch when he heard a twig crack. He froze. The mule lifted her head. A thousand thoughts raced through Louis' mind. Run? Hide? Shout? Nay. He could do nothing. He was at the mercy of whoever approached. The crackling increased. He reached down and lifted a large rock, which he held in the folds of his robe.

The brush below parted and a figure swung through. A young man who wore a hat strode toward Louis. His simple green tunic came to his knees and he carried a pack on his back and a staff in his left hand. In his right hand he held the reins to a mule.

"Samson John!" Relief flooding Louis heart like sun rays filling the sky. He dropped the rock.

The boy looked up, smiled, and climbed the rest of the way.

"How ... I guess you cannot tell me how you came. But I am glad to see you, boy."

Samson John's wide grin revealed his two dimples. He acted out how he tracked the mule, how he camped the night down below and came on in the morning.

Louis nodded, and told the boy about his wound. "But I got it out. See? Here is the arrow. You may keep it if you like."

Samson took the arrow and stowed it in his pack.

Louis tapped him on the shoulder. "Have you eaten?"

The boy shook his head, rubbed his stomach.

Louis unpacked the food and joined him in a second breakfast. Suddenly the way was not as hard, nor as long, nor as tedious as before. It was amazing how a companion lightened his load, even if that companion was a deaf-mute boy.

When they finished, Louis packed the saddle and picked up the reins. "We shall pray that our blessed Lord will lead us to a place of safety. I saw a village to the south and our journey leads that direction. Shall we try for the village, or do you think our enemies are there, watching the way from the mountain?"

Samson John shrugged his gaunt shoulders and tipped his hand to the south. "Yeh." He pointed to the sky and nodded with a grim smile.

Louis smiled, too. "Yes, I know. It is getting late. God will protect us. Lead the way, boy. If you found me in this forest, I trust your judgment. Only, pray don't cross the river. Once is enough for a lifetime."

***

Orleans, France, March 1201

Adrian swung the ax with a practiced eye and with one mighty stroke slew Baron FitzRauf who fell into three pieces. He leaned over with a rueful smile, picked up the wood and threw it on the pile. "That is what you deserve, my enemy. Now let me show you what I can do to thee, Sir Frederick! *En garde!* I shall hew thee into three pieces as well!"

He stacked the wood by the hut and glanced up as Grandfather walked by, carrying an apronful of eggs, humming a song. Adrian smiled and noted the pair of robins who built a nest in the crotch of the old oak tree; they seemed flustered and excited. Was it the arrival of the eggs? Privately he had named them, for the female reminded him of his mother—a busy, cackling little thing who loved to boss everyone around; and the male reminded him of DeArmond—full of himself, but meek in the presence of his mate.

He resumed his task, yet realized even as he worked that he was not the same as he had been. He loved this life. He loved to watch the stars on an evening as Grandfather instructed him in their names and forms, to learn the gentle rhythms of the days and the seasons, to discover the myriad skills that put food on their table and warmth in their home.

At times he made forays into the forest and took his temper out on innocent trees, but these incidents became few and far between as something inside him stilled. It seemed he was listening now, listening with his heart as well as with his ears.

People came to Old Bric there at the cottage, people with needs of all kinds. They came with broken wagon wheels, broken tools, broken bodies and broken minds. Many came and stayed and spoke with him over mugs of ale and stale bread. These visitors paid

142

Adrian no heed at all, for once people established his relationship to the old man he might as well have been one of the chickens scratching in the dirt at the cottage door.

Grandfather's faith in God was a matter of constant mystery and amazement to him. Adrian believed himself to be a religious man, loyal to God, to his liege lord the king and to his conscience. But as he watched Old Bric pray and worship his God, as he saw the good works that flowed from his hands like water to thirsty souls, he knew his definition of Christian was faulty. Old Bric lived in a different world and embodied a different spirit than Adrian had ever seen.

Spring came early that year. One morning he helped Grandfather mount sturdy canvas over the wagon and then watched as the old man supplied it with all sorts of goods. He showed Adrian bottles and flasks containing cures for every ailment—wormwood for fleas, sage for headaches or fevers, green leeches for bloodletting, agrimony boiled in milk as a cure for lust, senna as a laxative.

As Adrian worked, a fever boiled hot in his heart. He fled to the forest, stamping about, shouting, giving vent to his anger on whatever lay in his path. When he returned, Grandfather looked up from his task of carrying a box of food to the wagon.

Adrian shook his head. "What is it, Grandfather? Why do I feel this way? I feel as if ants are making holiday in my hose and bees swarm in my head. I cannot rid myself of this fever. I fear sometimes I am losing my mind."

Grandfather chuckled and led the way into the cottage where he began laying out their midday meal. "Tis the season, my son. Spring is ever the time when kings ride to battle. It is in your blood. Don't fret about it. It will pass."

But Adrian could not let it go. He thought more and more of his old life, of the affairs of the kingdom, of Mother and his wife, Maria. He thought about DeArmond, Mordelias, tournaments, fine clothes and ribald feasts. One day he heard from a villagers who came to visit that his mother was dead. Running from the cottage, he found solace in the sweet-smelling hay of the barn. Several hours later Grandfather came and laid a comforting hand on his back.

So Ma Mere was gone. Adrian had never been close to his mother, but now another tie to the past was gone.

That evening heavy clouds brought lightning and thunder. Chilled in the night, he climbed out of bed and threw a log on the fire. The wind howled with demon voices in the tall firs and lashed the latticed windows. He huddled before the fire.

Staring into the flames, he saw the spires of Mordelias, the winding river through the valley, could hear horns blowing, saw his horse, Kazimer, running like the wind. He saw Eleanor's face—his beautiful sister, the Pearl of Brittany. What had become of her? How did she fare? Mother's face appeared, beautiful, cold and bitter. She beckoned him. What did she want? He saw her mouth move. Ah. *Revenge.*

I can't seek revenge now, Mother. I am only a poor villein. Her face disappeared and John's came next. He wore a golden crown and strutted about like a peacock, laughing, lifting a chased silver cup. A beautiful woman clung to his arm.

John had won. Who would stop this evil man from his reckless career, destroying the kingdom his grandfather, Henry the Second, had worked so hard to build? Who would win justice for Adrian's poor mother, for his sister, for his people? How could he go on without at least trying?

He lifted his head, listening. Was that something outside? When he gazed at the fire again, the faces were gone. Resolve filled his heart, hot with the fires of hell, blinding him in its fury. He bent his head and wept, his fists balled tightly into the cloak he had thrown over his shoulders.

Oh, God. I will try. Yea, I will find revenge. I vow to kill John, even if I die in the attempt. His eyes closed, his head bobbed to his folded arms and he slept.

CHAPTER ELEVEN

When you are going through hell, keep going. Winston
Churchill

LaRochelle, France, February 1201

Judith vowed she would never forget the first day of Adar in the
Jewish year 4960, for it was the day her eyes rested on French soil.
LaRochelle at last! As she leaned her elbows on the rail of the ship
and the old city drew near, she allowed her mind to travel back to
Madrid.

She had allowed Miguel a few days in the city to look for his
relatives, but every lead turned to dust. Every evening he returned to
the inn with a longer face and an emptier purse. On the last evening
he heard of an old man who had just arrived from the vast rolling
savannah land to the south. On a hunch he went to talk with him.

Later he told Judith what he learned.

"My family was taken at the same time I was. Slave traders, I
suppose, sold them to the east. The old man said he heard my father
had been sold to the galleys. If that is true, he is dead by now, for no
one survives the galleys for long. I am sorry I delayed our journey,
mistress. My search has been as unprofitable as yours."

She nodded, tears stinging her eyes. "It is strange. Have you
considered, Miguel, how similar our situations are? I am not your
mistress anymore than you are my slave. You are my family and I
am yours. From now on you must not call me mistress."

He looked into her eyes deeply and sighed. "Your words cheer
my heart a little, Judith. Thank you. Now you must get your rest, for
tomorrow we shall begin our journey west to Valencia."

"Nay." Judith rose to pace to the small window which faced
east. "I have not been idle these days. There is a caravan that arrived
in the city today. They journey east, to the coast, over the
mountains." She pointed to the snow-capped peaks that reared up on

the horizon. "They are willing that we travel with them. We should find safety in their numbers, for they are heavily guarded. What say you?"

Miguel nodded. "Aye. It is a sound plan. I congratulate you on your wisdom and foresight. We shall travel to A'Coruna with this caravan of yours." He smiled, his wide, white-toothed smile, the first she had seen for many days. "And may Yahweh your God guide our steps home."

The trip across Spain was one she would never forget—the mountains, valleys and rolling prairies spread out like a beautiful palette of colors. In the port city of A'Coruna she sold a ring to pay for their board on ship to LaRochelle. She hated to part with it, for her mother gave it to her on her birthday. But it must go.

Life on board ship was torment with poor food, little sleep, and rough companions. Had the sailors known she was a girl, she would not have survived. Judith sat on deck, bending her heart to the north, praying that the miles would fly and they would soon arrive.

And so the morning came when she spotted the city of LaRochelle sprawled out on the hillsides above the sea. It was like all the other ports they had visited—dirty, crowded and expensive, but the air smelled different and the hills were clad in firs and pines and all about she heard people speaking French. It was dearest to her heart next to Hebrew.

From habit she picked up their bags while Miguel unloaded the horses from the barge and saw to their care. Then they began casting about for a comfortable but inexpensive inn as it was raining and Judith did not want to spend the night outside.

When the prices were quoted for a room, Miguel shook his head. "Judith, we must travel on. We have barely enough money left for food, and none at all for grain for the horses. This is not Spain where they can graze in the winter. Here we must provide for them." He stroked Saladin, his black Arabian gelding. She knew he would go without food himself rather than see his horse suffer.

"But which way shall we take?" She mounted Jocebed with the practiced ease of one who had ridden much.

"We shall ride inland, north to Tours, then follow the Loire River to Orleans, then on to Troyes. We decided this on the ship. Why are you asking me again?"

She could not explain the tightness in her chest whenever she thought of Tours. What was it that she did not like about that city? Something from her past, something sent red warning flags up in her mind and chills down her back. She sighed. "But I suppose you are right. Very well, we shall go north."

That evening they rode until Miguel spotted an abandoned shack some miles from the city where mice abounded along with cockroaches. Miguel found grain in one of the bins and gave the horses what he could scrape out. They ate a meager supper of dried figs and old cheese.

Miguel stretched. "I will take the first watch. Here. I'll fix you a bed above ground." He took two planks of wood and laid them across two barrels, forming a bed of sorts. She lay down and covered herself with her damp cloak, for intermittent showers had accompanied them on the way.

Yet she could not sleep. She heard the scurry of mice, the hoot of owls, the gentle pitter-pat of rain, the occasional stomp of a horse's hoof and Miguel's low voice as he sang a Spanish song.

What would they do if they were attacked? Miguel wore the sword at his side, but she knew he was no terrific swordsman. At least they might bluff their way out of trouble. And when they arrived in Troyes, what awaited them there? Did any of her father's relatives still live? Would they take her in?

Her fingers closed around the plain capsule hanging on a leather thong around her neck. Grandfather's scroll. What was written on it? She shuddered, cold fingers of dread shivering down her spine as if a dead spirit touched her soul. Why did it have to come to a small, insignificant girl like herself?

What of her other mission, finding her father? She had failed in this too. How could she accomplish the greater? Was there a curse on her life?

Against her will, her thoughts flew to the scene when her mother was murdered. The knights, their shouts, the blood, poor Nero lying there ... the knights, there was something she must remember about the knights. What was it? Slowly she sat and rubbed her head. A red bull on a black field. Yes! That was it. The pennant the knights carried on their lances and the emblem on their shields— it came back to her now, after all these years.

She remembered that Miguel said the knights who took her father also carried such a symbol.

The red bull pennant seemed familiar ... she seen it before ... many years ago, but where, oh, God, where? The memory eluded her and she fell into a fitful sleep, only to be awakened by a shake on her shoulder. Miguel stood there and at first her heart stopped, for she thought they were being attacked.

But he merely nodded for her to go watch. Before she got to her post beside the door, she heard his gentle snores.

The next morning they continued their journey, and the next, and the next ... every day like the one before with little food, cold and damp camps and long days in the saddle. The horses were tiring, their steps lagged and they did not hold up their heads.

She felt sorry for them, yet even she and Miguel were close to starvation. She knew it, for she had no energy and her skin was gray and sallow. He developed a worrisome cough.

The eighth day of their journey was the worst of all, for it rained a steady downpour and Miguel's cough seemed to shake his whole body.

"We must stop and get some help," she said. They pulled up for shelter under a pine tree, but the sodden drip of rain reached them even here.

He shook his head. "We have no money for treatment."

"There must be a monastery in Tours. We shall stop there."

After a bout of coughing, he lifted his head. "Even the monks want money, Judith. No, we must go on to Troyes. That is all we can do."

That night they camped in a small meadow on the banks of the river. She rolled into her bed, a dry spot under a huge fir, pulled the saddle blanket and her wet cloak up over her body and tried to sleep. But the rain continued and Miguel coughed throughout the night. She wondered what would happen if he died. How could she go on?

The next day they rode on, but Miguel was so sick he could barely sit upright in the saddle. He was feverish; his body shook as with ague and he could not eat nor talk.

"Miguel, we must stop." Judith helped him into the saddle after their midday meal.

He shook his head. "Canna stop. No money ... " Another fit of coughing seized him and she grabbed him to keep him from falling to the ground.

Riding beside him, she kept her arm around his waist. His face was gray and she knew it was only his iron will that held him upright in the saddle. Many times during the long ride they had to go singly, for the path narrowed here and there as they wound through the forest or followed a river—was it the Indre?—and she wondered how he stayed in the saddle.

Toward evening, they arrived at the city of Tours. It was a large city on the Loire River. They stopped at a vendor's stall on the main cobblestoned street through the city. She inquired if there was a monastery where they would treat an ill man.

"Continue on down this road, boy," the man said, "and you will come to our great cathedral, La Cattedral di St. Gatien. On the north side, you will find the Cloister de La Pralette. Tell them Patrick of the Silver Links sent you. They know me."

She thanked him and continued down the thoroughfare. Miguel took little notice of the city, but she began remembering this Church, that storefront, the bridge over the river, that stone house. When had she come to Tours before? Her memory failed her.

Then she saw it—one could scarcely miss it, for spires reached to the sky and it filled a whole large square with its old, gray stones and buttresses. On the north side, she found the cloister. She stepped down from Jochebed and rang the bell outside the gate. A black-robed monk approached sedately. It was all she could do to force herself to speak with him, for a tide of hatred flooded her vision when she saw the cross hanging from his neck.

He peered at her from under his cowl.

"I need help. I ... mean, we need help."

He nodded. "Yea? What sort of help, my boy?"

"My master is very ill." She glanced back at Miguel who swayed in the saddle and was suddenly taken with a fit of coughing. "We know no one in the city. A man told us to come here. He is Patrick of the Golden Links."

"Golden ... ah, Silver Links." He smiled. "I know of whom you speak. Come in, my lad, and bring your horses. We have shelter and help for you. Come in." He unlocked the gate and opened it.

Judith led both the horses, praying Miguel would not fall from the saddle. The monk held him upright until they reached the stables. The brothers helped Miguel from the saddle and while stable lads came to care for the horses, Judith supported him down the long halls until they arrived at last at a small cell where two cots lined the walls. Miguel tottered to the cot and fell upon it, sinking into a feverish stupor.

"You may sleep here beside him, boy," the monk said. "I will send our physician to see him. Have you eaten? No? Very well, I shall send a boy with food." He eyed their poor clothing with disfavor, but said nothing.

Judith remembered what Miguel said about payment even in the monastery. How was she to pay? She turned to look at him, for he moaned and thrashed on the cot. In the last light of the sinking sun slanting through the high window overhead, something bright glinted on his neck where his tunic fell open. She stepped to his side and lifted the gold chain that he wore that held a large ring. He had it when he came to them in Dijon. Now she wondered—would it be wrong to sell the ring?

Gently she lifted his head, removed the chain, and took the ring to the fading light. It was made of gold and silver; the emblem on it was a stag. It appeared very old. She shook her head. Nay, she must not sell this. But what of the chain?

The boy with a tray arrived. On it was a loaf of bread, a chunk of cheese and stewed cabbage in a bowl. She ate ravenously, and before she was finished, the physician came to tend to Miguel. While the monk worked, she slipped from the room, made her way down the halls and emerged into the courtyard.

At the gate, she nodded to the gatekeeper. "Please let me in when I return."

"It is not safe for you to venture forth into the city at night, boy," came the gruff reply. Nevertheless, he opened the gate and waved her through.

She was unsure of where to go, but found her way down the street and to the same vendor who had directed her to the monastery. Patrick was just folding up his awnings when she approached. "My lord." She tapped him on the shoulder and he whirled around, as if ready to do battle.

When he saw her, he laughed. "Ah, the servant boy who wanted to find a monastery. Did you find it? Is all well with your master?" His mustache was long and luxurious, his black hair caught in a knot at his neck. Business must have been good for him, for his robe was fine linen, blue and gold, and his leather sandals were adorned with silver buckles. On his stand she saw silver jewelry, chased silver mugs, belts, swords and other trinkets.

"All is well, master Patrick. Yet I must pay for his treatment. I have this chain. I wondered what you would give me for it." She pulled it from her neck and handed it to the man, praying he was honest. "I am not as simple or stupid as I appear," she said as the man let the chain run through his fingers. She saw avarice in his eyes. "I was raised in a wealthy family and fell into bad times, which is the reason I am now a servant. I know a good price from a bad one. If your offer does not please me, I shall take it somewhere else."

He laughed again, showing yellowed teeth. "Well spoken, young sir. Many fall upon hard times these days." He considered the chain for a while longer and named a price. It was very low.

She named a price far above anything she hoped to receive and so the barter began. When they finished, they were both satisfied that they had struck a good bargain. The man measured gold and silver coins into a leather bag and handed it to her.

He said, "You drive a hard bargain, boy. Your master should be proud. When do you think you will be ready to travel on?"

She shrugged, shoving the purse deep within the belt at her waist. "I know not. As soon as my master feels well enough to travel. God alone knows when that may be. I thank you for your kindness. God be with you."

"And with you." He bowed.

A week later, Miguel's health returned, but he was unable to do more than sit upright and walk about the gardens. Judith visited Patrick of the Silver Links often, but this evening she sat with Miguel in the quiet of the garden. She told him of selling the chain. "I am very sorry, but I could not ask you and I made a generous donation to the abbey."

He waved away her anxious words. "I am glad you sold it, Judith. I was saving it for our direst need."

"I put the ring in your pouch, inside your tunic. Where did you get it? I know you've worn the chain and ring since you came to us."

He nodded and his broad smile flashed. "I was able to hide it from the slave dealers. In my mouth. My father gave it to me. Said it was an emblem of our family." He sighed and adjusted the coverlet. "I am sorry I have detained your journey. How long … ?"

"You must not concern yourself about how long our journey is interrupted. The important thing is that you regain your health. I am afeared we nearly lost you."

Several days later, Judith learned of a party journeying to Troyes, and when she told Miguel about it, he urged her to go on without him.

"But we shall be separated, and how shall we find each other again in this wide, wide world?"

He smiled. They sat in the sunshine in the cloister garden, watching the monks work in the garden and listening to the low murmur of their songs. Judith had decided they were harmless, yet nothing could drive from her heart the loathing she had for them, and for their God, this Jesus of Nazareth, and His mother, Mary. She had been taught that Jesus was the product of a union between a village girl and a Roman soldier.

Miguel lifted his head to the song of a mourning dove. "I shall come to you at Troyes and ask for your relatives. If all else fails, I shall ask at the synagogue. Leave word for me there."

"Oh, Miguel!" She fell beside him on her knees. "I hate to leave you, but I long to find my family and be at home. Are you sure?" She received his assurances and the promise of his prayers while tears coursed her cheeks. Then she rose to pack.

That evening Judith visited Patrick and shared a mug of tea with him as they sat under the awning beside his stall. "I am leaving in the morning, very early. They allowed me to ride with them for a small fee. That leaves me with most of the money … " She gulped. " … or some of it, anyway, that I got from the chain." She smiled and he returned the smile, but suddenly something came into his eyes, something that reminded her of a stalking beast about to jump its prey. She shuddered and turned away, thinking surely her imagination was taking flight again.

"I am very happy for you," he said in his jovial way. "I shall miss our little chats in the evening. Pray be careful upon the road. There are robbers out there, you know."

She nodded and tried to smile, but again she felt something evil. She took her leave of him, hurrying back to the monastery.

The next morning when Jochabed was saddled and packed with provisions, Miguel came to the courtyard, leaning on a staff. Judith gave him a hug.

He released her and patted her shoulder. "Be well, Judith. This I pray for you every day. Be well."

"Thank you, my good friend. I shall pray the same for you."

After mounting Jochabed, she joined the company outside the cathedral. The party consisted of two Jewish families who were moving to Troyes. They rumbled out of the city with their wagons, mules, horses and two armed guards.

They followed the river, and she was pleased to see the beautiful Loire Valley spread before her in all its spring glory. At noon the party stopped beside the river for a short break. Judith removed her robe and tied it behind the saddle, then drank of her water flask. Her meal was a fresh loaf, figs, cheese and a bit of fried fish.

The others mounted and were on their way while she dipped her feet in the river and watched a family of ducks. When she returned to the camping spot, the others had vanished around the bend. Hastily, she gathered her reins and mounted Jochebed. Suddenly, from the bushes sprang four horsemen, surrounding her before she could kick the horse. They blocked her escape.

The men had not bothered to cover their faces. They were knights, but they wore no armor, only carried shields and wielded swords.

"Halt. You may not proceed this way!" The knight who spoke was young, blond of hair and had light grey eyes, eyes that pierced her through with an evil leer. He grabbed her reins.

Judith kicked Jochebed and made an attempt to flee, but they were too close. "What do you want? I am nothing. If you want gold, you should have taken it from those who rode with me. They have far more than I."

"But you are easy, my boy. Easy."

She shuddered, for she knew his face. "So you prey upon the weak and helpless. My friends, those of the company, will return for me."

The blond man leered. His eyes were dead, flat and glittering, like the eyes of a snake. "I don't think so. My man is stationed up the road—he is instructed to tell them that if they value their hides, they will keep going. No, son. You are alone and you are mine. I have taken a fancy to you, for you have more spirit than I thought."

He edged closer to her, feeling her tunic around the waist. "Give me your purse. I know you have gold."

She swatted away his hands and handed him the moneybag. "Keep your filthy hands off me. At least Patrick will get some of his own back."

The knight laughed. "You are intelligent, too. Come. We shall ride to my castle. You should feel fortunate, for I may make you a squire, and that would raise your standing. Don't be cast down, son. I have not harmed you, as I might. Learn this lesson and learn it well: I have all the power over life and death. You have nothing. Come along and be obedient and I will show you mercy. But try to escape, and I shall torture you within an inch of your life. I speak not in jest. I have personally watched the flaying of my enemies and have enjoyed every moment of it. I displayed their bleeding skins on my outer wall."

They tied her hands. Her body shook violently, but she was determined to keep up the brave front she had begun. "Who are you and where is your castle?"

He snorted. "You have too many questions for a slave. I am Sir Frederick. My father is Baron FitzRauf, the lord of this fief. We go to one of his castles. There you shall learn the meaning of obedience and not to have a saucy tongue in your mouth." He unfurled his banner—a red bull charging on a black field.

As they thundered away and Judith clung to the saddle, she remembered everything.

She must have been only five or six. She had gone with her father to Tours to deliver a golden brooch he made on order for Baron FitzRauf's wife. When they arrived at the castle and showed the brooch to FitzRauf, he refused payment, saying the work was far inferior to what he wanted. Father argued, and the baron threw them in a cell under the castle walls. They went two and a half days with no food or water before father said he would take no payment at all. FitzRauf let them go.

And even though she was a child, Frederick looked upon her with lust and asked his father if he could have her. Elias' face reddened and he pulled her close.

The baron burst into a great guffaw of laughter. "You do not want a Jew, you fool. Even though she is a lovely wench. Nay, son. You have many at your disposal. You do not want a Jew."

Now she knew that FitzRauf's men must have followed Father home that day, discovered where they lived and learned of Father's journey to Marseilles. FitzRauf fell upon the party as they returned from the trip with gold in their pockets, but he was not finished with his mischief even then. There was more gold to be gleaned from the Jews.

She pieced it all together, like an evil mosaic, a puzzle of the devil. This man's shield bore the same emblem of the knights who broke into their home in Dijon—the emblem that had been burned on her mind forever. She recalled that Mother had sold some of their jewelry just prior to the attack. The dealer who bought it had asked many questions, about mother's livelihood, where she lived, how her husband was occupied and did she have more valuables to sell?

Judith remembered the vendor's narrow face and the sudden sense of fear that came upon her when mother said her husband had disappeared. It all added up now. The dealer was the baron's man, just like Patrick. FitzRauf was the cause of all her grief.

She ground her teeth and vowed that when the right moment came, she would kill Frederick and his depraved father. Even if it meant her death.

***

Before the sun rose over the treetops, Adrian harnessed Old Bess to the wagon and tied the mule, Georges, to the back. Grandfather mounted the wagon seat and snapped the reins over Bess' head.

They followed the Loire River, passing castles and villages on the way. Adrian had never been so far south and he marveled at the beauty of the valley—the sweet, green grasses; the array of flowers and birds, the fertile fields where villeins tilled the soil for their masters, the fruit trees all in glorious bloom.

Several days later, they stopped beside the road for a midday meal. Grandfather snored softly while Adrian gazed up at the turquoise sky through the branches of an oak tree. It seemed a few moments only and Grandfather rolled over with a moan. *"Eh bien."*

He sat and stretched. "Let us gather our things and be on our journey."

"Aye, sir. I will fetch Bess." While Adrian was at the task, he heard the sound of hooves on the baked and rutted road. A party of knights, covered chairs and a train of servants approached.

He took special interest in the horses, the knights, the armor and the banners. His heart skipped a beat. Two lions, rearing, on a red field. The Plantagent banner! The duchess of Brittany, Maria! Remembering his place, he lowered his head and pulled on his forelock. They rode past without a nod or gesture, just as he would have done a short while ago if he had passed a tinker and a servant boy.

He had heard precious little of Maria. Had the king married her to another? Would he catch a glimpse of her face? The curtains on the chair were tightly closed, and he caught nothing save a whiff of fragrance. *It is Maria!* He held himself stiff and still, for all his instincts, heritage and desires urged him to run after the train, to call for Maria.

The last of the line, a weary palfrey carrying an overweight monk, disappeared. Adrian finished harnessing Bess, led her to the wagon and hitched it up. Grandfather stepped up onto the wagon seat, but Adrian opted to walk.

They had not gone far when Grandfather smiled. "It was your wife's train, was it not? The Duchess Maria?"

Adrian looked up in surprise. "Aye."

"You are doing well. Two months ago you would have run after them and asserted yourself. Surely the good Lord is pleased."

Adrian smiled. "You do not know how close I came to that, sir. I have learned a measure of patience from your example. Do you know why they come this way?"

"They go to FitzRauf's castle, the Chateau Renault. Sir Frederick is to wed the duchess in a month's time."

"Maria! To wed ... " Adrian stumbled, stopped dead in his tracks. The cur! The brigand! To marry my .... He glanced up and hurried to catch the wagon. "And whither are we bound, sir? The city of Tours?"

"Nay, the village near the castle. I have some business there."

Adrian's heart leapt. Perchance he would see FitzRauf and his son, perchance he would have opportunity to … He cast a quick glance at Grandfather, but the old man gazed straight ahead.

Suddenly Adrian was cast back; memories flooded his mind as a wave of the sea crashed against rocks. The feel of silk and brocaded velvet and furs; the smell of roasted duck and pork and the light, crusty pies he loved so much; hot baths poured by servants in tubs as large as Grandfather's cottage; a squadron of squires and servants who dressed and combed him; splintering lances on the tilting grounds—ah, the snap of banners against a cobalt sky, the feel of fine steel in gauntleted hand, a spirited steed beneath him.

"You are quiet,"Grandfather said in a low voice.

"Is that a fault, sir?"

"No, lad. Only that I know a little of what passes through thy mind. Baron FitzRauf rules all this land, does he not? If the rumors I heard about you are correct, you have a blood feud with his son, Frederick. Am I close to the mark? Does the name of his castle arouse all your old passions, boy?"

"Aye, sir."

The old man pulled back on the reins and motioned Adrian to climb into the wagon.

Adrian wondered if he was to receive a reprimand, but Grandfather continued in a mild voice and his question surprised him.

"What say you? Is this road too hard? Would you rather that I left thee in prison to die? As the Scripture saith, 'No one after putting his hand to the plow and looking back is fit for the Kingdom of God.' Do you desire to be the ruler of Brittany … of England?"

Adrian shot him a look. "Of course I long to avenge myself of the wrong that was done to me. I think of little else. This life has its advantages. I appreciate what you have taught me. Yet, I miss … "

"Aye? You miss what? I will not scold you for your confession, for confession makes the soul glad. As the Scriptures saith, 'He who confesses and forsakes his sin will find compassion.' You have sat on your grief long enough. Speak now."

"For certes, I miss my horse." Adrian grinned. "It may seem strange to you that I should miss my horse, perchance even more than I miss my family, but let me explain. I was born to sit astride a fine animal and this was the finest of them all. Ah, my beautiful

Kazimer!" He sighed deeply. "Of course I miss my mother and wonder about my sister, Eleanor. Have you heard aught of her, Grandfather?"

"Nay, son. At the village we may hear news. But be careful not to ask too many questions. A servant would not even know the questions to ask."

"Yes, sir. And do you think that I shall regain my former position?"

"According to the will of God. Your former position may be the least that you desire some day." Grandfather clucked to the horse. "There is great unrest in this land over the rule of the English. John is hated by all, from the lord who sits in his castle, to the serfs in the fields. What do you ken of this?"

Adrian lifted his head, his heart strangely moved by Grandfather's words. "It is a dark day for our country, for certes. My people need a strong leader who will fight for their rights. I shall be that leader one day, Grandfather. I shall! I know it!"

The wagon jolted over the ruts. Grandfather nodded. "You may, son. But to be a good king, you must rule with love and you must be willing to sacrifice your own life. If you can do those two things, you will be the best ruler in all of history."

CHAPTER TWELVE

Once the game is over, the king and the pawn go back into the same box. Italian Proverb

Orleans, France, March 1201

It was evening when Louis and Samson John approached the Loire River. All day they had followed a long valley that was largely unpopulated, traveling off the road, for Louis was afraid his enemies were watching the roads. He had learned to trust the boy's sense of direction, even though the valley they followed wound hither and yon.

Each morning he washed his wound, applied a salve and wrapped it again. Do what he may for it, though, red and swollen tissue grew around it and a fever raged through his body. He knew he must stop and have it cared for, but there were no places of rest, no one to tend to his wound.

Now, as they reached the river, each step was torture. His body afire with infection, his mind cloudy, his breath coming in gasps, he struggled to stay on his feet. Samson John did everything he could, but the boy knew little of medicine.

At least it did not rain. That was a blessing. They camped that night in a place near a village. Louis sent the boy into the village with a note, asking for help, but he soon returned. From his motions, Louis understood that they set dogs on the boy and threw stones.

He ate what little he could—only a morsel of bread, washed down with water—and settled under a beech tree, the sound of the river in his ears, the damp smell of moss and water in his nose. He had given instructions to Samson John, hoping the boy understood his intent, that if he could not rise, or if he died, the boy was to take the mule to the abbey at Orleans and hand the box and a note Louis had written to the abbot father.

That night he fell into a fevered dream. He knelt in a wind-swept meadow, knees pressed into the damp soil, a young boy again, and watched as a knight drew sword and lunged at his mother.

The last rays of sun caught and glinted on the sword. Louis did not close his eyes, nor cry out, yet he drew blood from biting his lower lip while tears coursed down his cheeks. Mama leaped from the sword; he heard her mocking laugh, then she swung the mattock and connected solidly with the knight's head. There was a dull thud; he went down like a felled tree.

The other knight leaped from the saddle to aid his friend. Louis gripped the damp soil and cheered silently for his mother. She took to her heels, but the knight she struck regained his feet, and his sword flashed in the failing light.

Suddenly someone shook him. He pushed the hands away, felt water on his lips, running down his neck. He opened his eyes and groaned. Samson John knelt over him, holding a cup. The boy's face was pale and drawn, as if he had little sleep. Louis lifted himself and drank.

Early morning sunlight dappled on the grass and the river chuckled beyond his bed. It was time to be on his way. He tried to stand, but his legs failed him, and after a few moments, he lay back, panting. Sharp pains issued from his shoulder, so much so that when he moved even the slightest, he nearly fainted.

Samson John sat on his heels, stirring a small fire, a piece of bread in one hand and a cup of water in the other, his eyes never straying far from his master. Louis motioned for him to come. The boy knelt beside him, uttering gutteral sounds in his throat, motioning to the mule and the road.

Louis pointed to his wound. "I cannot travel today, boy. You must go on." He motioned down the trail. "Find help. Orleans, if you have to—here, take the note I wrote." He drew out the parchment that was tied with a cord. "Get help. Come back. It is all we can do." He lay back, panting, pushing back against the grey mist enveloping his mind, darkness almost overcoming him. "Leave me … a flask of water and … some bread. Then go, boy. Go!"

Samson John shook his head, reluctant to leave. Louis lifted a hand and waved him away, then lay back on the damp grass. With tears pouring down his face, Samson John brought the flask of water and the bread to Louis' side and bowed his head for silent prayer.

He picked up the pack and plodded away from his master. At the turning of the lane, he looked back. Louis roused briefly and waved. The boy waved back and set out down the lane.

***

In every small village and hamlet, Grandfather halted the wagon and when a crowd gathered, he sold his wares from the back. Adrian learned to barter under Old Bric's tutelage. Two days of travel were consumed, with camps beside the river where the low gurgle of water soothed Adrian's nerves.

On the third day from the cottage, Grandfather packed the wagon and glanced over at Adrian who helped pull the canvas tight over the top. "Today we shall be in the village near the castle. I have business there."

"What sort of business, Grandfather? Selling our goods?"

Grandfather grunted. "Nay, Son. This is business of another sort. There are some of us ... I should say many of us ... who are working toward freedom. Do ye ken that word?"

Adrian nodded. "I know what freedom is, sir. But Brittany and France are free, are we not?" He climbed onto the wagon seat.

"It depends upon which side of the fence you are on." Grandfather hoisted himself to the seat of the wagon and took up the reins. He flicked them and Bess ambled down the trail. "You may say that Bess is free. She is gainfully employed, all her needs are met and she is treated with kindness. Yet she is not free—she is a beast of burden and that is well for her. It is not well for people."

Adrian wondered where Grandfather was going with this talk. There were movements among the common folk—brigands, knaves—who fought their private wars against injustice and inequality, but he had been trained to view this as the worst sort of insurrection and treason. To give loyalty to your liege lord, and to serve him until the end of your days, never questioning his judgment was the code that governed his life.

Grandfather stroked his beard. "It is not well for the common man, for the Lord God gave humans a sense of freedom. Freedom, Adrian, is the right to choose your own path in life, to have justice, to rule your own affairs, to work hard and be paid a good wage for your labors, to have a hand in making the laws, to be able to own a few acres of land and not to have to work for an overlord. It is not freedom, nor justice, when there is a law for the rich and another law for the poor."

Adrian nodded. "Aye. I know of such things."

"This is not what we have in France." He snapped the reins as they approached a hill. "You have seen the abuses of the system, yet you have not suffered as the common folk suffer every day. Evil masters who call themselves barons and earls own many castles and much land, yet the power they wield can bring harm to the poor. Barons may deflower a young woman of a low class and think nothing of it—the evil practice of *droit de seigner*. You know of this. It should not be. God has called me to help right these wrongs. I meet with other men in the villages. We call ourselves the Longbeards after a brave man in England who died for the freedom he fought for. This is the business I have in the village."

"But, sir. This business is dangerous. You must know that the barons cannot endure such a thing. They fear an uprising from the common people more than anything else. You cannot be successful. They will kill you."

"*Eh, bein.* They will kill me, then. *Dues lo volt,* as they say on the Crusades." He chuckled. "Do not be so downcast, Son. I will take every precaution to stay alive as long as God allows it."

They rounded a bend, and there, standing not twenty paces away, was a young man in a green tunic and tattered cloak and a large floppy hat. When he saw them approach, he removed his hat, waving it frantically. His face was flushed as if he had been running.

"Hail!" Grandfather called. "Whither art thou going, young man?" He pulled back on the reins as the boy stepped closer.

His mouth worked, but he uttered only guttural sounds, much like an animal. He motioned wildly back into the forest and began weeping. But then he remembered something and, digging in his cloak, he brought forth a rolled parchment tied with a string. This he handed to Grandfather as he wiped his face.

"Peace." Grandfather laid a hand on the boy's dark head. Looking into his eyes and making sure the boy could see his lips, he continued, "We will help you." He turned to Adrian. "Give this young man a drink, and I shall see what message he brings."

Adrian did not want to touch the boy's eager hand as it reached up for the flask. He shrank from this commoner, this person who was maimed, for he believed that it was the devil who made him so. Yet he remembered Grandfather's kind words, words that already calmed the boy's face and brought hope to his dark eyes.

Grandfather perused the missal, then turned his face to the boy and spoke distinctly. "We shall come to your master's aid. It says here that he is very ill and needs assistance. I think the good Lord directed your steps, for we are able to help him. Come along, hop up into the wagon and show us where he is."

A mile or so down the trail, Grandfather pulled back on the reins, for a fallen tree blocked their path. They climbed out of the wagon and Grandfather tied Bess to a tree, gathered some provisions and followed the boy's slender figure into the forest.

Adrian followed behind, frowning, swatting at flies, muttering under his breath. *Why he thinks we must delay our journey to help this ... this halfwit boy and his master is beyond me.* He turned his thoughts to the castle, to the wedding that would soon take place. That his ex-wife would be married to his enemy, the craven and doltish son of Lord FitzRauf, nettled his mind. He wondered if there was anything he could do to stop the wedding.

The path led to the Loire River, to a loop that ran north. In a small meadow they saw the prone figure of a man. As Grandfather knelt beside him, Adrian saw it was a monk who seemed asleep, yet was burning to the touch. The monk looked familiar—where had Adrian seen him before?

"His name is Brother Louis." Grandfather glanced up at Adrian. "He has been wounded and the wound has festered. We cannot move him like this, but I think some things I brought with me might help. Build up the fire. We will need hot water."

Brother Louis! Adrian studied the man's wan face. He recognized him now—a monk who served at St. Jacques' and also at the chapel in the castle at Mordelias. He drew Grandfather aside. "I cannot let the monk see my face. He served at the castle. He will know me as Prince Arthur."

Grandfather smiled grimly and shook his head. "If he knows his own mother, that would be a miracle, Adrian. Nay. He shall not know thee as Prince Arthur. Look at thyself. You may look like him, but no one would take you for the prince now." He turned back to his work.

Adrian stepped to the river, found a pool that was still and stared at his reflection. His hair had grown and was uncombed, falling about his face. Facial hair grew in soft, golden wisps on his chin, and one eye was black from the blow he had received from a low-hanging branch. He looked down at his clothes—he wore no hose at all, only rough sandals, and a tattered tunic. His robe was of the roughest material he had ever felt. It was true. No one would recognize him as Prince Arthur. Not even his mother, if she were still living.

Samson John did Grandfather's bidding, but Adrian sat by the fire and watched as Grandfather's skilled hands worked over the feverish monk.

Night descended with the hoot of owls and the song of the katydid. Grandfather sent Adrian back to the wagon. "Take care of Bess, and bring me the small box that is under my cot in the wagon, the one with flames painted on the lid. We shall have to spend the night here, so bring some food. Bring also that piece of canvas, for we may need to carry him out."

Adrian did not pull on his forelock or bow. He merely turned and trudged back to the wagon.

Brother Louis remained in a dreamlike state most of the night. When Adrian woke the next morning, the monk was speaking in a low, urgent voice to Grandfather. Adrian brought water to Grandfather, whose hair was askew and eyes red-rimmed. He had not slept.

Brother Louis seemed more concerned for his mule than for anything else, and kept saying something about a gift he carried to the monastery in Orleans. "You must give it to the abbot, along with this letter. Promise me."

Grandfather assured him he would see that the parcel was delivered safely.

Brother Louis sighed, closed his eyes and slept.

They carried him to the wagon that day and placed him in it with great care. Samson John, for the note so named him, never left his side, but hovered over him, his eyes overflowing with tears at times. Whenever he looked at Grandfather, he beamed his gratitude.

Adrian kept his distance from Samson John, but the boy seemed not to notice. Adrian appreciated his love and loyalty for his master and so as the day wore on, he spoke to the boy, making sure he saw his lips and could follow his words. He found him intelligent, personable and a good companion. Samson John was able to understand and also able to communicate with his hands—dexterous, slim, agile hands.

They came that evening to the village below the castle. It was a small but busy center of activity. The people of the village—the blacksmith, miller, farmer, clothier, seamster, cooks and those who raised livestock—provided the staples for the nobles when the castle was occupied.

The wagon was greeted by a swarm of dirty little boys who clamored for a ride, then ran alongside until Grandfather pulled to a stop on the village green. "Our first order of business is to see that Brother Louis finds the care he needs. I know the medicine woman here. She is able, kindly and of a good heart." He glanced at the monk, who seemed to be sleeping peacefully. "I guess it will not hurt to let the villagers buy a few things from us before we go to her house. Come, Adrian, open the wagon."

It was not long before the villagers crowded around. Adrian kept busy filling the orders as they came, but he paused when a young girl approached the wagon, a girl of extraordinary beauty. Her golden hair was clean and neatly braided, and her bright blue eyes snapped with intelligence and something else.

He nodded to her. "How may I help you, my lady?" It was a simple question, one that he'd been saying for the past hour, but now it was wrought with undertones, none of which were lost on the girl.

She giggled. "A pound of your linseed oil, if you please, and my grandmother would like a pot. I think that one there." She pointed upwards, her long sleeve falling away from a shapely arm. The bodice of her gown was cut low, granting Adrian a sight that he appreciated most thoroughly.

He hurried to get the items, but the girl fumbled with her coins and dropped one on the ground. Leaping from the wagon, he retrieved it. From this proximity, he saw she was dressed in a clean frock, had well-shaped ankles and a slim waist.

"Thank you, kind sir," she said primly, for she knew her good looks and seemed accustomed to attention. "Will you be staying long in the village?"

"I know not, madam." Adrian bowed and she giggled again. He handed her the coin and when he did, he allowed his fingers to touch hers and linger just a moment. "What is your name, please? It is not every day I see such a beautiful face in the midst of a motley crowd."

She winked. "Find out." Swirling her skirts, she was soon lost in the crowd.

"Adrian!" Grandfather's reprimand recalled him to his duties.

After a time, a matronly lady appeared and invited them to partake of the evening meal in her home.

Grandfather nodded. "Thank you, Madame LaVerne. I have a very ill man for you to see. He has a wound that festered. I have treated him with all my skill and he seems to be resting easier. Would it be convenient to bring him to your home?"

She took a quick look at the monk and nodded. "Aye. Please do."

Grandfather folded up shop soon afterward and directed the wagon to a spot on the riverbank to bathe, for it afforded some privacy. After they bathed in the cool river, Adrian pulled on the only pair of hose he owned, an old, loose pair Grandfather found in his belongings, and donned a dark green tunic Grandfather had found for him. It was too large, and he sighed as he patted it down, longing for the finery he wore as prince. Grandfather wore a white tunic embroidered at the neck, dark blue hose and a blue robe of soft material from the east—*baldikin* they called it, for it came from Baghdad.

LaVerne's home was the largest house in the village, a thatched cottage off the village green with a stone-walled fence and a croft in the back. The croft sloped gently to a small creek. Her cottage commandeered not only a portion of the stream but also sat near the mill. The advantage to this was that they did not have to travel far to grind their meal, for none could grind meal nor bake bread at home. The baron received a small fee each time they made bread.

Grandfather and Adrian carried Brother Louis into the cottage and helped LaVerne settle him on a cot in a small bedroom at the back. Adrian noticed a comely lass bending over the pot at the fireplace and realized it was the girl he had spoken to at the wagon. She peeked at him from under long lashes, but turned away abruptly when he would speak with her.

Outside, he and Grandfather sat on a bench under a spreading oak tree. A large black dog settled itself at their feet. Adrian scratched his ears and the dog cast him a grateful glance, leaning solidly against his legs.

LaVerne, a tall, heavy-set woman with graying hair and the sharp eyes of one who rules her household, her husband and village affairs, brought them flagons of ale and dried apple slices. She sat down beside them and plied them with questions about the monk. Then she turned her inquisitive eyes upon Adrian. "Your grandson, ye say?" She frowned as if Adrian were at fault for his existence. "Think that ye can raise such a one?"

Adrian did not like the woman's forward tongue, but Grandfather answered her meekly with a *grumphing* chuckle. "He's had a bad time of it in life. His father and mother died. He was friendless and nearly dead when he came to me. I know not how he was able to make the journey, but I took him in and he has been a blessing to me in my old age."

Adrian smiled. It was an unusual way to say it, but Grandfather did not err from the truth.

She snorted. "He will probably help himself to your coin, too, I'm thinkin'."

"Yea, thou knowest the ways of the world, Madame LaVerne. And how art thy children? What is new?"

She launched into a long narrative about the many difficulties of her grown children and their families. The girl in the cottage, she said, was her granddaughter. Suddenly she called out, "Come out and greet my guests, Aimee!"

The girl's cheeks were rosy and she kept her eyes lowered. "Good day, sirs." She favored Adrian with one glance, then curtsied and ducked back into the cottage.

Grandfather chuckled. "Very pretty. She has a beautiful name. Beloved. I see she took special interest in our young man here." He prodded the boy with his knee and smiled.

Adrian blushed and hid his face in the mug of ale, the best ale he'd tasted in a long time. Life suddenly seemed very satisfactory.

"The good man will be home soon," LaVerne said, standing and shaking out her skirt. "I shall look to the meal we have prepared. Afterward there is a meeting down by the river." She disappeared into the cottage without any further word.

"A meeting, sir?" The dog stretched out, begging for his stomach to be scratched. Adrian obliged him.

"Aye. It is a very private meeting, but you may attend if you like. Sit to the back and make not a sound. Keep the knowledge you learn to yourself. Will you keep silent about what is said, boy?"

Adrian frowned. "I may look a fool, Grandfather, but my wits are the same as when I ... " He dropped his head. "I am sorry, sir. I will do what you ask of me. Please forgive my impertinence."

Grandfather smiled. "You may think it strange that we speak of freedom for the common man and yet I hold you so strictly to an ancient form of servitude. It is for thy training. Just as you were trained in swordplay, in riding and in jousts, so you are being trained to be humble. In due time your training shall be completed and we shall be equals. Indeed, you shall surpass me, for you have a bright mind and you possess virtues of courage, valor and honor. Others will discover the man behind the foolish boy you pretend to be. As the Scriptures saith, 'When He has tried me, I shall come forth as gold.' *En viola!* You will become such a man!"

Adrian saw tears in Grandfather's eyes and was unable at first to respond. "I? Surpass you? I may one day occupy the throne or some other lower position, but I will never surpass you in wisdom and faith."

Grandfather smiled at his bewilderment and patted his knee. "Time will tell. As the Scriptures saith, 'Sufficient for each day is the evil therein.' Now I see wood at the back of the cottage that the good man has not had time to chop, and perchance there are a few other chores you may find to do. Your training is not finished yet."

Adrian stood and stretched, laughing at the old dog stretched out on his back with his legs in the air. "No, I do not suppose it is."

Twice while Adrian chopped wood, he caught sight of Aimee— a glimpse of her swirling skirt as she turned from the doorway and the flash of her hair as the sun touched it when she set a milk jug outside the door. He picked it up and milked the cow, thinking while he did not only of the maid in the cottage, but also of the castle so close, the place where if anything were ever to happen, it would happen there.

LaVerne's husband, a lean, silent man, arrived just as he was finishing. Adrian washed his hands, sat at the rough table and enjoyed the woman's plain fare--lentil stew, fresh bread, curdled cheese and poached eggs seasoned with parsley. But he could not help comparing this with the food he used to eat.

Up there in the castle they were sitting down to a feast of crisply roasted quail dipped in honey sauce, haunches of beef dripping with fat and nestled with gravy, peaches and cherries from the south, delectable pastries stuffed with dates and dipped in honey. They were entertained with dancing and acrobatic troupes and music in the gallery. They were laughing about how the king of France fled the Crusades. They were making love under the rose arbors. Up in the castle his enemy courted Maria.

After the meal, Adrian wandered to the croft and sat on a wooden bench. The black dog ambled over and settled against his legs. It was not long before Aimee came sauntering across the grass, her hips swinging.

"It was a good meal," he said.

She glanced his way, as if surprised to find him in her garden. "Aye, it was." She sat beside him, lifting her skirts to show trim ankles. "So, you learned my name."

He laughed. "Yes, my girl. It is a lovely name, like its owner."

She nodded, pleased. "You must tell me whither you have been and what your life is like. I get so little news about the outside world. I am not a common lass; I lived in Paris once, you know." She raised her chin.

"In Paris?" He hoped he sounded impressed, but in fact, he was not. He had lived in Paris, too, and all his memories of that city were those of a bad dream.

I wonder what she would think if she knew who I am. The temptation to tell her was strong, for he knew she would swoon with delight if she believed him. But, nay. She would not believe.

He gazed into her eyes— beautiful eyes, cobalt blue like his mother's—and told her about the places and castles he had seen, of the knights and kings and courts he had visited, of horses and battles and weapons and banners.

She pulled on his sleeve. "But what about the women? What do they wear in Rouen these days? How do they fix their hair? What are they talking about?"

"Well, as to that, I confess I cannot help you." He scratched the old dog's ears. "Do you attend the meetings they hold here, Aimee?"

She preened a bit when he used her surname. "Nay. They would'na let such a one as I, and a girl besides, come to their precious meetings. But I know fair enough what it is they speak of, for their voices carry and I can hear them when I lean out my bedchamber's window. See? It is in the loft up there." She pointed. He noted the small window in the eaves of the cottage. She lowered her voice. "Would you like to come to my room?"

"Very much so, my lady." He took her hand in his best courtier manner and brought it to his lips. She giggled.

Grandfather's voice boomed from the back of the house. Adrian dropped her hand and stood as Grandfather marched into the lower garden, followed by a group of men.

Aimee nodded to the first of them, then flounced away with a swirl of skirts. Most of the men wore the heavy tunic and square-toed shoes of the villein but a few were well dressed and shrewd of eye.

When all had gathered and the general talk subsided, Grandfather stood at the foot of the croft and spoke. Adrian was surprised, for he had never heard him address an audience and he suspected Grandfather would speak in fiery tones to stir the hearts of his listeners to action against the injustices they suffered.

Grandfather's voice was low and modulated, just loud enough to carry to the top of the croft. He spoke of suffering and love and kindness to all. He spoke of God's love; he spoke of entering the kingdom of Heaven as a small child; he spoke of equality for all men.

That evening as they settled themselves in the wagon that was parked near the river on the village green, Adrian rolled over and stared at the canvas roof over his head. "May I speak my mind, sir?"

Grandfather murmured his assent.

"Why do you hold these meetings? For certes, it is suicide for the common man to rise up against their lords. They have no training, no weapons, no armies and no finances. You know that this kind of talk will lead to a rebellion. How can you give them hope for freedom and equality when there is no hope?"

After a pause, Grandfather spoke in his low, rumbling voice. "You are right about the plight of these people, but wrong about one thing. Each man, no matter how low or how ignorant he may be, needs hope. You say there is no hope, but a day is coming when the common man will have freedom and equality. I shall continue the meetings, my son, until the good Lord tells me to stop."

Adrian let it be and rolled over to sleep.

***

Louis remembered little of the old man and his servant who came to him in the meadow or of the journey in the wagon to the woman's cottage. He awoke one morning and saw Samson John in the corner of a small room, bent over, sleeping in his clothes. The walls were wattle and daub. A rooster crowed and the voice of a woman ordered someone to get water. A fire crackled; he smelled freshly baked bread, heard the moan of old timbers as someone slammed the door.

He sat up and found to his surprise that his arm was not nearly as sore as it had been. The bed creaked beneath him. Samson John awoke, straightened, and looked his way. How he knew Louis was awake was a puzzle, but it happened every morning—as soon as Louis wakened, the boy would open his eyes.

Louis turned his face to him. "You have slept in your clothes on the floor, my son. That must not have been very comfortable."

The boy leaped to his feet and was beside Louis in a flash. He touched Louis' face, patted his shoulder, made noises in his throat, motioned to the water jug.

"Yes, I believe I would like a drink. Then you can bring me my clothes." The water tasted good on his parched throat. How long had he been sick? Where was he? And what of the mule and his pack? "Where is my pack, boy?" He finished the water and looked about for his clothes.

The boy grunted, then pointed to a corner of the room where his pack lay undisturbed.

Louis sighed and lay back on the bed. The effort to sit up drained his small store of energy. "Ah, well. I am glad you remembered it. I would not have wanted it left in the stable." He eyed a lizard that lived near the beam of the roof. It made its lazy way down the wall. Now he heard men's voices from the other room.

"Would you fetch me someone? Someone I can speak to and ask questions of? I am fairly dying with curiosity to know what happened to me."

The boy grunted and went flapping through the door. Louis saw flashes of movement, but he could not make out the people. The woman's voice was predominant.

The old man he had seen as if in a dream entered, smiling. "Greetings, brother monk. Your name is Louis? I am pleased to meet you. My name is Old Bric." He held out his hand.

Louis shook it. "You have my eternal gratitude, sir, for rescuing me. My servant and friend, Samson John, found few who would read my missal and no one who would take the time to help. Could you inform me as to my whereabouts? Am I near Tours?"

Old Bric nodded and pulled a bench closer to the cot. "Aye, my good monk. Tours is only five furlongs or so to the south. This is the village of Montebank, near the castle of Baron FitzRauf who rules the fief. I am a tinker by trade."

Louis gazed at the old man and nodded. "I ... suppose I spoke in my dreams. Did I speak of a parcel I must deliver to ... someone of great importance?"

"Aye, you did, but you gave no hint of its contents, or even to whom it was intended. The only thing I know is what you wrote in the message that you wanted to get it to the monastery in Orleans."

Louis exhaled with a whoosh. So the package was safe and it seemed his enemies had lost sight of him. Perchance it was God's will that he got sick, for he came into the village in a covert manner.

The old man stretched and stood. "You are in the home of LaVerne and her husband, Guillaume. LaVerne is the village medicine woman and she is very capable. I will send my servant in with a meal so you may break your fast. Are you well? Do you feel up to sitting outside for a spell this morning?"

Louis smiled. "I feel better than before, but my legs are as weak as a baby lamb's. Still, if it be no trouble, I would like to sit outside. I must get to Orleans as soon as possible. Or at least to Tours. Do you think you could find a way to Tours? I can pay."

Old Bric nodded, stroking his long, white beard. "Aye, my old Bess and the wagon can take you. We would not charge you a franc."

Louis lay back and smiled his thanks. When the old man's servant came in bringing a tray, Louis smiled. "Thank you." He peered up into the boy's face. It looked familiar. "Have I seen you somewhere, boy? Did you live in Mordelias for a time?"

Adrian bowed. "I am from southern France. I have come only recently to stay with my Grandfather. We spent the winter in his cottage upriver. I shall come for your tray when you are finished."

"You look very much like another young lad I once knew in Brittany."

The boy tugged on his forelock. "I am related to a great many people, Brother, but they all live far away."

Louis sighed and turned his attention to his food. The mystery would unravel itself as he regained his strength and mind, but still it teased his mind. Who was the young man? He did not speak with the soft twang of the *languedoc* of southern France but with the clipped accents of Brittany. Why would he lie? Did he hide a secret?

He glanced up and smiled at the lizard. In God's good time he would know.

***

Adrian ducked into the other room and pushed back his hair. Whew. That was close. The monk did recognize him and Adrian knew his stumbling reply did not appease the man's avid curiosity.

Two days later he drove Brother Louis and Samson John to Tours. During the whole of the trip, he caught Louis eyeing him with curiosity and puzzlement. He avoided conversation and concentrated on driving. In the city, the spires of the cathedral rose over all the other buildings. He was glad for the bustle of traffic and the sights and sounds of the busy city. They crossed the river and came at last to the monastery.

There he was directed to the north side of the Church, to the cloister and hospitium. Adrian hopped down from the wagon and rang the bell. A few moments later, he helped Brother Louis from the wagon and tugged on his forelock in farewell. As he drove away, he smiled. Ah. I am free. Or was he? What lay in his future? His heart tugged him toward the castle but Grandfather's gentle words held him back.

He sighed and clapped the reins over Bess' back. She flipped back her ears, annoyed. I am doing all I can, she seemed to say with a low nicker. "Yea, I know, Bess. Does not God call us all to do that?" He laughed. "Now I speak like Grandfather."

CHAPTER THIRTEEN

*Every normal man must be tempted at times to spit upon his
hands, hoist the black flag and begin slitting throats.* Ambroise
Bierce

Monteback, France, April 1201

The dank smell of the river, of moss and moist earth, rose to
Adrian's nostrils as he sat alone beside the river one evening a few
days after taking the monk to Tours. He came here, for it was a place
of silence where he could think and pray. He thought tonight of the
last meeting at LaVerne's. A villein stood and called for action.
Others joined in with words about weapons and warfare and the
majority agreed it was time for a revolt. Adrian was troubled in spirit
and tried to pray, but it seemed his prayers fell short and bounced
back to him lifelessly from the low clouds overhead.

The creaky sound of tree frogs joined a choir of crickets. Out in
the river a fish jumped. Tiny waves lapped against rocks along the
shore. He swatted at a mosquito. The peace he sought seemed
elusive; instead, danger seemed to tremble on the still evening air.
Someone approached; he heard soft footfalls and the clink of metal
on metal. Turning slightly so he could see through the brush, a man's
form came into view and another man followed. He could not see
their faces.

"I think we are alone here," he heard one of them say in a gruff
voice. "There is something I need to talk to you about, and I don't
want any of those rufflers who gather at the woman's house to hear
me." His accents revealed he was of a high class. Adrian saw the
glint of light on a sword at the man's side.

Adrian held himself still. The two sat on the rocks beside the
river—one with fine black leather boots, the other with the coarse
shoes of a serf. He didn't hear every word, but the gist of the
conversation was that someone of nobility had gotten word of the

meetings of the Longbeards and they wanted it stopped. Through the sparse brush, he could see the backs of the two men—now he recognized the larger one—it was Morgan Barnwell, the bailiff at the manor house. Adrian did not know the other speaker and could not see who it was.

"Whatcher want me to do about it?" The other man's speech was rough, that of the lowest of class, perhaps a slave.

"I want news of their meetings." Morgan Barnwell lowered his voice. Adrian heard only snatches of his words. "If we can ... burn the house and kill ... a reward for the old man ... torture ... an example to others."

Silence. Material rubbed on material as bodies shifted.

Morgan Barnwell raised his voice. "It means gold, me lad. Get me the information I seek. Then we shall see. Mayhap it will be enough to buy your freedom and a piece of land. Would you like that?"

"Aye." The younger man breathed heavily. "I wants to be free, sames as all o'them. But I can't, unless I get a boon. Who's to say you won't take it all? Pardons me for askin', sir."

Adrian imagined the man pulling at his forelock and dipping his head. He heard the clink of coins.

"Here's the feel of real gold. Don't lose it or spend it foolishly, boy. You will get your boon when you have completed your task. Aye, my lad. You will get a sack full of these."

"By St. Martin! 'Tis done, my lord! When do ye ... " Their voices sank to conspiratorial whispers, then they rose from their perch and left.

Adrian waited by the river for a time after they left, then scurried back to the village green under the cover of darkness. Breathless, he lay down on the crude bed in the wagon. Grandfather snored, so he did not awaken him. Adrian slept little that night.

It was while they were breaking their fast with a bowl of pottage and cold bread over their campfire, and washing it down with a mug of ale, that he broached the subject. "We are in trouble, Grandfather. Last night I overhead two men talking down by the creek. The baron has discovered where you hold your meetings with the Longbeards. They said they will kill everyone. They mentioned you and said you were to be taken alive and tortured. I slept very little, for I thought they might come even as we slept."

The old man laid a hand on Adrian's knee and pierced him with a bright, blue glance. "Son, you are full of fears this morning. As the Scriptures saith, 'I will not fear what man can do unto me, for my trust is in the Lord.' Our Lord has promised to give us freedom from fear and worry, if we will only trust Him."

"For certes, you speak the truth." Adrian strove to beat down the panic that rose sharp and bitter in his heart. "But what about the plot against the Longbeards? I know how the nobles think. They fear nothing more than an organized uprising of the common people. We are in grave danger. Did you not hear me say they intend to kill us?"

Grandfather nodded slowly and rinsed out his trencher. "I hear thee, yet I know my God is larger and stronger and wiser than any of the nobles. He can keep us safe from all the plots of the wicked. As the Scriptures saith—"

"I care not what the Scriptures saith!" Adrian leaped to his feet. "Our lives are in danger! And our friends' lives! And all you can do is quote Scriptures?" He stalked off, ashamed of his outburst, ashamed of his fears, almost frantic with worry.

But what could he do? He could not muster an army or defend himself. He fumed with this sense of impotency, glancing more than once at the castle.

That morning he helped Grandfather build a stone wall around the abbey Church. When the sun was high, they sat under an oak tree to share a meal the monks brought out to them. He glanced at the old man. "Who paid for my release?"

Grandfather, not in a hurry to answer, bowed his head and said a prayer before opening the box and drawing out the food. He shook his head. "I know not, my son. Here. This cold mutton is good. We don't get paid much for working here, but they feed us well. Here is a fresh tomato! Oh, la, la! Wine! Look, lad!" He drew out a flask, opened it and took a drink.

"Grandfather, will you listen to me? Do you know aught of my escape? Please tell me or I shall perish!"

Old Bric slewed his head around to gaze at him. "What is going on in that mind of yours? Ah, I perceive! You want to rise to your former position, raise an army and defend the village."

Adrian sighed and settled back against the tree with a piece of mutton and the flask of wine. "I know it may be as a tale told to children, yet it could happen. It could happen in time to save some of our friends, if you would only tell me what I need to know."

Old Bric munched for some time on his leg of mutton, then gazed up into the branches of the oak tree. "I will tell thee the truth, for certes, my son. I was approached late one night by two men who rode tired horses. I could see they were of nobility, yet their faces were covered. When they told me of the task I was to accomplish, I agreed to work with them to save you from death. I did not take the gold they offered."

"Is that all?" Adrian passed him the wine.

"A fortnight later, a messenger arrived, a young boy whom I did not know, with instructions written on parchment. I memorized them and burned the missive. I followed the instructions, found you, walked out of the castle and arrived at the cottage. Two men appeared by my side to help carry you. I had never seen them before and have never seen them since. I swear by all the saints, and by the Holy Mother Herself, that is all I know of the affair." He finished the wine and stood.

"But there must be—"

"We can tarry no longer." Grandfather gathered up the food. "Or we shall be working on this wall when the Lord comes for His Kingdom." He laid a hand on Adrian's shoulder. "Do not trouble yourself about my safety, or the safety of our friends. God will take care of us. This I know."

Adrian heaved himself from the soft earth and took up the handles of the cart to fetch a load of stone. His thoughts strayed to the castle on the hill and he found himself praying for a chance to wield a sword against his enemies.

Two days later, Adrian perched on a log stool across a low fire from Grandfather after their work was finished. Crickets began their evening chorus alongside the riverbank, first one, then two and then a dozen. Dragonflies darted over the swiftly moving water. The sun descended majestically behind the pine-crested ridge to the west and Venus, a bright little star on the horizon below a crescent moon, appeared.

Adrian's glance returned time and again to the turreted castle where lights blazed from many windows and he thought of the festivities there—the lords and ladies dancing to music being played from the balcony of the Great Hall, the food and wine, the laughter and camaraderie of the knights. "Tis said they are having a grand fete in the castle in a fortnight. It is to honor the wedding of Sir Frederick and the duchess Maria. It will be a grand affair."

Grandfather glanced up from the Scripture texts he was reading by the light of a candle. "I was hoping to keep you busy enough that your mind would not dwell upon it." He studied Adrian for a moment and put away his parchments. "Would you like to go inside the castle? To see some of the guests?"

"Aye." Adrian prodded the fire with a stick, trying to appear nonchalant even though his heart thudded heavily. "Is it possible?"

"It is. As you know, there will be many village people entering the castle throughout the day of the wedding. Some of them will work in the kitchens and the stables. I can see that you find employment, but I need to know if this is what you truly desire. Will it not arouse your passions? Fire your worldly imaginations? As the Scriptures saith, boy, 'Watch over thine heart, for out of it cometh the affairs of your life.'"

The old anger surged in Adrian's veins, and he longed to jump, to yell, to break the bonds of his servitude. Yet he pushed it down and sat thoughtfully, staring into the fire. "Do you not trust me after so long a time, Grandfather? Please tell me what I should do to find employment in the castle and I pledge to mind my ways and keep to the business set before me."

The old man did not answer at once, but gazed into the fire. "FitzRauf has increased his holdings and rises in power. I hear that he has set his sights on being King John's right-hand man. He is wicked and must be stopped."

Adrian nodded. "Aye. He sets whole villages alight and takes what he wants. I shall fight him, then. Perchance it is he who threatens the Longbeards. I shall fight him and I shall win." He stood in the old fighting stance, arms akimbo, back straight.

Grandfather shook his head, laying a hand on Adrian's tattered sleeve. "Nay, the time is not right. The good Lord will bring your enemy to you. Until then, leave the matter with Him." He chuckled. "Besides, you have not touched sword or rapier in many days. You are out of form, my son." He disappeared into the wagon, rummaged in it for some time, then returned.

Adrian looked up in surprise, for the old man carried a sword. It was in a golden gilded scabbard. The hilt was intricately wrought.

When Grandfather handed it to him hilt first, he took it reverently, for it reminded him of his father's blade.

"This be my sword, and I need it not, for I am past fighting for myself. I have kept this back, waiting for the right moment to give it to you. That moment has come. I beg of you not to wear it just yet. Practice only in private. As I said before, God's time will come for you to use it against your enemies."

"Grandfather, I know not how to thank you. This gift ... " He wiped tears from his eyes and sank to his knees. "I pledge thee, my lord. I shall use this sword only for knightly purposes. I shall make you proud of the one you saved from death."

For a week Adrian practiced in the forest. Grandfather found an ancient blade from a friend and parried with him. Adrian discovered that the old man was no mean swordsman and was able with little effort to thwart his advances and disarm him.

"Slow! Slow!" Old Bric's voice rang out. "Let it come. You are too eager. You must learn to time your advances. Watch your enemy's eyes. Handle your blade with a light touch. See? See how little effort it takes to disarm? Let it come into your circle."

Occasionally Adrian would hear "Well done!" from his master and feel a rush of pride. Soon it became apparent that his old skill, combined with the new strength of his arms and hands and the instruction of his teacher, brought him to a height of proficiency that he had never gained before.

One morning as it approached the first of May, a day when the village folk celebrated with a grand fete in the village green, Grandfather gave Adrian a task. "We are having a meeting tonight," he said when they broke their fast that morning. "And I need someone to tell the men in LaRoche. Dost thou know where that is, boy?"

Adrian glanced up from his porridge. "Aye."

"Go to Peter's house. He be the headman. His house is on the village green. Tell him that we will hold the meeting here, tonight, at LaVerne's. There is something of great import that we must discuss."

"What?"

The old man shook his head. "I canna say. If you come to the meeting, you shall hear. Suffice it to say that we are in grave danger."

Adrian's heart stood still. Blood pounded to his face as fear gripped his mind with cold fingers. He leaped to his feet. "It is as I said, Grandfather! We must flee. Why do you need a meeting? It is you they are after. Come, let us pack up the wagon. Today! Now!" He took a step toward Bess.

"Stay!" Grandfather rose, his face flushed. "I am the one who gives the orders, boy. You are free to go whither you would, but I will stay here. I fear no man. No, not even the fornicator in the castle. The danger I spoke of was not for ourselves, but for the maidens of this village. We have word that Sir Frederick has seen Aimee and intends to take her. Now, run, boy! Run as if your life depended on it!"

Adrian bowed, then took to his heels down the lane toward the village of LaRoche. He knew it was not far, yet it would take him most of the morning to reach it, deliver his message and run back. Even as he ran, fear pricked his heels, making him run faster and faster till there was little breath in his lungs.

He halted by a spring, caught his breath and drank. Then he ran on. The sun, mildly warm that morning, was now his enemy. Sweat trickled down his back; he was not taking enough breaks or drinking enough water. Fear increased as he ran, as if a thousand howling demons were circling, jabbering, torturing his soul.

The village lay sleepily in the late morning sun, its thatched roof houses and scraggily village green like any other. He found the headman's house without delay, for it was the largest near the village green. He delivered his message to the man himself, who had just come in from the field for his noon-day meal. "I am ... Adrian, Old Bric's grandson. He has ... sent me to tell you there is a meeting ... tonight ... in Montebank." He accepted a cup of ale. "It ... is of great importance."

Peter nodded slowly. He was thin and tall, dressed well and carried himself with importance, for he was a freedman. He swiped his forehead and beckoned for Adrian to sit. "Join us in our meal that the good wife is preparing. I remember thee. How is Old Bric?"

Adrian's head swam; he had trouble keeping the man's face in focus. "He is ... " He knew he was falling, but could do nothing to stop it. He heard the clang of the cup on the hard-packed ground. He did not see lights or hear bells or see visions. Blackness enveloped his mind with the suddenness of a falling curtain.

When he awoke, he sensed that the sun was beginning its swing to the west, shadows were longer, the breeze was cooler. He lay on a bench under the huge locust tree in the headman's toft. Two dogs lay beside him, as if keeping guard. He sat up, waited until his head cleared, then stood.

The good wife ran to him. "You must lay down again, young sir. Peter said you must stay the night, that you are very ill. You are as pale as the new moon."

Adrian shook his head. "Nay, I must be off. Thank you for the ale. Fare well."

"Wait! Please do not leave." She disappeared into the house and returned with a flask and a cloth bag. "Here. Take this and welcome."

He thanked her, bowing courteously, and began to run back to the village. He ran only a furlong and had to stop, for his legs gave out and his breath failed him. He stopped to rest and drink the ale and eat a bit of the food.

The sun was sinking when he topped the last rise. A pall of smoke hung over the village and with bursting lungs, he ran the last hundred feet. Cottages were burned, debris lay scattered heedlessly, dogs and small children wandered helplessly, wailing filled the air with the acrid, stinking smoke.

Too late! I am too late!

He ran into the village, past the cottages of the folk he had come to know and love. Remnants of clothing, broken furniture, tools...and bodies. They lay in bloody heaps, grotesque and misshapen, awkward in death, like broken dolls a small and impish child might toss about a room.

His focus was LaVerne's home, for Grandfather had been a guest at her home that evening, as they were most evenings. It was burned and gutted. He ran into it, shrieking aloud for Grandfather, for LaVerne, for Aimee. No answer.

In the croft he saw a foot lying beneath a rubble of brambles. Closer inspection showed it was LaVerne, dead. Beside her, in a twisted heap, lay Aimee, beautiful and bloodied, with a hoe in her hand as if she had attempted to save her grandmother. The black dog huddled beside them, silent in his misery.

Adrian swiped at his eyes, for a mist seemed to enshroud his vision. He had seen a lot of deaths and had killed many on a field of battle, yet this was beyond anything he had ever experienced. He wanted to scream, to shake the dead bodies and bring life back into them.

He glanced up at the castle spires and shook his fist.

Where is Grandfather? Blood had dripped on the ground. He followed the trail. Near the creek he found Guillaume, his head split open, blood puddled around him. Adrian retched, bending over a small bush, then retched again. When he returned to the cottage and pulled at the burnt beams, he knew Grandfather was not there.

He screamed, his voice a long wail, piercing the evening air as the sun sank behind the hill and darkness crept over the sky.

It was his fault. If only he had run faster. If only Grandfather had moved the wagon. *The wagon!* Wiping tears from his face with blackened hands, he bolted in blind fury across the village green to the fringe of trees by the river. The wagon was burned—an empty shell.

He pawed through the smoldering ruins, calling out for Grandfather. He came upon a pair of sandals. Grandfather's good sandals. He caressed them. Surely, surely Grandfather could not be dead. He searched under the wagon and behind the bushes, sobbing, desperate, dropping one sandal in his haste.

"Grandfather!" His voice was hoarse, so often had he called. Then the truth dawned upon him. Grandfather was gone. "Nay!" He threw the shoe as far as he could.

"Aye," a man's voice sounded behind him. Adrian jumped and turned. It was Peter, the headman from LaRoche.

Peter retrieved the shoe, walking slowly across the green, returning just as slowly. He reminded Adrian of Grandfather in his unhurried manner. "I say aye." Peter handed him the shoe. His brown eyes flashed with anger and his lips were a thin, white line. "This has happened. We grieve. But God's grace is sufficient and we must go on."

"But what of Grandfather?" Adrian sat hard on one of the stumps where he and Grandfather had partaken of their meals. It seemed like just minutes ago when they had eaten here last. "Do you know what has become of him?"

Peter pulled the other stump close and leaned over, whispering. "For certes, my son. He was taken. I saw them with my own eyes. He was taken to the castle." He lifted his eyes to the pennant swaying in the evening breeze from the donjon of the north tower. "It was Sir Frederick."

Adrian shuddered. "I could not run fast enough. It is my fault." His throat closed and he lowered his head to his hands as great sobs shook his body.

Peter let him weep with no comment.

After awhile, Adrian lifted his head. "What did you say of Grandfather?"

"They came looking for him, for all who were involved with the Longbeards. That is why LaVerne and her husband were killed and the cottage burned. I had just arrived in the village and scrambled up a tree, but there was naught I could do." His voice wavered and he looked to the horizon where a blaze of color lit the sky. Tears glittered on his cheek.

Adrian straightened. "It was not FitzRauf and his son alone. The other night I was down by the river and I saw and overheard two men discussing a plot." He told Peter what he overheard and that it was Morgan Barnwell who betrayed them.

The old man nodded. "Aye, I know where Morgan Barnwell stands, for he is a Norman. The baron has his hallmote in a month. Will you testify against Barnwell if we bring charges?"

Adrian nodded. "I will, if I am still here. But will FitzRauf listen?"

"Aye. He will listen. He must listen." Children still cried for their mothers from the village. Every now and then someone lifted a wailing voice. A mourning dove cooed for its mate. "That does not solve our problem. Old Bric is in the castle and no one escapes from the dungeons of the castle Renault. I have lived here all my life and no one has ever escaped."

Adrian nodded, for he knew how secure those places were. "What may be done to save Grandfather, then?"

"Naught can be done, young man. Even your grandfather would say that the Lord has destined him for such a thing. He would not want men risking their lives to save him."

"But, man, you do not know what they will do to him!" Adrian stood to his feet. In his ears he heard the hideous wails of men whose eyes were burned from their sockets. "If FitzRauf can elicit information from Grandfather about the activities of the Longbeards, he can use that information to win the favor of the barons of

Brittany. And then it will be easy for him to take the reins of this country, especially if his son marries the duchess, and ..."

Peter looked at him with a new light in his eyes. "You do not speak as a servant. How do you know so much? Who are you?"

Adrian knew he had spoken rashly, but his heart was heavy and his pain drove all caution from his mind. "This is no time to ask questions. Perchance I am more than a servant boy. You may ask Grandfather when he is free."

"And how do you plan to accomplish this thing? If you are to be successful, you must act quickly."

Adrian sat down again and cradled his head in his hands. "I have no plan, save that I must rescue him. Wait. The wedding is to be held in ... ten days, is it not? I can enter the castle then, for they will be looking for people to work. And then ... "

"And then? You will free your grandfather alone?"

Adrian looked at him and nodded. "Alone, if need be. I pray thee, lend me whatever aid you may."

Peter stood and bowed. "I will see what I can do. Meet me in the meadow by the twin oaks when the moon clears the trees."

CHAPTER FOURTEEN

One hand cannot clap alone. Arab Proverbs

Tours, France, April 1201

"I must travel on to Orleans as soon as I may, Father." Louis stood in the abbot's office, his hands gripping the back of the chair to keep himself upright, for he was so weak he could not sit nor stand for long.

Abbot Bernard was a portly man in his early sixties. While Louis forbore to judge his superiors, he had taken an instant dislike to the man, primarily because of his love for the fine things of the world that were denied, and even harshly condemned, for the lower ranking brothers.

Louis had stepped into a different world when he entered this office. In one glimpse he saw heavy brocaded drapes at the window, an oak desk, a chair made of mahogany, thick carpet underfoot and gold glittering from the cressets on the walls and the quill on the desktop.

He brought his mind back to what the abbot was saying.

"… and therefore, I feel it would be unsafe for you to travel at this time. You may rest here, Brother, and heal, for I know thou hast not fully recovered from your wounds. Whatever messages you must send to Orleans may be sent through one of my couriers."

Louis gazed at him. The abbot's eyes were like black diamonds, cold and hard and glittering; his face was flushed, his fists were clenched. What have I done to arouse his anger? "Nay, Father, I seek nothing but to continue my journey. I was sent to visit the monastery in Orleans. There is a great physician there I would like to consult as part of my training. I am from Mont St. Michael's, you know. I am studying to be a physician and would like to go on to Alexandria. I feel well enough to travel, if you would be so kind as to arrange a wagon, as I do not care to travel horseback. Is that too much to ask, Father Abbot?"

Abbot Bernard stood, adjusted his robe and paced around the desk to stand in front of Louis, piercing him with a long, steady gaze, as if to search his very soul. He nodded. "I would that thou stay with us for a time, Brother. As I said, you are unwell. What is a month? Is this journey of yours so urgent that you must hasten?"

Louis took a step backward and dropped his eyes. His palms were sweaty; he strove to keep his breath steady, though his heart thumped hard in his chest. It came as a shock—his enemies did not only lie in wait for him in the forest, but were in the blessed Church he served. This man suspected that he was a spy. Evidently Abbot Bernard knew of the message to the pope, of the rumors about the new crusade and did not want the message to reach the holy father. Why? Was it money? Did he have partners who would send him gold from the cities the crusaders ravaged?

"I hear and will obey, Father." Louis bowed. "I ask permission to leave."

Father Bernard laid his hand on Louis' shoulder. "Let me bless thee, my son. Then go and rest and be at ease with the burden you carry. Again I say, if there is a message you would like to send to the abbey in Orleans, please see me. We have the finest couriers in the world, and the safest. You will do that, won't you?"

Louis nodded. "Yea, Father. I will do all you say for I am only a lowly monk and I have pledged myself to the Church to serve her. Nothing shall stand in my way." He knew immediately he should not have added the last. Why had he said that? Even to his ears it sounded defiant.

But the abbot seemed not to notice. "Very well, my son. Kneel and I shall bless thee."

Louis knelt, but his flesh crawled with the touch of the abbot's hand on his head. How could it be that he would feel like this about a priest, a revered member of his order?

Back in his room, Louis paced while Samson John sat on the cot, his knees caught up to his chin. The walls of the monastery closed about Louis, as would a prison. He looked at the pack beside his bed and turned to face the boy. "Has anyone touched the pack, Samson John? Anyone at all?"

The boy's eyes widened and he shook his head.

"You have never left it out of your sight, as I told you?"

Again the boy shook his head.

Louis sighed and slumped down on the bed. "You have done well." He leaned closer to the boy. "We must get out of here—soon. Our enemies are within these very walls. I do not feel safe here any longer, for they may ... " The sound of feet approached in the hall, then went on. "We must leave."

Samson John's eyes widened even farther.

Louis collapsed on the bed while Samson John went for water. His shoulder throbbed again and he felt hot and sweaty. But he could not give in to his sickness. How could he flee? There were guards at the gate. Could he bribe them? He sat up, cradling his head in his hands. *Oh, God. I do not want this life of spying and playing at the game of politics. I am just a common man. Oh, Lord, what should I do?*

The answer came quickly. *Do what you have been given to do, even though you like it little.*

But how could this thing be accomplished? *Eh, bein.* He would escape and flee. If this was God's will, God would provide him the way and the means. Yet his spirit cringed at the thought. He would become an outcast monk; Father Bernard would blacken his name to prevent him from gaining help from other monasteries. It had happened before—it could happen to him.

Nevertheless, he must do it.

***

The Castle Renault, April 1201

Judith was not held in the dungeons, but she was not allowed freedom, either. Upon her arrival, she was led to a courtyard with five other slaves and told to strip. A group of the servants stood close about her, both men and women. A tub of cold water with lye in it stood ready.

When it was her turn to strip off her clothes and step into the water, her face grew hot and she felt shamed beyond anything she could have imagined. Strange, hostile eyes glared at her. Was there no friendly face in the crowd? She clenched her fists and stared straight ahead, as if it didn't matter. But it did. Pulling her cloak of hatred down over her soul, she reminded herself they were accursed heathen Christians and she hated each of them—hated them, hated them.

She was able to slip the capsule into her mouth, remembering Miguel's account of how he hid his chain and ring. The capsule was preserved, but the long-held secret of her gender could not be hidden.

"We thoughts you be a boy!" An older serving woman declared through missing teeth. "I'se thinkin' thas's what the masser thught, too." Her bold stare at Judith's maturing body sent a cold chill through the girl.

"Wait til he finds out he's got hisself a maiden." This from a girl.

Judith lifted her eyes to the speaker. The girl was about her own age, her face badly scarred, disfiguring her natural good looks. The girl kept her long black hair hanging down over her face, but Judith looked directly into her eyes. Blue eyes. Mocking eyes.

"Will you tell him?" She lifted her chin and stepped into the water, grateful that it was murky and hid her body.

The girl ducked her head and said nothing. The others hooted ribald remarks, but none said outright that they would betray her to the master. Something beyond fear—perhaps it was terror—gripped the servants whenever they spoke of Sir Frederick.

Judith lived with ten other servants in a long sordid hut where cots lined the walls and the floor was dirt, uncovered by rushes. Her duties began before the sun rose, even before the cock crowed. She fetched water, helped in the kitchen, turned meat on spits in front of the hot fires, ran errands, cleaned hallways, tended the chickens and pigs, washed clothes. Each evening she fell into bed, exhausted, sore and dirty.

Of Sir Frederick, she saw nothing at all. The servants whispered that he was away to the northeast at the bidding of his father. But in a fortnight's time he would return, to wed the duchess of Brittany. Then the castle would be cleansed from top to bottom, a feast would be prepared and barons from far and wide would come.

Judith decided she must escape before that day, for above all, she feared being taken to Sir Frederick as a girl—a girl he may desire to humble in more ways than one.

Her hatred kept the other servants at arm's length, but she allowed a friendship to develop with Meredith, the scarred-face girl who occupied the bunk next to hers. The girl was not the beaten down, poor specimen of humanity that Judith thought at first. She was witty, willful and desperate to escape.

"The master will not keep me when he learns of my face," she told Judith once as they washed the clothes together in the moat. "It happened months ago, but I have been able to hide my face from him so far."

"What will he do with you?"

The girl shrugged. "He will not sell me, could not sell me. Nay, he will lock me away and I shall starve to death. That is what he does with those he cannot abide. And that is why I must escape." She turned to Judith and her eyes flashed. "I feel that you have the same thoughts. That you are planning an escape. Can we do this thing together?"

Judith shushed her, for Berthe, the older serving woman, their supervisor, approached. As soon as she was gone, Judith confided in Meredith that indeed she did want to escape. But before she fled the castle, she had to learn the fate of her father. "Could you ask someone, perchance one of the older men, for me? My father is a Jew, a wealthy Jew, who traveled from Dijon to Marseilles in a group of four other men. I suspect he was sold as a slave. This was nearly three years ago. When we are free, I shall reward you handsomely, for my father's relatives descended from the great Rashi and they are very wealthy."

Meredith shrugged again and lifted her load of wash. "I shall see what I can do. In the meantime, think up a plan to escape. The master will return soon and I must be away."

"And so must I." Judith brushed back her hair and lifted her load, her legs and back screaming with pain. How could they escape? Where would they go? *Oh, Yahweh, please look down upon Your handmaid. I plead with You. You saw Hagar, Lord. Please see me.*

***

Adrian returned to LaVerne's cottage and dug shallow graves near the stream. A few neighbors stood at a distance with lowered heads as he turned the last shovel of dirt and prayed aloud. Opening his eyes, he looked again at the castle.

It was time—time to use his sword. He ran to the secret hiding place near the stream where he kept his sword and tied it about his waist, then made his way to the twin oaks by the river. The sun's last rays cast a pale pinkish streak on the western horizon. Venus and a few of her friends appeared in the pale sky. He perched on a log, mapping out his plan.

Hoof beats. He looked up. Peter trotted down the lane, panting with the effort of keeping up with the energetic strides of a horse—a long-legged bay with noble blood in his veins. Adrian leaped up, greeted the horse, rubbed his neck and ears, taking note of his intelligent eyes and rippling muscles.

"Ah, Peter. This is a fine steed. Where did you get him?"

"He belonged to a knight who was unhorsed at the last tournament and unclaimed by the victor. Some of us have taken care of him and I knew where to find him. I am sorry I have only a saddle … "

"Be that as it may. I care not for a knight's emblems." He leaped to saddle and rode in a tight circle, both horse and man testing each other's mettle.

"What be your intent, my lord?" Peter grasped the bridle when Adrian halted.

"I must get into the castle. Can you help me?"

Peter nodded, his dark eyes twinkling. "I canna promise you the outcome, but I know a man. If I can find him, shall I tell him to meet with you? Here? Tonight?"

"Good friend, if you can find this man, I shall wait the night for him. Thank you! You do not know how much you have proven your friendship to me … to Grandfather." His throat tightened. He dismounted, keeping his back turned, not willing for Peter to see his face.

Peter slapped Adrian's back. "While you wait, here is some food my good wife prepared." He handed over a packet wrapped in oilskin.

Adrian received it, thanked him again. "When you say your prayers, please say one for me."

"That I shall, lad. That I shall."

The night was still, except for the occasional hoot of an owl and a chorus of crickets. Adrian said his prayers, as much of them as he could remember, and spoke in low tones to the horse that he named Bret for the land he loved. Bret seemed to enjoy the sound of his voice, for he tossed his head and nickered low.

The evening drew in. A wind freshened from the west, the clouds parted and a moon sailed high in the sky. As Adrian drank from the river, a hand gripped his shoulder. He leaped to his feet. A man stood behind him with thumbs tucked into his belt and a somber look on his face. His dark hair lay flat on his head; a trim beard framed his jaw.

"By St. Anne! I heard you not! Are you a spirit?"

The man bowed, a ghost of a smile playing on his lips. "Leon Fitzgerald at your service."

Adrian bowed. "Adrian D'Arcy at your service. I pray you may help me, sir."

"That depends upon the good Lord's will. What be your problem?"

Adrian took a deep breath and looked out over the river. "Baron FitzRauf and his son Sir Frederick razed the village and took my grandfather, Old Bric, prisoner to the castle." He glanced up, for the torches were lit in the highest towers. "I am only a servant boy, yet I must free my grandfather. I entreat you. Will you help me?"

In the dim light, he saw the man nod. "You speak well for being a village lad. I wager you are something more than that." Leon glanced over his shoulder and, for the first time, Adrian noticed several other men standing a little distance away.

"And you, too, my lord," he said in a low voice. "You are something more than a trailbastion, an outlaw. You are the son of Baron Maurice Phillip Fitzgerald, sixteen generations in a line descended direct from the great king Henry Capet. Your family owns vast lands and holdings in Picardy and Artios. Your father fought with King Richard in the Crusades. Shall I continue, sir?"

"Stay!" Sir Leon held up his hand and bent his head to peer into Adrian's face. Adrian drew back, yet he saw recognition, disbelief and amazement flashed in swift succession across Sir Leon's face. "You know much for a mere village lad, Adrian," Leon said, his voice heavy with sarcasm. "Is this the name you have taken? And how did this miracle occur when all the world thinks .... No matter.

Your secret will be safe with me. I care nothing for kings, politics, or the quarrels of nations."

Adrian bowed. "I am glad to hear that."

Leon walked to the riverside. "Be that as it may, what you intend to do is impossible. You may as well say your prayers for Old Bric and go about your business, for his fate has been sealed by the great God above. I know whereof I speak."

Hope drained from Adrian's heart as surely as if a bucket of water suddenly sprang a hole. *Impossible. I know whereof I speak.* The words seemed to echo in the clearing. Yes, it was impossible. Who was he to dare such a thing?

An owl screeched in the quiet that descended on the small clearing, and the river gurgled as it flowed over its smooth stones. Something turned in Adrian's heart. He lifted his eyes to the red windows of the castle. He could hardly breathe. It felt as if he was crossing a bridge that would crumble beneath his feet as soon as he stepped out.

Then, in a flash, his courage returned. "I know whereof I speak, too, my lord. I will do this thing or I will perish trying it. My life is forfeit and would have ceased, had it not been for the kindness of that old man. All I ask is that you speak naught of my mission, and aid me however you may. If you cannot aid me, then step aside and say a prayer for me, for I will not be turned."

Leon stared at him, his eyes glinting, his face still. Experience, wisdom and integrity were etched on that face. He smiled and it seemed as if the sun came from behind the clouds. "I will aid you, and so will my men, for we are all loyal to the cause. Come, sit, and we will talk." He turned and raised his voice. "Come, my good men. Meet my new friend. We have work to do."

His words drew men flocking from their hiding places. Someone brought a light, someone else laid wood and soon a bright fire sprang up. They ate a fair-sized meal of the baron's deer, fresh loaves of bread, and cheese. They drank gallons of ale.

Leon surrounded himself with a crew of hardy and seasoned men. The chief of these was a huge bulk of a man. "Come, Tate," he called.

Adrian was staring up, up, up … the man seemed to tower above him, and held out his hand. Tate crunched Adrian's fingers in his massive paw. The other men laughed when they saw pain on

Adrian's face. Tate's long black hair stuck out on all sides of his head, and his bristly beard accentuated a square jaw and dark eyes, eyes that gleamed fiercely.

Luthar came next. He was a cold hard man who carried a longbow like it grew from his shoulder. He eyed Adrian with suspicion and did not offer his hand. Adrian knew it would take many days and many miles to prove his worth to this man. Hager, a seasoned fighter, wore an eye patch. The hatred that blazed from his good eye scalded Adrian from head to toe. He carried an ax, and there was no doubt he used it for things other than trees.

One other man came from behind and gave Adrian a slap on his back that nearly knocked him over. "I am Gabriel, and regardless of my appearance I am not an angel." The others laughed. "I am last for meals, last for the women, and last for the gold." He was young, perhaps Adrian's age, with brown hair tinged with blond that he wore in a long braid down his back.

"Gold," roared Tate. "When has anyone here seen the color of gold? And women? What has been withheld from me, Leon?"

"Nothing, nothing." Leon laughed. "Go sit down and finish the baron's deer."

Adrian's heart gave a leap. In this company, the task seemed possible. There were other men who sat farther from the fire, their faces in the shadows.

Leon leaned closer when they had finished their meal. "Sir Frederick arrived yesterday. What is your plan, Adrian?"

"I have no plan." Adrian shook his head. "I only know we must strike soon."

Leon considered this for some time, then lifted his head. "In a week they will feast and celebrate as never before, for Sir Frederick will wed his betrothed, the Duchess Maria. We shall strike that day, for their guard will be down." He nodded. "This is good. It will give us a chance to plan."

Adrian shifted his feet. "But I hate to think of grandfather in the dungeons that long. Will he be safe? Will he survive?"

Tate grunted. "They will do nothing to the prisoners until after the wedding. This consumes all their thoughts. I know, for my friend is a squire to one of the knights. He gives me news."

Leon patted Adrian's knee. "Your grandfather, as you call him, is of tough material. He will survive. That you can depend upon."

193

"Very well." Adrian took a deep breath. "I shall camp here with this fine horse that my friend brought to me. On the day of the wedding, will the village people bring supplies into the castle?"

"For certes." Leon stoked the fire. "There will be a constant flow of villagers into the castle. It will begin with the first light."

Adrian stood and looked around at the twenty or so men who talked among themselves further back. "Can these men be trusted, my lord?"

"Aye. They are from the villages nearby. We come together, for the baron's lusts have reached to heaven, along with the cries of the innocents. Every man here has lost a wife, or a daughter, or a mother to the fornicator up there. You may count on them."

"This, then, is my plan." Adrian raised his voice. A hush fell. "We must wreak God's vengeance on this man, for he murdered many in Montebank. We must infiltrate the castle and free my grandfather who was taken a prisoner. There will be men inside and outside. We will need someone who knows the castle, a servant, perchance. While the wine flows and the food is consumed and the noble barons and lords make merry, we will do our work. What think you, Leon? Is this a fair plan? Can we work it on short notice?"

Leon studied the flames flickering down into a rosy bed. He nodded. "I have the men. You outline exactly what we are to do and we will do it. I can say thus: we will free the prisoners—all the prisoners—from their wretched fate or we will perish in the attempt. What say you, my men? Some of you may die. What is your wish?"

As of one voice, they spoke the word, "Aye!" with such vehemence that Adrian did not doubt them from that moment on. Slowly they drifted away as the night deepened and the moon laid herself to rest in the west.

Soon all were gone but Leon, his friends and Adrian. Silence descended as they allowed the night to gather itself around their heads. Gabriel, who at one time had been a monk, led in a prayer.

They watched the fire die as the stars peeped out and the crickets went to bed.

***

"Here. Take this to the old man, the prisoner they hold in the farthest cell. Titus will show you the way." Berthe set a bucket of slop and a flask of water on the ground. Behind her stood her husband, a slovenly man who tended the pigs.

Judith looked up from the chicken she was plucking. She stood slowly and bowed her head. "Yes, my lady." The bucket contained a sloppy mess of porridge, pieces of vegetables and fish eyes. The smell turned her stomach, but she picked it up and followed after Titus.

He lit a torch and led off down the hallways, through arches and past numerous doors, descending into the bottom of the castle and coming at last to a locked door. A guard opened it.

Beyond the door was another hall, cell doors lining each side. The guard opened a heavy iron door of the last cell and stepped back. Judith entered. Titus stood outside, his torch held high so she could see.

The smell nearly took her breath away. She did not want to see, but there along the wall sat an old man, his feet manacled to the wall. His hair was matted and dirty with straw, his beard gray-black with filth, his clothes tattered and soiled. His eyes held hers.

"Good even, daughter. I would bow before you, but as you can see, I am not allowed." His voice was low and he displayed no despair, grief or pain. Yet she knew the cruel manacles must hurt.

In that second when their eyes met, she thought of her own beloved grandfather. This was someone's grandfather and he was being treated worse than an animal. Tears sprang to her eyes as she knelt beside him in the reeking straw and carefully set down the bucket. Then she glanced at Titus.

"Leave me, Titus." She stood and approached him, laying a hand on his arm. "Please. I wish to speak to him whilst he eats. I know the way back and shall bring the bucket when I come."

Titus frowned. "It is not allowed, Joseph." He sighed, glancing back down the tunnel and shifting his feet. "Very well. I shall tell the guard to let you out." His gaze shifted to the old man. "He canna' go far, chained as he is to the wall. Yet it puzzles me why you would stay in such a pigsty. How can you abide it?"

She flashed him a smile, thinking of the name the other servants had given her to hide her identity. "I had a grandfather once and my heart goes out to this one. Thank you." She returned to the old man and squatted beside him, pulling her tunic over her knees. "You had better eat, Grandfather. You must keep up your strength."

"Aye, I will. Yet I would rather you do not watch me, for it is a messy affair."

"As you wish." She turned her gaze to the far wall where someone had scrawled dates. She waited while she heard the slurping progress of his meal. "Have you been here long?"

"Long? How do you measure time? For me each day is an eternity, yet I have hope."

The guard appeared at the doorway, his torch sputtering. "When he is finished, you must leave."

Judith bent her head. "Very well." She waited while the guard disappeared and the darkness closed in again. She shivered. How could the old man bear the darkness, the chill and discomfort? "Hope? You have hope, good sir?"

"Aye." His voice was a whisper. "I have friends. They will come for me. My grandson will come for me."

"I, too, must escape, for even though I am not confined to a cell and chained to the wall, I am just as much as prisoner as you. I must flee. I am a girl and I cannot allow the master to find me out, for he is very wicked. My real name is Judith. Sir Frederick has returned and I hoped to be gone by now. I am seeking information about my father who was taken as a slave and … well, I do not want to burden you with my misfortunes. What is the name of your grandson who will come to your aid?"

The guard's footsteps approached.

The old man finished his meal and drank from the flask. He wiped his mouth. He leaned close and whispered. "Adrian. He is only a young man, yet I know he will come." His blue gaze studied her face. "Judith. It is a Jewish name, no?"

"It is, grandfather. I am a Jew, yet few here know it. My father was taken and sold as a slave and my mother was killed. Baron FitzRauf did this. I have vowed to … "

The guard was at the door.

She rose. "I go now." Her heart wrenched to leave him like this. "My prayers shall be with thee."

"Thank you, Jospeh. You are a ray of sunshine in my darkness. Because of you, I shall hang on and wait until either my grandson or the blessed angel of light appears. *Au revoir.*"

She bowed, picked up the bucket, and fled.

***

An early morning breeze stirred Adrian's fair hair as he lay in a crease of the ground, covered with his saddle blanket. A raven cawed harshly in the tall pines. He opened his eyes and rolled out of his bed just as a rosy light tinged the east.

This is the day. Oh, God. Please be with me. God? Which God? He shrugged. Any God would do today. He strapped his pack behind the saddle, led Bret to the village and tethered him behind the blacksmith's shop.

Leon greeted him at the door of the village inn. They ate a simple breakfast of brown bread and warm pottage and drank a tall cup of ale. Adrian noted the stir in the village, the stream of folks already making their way to the castle gate.

After Leon paid the bill, they walked to the back of the inn and stopped under a giant oak. He pressed something into Adrian's hands. It glinted golden in the light of the new day. It was a horn. "Since you will be among those inside the castle, sound the horn the moment we are to enter. We will be in the woods just beyond the postern gate. Our men inside will see that it is opened for us. We will cover your actions with a distraction—a very fine distraction. A castle is not made entirely of stone and mortar. Wood still burns, even FitzRauf's."

Adrian nodded. "Swords and weapons have already been smuggled into the castle. I promise you, when you hear the horn, we will have Grandfather."

"What then? We need a place for the prisoners, for if not, the baron will gather them again as surely as a mother hen finds her chicks."

Adrian thought of that problem for a time, then he smacked his hands together. "We will need wagons. Load the prisoners into the wagons just inside the wood and drive them with all speed possible to the monastery in Tours. We will find sanctuary for them at this place. I shall ride there with grandfather."

Leon nodded. "It is a good plan. I shall meet you there and afterward we shall talk."

More of the village people were making their way towards the castle with carts and wagons of coal and food. It was time. He turned to Leon, met his eyes squarely and shook his hand. "Aye, good friend. My prayers go with thee."

"And mine with thee."

***

Judith turned the pig on the spike over the fire, wiping her face, thinking about the old man held prisoner below her feet. Each night she brought him his supper and spoke quietly to him while he ate. Now it was the day of the great wedding and she was kept so busy she could not think of her plans for escape.

"Take this tray to my lord's chambers, girl." Berthe stepped to her side, bearing a tray loaded with mugs and sweetmeats. "Then come directly back."

Judith's heart fell, for she knew the woman was speaking of Sir Frederick, who entertained guests in his rooms. "I ... I do not know where his chambers are. I have never been in that part of the castle."

Berthe beckoned to Claude. "Go with Judith. Here, you can carry the wine. I am too busy this morning to ... " Her words were lost as she turned to her tasks.

Claude lifted the flask and started off through a doorway and up a flight of stairs into the castle proper. Judith lagged behind, trying to think of a way out of her dilemma. The thing she had vowed to avoid at any costs was happening. Sir Frederick must not see her as a girl, must not recognize her. She wore a simple tunic and had kept her hair shorn, but she feared her breasts would show through the thin material, that something in her face would betray her.

The apartment was crowded with people, both men and women, so she set the tray on a shelf near the door and turned away.

"Stop!" The voice held the ring of authority.

She was tempted to flee, but she knew she could not get away. She froze.

"Who do we have here? I do not recall this fresh young face among my slaves." Sir Frederick lifted her chin to study her face. "Ah. Perchance I do. I thought you were a boy, but you are a maid. And quite a lovely one."

"I think you will be too busy for slaves tonight." The comment came from one of the young men assembled in the room and was followed by a burst of laughter. Several of the young ladies colored and waved fans in front of their faces.

"I know." Sir Frederick held her still. She hated the touch of his fingers on her face and thought again of her vow to kill him. His short sword hung only inches from her hand on his belt … surely she could snatch it from the scabbard and plunge it into his heart.

"But this one fascinates me. It seems I know you from somewhere. What is your name, girl?"

Judith felt her face flush. She jerked from his grasp. "Judith Itzchaki. My father is Elias, the jeweler. I was here in your castle when I was a child." She lowered her voice to a whisper. "I have proof that you killed my mother and our servants. I recognized the emblem on your shield. I swear, I shall go to the king with my knowledge and you shall pay."

He stepped back from her as if he were stung. "I know not what you say, girl, but if I were you, I would keep a still tongue in my head. Remember, I have all the power here." He laughed suddenly, for the room had grown still. His friends seemed to lean closer to hear their conversation. "This one has spirit, I will give you that. It is why I keep her." He turned away. "Ah, well. Tonight I shall be wed, and that shall keep me busy for a while. But afterwards … " He snapped his fingers. "I shall humble that one."

The room burst into a roar of laughter as they reached for the wine goblets.

Judith fled, berating herself for her bold tongue. Why couldn't she have endured his taunts and escaped his presence? Now he knew her, and he knew the threat she posed to his well being. Would he set a special guard over her? She thought not. For a few hours she would be unguarded, for Frederick had his mind on his wedding.

She must escape. Today.

***

Adrian was among the first to be smuggled into the castle. Luthar, Gabriel and five other men from the village posed no problem, for they were well known to the guards at the castle gate and were often seen carrying live chickens and herding pigs past the gates or coming to tend the horses or rebuild a crumbling wall. But Adrian had to be stowed in a wagon under a pile of onions and cabbages and carrots. It was far from comfortable, and while the wagon trundled along, his mind raced ahead.

Would the plan work? Would he be able to free Grandfather? A great wave of doubt washed over him. How could he believe that a handful of village men with pickaxes and sticks could overcome the soldiers and knights of the court, free a prisoner from the dungeons and come out alive?

Last night the brave men of the village met again and filled him with comfort and encouragement with their talk around the campfire. But now ... now he trembled. Surely they would all die this night. Oh, for the soldiers he once commanded or the brave knights who carried his banners. He would give his very soul for the comfort of knowing his old friend, the Baron Hugh de Brun, fought by his side.

He listened as they rumbled across the outer drawbridge, as the gate clanged shut. The cart rolled across stones, down corridors and stopped at last. He leaped from the cart and found occupation in helping stable the horses of the guests who were streaming into the castle for the wedding that evening.

A voice rang out in the courtyard that he knew, but he did not turn to look. He helped a lady dismount, then casually glanced in the direction of the voice. DeArmond! Blinking back tears, he studied his former teacher. DeArmond's hair was peppered with white, yet his gait was the same, full of purpose and confidence, chin up, back straight.

A little later, while herding some pigs into a pen, Adrian felt a tug on his tunic. It was a short man with greasy hair. "Come with me. I will show you where the cells are."

Adrian followed behind the man down long stairways into the bowels of the castle. He carried a pot of porridge and a loaf of coarse bread in one hand, a candle in the other.

After following a labyrinth of narrow hallways, the man stopped at a metal door which barred their way. He banged on it. The dank stone walls echoed eerily and the candle sputtered. A guard eyed them through a small portal.

"Dinner for the prisoner," the man said. "For the old man. Open up!"

The door opened with a screech. Unlocking the last door in a long hall, the guard stepped aside so they could enter.

Adrian nearly cried aloud when he saw Grandfather sitting on a pile of putrid straw, chained to the wall by his ankles. He deposited the food dishes and the flask of water on the floor and gathered up the ones that were empty.

Grandfather looked up, but gave no cry; only his brows lifted and he smiled. Weariness etched his face, yet he seemed in good spirits. Adrian's heart lurched. He strove to control his emotions, for tears threatened and he had an insane desire to bash the guard on the head and free Grandfather then and there.

"God bless you," Grandfather said gently, reaching for the food to the clank of his chains. "I was afraid they had forgotten me today. You must be new, young man. For a week it has been a young maiden who…"

"Shut up, old man!" The guard hustled Adrian and the man into the hall. As Adrian left, he heard Grandfather say, "My prayers are with thee, my son."

The day wore on, tediously, as if reluctant to leave. Adrian waited in the kitchens, keeping occupied with whatever duty lay at hand. He noticed a young girl whose large, round eyes followed him from the fire to the pots to the animal sheds. Something about her drew his attention—not her looks, for her face was dirty and her clothes tattered. It was something in her eyes; they pulled at his heartstrings.

When he went to draw water, she followed behind. "Good sir," she said in a low voice. "You are new. There are many new faces here today. May I ask what is happening? I hear the servants whisper. They say—"

"Nothing is happening, save the wedding. I am from the village and was hired to work a day's labor in the castle to prepare for the wedding feast. It is the same with the others." He turned away, for he could not lose his focus. Many people had needs. He was here to free Grandfather.

She tugged on his sleeve. "Sir, please listen. I was taken against my will and am being held a slave to Sir Frederick. He is a demon. He—I have no time to tell you what he has done to me—but I beg you, aid me. I must escape before he … "

The burly overseer, a man who wielded the whip if the slaves tarried, poked his head from the kitchen doorway. "Hey, you! Get over here with that water, or you shall feel this whip!"

"I can do nothing for you, maiden." He turned away, but even as he did, he glimpsed the depths of her eyes, eyes that were filled with desperation.

She was not as she seemed, she had seen a different kind of life, perhaps a gentle and noble life. Her face held a winsome kind of beauty, yet she smelled of the pigsty and wood smoke. He brushed off her hand and hurried back to the kitchen. Nay, he could not help every waif that came to him for aid.

Toward evening, when shadows began to lengthen, Gabriel beckoned from the stable and led him into a vacant stall. "We need to know what is the state of the baron and the castle. You must serve the guests. Here, we found valet garments. Margarita will give you a tray of sweetmeats."

Adrian served the men's quarters without incident, not seeing Sir Frederick or his father, averting his face whenever a knight or baron of his acquaintance appeared in the hall.

Beside the door of one apartment, where a party of women dressed for dinner, he paused.

A serving woman saw him and beckoned him with a broad smile. "Come, Valet, come! My lady is in need of some refreshment!"

The women showed no distress at his entrance, even though some of them were in the process of disrobing. He kept his eyes downcast, but even in that position, he saw delicate undergarments cast on the floor. When he announced his errand, the ladies giggled and held out their white, dainty hands for the drinks.

One lady, upon whose slender hand rested an enormous emerald, laughed aloud when she caught a glimpse of his face. "Look, my friends. This valet is quite handsome. Oh, la, la! He blushes! Come, *mon chevalier.* You must remain with us, for you have taken our fancy."

"I cannot, fair lady." He shook his head, still not looking into the eyes of the speaker. "I am required to return to the kitchen as soon as I have finished." He bowed and tried to make a hasty retreat when the lady gripped his arm with surprisingly strong fingers.

"*Soit!* You must tarry with us. We perish of tedium. I shall speak for thee, *cherie!* Come now, look me in the eye. Am I so poorly to look upon that you turn your face from me?"

He lifted his eyes and looked into the soft color of windswept sea waves breaking upon a stormy shore. Shining coils of brown hair were piled high on her head; her full, sweet lips curved naturally into a smile; her delicate, arched eyebrows accentuated her eyes; her smooth, white skin seemed to be made of porcelain. "*Merci*, my lady. I kept my eyes lowered because of my position, not because I thought you were lacking in appearance. Please forgive me." He lifted her hand to his lips.

She laughed as if she had discovered a marvelous wonder. "*Viola!* A courtier and a knight in the garb of a servant. Whence is this, my fine young man? Will you tell me your story?" The ladies clapped their hands, but at that moment, a distant gong sounded.

"We must go, Lady Matilde," one of the older women said, trying to draw her away from Adrian. "He is nothing more than a servant. You must not waste time on such as he. Come, *mon ami*. We will be chastised if we are late."

Lady Matilde turned to him. "Wait for me here, Sir Valet," she whispered. "I want to hear your story, for I see it in your eyes. Wait for me outside the apartment. There is an anteroom. Pray say you will."

How could he resist? She was beautiful, charming, and what was more, he knew her to be his relative—a cousin once removed, the granddaughter of his father's sister, Joanne. "I promise to tell you my story some day, my lady. Not tonight, for now I must go."

The ladies bustled from the apartment. Lady Matilde pressed his hand and gave him a backward glance as she hurried down the hall. With a sigh, he started for the kitchens, moving carefully down the stone corridor where torches gave a flickering light from cressets high on the wall.

A voice boomed down the corridor and he looked up. Baron FitzRauf with several lords and ladies approached. *Hide!* Close by was an indentation in the stone wall which was used by the servants for storing supplies from the kitchen. Ducking into it and pulling a thin curtain across the opening, he waited. A wooden cupboard had been built within, the bottom of which was devoid of shelves.

The baron's party moved down the corridor. Adrian was about to see if the way was clear when he heard a man's voice. "Stay! I would speak with you. Here, in private."

Peering out, he saw two barons who stood nearby, very close to the closet where he hid. The darkness hid their faces.

"Do you think your plans will succeed?" The smaller man's voice was high and womanish. He fiddled with the gold tassels on his tunic.

Adrian cast into his memory for recognition of the voice but no name sprang to mind.

The larger of the two, an older man by the sound of his voice, was more confident. "If I did not think so, we would not attempt it." Adrian knew this one—the Comte Henri de Grand Pre, a pompous fool who extended his boundaries much as FitzRauf did. He leaned closer, their linen tunics mere inches from his nose.

Comte de Pre continued in *sotto voce*. "You can join us, my friend. How many men have you?"

"Two score."

The Comte chuckled. "We can use them. Listen. I have men at arms positioned at the barbican gate. There are soldiers in the wood outside, to the north. Two of my men wait inside at the gate to lower it on my signal. The order is to kill FitzRauf, his son, his bride-to-be, and his guests. Then we shall ... " He dropped his voice.

Adrian pinched his nose, for a sneeze threatened.

The Comte said, "Will you join us? The sack of the castle will be divided between us."

"When do you propose to strike?"

"When the chapel bell tolls the hour of Matins."

The young lord drew in his breath sharply. "Midnight! It does not give us long, does it?" Silence. "I shall join you, de Pre, if you give me half of the booty."

"Half! I say a third. It was I who did all the planning, remember."

"Very well. Shall we toast our *coup*?" They laughed and departed.

Adrian eased from the cupboard, waiting a few moments only, his heart thudding a hard beat, skin tightening on his back. He had failed in a military endeavor before and it cost him everything he held most dear. Now he was being given another chance. He must not fail.

He hesitated. Should he run to the kitchens and warn his friends, or find Lady Matilde and warn her? He had no concern for FitzRauf.

If the baron was killed, the world would be cleansed of a great evil. But his friends—Lady Matilde, Princess Maria, DeArmond and Baron le Brun—he could not go about his business of rescuing Grandfather and let them perish.

He turned to the stairs leading to the Great Hall where the sound of music and voices drifted to him. All those people, slaughtered like so many cattle. Nay, he could not do such a thing.

Nipping a tray from an alcove, he joined a line of servers. The Great Hall was festooned with banners in colors of bright green and red and gold, and in every corner and on every table sat flowers of varied hues. The noise was deafening. Princess Maria and Sir Frederick sat on the dais under a canopy. Beside them, Baron FitzRauf lifted a silver tankard. Other nobles and barons, including DeArmond, Baron le Brun, Comte de Pre, and beside him, Lord Phillipe, ranged themselves at tables nearby.

Phillipe. So that was who planned the coup with de Pre.

Adrian's eyes were drawn to Maria. As he sought a clear view of her face, the noise of the Great Hall dimmed in his mind as if he dreamed. She was as beautiful as the day he wed her. His heart hammered in his ears as he remembered the sweet touch of her hand, the way her eyes would flash when she looked upon him, their tender intimate moments … He wended his way closer, unheeding the calls for wine. Upon closer view, he saw her face was sallow and gaunt, the ravages of grief and unhappiness drawn as plainly as if in paint.

She lifted her head just then and looked his way. Their eyes met, yet she did not recognize him, did not even see him. Baron le Brun, his old friend, seemed heavier and darker, his expression filled with contempt. Adrian almost called out to him, but caught himself just in time. *I cannot speak to Baron le Brun. He wouldn't know me and wouldn't listen to one such as I have become. The lady is my only chance.*

Time was running out. Where was she? Then he saw her, sitting beside a heavy woman, the wife of one of the barons. She hid a yawn behind her hand and looked toward the doorway of the hall. Carefully, Adrian made his way to the dais and leaned over her shoulder. "More wine, my lady?"

She waved him away impatiently. "No more wine."

"Lady Matilde!" He whispered in her ear.

She turned, her lips drawn into a thin line, but when she saw him, her eyes widened.

"Meet me in the hall, near the north door. I have something of great importance to tell you. Speak to no one of it." She began to question, but left her without explanation.

In the corridor he deposited the tray and waited. Sweat oozed down his back, anxiety twisted his gut like a tightly wound spring and every moment dawdled by like the first hour of the world. When it seemed he could wait no longer, he let out a breath and turned to hurry off.

Then he heard the soft rustle of skirts and caught the scent of honeysuckle.

Lady Matilde gripped his arm. "Ah, it is you, Sir Valet!" Her breath tickled his ear. "Why did you ask me to meet you here like this? I must admit, I—"

"You must flee, my lady! There is a *coup* planned. It will happen very soon. Come." He pulled her aside, out of the stream of servants. "The castle will be attacked tonight. It is Comte de Pre and Lord Phillipe. I overheard their conversation just now in the hall. They mentioned killing Baron FitzRauf, the duchess, Baron le Brun, and all the guests." He drew a breath, steadied himself to speak slowly and distinctly. "They have men positioned to attack the castle in the outer wood. You must warn Baron le Brun. Then you must flee. I have friends who will saddle your horses. I am not whom I appear, Lady, but I can say no more." He swallowed. "Please heed my words."

Her blue eyes widened, the hand on his arm tightened, but she was not given to shrieks of hysteria and did not panic even now when her life and many others hung in the balance. "I believe you. But it may take some time." Her breath came in gasps, as if she were drowning. "Let me think."

He willed her to hurry, yet said nothing.

Her brow puckered. "I shall not be sad to see the last of Ahab FitzRauf. He casts too many bold glances my way. I was accompanied here by some of my uncle's knights; they will leave with me. First, I shall warn Baron le Brun. He will aid the duchess." She nodded, as if making up her mind. "Thank you, kind friend."

He moved as if to go, but she pulled him back, her eyes large, her face the color of putty. "What is your name? So I may thank you properly some day."

"Adrian D'Arcy, but I doubt if you will ever see me again. Fare thee well, Lady Matilde. May God grant you safety." He kissed her hand.

Her eyes glittered with unshed tears; she turned away with a flurry of skirts.

Adrian retraced his way to the kitchens where servants flew about their duties in the inner bailey, where hot fires roasted whole pigs and the chief cooks and bakers drove their slaves with shouts and curses. He found Gabriel and Luthar in the stable. "I have news," he said, bending over to inspect a horse's hoof. The two men leaned closer. He told them what he overheard. "They said they would wait for the chapel bell to toll Matins. It must be close to that now. We do not have much time."

"Where are the village men? Are they in position?" Gabriel's fist tightened on the horse's mane, his eyes glittered.

Adrian nodded. "Leon and Hager and the others from the village are outside, near the postern gate, awaiting the call of the horn. We will use that gate." He looked up. "There is one further thing. I met a lady. She showed me kindness and I have promised to help her. Would you see that the lady's horse, and those of her party, are saddled and ready to leave?"

They glanced at each other. "Her name is … ?" Luthar's lip twisted.

"The Lady Matilde, the great-granddaughter of King Richard."

Gabriel laid a hand on his shoulder. "Aye, Adrian, we shall see to your bidding."

"Do it quickly. Time is working against us. Luthar, gather a few able men and come with me. Gabriel, watch here and guard our escape." Catching up a bucket and a torch, Adrian turned, but Gabriel laid hold of his arm.

"Wait. I have something for you." He rustled in the hay of the manger and lifted out Adrian's sword. "We smuggled this in for you. You may need it for the work below."

Adrian wanted to kiss him, but forbore and tied the sword belt around his waist. "*Merci!*" He tore down the hallways, the men pounding behind, their boots thudding on the stone, as if it was a game of chase and tag like he played as a child in the castle at Mordelias. Yet this was no game. He arrived at the first locked door and, without pause, banged on it.

The guard opened a small window, looked out and shook his head. "He has had his dinner already."

"A last meal, the best from the table, for they call for his death." Adrian held up the bucket. "Baron FitzRauf will have your head, as well, if you do not let me by."

The guard's face blanched and the key turned in the lock. As soon as the latch lifted, Adrian jumped against the door with all his might, pinioning the guard against the wall. The guard started to scream, but Luthar plunged a dagger in his throat and his scream was only a gurgling cry that ended abruptly as he slid down the wall.

Adrian searched the man for a key but found none. Gazing into Luthar's cold blue eyes, he felt the first fingers of fear clutching his heart. "Go back down the hall. We must find the ... "

Luthar was gone. Adrian turned to a tall villager who stood behind him. "Go with him. I shall run this other way. The rest of you, stay by this door."

Down the hall, he found an open doorway, entered and came upon a man who wore the garb of the royal guard. He was far into his wine and looked up groggily as Adrian grabbed him by the hair, pulled back his head and put a knife to his throat. "The keys to the cells or you die!"

Now fully alert, the man's eyes widened, but he shook his head. "I have no keys."

"Do you know where the keys are?" Adrian pressed the knife harder against the throat and drew forth a thin line of blood.

The man's eyes stared from their sockets. "The captain has the keys."

"Where is the captain?"

"He went to the garderobe a few moments ago. He ... has not ... returned. Please, sir ... Let me go! I shall not harm you!" His face was as white as the pastry going into the ovens.

"I shall, when you take me to the captain."

Luthar and the other man returned, panting, to report that they had found no one. Sweat trickled down Adrian's face. Without removing the knife, he prodded the guard down the hall to the privy.

Inside the small room they found the officer. He was lying on the floor—dead. Luthar searched the body but found no keys.

"*Oh, God.*" Adrian released his captive and made his way back to Grandfather's cell. In the flickering light of the torches, he stared at the door, then at Luthar. The fierce little man glared back and raised his eyebrows.

A door far down the hall crashed open. Heavy boots pounded on the stone floor.

The guards!

Adrian crouched low and drew his sword. The other men bunched together. Luthar's bow was in his hand.

A strange, sinking sensation smote Adrian's heart, similar to what he felt at Mordelias when he saw the English riding over the hill. His plan had failed. They would perish here like a bunch of skewered rats.

CHAPTER FIFTEEN

After I am dead, I would rather have people ask why I have no monument than why I have one. Cato the Elder (234-149 BC)

Tours, France, April 1201

The fever hit again, this time with a vengeance. All Louis knew in those days was the quiet murmur of voices and Samson John's face above his, mouthing words, uttering guttural noises. It seemed the boy was trying to communicate something of great importance, but he could not comprehend what it was.

Then one day the walls of his small room came into focus. A ray of sunshine slanted through the high window. Louis turned his face to the sunshine and looked about. Samson John sat in the corner, on the floor, asleep.

Slowly Louis sat up. What day was it? What hour? He was weaker than a newborn mouse dry of throat; even the effort of raising himself from the bed caused his heart to pound as if a thousand drums boomed in his chest. It must be morning, but of what day? Setting his feet on the floor, he pushed off the coverlet and rose, steadying himself against a wave of dizziness.

He noticed the empty corner wherein his pack had lain. *My pack! The letters!* He stumbled to Samson John and shook him. "Samson John!"

The boy was wide-eyed in a moment. He leaped to his feet and steadied Louis with one arm, gesturing for him to return to the cot.

"Where is my pack? How long have I lain on the cot? What day is it? Where is my pack?"

Samson John could not follow the rapid questions but knew their intent. With many imploring gestures, he persuaded Louis to return to bed. When Louis was safely seated, he motioned. *Wait here. I will be back.*

210

A long twenty minutes later passed; a tortuous time for Louis as he sat helpless on his bed, praying, weeping, calling out to God and the Virgin Mother for help. Where had the boy gone? Why was it taking him so long?

The urgency of Louis' mission pressed itself upon his mind. He remembered the look on the abbot's face at Mont St. Michaels. "If you do not go, and go quickly, many people will die." Had he failed before he had barely begun?

The door swung open and Samson John entered. He laid the pack on the bare wooden floor beside Louis' feet with a bow. *Here it is. I kept it safe.*

"My pack, my pack. Oh, you blessed child!" Louis fell to his knees and clung to the dirty sandaled feet of his servant. "How ... where ... oh, you blessed boy. May all the saints in heaven praise you!"

Samson John laughed.

Louis stopped and looked up in amazement, for he had never heard him laugh before. He lifted his arms and they laughed together; the boy raised him up and they fell upon the bed in a pile of glee. Disentangling himself, Louis wiped his eyes and made the boy look upon his face. "Where did you hide it?"

Samson John acted out carrying the pack, horses, eating, burying, checking it and burying it again. Louis understood the boy took it to the stable and hid it in the hay, but when the monks who cared for the animals dug too close, he would bury it again, then again.

He patted the boy's back. "You have done well. How long have I been ill?"

Samson John lifted one finger after another until six were extended. Six days.

Louis lay back on the bed. "Six days, this is the seventh. I have been running and ill for nearly a fortnight. Why, in that time a whole city could be consumed. Indeed, it may have been. I wonder what has been happening in the world?" He rose on one elbow and pulled the boy's face around. "Samson John, we must escape. Tonight. During Matins. Can you get some food?"

The boy nodded.

"Good. We shall pack the mule and buy our way out of the gate. It must be tonight, for I have lingered too long in Tours. I have lingered too long in France. I should have been in the Holy See, where our Holy Father—", he crossed himself, "can deal with the message."

He gripped the boy's shoulders. "Tonight."

***

Castle Renault

It was not guards who turned the corner and advanced. It was Tate. His antaean form seemed to fill the hallway. "Why stand you thus?" He halted, hands on hips.

"The keys!" Adrian managed to croak from a dry throat. "The keys, for God's sake, Tate. Or we shall all perish in this rat hole."

Tate laughed and held aloft a ring of keys. "I found them on the body of a captain. I have been looking for you."

Adrian indicated the locked door. Tate inserted the key, but the lock did not turn. He tried another key and another. The last key on the ring stuck and would not budge. He murmured curses; his breath came in gasps.

Pushing Tate aside, Adrian took the key. "Here. Let me do it." With a prayer as he had been taught to the Lord of All, he pulled back gently on the key, eased it into position, and twisted. With a soft *click!*, the lock turned.

Adrian lunged into the cell, unlocked the chain that held Grandfather to the wall and raised him up. A rat scuttled away into the darkness.

The old man grasped him. "Praise to the Father! I saved thee once and now God has used you to save me!"

"We are not safe yet, Grandfather." Adrian received his fervent hug and kiss. "You must move quickly. Can you run?"

"I will keep up." Old Bric pulled himself erect. His eyes glittered. "But first you must free the other prisoners. Down the hall—women and children, innocent victims. And there is a girl in the kit—"

"You. Go with Luthar." Adrian pointed to a burly villager, the blacksmith. "Free the prisoners. Catch up with us. We shall go the way we came to the first stair."

Taking Grandfather's arms, he and Tate hastened down the passage, but they had not gone far before they heard the clang of weapons and the shouts of men from some distant point in the labyrinth of corridors. *Soldiers!*

Adrian paused. "We must turn back. Hurry."

"There is a girl in the kitchen who must be rescued." Grandfather tried to pull Adrian to a stop, but Adrian paid him no mind. They passed the cells and joined with Luthar who led a score of prisoners—men, women and small children.

Adrian beckoned. "Come. This passage must lead somewhere." He opened the door at the far end of the hall, darting along as fast as he could with Grandfather on his arm, stopping now and then to let the weakest ones catch up, then dashing off again. It seemed a bad dream as they wandered the bowels of the castle down the labyrinth of tunnels.

Grandfather kept up as best he could, but suddenly he sagged to the floor. "I ... I cannot go ... any farther. I ... I must rest. Go on ... save yourselves."

Tate lifted him gently in his arms and they were off again. The clang of iron boots on the stone floor drew closer. Adrian stopped and entered a small room, glancing up as he did so. They must be just under ... the kitchens, or perchance the stable. He was good at directions and even as he ran through the underground halls, he remembered their position in relation to the castle above.

"Here. Come in here. Quickly." He led the way while the others pressed behind, until the small room was jammed so tightly he could barely breathe. On the far wall was a door, old and unused. He tried it, his heart pounding, his breath labored. It would not budge.

The sounds of booted feet grew louder. Moans and cries erupted from the throats of the prisoners as all looked about with widened eyes.

Oh, God. Virgin Mother Mary. St. Agnes. St. Joseph. God of the ugly face, Dagda. Sweat trickled into his eyes. He brushed it away. "Tate. Here. Take a hand with this door."

At Tate's first try, the door did not budge, but then he threw his weight against it, and it creaked open with a flurry of dust and rotten wood, revealing a narrow, twisting stair leading upward.

Tate led the way up without hesitation, and Adrian followed, pulling along Grandfather. The prisoners came behind accompanied by the whimpered cries of the children, quickly muffled, and the scuffle of feet. No one spoke and no one stopped on the narrow steps.

After the first dozen rapid steps, Grandfather's face became white with effort and his breath exploded in short gasps. Adrian thought his arm would fall off in his effort to lift the old man up the stair. Against the sweat pouring into his eyes, he squinted down. "Close the door behind the last one. Pass it down!"

The whisper passed down the line and the door scraped shut. Tate stopped suddenly above him, grunting like a pig in heat. A screech of wood on wood and a shower of dirt filled the air as he lifted a trapdoor and threw it off. He leaped out and disappeared.

Adrian pulled Grandfather out of the hole, rolling over on bare boards, groaning from the pain in his arm. He heard Grandfather's prayers of thanksgiving. One by one the others emerged into the semi-darkness of a room with close and fetid air, ill lit by torches, smelling of hay and horses. The stables!

"The horn!" Tate lifted Adrian to his feet. "You must wind it and escape this place. I am afeared that the attack from without has begun."

Adrian nodded. "The horn is near." He had hidden it that morning in one of the unused stalls. As he held the cold metal of the horn, he felt an exultation of spirit such as he had never felt before, not even when he commanded hundreds of knights and foot soldiers. He ran into the inner bailey and winded the horn, once, twice, thrice—a sound that seemed to rattle the ancient stones of the curtain wall.

Grandfather pulled on his sleeve. "There is a girl in the kitchens, my son. I will fetch her. She must be rescued."

Adrian turned. "I care not for a beggar girl. Look. The battle has begun. I am needed. Go with the others, Grandfather." He turned to Gabriel. "Guard the hatch in the stable. There may be soldiers who ascend there and you will find a harvest for your sword."

Gabriel nodded and scurried back into the stable, taking the blacksmith and two other men of the village with him.

Old Bric planted his feet and shook his head. "I shall not leave until I find Judith."

Adrian threw up his hands, but in that moment, a slip of a girl lurched through the darkened courtyard and clung to Grandfather.

She wore a cloak, its hood pulled over her head. Adrian could only see her eyes—large, wild and angry—the eyes of a caged animal.

"Now I will go." Grandfather put his arm around the girl and together they followed the line of prisoners.

Adrian drew his sword and leaped to the lower bailey where the battle was already hot. This was work to which he was accustomed—not the step and feint of rapier dueling, but the hack and slash of real sword fighting. Soldiers bearing the colors of their lords—some in maroon and black, some in gray and gold—engaged in sword fights while the village men defended the retreating line of prisoners with axes and hoes and cudgels.

Men on the walls sent arrows whizzing into the melee, while the sounds of battle filled the air—the clash of sword on sword, the shouts and screams, the twang of bows and the *thunk!* of arrows landing, the groans and grunts and oaths of men in deadly combat.

The prisoners, including Grandfather and the little serving girl, swarmed through the rear postern gate, past the stream feeding the mill and through the outside gate. Wagons and horses and drivers waited for their precious cargo and a swift run to Tours and the monastery. All was going as planned.

"*En garde!*"

Adrian whirled and faced a large, bearded man who swung his sword downward, a slashing blow intended for his neck. Before he could think, his sword was in his hand and he blocked the weapon that descended with a scream of steel on steel. He saw surprise in the man's eyes. Perhaps the man thought he was easy prey, for he still wore the livery of a servant.

Adrian's old battle skills rose to the fore, everything else was blotted out—he saw only a man's bearded face, knew only the old killing rage. He leaped upon a stack of hay and delivered the fatal blow to his enemy, but had not a moment's reprieve. A dozen soldiers swarmed into the place where the man fell.

The village men began lighting the castle afire while others leaped to the gates to guard against the invasion of more soldiers.

Adrian heard a high and melodious note above the din. He glanced up and saw the tall, slender figure of a man clad in brown and green leap onto the dog kennels, swinging his sword in a circle. Leon.

"Give him a taste of steel, my lord," Leon called, turning to engage his own opponent.

"What took you so long?" Adrian cocked his head upward with a grin. He engaged a man who was taller and stronger than he, a man whose eyes widened and his mouth hung open a few seconds into the fight when Adrian easily pierced his defenses and without much ado sent him to the regions beyond.

Smoke burned Adrian's nostrils from the fire licking eagerly at the castle. He glanced about but did not see Lady Matilde. Suddenly a whole squadron of soldiers closed about him.

They were too many. Glancing up, he saw a rope hanging down the castle wall and, catching it, he swung out, above their heads, to land in a cleared space. From there he confronted one at a time while Leon, Tate, Luthar, Hager and Gabriel took on the others.

It seemed there was a never-ending flow of de Pre's and FitzRauf's soldiers. Adrian wondered how the battle went inside the castle. When there was a space free, Adrian leaped over bodies to flee to the rear of the lower bailey.

Leon met him there, smiling grimly, panting. "Fine fighting ... but we must leave ... the prisoners are safely away. Come!" Fitting action to his words he bounded away like a deer. Adrian followed.

Outside the postern gate, in a small copse of trees, the prisoners were loaded into four wagons, the last of which was Grandfather's, having been repaired. Adrian rushed to it and gripped his hand. "I shall come presently, but I have to see to a lady first. I shall meet you in Tours."

Grandfather tried to say something but Leon appeared with Bret. "Here is your horse."

Adrian mounted and turned back to view the burning castle. He shook his head. "I have to make sure Lady Matilde makes it out safely. Do not wait for me!" Without waiting to hear their cries, he kicked Bret toward the castle. In a wood just before the drawbridge of the Great Gate, he stared agape at the castle, for the whole of it was alight with fire. Men fought hand-to-hand battles, bodies fell from the battlements, screams of women and horses filled the air...and the fire roared.

The drawbridge was down but unguarded and the heavy metal links of the barbican gate were not lowered. Then he saw her. She and five others—two ladies, two knights and a groom—approached the barbican gate.

It was being lowered with the creaking of heavy chains. The others of her party kicked their mounts under the barricade and across the drawbridge, but the lady rode more timidly. She would not make it. She glanced up, terror flooding her face. Two men in maroon and black, FitzRauf's men, turned the wheel beside the gate.

Adrian kicked Bret and thundered across the drawbridge. The linked gate lowered slowly—he rode under it just in time. Barely had he cleared the wooden planks when he flew from the saddle and spitted one of the soldiers on the end of his sword. The other turned to him and slashed at his legs. "Flee, my lady!" he cried even as he parried and stabbed and lunged. "Your horse can make it under the gate!"

He had the satisfaction of seeing the flash of her eyes as she kicked her horse and fled the castle. But now he was in trouble, for more of FitzRauf's soldiers poured into the open square before the gate and came to the aid of their companions. As they surrounded him, he heard with sinking heart the rattle of chains as the gate was lowered.

There would be no escape, for certes. Still he fought like a wild man, not deterring even when the soldiers formed a circle about him and mocked him as he hacked and hewed at his opponent.

"Stay!" The command came from the rear, and he knew at once that it was Sir Frederick. The baron's son came through the smoke like the evil captain of the dead. He wore no mail, but only a leather jerkin and a light helmet. He called to his soldiers, and they stepped back, giving him room. Dismounting, he turned and raised his sword. "Who is this knave, this ... " As he neared Adrian, he stopped in stunned silence. "How can this be? I thought ... "

"I am Adrian D'Arcy, my lord." He took the stance. "*En garde!*"

Sir Frederick smiled showing white teeth in a dark face. "Am I dreaming? Is it truly you, mine enemy, whom I have longed to kill? Ah! Defend yourself, knave, for you shall die this night!"

"It is you who shall die, Sir Frederick!"

He shrugged. "Adrian D'Acry. Is this what you call yourself now? Nevertheless, I ask nothing more than to sink my blade into your heart. You bested me once—that I freely acknowledge. I have lived only to have the chance to parry blades with you once more. I know not how this miracle has occurred, but I trust you are a better swordsman than Prince Arthur, for I have vowed to kill him. And I shall!"

Adrian nodded. "And I shall avenge the death of my friends in the village of Montebank." He saw surprise flicker across Frederick's face.

The knight lunged quickly, yet it was not the wild and untrained lunge of a maddened beast. Adrian was surprised to find that Frederick had improved his skill, and realized that his opponent was now much his superior. The soldiers made hurried bets, cheering on their *chevalier*.

Frederick's eyes glittered with hatred; he gritted his teeth and spoke between them. "Can we never be done with ... Geoffrey's whelps, the sons of the devil? Thou fool. I have lived for nothing more ... than to spit thee ... as I would a dog."

"You will ... have to work harder ... than that!" Adrian found a space inside the knight's guard and drew blood, a cut to his inner arm. "Did you ever get the truth from your lying father about the death of your family?"

"Ah!" Frederick's screech came from his very soul. "Thou shalt die!"

The fight seemed interminable. Sweat poured into Adrian's eyes and his hand was slippery with it. His arm ached abominably, but Sir Frederick seemed fresh and strong. Adrian looked vainly for some sign that he was tiring, but the vigorous attack continued.

As he fought—parrying, lunging, circling, trying every trick Grandfather taught him— smoke billowed into the outer bailey and the battle raged in the castle. Now it seemed the tide had turned, and more of the Comte le Pre's green and gold flooded the bailey. Adrian noticed now and then a midnight blue and gold soldier—le Brun's!

A horn blew and Sir Frederick's men left to aid their failing brothers in the castle.

Back, back ... Adrian gave ground until his feet gripped the verge near the moat. He knew he was in trouble, knew his guard was down, knew the grass was slippery. Sir Frederick's sword found his arm unguarded and slashed deeply, drawing blood. Adrian switched to his left.

Sir Frederick came on, possessed by a demon of spite, his eyes glittering in the torchlight. Adrian heard the rattle of chains and cast a glance at the gate. A man knelt beside the winch, was turning it, lifting it. *Leon!* Adrian whirled to avoid the blade of his opponent.

How did Leon manage to come back in through the castle, now that le Pre's men overran it? The sight of his friend lent strength to his failing left arm. He took the fight back into his court.

Sir Frederick gave ground. His eyes widened, his nostrils flared, his breath came in heaving gasps. Then, in a moment of fighting, when Adrian knew it was either do or die, he pressed hard, and Frederick slipped on the wet grass and fell.

Adrian plunged the sword into his chest. The knight's eyes widened in surprise and pain. Adrian pulled his sword free and stood before him, panting heavily, too tired to move. He watched death steal across Frederick's face, was going to plunge the sword in the second time, but someone pulled on him.

"Come!" It was Leon.

He looked up. Running across the upper bailey, three maroon and gold soldiers approached. One winded a horn. Adrian gave Frederick one last glance and then accepted Leon's help to mount his horse. Leon leaped up behind. They cleared the bridge in a single bound.

***

Judith clung to the old man as the wagon lurched down the rutted lane. Her eyes turned steadily to the rear, expecting to see soldiers approaching, feeling deep in her bones that she could not escape so easily. But the road remained empty and the moon sailed high in a scuddy sky, and soon the lights of Tours came into view as they headed down the last hill into town.

She kept her arm around Old Bric's shoulders, for she felt him droop, as if he had expended all his energy and kept upright only because of her arm. "Was the young man, the one you spoke to, was he your grandson, sir?"

"Aye. His name is Adrian." He shot her a bright look from under shaggy brows. "I told you, didn't I? He would come for me, and he did. I wonder why he did not ride with us."

"He said he had to take care of a lady. He knows where we are going. Surely he knows." A desire to see the young man again rose in her heart. She pushed it away. He was a heathen, a Christian, of the sort who killed her mother. But he was also very good to look upon. Even in her fear and despair and wild anger, she had seen that.

Old Bric nodded. "Aye, he knows. He is clever and capable. But you, child. What of you? Have you family in Tours?"

She shook her head. "Nay. I have no family. I have only a servant. I left him at the monastery until he was cured of an illness, but I imagine he has gone. We were to meet in Troyes or Dijon."

He nodded, for she had told him much of her life when they sat together in the dark cell. He fell into silence and his head bobbed to rest on her shoulder. She held him, then, until they reached the city and rumbled over the bridge.

"Halt!" The command came from up the street where the first wagon stopped. "Who goes there?"

Judith craned her neck. It was the night guard for the city, but two men only.

"Pilgrims, friend," the driver in the lead wagon said. "We have come from Orleans to visit your wonderful Cattedral di St. Gatien. We lost our way and so have arrived late. If you would, please escort us to the gates and we shall say a prayer for you."

The guard squinted down the line of wagons, then turned to his companion. "Let them pass. They appear harmless."

Judith breathed again as the wagons rolled down the street. There, beside the fish market, was where Patrick set up his stand. She turned her eyes away, for she had no desire to see the man. She sighed, glancing at Old Bric who opened his eyes and straightened. "Are you staying on at the monastery?"

"I do not know, my dear. Ah. Here we are." He turned to her and laid a hand on her arm as the wagons entered the massive gates and ground to a halt. "I want to hear all of your story and perchance I may be able to help you. Please do not leave without seeing me. Do you promise?"

Judith nodded. "Kind sir, I shall see thee if hell itself burns over." She took his hand and kissed it. "You are a savior to me. Someday I hope to repay you for the kindness you showed me. Good even, Grandfather."

***

Samson John picked up the pack. Louis wrapped his cloak about his body, for at times he felt a chill and feared the fever would strike again. But not tonight. *Dear God, not tonight.*

The moon played among silver clouds as he led the way from the cloister, through the garth, down a long arched hall, then to the cobbled courtyard. Every rustle in the long grasses, every movement of mouse and bat, every scrape of tree limb against tree limb made him jump. He paused before starting across the open space of the courtyard, listening. Did he hear footsteps? The rustle of a robe?

"Who goes there?" A dark-robed figure emerged from the shadows near the archway leading up into the cathedral. Father Martin, a priest who curried favor with the abbot, marched into the moonlight.

"I am Brother Louis. My servant and I are taking a stroll in the cool of the evening. Is there something wrong, Father Martin?"

The priest approached. He was a younger man, his brown fuzz of hair framing a narrow face. He studied Louis carefully. "You are dressed strangely for stroll, Brother. You look as if you are leaving on a journey." He chuckled. "But surely not. Not in your condition."

Louis shook his head. "A journey? How can you think such a thing?"

Father Martin straightened. "I came to find you, and your cell was empty. Father Bernard wants to see you in his office."

"I will come tomorrow morning. I feel too weak tonight."

"Now. Bring your pack." He eyed the pack that Samson John wore strapped to his back. "Come." He turned and began to stride across the cobblestones.

Louis cast a glimpse at Samson John, then followed. Suddenly he halted, doubled over, groaning, grasping his side.

Father Martin turned and surveyed him. "Now, none of that. You must come with me."

Louis cast himself onto the stones, the bite of them hitting his muscles like sledgehammers, pain shrieking through his wounded shoulder. He emitted a shriek and then went limp.

Father Martin came to his side and kicked his ribs. Samson John hurled himself at the man but was pushed away. "Leave me alone. I say he is pretending. Well, I shall make him get up." He withdrew a slender dagger from his belt and plunged the tip of it into Louis' arm, where his robe fell back to reveal bare skin. Blood flowed from the wound.

Samson John howled, renewing his attack upon the priest.

Louis had seen the dagger coming and so resisted the flinch he knew the priest was looking for. He gritted his teeth and held himself still and slack, even though pain shot up his arm. His good arm. *Oh, God. Give me strength.*

The priest stood, panting. He stared at Louis' prone body as if willing him to react. Samson John, howling like an insane animal, pulled at the priest's robe in supplication. The priest backhanded him, sending him sprawling. "Get away from me, fool!" He took two steps backward, breathing hard. "I must go get help. Stay here with your master."

His footsteps pattered away.

Louis counted them. He held himself still even when the sound of the steps faded away, for there was a balcony overlooking the courtyard. Perchance the man went there to see if he was shamming. When he could stand it no longer, he lifted himself and gripped his arm, staunching the flow of blood. "Let's go."

Samson John motioned to the stables.

Louis shook his head. "Leave the mule. We must go now, or we shall never get away." Struggling to his feet, one hand gripping his arm where blood still flowed from the wound, he led the way to the gate. Two guards, hired by the monastery, stood beside the massive gates, their spears and shields glinting when the moon shone from behind a cloud. Louis reached into his scrip and pulled out a handful of francs.

A noise erupted on the street—a voice loudly ordered the gate to be opened, horses neighed, people cheered—it sounded like a war and a party combined. Louis knew not what to do. Make a dash for freedom as the gates opened? Yet wouldn't the guards be doubly alert at such a time?

He shrank back into the shadows and watched as four wagons, loaded with people—men, women and children—rolled into the courtyard and stopped. Accompanying them were three men on horseback. The gates clanged shut behind them. Louis' chance was gone.

A priest emerged from the cathedral. Father Martin. With him were a score of the younger monks. He carried a torch and studied the group before turning to address the leader, a burly man who was dressed as a blacksmith.

"What is the meaning of this? Who are these people?"

"We claims sanctuary." The blacksmith waved his hand to the people who piled out of the wagons with noisy chatter and loud praises to God.

"All of you?" The priest seemed out of his depth. "I do not know how we will ... "

"All of us. It be our right and we claims it."

The priest seemed to gather his wits. "Very well. I will send a servant to see to your animals. Stay here until I return. I must speak with the abbot and learn where you shall be housed."

"Just shows us where to bed them and we shall care for our own beasts."

Louis motioned for Samson John to continue along the far wall of the courtyard, hoping to arrive at the gate and escape undetected, for the moon had gone under and the priest had disappeared with his torch. As they went, a familiar face materialized out of the dim light.

"Brother Monk. Louis. I thought I recognized you."

It was Old Bric from the village. Louis nodded. "It is I. What is this about? Who are these people?"

"It is a story that will be told for generations. I was captured and held in the castle Renault, Baron FitzRauf's castle, for no other reason than that we held peaceful meetings on the cause of freedom. Many others were being held without trial and we faced certain death. Some of these with us are servants in the castle who fled because of the baron's harsh treatment. We were aided by the three men you see over there on horseback, and my grandson, Adrian. Surely you remember him. He drove you here when you were ill."

Louis nodded, wishing he could rid himself of the old man and make his escape. "Aye. I remember the lad. And what will you do afterward? These people cannot stay here forever. The baron will find them."

"I know, but we have ways. We have a secret way for them to find safety and to relocate them."

"And if they have family here?" Louis eyed the gate, anxious to be away.

Old Bric shrugged. "They must chose. Family or freedom. But what of you? Are you leaving?"

It was a question and must be answered, but Louis was loathe to discuss his private affairs with anyone. "I am. At once. The place where you find a sanctuary, I find a prison. They are seeking me even now. I am carrying ... but I cannot tell you now. Suffice to say I carry a message of great import to the Holy Father in Rome."

"The Holy Father! You mean Pope Innocent III?"

Louis removed the hand that gripped his sleeve and made to shuffle off, but Old Bric grabbed his arm again. "I cannot let you go." He released Louis' arm and noticed his hand was stained with blood. "You are wounded. Come aside here where I can help you." Old Bric led him to an alcove where the shadows were deep. He ripped a piece from the bottom of his robe and tied up Louis' wound. "I have a cottage in the woods some ways north of here. Toward Orleans. You may find refuge there, but I doubt if you can find it yourself. I shall go with you. Then I shall return and see to the safety of these people."

"But you are weak and tired." Louis tried again to free himself. "Please. Tell me the way and I shall find it."

But nothing would dissuade Old Bric. "We will use one of these wagons and that young man with the golden hair will drive. Wait here."

He was gone before Louis could stop him.

***

Judith crawled from the wagon and stood beside it, a lone, pathetic figure wrapped with the cloak she had stolen just before she ran to the lower bailey and found Grandfather. It was warm and fur-lined and long; a comfort to her soul, a reminder of days long ago when she had clothing like this.

She watched Grandfather's bent figure as he made his way to a monk who stood beside the courtyard wall. Who did he speak to? He waved to the man who drove his wagon. The man brought the wagon around. Was he going to leave again, so soon after arriving?

She let her eyes rove through the darkened courtyard. She must inquire about Miguel, if he lived, if he was still here. But there was no time. Even as she hesitated, she saw Old Bric speak to the driver of the wagon and wrap his cloak around his body. She must not lose Grandfather!

Dashing across the courtyard, she smacked hard into someone who was running the other way. Judith peered under the lowered hood. "Meredith! So you made it out, too."

The girl nodded, pushing her away, as if anxious to join the group heading to the cloister. "Yes, Judith. I must go, for they—"

"Meredith. Stay a moment. Did you find out anything about my father?"

"I have to go. They leave!"

Judith gripped her arm. "I will not let you go until you answer."

"Yes. I found that he was taken and sold as a slave. They say he was sold to an Arab dealer and probably wound up in Palestine. That is all I know. I swear! Now let me go!" She twisted her arm free and flew across the courtyard.

Judith stood frozen, her mind blank, her heart racing. Her journey of the past year had not gone far enough. Palestine! Was he still alive? Did he toil without hope in some dark cavern or in the belly of a ship or in the fields?

A wave of grief and despair swept over her soul, so much that she shook as if in a high wind. Father needed her. Now. But how could she get to him? Who would help her? She gazed across the shifting shadows of the courtyard. Someone was helping Grandfather into the wagon. Others were climbing in. Her only friend was leaving the monastery.

Without thought, without murmur or prayer, without hope or comfort, she darted across the open space and climbed into the wagon.

***

Louis helped Old Bric into the wagon, then scrambled in himself. Samson John clambered over the side. Louis pulled a coverlet up, but just before he yanked it over his head, a small figure crawl into the wagon. Who was that? No matter, at least he was leaving the monastery.

The driver of the wagon, a young man with a long braid down his back, told the guard at the gate they were going back to fetch some of their party who had been left behind. Louis peeked out again. A large man with the black beard mounted his horse and followed. He thought they called that one Tate. What a strange name.

They cleared the last of the town when Louis heard a shout and the driver pulled the horse to a halt. The sound of hooves on the hard-packed ground grew closer and closer. The driver of the wagon spoke in a low voice. "Who goes there?"

"It is I. Leon. Gabriel? Is that you?"

"Yes. I am glad to see you made it away. Who do you have with you?"

"Adrian. Why are you traveling north? I thought we were to rendezvous at the monastery."

Old Bric spoke up. "The others are at the monastery. Go there and I shall return. I am lending aid to a monk. Taking him to my cottage."

"I shall come with you, Grandfather." Adrian lifted his head from behind Leon and slid to the ground.

"But I will come back, my son. You do not need to make the journey with me."

Adrian stumbled to the wagon. "I do not wish to be separated from you again. Ever."

Leon boosted him to the wagon, and Louis scooted over to make room. The small person who had clambered into the wagon at the monastery shoved off her hood. It was a girl. She sat in one corner, her feet drawn up tightly to her chest. He glanced her way and smiled, but she glared at him.

"I, too, shall accompany you, sir," Leon said. "The baron may be searching for his servants. You may need my arms and my weapons." He mounted the horse and turned. "Lead the way, Gabriel. Tate and I shall follow."

CHAPTER SIXTEEN

Ah, but a man's reach should exceed his grasp, or what's a heaven for? Robert Browning

Tours, France, May 1201

If Judith could have oozed her body into the cracks of the old wagon, she would have, rather than share the space and perhaps touch the two who occupied the space across from her—a man of the Church and his servant boy. The boy seemed harmless enough, but there was something wrong with him. He did not speak.

Her fists closed over the buckskin cover as she pulled it up to her chin. And now another man, the one she had spoken to at the castle, lay at her feet. She felt pity for him, for he was young and good to look upon and wounded. He made no move, nor opened his eyes. Blood soaked his tunic and the sleeve of his undergarment on his arm.

As the wagon left the city and entered the forest, fear seemed to drip from the trees and lurk in the shadows. Even now she did not feel safe from the clutches of Sir Frederick or his father. She struggled to stay awake, to watch for riders from the rear, but weariness overtook her, her head bobbed to her knees and she slept.

***

Adrian lifted his head and heard the low murmur of a voice reciting a prayer. Turning, he looked into the wide eyes of a man, a monk of the church, and knew him immediately. It was Brother Louis, whom he had deposited at the monastery a week ago, and his servant, the deaf-mute who stayed by his side like a stray chick. What were they doing here?

"Cross the river here." Old Bric nudged Gabriel and indicated a small path leading away from the main road. "If any follow, I hope to throw them off. It is a rougher road, but few know of it."

Gabriel turned the horse into a small lane and stepped hard on the wagon brake as they descended a sharp bank, rattled across stones and dipped into the Loire. They floated with the current and the horse swam with all her strength.

After a time the horse found her footing on the sandy shore and pulled the wagon up a steep bank. Adrian dozed on the long trip, but awakened as the wagon slowed, then stopped.

The cottage was a welcome sight, yet he was too weak to get out of the wagon. His clothing was soaked with his own blood and it felt as if a thousand rapiers pierced his skin. Tate lifted him out and carried him to the cottage where he sat at the bench by the table. The others made their way into the cabin. He was surprised that although he was dirty and tired, and his arm and side hurt like the dickens, his spirits had revived and he looked about with interest as Grandfather rummaged in the cupboards for something to eat.

Old Bric produced dried apples, smoked venison, a loaf of stale bread and a jug of ale. He chuckled as he set the food on the table. "It seems we will not die of hunger, anyway."

The monk and his boy seated themselves, but the young girl, whom Adrian noted was the serving girl from the castle, stood near the door, her eyes upon Grandfather.

Grandfather straightened and cleared his throat. "This is Judith. She showed me kindness at the castle, risking her life to speak with me and give me encouragement. Judith, this is my grandson, Adrian, of whom I spoke, and these are his friends." He smiled. "I am sorry, sirs. I know not your names."

They stepped forward one by one and introduced themselves. Tate, Leon and Gabriel.

Grandfather bobbed his head to each man, then ... "This fine man of the Church is Brother Louis, and his servant. I'm sorry, I do not know your name, either."

"Samson John," Louis said. "He is deaf, but he reads lips and is not dumb."

Grandfather beckoned to Judith. "Come, Judith. Sit and we shall eat."

She stepped delicately to the table and sat near him.

Adrian took a swallow of ale and a huge mouthful of bread. "Where is Luthar?" He had not seen the little man with his longbow, and knew he fought the bravest of all in the castle.

Leon shook his head. "I know not. I only know that he stayed behind to keep our pursuers busy." He turned to Grandfather. "Did you leave word where we were going? I would like to speak with him if he comes."

Grandfather passed Judith the venison. "I told Jean, the blacksmith. He knows where I live and he can give directions."

Leon took a swallow of ale as the jug was passed down the board. He shook his head and sadness drooped his shoulders. "Hager was killed, Adrian. We could not stop it. He was taken down by ten soldiers."

"Ten! It took ten!" Adrian bowed his head. "I am sorry. He was a fine warrior."

After they finished eating, Grandfather rose. "I cannot offer you much in the line of comfort, but there is room on the floor to sleep. Judith will have your bed up in the loft, Adrian. In the morning I shall go back to the monastery to help our friends there."

Adrian shook his head. "Nay, Grandfather. You are too weary. Send one of these fine gentlemen. You must rest, or you shall be the one in need of help."

"I shall do what God wills, young man. Now it is time to get our rest. Judith, come with me, my dear." A candle in hand, he led Judith to the loft.

Louis beckoned to Adrian. "Come, my friend. I must tend to your wounds. I have some skills, too. Does your grandfather keep medicines here?"

"Aye. Up in that cupboard."

Louis rummaged in the cupboard. "Ah. Ah. A fine supply, I should say. Yes, with these I may cure about anything."

Adrian stripped off his tunic and the monk went to work. Tate and Leon continued to drink Grandfather's ale while Gabriel fell asleep, curled up in the corner with his cloak. Leon told the story of Adrian's fight with Sir Frederick.

"So that is one we do not have to deal with." Tate let his fist fall on the board.

Adrian was tempted to see if it left a dent. "Was FitzRauf killed?" He tipped the jug of ale and emptying it. Several shook their heads; it seemed the fate of the baron was unknown.

When Brother Louis was finished, Adrian yawned, for the room was spinning and he could stay awake no longer. He found an empty space beside Gabriel and fell asleep, listening to Grandfather's droning voice as he spoke in low tones to Leon, Tate and Louis.

The next morning he awoke before dawn to stirrings in the room. Gabriel was gone and the girl, Judith, added wood to the fire, then brushed off her hands and kneaded a lump of dough. "Good morn," he said, but she did not look up or answer.

In the far corner of the hut a makeshift bed had been laid on the floor. He recognized it as the cot and mattress from the wagon. Louis was kneeling over it and low on the still air he heard someone moaning. "Grandfather!" He leapt up and dashed to the bed.

Louis looked up, a worried frown on his lean face. "He took ill in the night. He has a high fever and very much discomfort in his ... bowels. I need some water."

Fear clutched Adrian's stomach like a sledgehammer. He grabbed the bucket and ran to the well. From there he peered into the stable and noticed a horse gone. Tate's. Had they sent for help?

Back in the cottage, he knelt again beside Grandfather and took his hand. It was hot and his face was flushed, the color of old bricks. Grandfather vomited into a basin by his head. When he lay back, he groaned as if in deep pain.

"What is it?" Adrian shifted to allow the monk room to work.

"I do not know. I suspect it is some kind of food poisoning. Perchance something he ate at the castle." The monk glanced up. "You might say your prayers. He is old and may not be able to shake this off, for it is violent and comes with a fever."

Adrian nodded. He and Leon erected blankets on ropes to allow privacy so the monk could strip him and cool him with water. Adrian looked at Grandfather's body; it was bruised, bleeding and thin. Tears stung his eyes.

Judith brought bread from the fire and laid it on the table. It smelled good. They sat at the board while Judith poured ale and brought forth a dish of eggs and salted pork.

"Where did you get the eggs?" Adrian helped himself to the dish and passed it along. "Grandfather gave his chickens away before we left."

"A lot of them returned, then." Judith wiped her hands with a cloth. "I found them in the barn and raided the nests."

Leon smiled at her. "You better sit and eat, too. It looks as if they did not feed you very well in the castle."

"Nay, they did not. I thank you, kind sir." She bowed and sat at the end of the bench, pulling her tunic about her legs as if she did not want to touch anyone.

Adrian passed the dish to Samson John. "Where are Tate and Gabriel?"

"They left this morning for Tours. Fortunately Old Bric left instructions as how to help the villagers." Leon glanced at the old man. "He will not be fit to travel for many a day."

"But I must travel." Louis seated himself at the table. He helped himself to the eggs.

Leon frowned. "I am afraid we need you here. Where are you going and what is your urgent business?"

"I have been sent from the monastery of Mont St. Michaels to deliver a message, a very important message to the Holy Father in Rome. For a fortnight I have been delayed, so I must be on my way immediately."

"Immediately." Leon turned the word over carefully as if he was turning griddle cakes.

Adrian leaned forward. "Your plans could not be as important as the life of my Grandfather, Brother."

Louis lifted a sober face. "The message I carry concerns not a few people but many who live in cities far away. It could mean their very lives. I shall tell you how to treat the old man. There is nothing complicated about it."

"I shall tend to him." Judith looked up eagerly. "I know something of medicine."

Adrian glared at her. "You know nothing. You are a foolish girl. The monk will stay and care for Grandfather. He is my grandfather, so what I say must be done." He eyed Judith and their glances met—met and fought, as if parrying with swords. He was surprised at the strength of will in such a slight maid. He dropped his eyes. "Very well. You may stay, but I want Brother Louis here to render his skill. He sewed me up once ... "

The monk raised his eyebrows, astonishment on his face. "I ... do not remember such a time, Adrian. Refresh my memory."

Adrian turned away. "I think I am mistaken. It was long ago and I was a child. We traveled through the northern provinces, for my parents were sold to a baron in Brittany. I thought it was you ... but I may be mistaken."

To take the attention from himself, he turned to Judith. Now that the dirt was washed from her face and she was clad in clean clothes, she was fair to look upon. "I am sorry I spoke so harshly, maiden. Please do not judge me this morn, for I am sick with worry for Grandfather and I want the best for him. You are not a foolish girl. Where are you from and where do you go?" He paused, his face burning. How could such a girl cause him discomfort? She did not seem of much account. "If you do not mind telling us."

Judith stood, carrying food to the counter. "I do mind, sir. Yet I will tell you this. My father was taken as a slave, and I have pledged myself to find him. Last night I learned he was sold to an Arab dealer and may now be in Palestine." She turned to face them. "And so I must go to Palestine. I vowed to find my father, and so I shall. Whether I must crawl on my hands and knees to do it, I shall go."

Adrian was struck with the force of her will. *The Beautiful Iron Maiden. I wonder what makes her so.*

Old Bric's recovery was tedious, yet every day he improved. Adrian returned from the creek one morning and stopped in his tracks. There, on the bench outside the cottage, sat Grandfather and Judith, their heads close together, Grandfather's book of Scriptures spread in his lap. It looked like they were sharing secrets. Judith spoke fervently in low tones, waving her hands for emphasis. Grandfather nodded and patted her shoulder.

Adrian's first reaction was to pull Judith from the bench and declare that Old Bric was his grandfather ... the two of them shared secrets ... that place on the bench was his place.

But at that moment Grandfather raised his eyes, smiled and indicated a stump nearby. "Come, sit, Adrian. You have been working too hard. See? I am up for the first time. This calls for a celebration, no? Bring me some wine, if you would. And cups for all of us."

Adrian fetched the wine from the cellar behind the house, but the issue of cups was impossible, for Grandfather only possessed two. He brought them out. "Go ahead. You and Judith. I have things to do."

Grandfather shook his head. "Nay, son. Sit. Judith was telling me of her life before she came to us."

Seating himself, Adrian shared the cup with Grandfather, glancing at Judith to see if she would continue her story. But evidently his presence dried the fount of her self-disclosures, for she set down her cup and excused herself to prepare their midday meal.

Adrian lifted his head, for the sound of hooves echoed on the still morning air. Leon appeared from the stable with a hammer in hand, watching the road. Tate, who had returned from Tours the day before, emerged from the cottage, a knife in his grip. Gabriel poked his head from the chicken coop brandishing a shovel.

Only a mule plodded down the lane, and on its back sat a man. The mule halted in front of the cottage and the man fell to the ground. His clothes were in tatters and stained with blood. He lifted his head and tried to stand. "I ... escaped their foul ... prison." It was Luthar.

Adrian reached him first, then Louis and Leon arrived. They bore him inside, to the bed, stripped the rags from his poor tormented body, bathed him and gave him something to eat. He could only take a few mouthfuls of soup and a little ale before he closed his eyes and slept.

The next day Luthar opened his eyes and told his story. He had tarried the night of their escape, and was captured by FitzRauf's men. Held in a makeshift jail, he had been tortured for days. But he would tell them nothing, and after a time was able to kill his jailer, escape, find the mule and ride to the cottage.

Adrian leaned forward. "How did you know where to come?"

"The mule knew the way. I let him have his head, yet I do not—"

"It is because he is Georges, my mule." Grandfather chuckled. "Some of the villagers must have loosed him, for I had him with me in the village."

"Aye, it was near the village where I found him."

Adrian gripped the edge of the man's tunic. "Luthar, can you tell me one thing? Does Sir Frederick live or die? I must know. I plunged the sword in his foul heart, but I did not tarry to make sure."

Luthar shook his head. "I am sorry to tell you, lad, but that son of the devil still lives. I heard this and hoped it was an evil rumor, but I saw him with my own eyes, born on a litter. They say the druid gods kept him alive."

"What of Baron le Brun? Does he live?"

"Aye. He lives, but the duchess was murdered by those foul fiends. Many of the other guests were killed. The baron was warned by a lady who received word from one of the servants." He lifted a brow and glanced quizzically at Adrian. "They are searching far and wide for this young man by the name of Adrian D'Arcy, whom they say is the leader of the villeins. Do you know aught of this affair, Adrian?"

Adrian shrugged and looked away.

Luthar continued. "There is a price on your head, me lad. A hundred silver coins and a knighthood and lands for the one who brings you in. That ought to keep you on your toes!" He chuckled suddenly.

It was the first time Adrian had seen him smile. "Do you have news of Lady Madilde?"

"Aye, lad. You can sleep well on her account. She escaped. She, too, searches for you." He leaned closer to Adrian and placed a warning hand on his knee. "I do not wish to alarm you, son, but FitzRauf is enraged ... furious about the injury you inflicted upon his son. He seeks you and says nothing will stand in his way until you are dead. I am afraid you have become an outlaw and a hero in one fell swoop."

Adrian was dumbfounded.

Luthar leaned back and smiled grimly. "Your name will be sung in songs. Stories will be told of you in hamlets across the nation."

Adrian rose to pace the small room. "That is of little account if I am dead. I must flee. But where shall I go?"

Leon cast an amused glance to Grandfather and nodded with a knowing air. Judith's dark eyes followed Adrian's every move from the shadow in the corner, but her face held nothing save contempt.

He fled outside. Pacing under the trees, his spirit springing from great joy to the depths of agony—made a hero and yet wanted for murder, lauded by the common people and yet hunted as a common criminal—he groaned aloud, wishing for the quiet life he had led a few weeks ago.

Should he make his bid for the kingdom now? Where could he find the money, the backing, the men? He thought of Lady Matilde. One of her rank would be able to finance his venture. It would be an easy thing to convince her of his lineage and right to the throne—he was sure he saw a look of recognition in her eyes that night. But could she persuade the other barons?

Later that evening, he sat beside Grandfather outside on the bench.

Grandfather studied the stars in the black sky, then nodded to him. "Tomorrow I shall ride to Montebank. Tate, Gabriel and Luthar will come with me."

"Is Judith going with you?"

"Aye."

"I would like to ride back with you, too."

"Nay, my son. God has set before thee many tasks in this world. You have outgrown your servanthood. Do you remember I have told you that you shall surpass your teacher?" His wise old eyes glimmered with tears. "It has come to pass. Save in this." He tapped his heart. "Only in your knowledge of the Word of God and your love for the Almighty. In these you shall grow like a young tree planted by the river of waters. It is time you made your own way in the world."

"But what shall I do? I have no money and no army. I may no longer ride the paths in Brittany or even of France. There is a price on my head."

Grandfather struggled to his feet. "God is setting you free, my son. You must broaden your horizons and seek your fortune in other lands. Just think, lad. You may ride to Spain, to Italy, even to the Holy Lands. Oh, that I was young and could ride with you."

Adrian shook his head sadly. "I will not ride far with an empty purse."

Grandfather reached inside his robe and pulled out a leather bag. This he handed to Adrian. It jingled. "It is not much, but I saved it for just a time like this."

Adrian tried to return the purse.

Grandfather shook his head. "Take it. I have little else to give you as an inheritance. My only request is that you use it to do God's will. Pledge me, boy!"

Tears blinded Adrian so much that he did not look up for several moments. "But I do not deserve—"

"Pah! Deserve! Who has ever said anything about deserving? We live and breathe by grace alone. God's free gift of salvation is by mercy. Do not speak to me of deserving. Receive the gift and give glory to God. Now pledge me."

Adrian fell to his knees. "I pledge that I will try to find God's will and do it with all my heart." He glanced up. "Is that enough?"

Grandfather kissed his forehead. "It is sufficient. Go with God, my son."

Adrian laughed and pulled himself to the bench where he sat with Grandfather. They spoke of many things until "the troop", as Adrian affectionately nicknamed his friends, joined them around a low fire. They watched for falling stars while Grandfather smoked his pipe and Gabriel sang ballads and Tate told stories. Adrian mentioned that he was leaving in the morning.

Brother Louis passed around a jug of ale and returned to his stump. "Where are you going?"

Adrian shrugged. "I know not. I shall have to travel at night and by the back roads." He studied a bright star on the horizon for some time. "I think ... I would like to go to Palestine, perchance even Constantinople. I have heard that one may scoop up gold on the streets in that great city."

Brother Louis sucked in his breath. "Will you be passing through Rome?"

"I could do that. What do you have in mind, Brother?" He gazed steadily at the monk, whose brown hair had grown over the top of his head, making him appear more of a man, less a monk.

"I ... I must get to Rome as soon as possible. It concerns the crusade bound for Palestine, but I know not what the message is that I carry to the Holy Father. Only that time is the essence." He glanced around the circle, including Judith who sat in the shadows, as usual. "I trust all of you to keep a still tongue in your heads concerning this matter. I have already suffered harm from enemies who do not want this message delivered. There are those in league with Venice—"

"Venice!" Leon straightened.

"Aye. Venice. The leaders of the crusade made a pact with the doge of Venice for ships to carry them across the sea. In any case, I have learned that I cannot travel alone. I need guards, guards I can trust. I can pay, not only for my own expenses but for yours, as well. I need not a large party—Adrian, you and Leon would do. We will travel with all speed to the nearest port and take ship to Rome. From there, only God knows."

Silence descended, except for the katydid's song, the swoosh of bats and the occasional hoot of an owl. Adrian noted that Judith leaned forward, her studied expression of disinterest and disdain replaced by something else.

He nodded. "I am in." Hope, like one of those elusive winged bats, swooped into his heart, lifting it with a sudden joy. If he could get to Palestine and join the crusade, he would have a share in the plunder. He would return home with more wealth than King John— enough wealth at least to set up his fief.

Leon chuckled. "I have nothing better to do. I am in, too."

Louis smacked his hands together. "Fine. We will begin in the morning. Which way would you suggest, Leon?"

"LaRochelle is the closest port. If we ride hard, we may be there in five, six days. And then we can—"

"Take me with you." Judith stood, entering the circle of light cast by the fire. Her face was drawn, but her eyes gleamed with passion. "I would go with you. I can pose as a boy. I want to journey to Palestine to find my father. I will serve you ... do whatever you ask."

"Nay!" Grandfather shook his head. "I am sorry, child, but it would be too dangerous. Didn't you tell me you have family in Dijon? I shall pay your way to Dijon and arrange an escort for you. Give up seeking your father."

She lifted her chin. "Yahweh, my God, will help me as He did Hagar in the desert. I have His promise and I must take this chance. I love you, Grandfather, and do not want to hurt you, but you cannot understand ... " She turned her face away and composed her voice. "He is all I have. I must find him."

Once again silence descended, but now it was an uneasy silence. The girl sat back in the shadows, suspicion and disquietude playing on her fine features.

Adrian shook himself and stood. "Grandfather is right." He saw Judith's face fall, her eyes flash. He glanced at Leon for support. "We have neither the time nor inclination to tarry for a girl ... a girl who would slow us down."

"I will not slow you down." Her voice was hard, etched with anger, her face white. "If you care for those less fortunate than yourself—"

"I am sorry. I would like to help you. But we cannot. We shall all depart on the morrow—Grandfather to Montebank, where he has business, and I and my friends to LaRochelle. I pray that God will give you peace and patience and that you will one day find your family, Judith."

"Like you care." She stomped off into the cabin.

Grandfather stood, wrapping his warm robe about his body. "I will talk with her, Adrian. She must see that this is for the best."

Adrian shrugged. "Do not waste much breath, Grandfather. She is worth less than nothing in the light of what we must accomplish."

Old Bric stepped closer and gripped Adrian's tunic at the neck, pulling his face close. For the first time since he had lived with the old man, Adrian saw anger flash from his eyes. "She is worth more than all of us combined, you young fool! Have you learned nothing at all from me? Nothing?" He shook Adrian as a dog shakes a bone. But then he gave a great sigh and released his hold. "Ah, well. You shall learn the hard way, boy. I shall see thee in the morning."

The next morning came in fine, with an early mist rising from the low-lying creek, trailing wreath-like from the trees on the hillsides and floating like smoke on the hills. Adrian rose and looked about, for Tate, Leon and Gabriel were gone and no one built the fire or set food upon the table. Luthar slept. Where was everyone?

Hurrying outside, he found Grandfather sitting on his bench by the cottage reciting verses from the Scriptures.

Grandfather looked up. "Good morn. It looks to be a fine day." His calm words belied his inner emotion, for he rubbed an old wound on his thigh.

"What's going on? Where is everyone?" Adrian stood with arms akimbo.

Grandfather seemed old and worn, the worry lines in his face deep and numerous. "Judith is gone. So is Georges and a few stores." He attempted a smile. "She left a coin in the cottage and a note. Here."

Adrian was surprised that she knew how to write. It read, "Mon Cherie Grandfather, I am sorry for leaving this way, but I must find my father and if none of you will help me, I shall go on my own. Please remember me to your God. Merci. Au revoir. Judith." He returned the parchment. "So is that where everyone has gone? To find Judith and the mule?"

Grandfather nodded. "To look for her, but I doubt if they will find her."

"Have you eaten this morn, Grandfather?"

The old man shook his head. "Nay. Food does not appeal to me at this moment."

"Yet you must eat. I shall bring you something." Adrian hurried inside and laid a hasty meal on the board—cheese, smoked fish and a loaf of bread Judith made yesterday.

Grandfather came in just as Adrian finished and soon after, Gabriel, Tate and Leon entered. Silence accompanied their meal, and when it was finished, Grandfather said a prayer for Judith. "Now we must go forward with our plans," he said, looking around the table. "I shall miss her very much."

Louis lifted his head. "Grandfather, you shall have Samson John to take her place." He laid a hand on the boy's shoulders. "Samson, would you like to go with Grandfather?"

The boy shook his head and made anxious, guttural sounds.

Louis shrugged. "He is determined to come with me. I fear it would be like Judith. I am sorry, Grandfather."

"Ah, well," Grandfather said with a low chuckle. "I have three men to accompany me. How could I lack anything with these? Perchance God has a great deed for this humble boy to perform. Who knows?"

After they had cleaned the cottage and saddled horses, Adrian bade Tate and Gabriel fare well. The two men mounted and started down the road. Luthar, much improved, rode in the wagon with Grandfather. Adrian waved until the wagon was lost to sight.

He stood by the path, listening to the horse's hooves and the creak of the wheels and Grandfather's final words of advice until all was silent. A whippoorwill called to her mate, a thin and delicate sound, muted by the mist. He took a deep breath and laid a hand on his sword hilt. A tingling sensation radiated down his back much like the time he first sighted Mordelias.

A new beginning. The start of a new life. What lay ahead? The fulfillment of his dreams— or disaster? He shrugged philosophically and turned to the stable. Only God knows, as Grandfather would say.

Bret whinnied a welcome and Adrian set about saddling. They would have to buy Louis a horse in Tours, but for now, the monk and Samson John would walk.

"Are you ready for an adventure, young sir?" The question erupted from the next stall, where Leon readied his Andalusian stallion.

"Aye. As much as lieth in me." Adrian pulled the cinch tight and made sure his sword sat firm in the scabbard. He looked up and found Leon's eyes across his gelding's withers. "Where does your path lead?"

Leon smiled, revealing straight, white teeth in a dark face. The light of adventure shone in his fine eyes. "I would like to visit Greece."

They led their horses out into the sunshine. Brother Louis and the boy had started out already and were lost to sight.

As they trotted down the lane, Adrian said, "I am in search of good men for my kingdom and it seems I have made a fine start."

"Your kingdom, eh?" Leon shot him a surprised look. "I thought you had given that up, that you joined the rest of us in seeking to break out from this evil system."

"I would be a fair king, one that would bring justice to all."

Leon snorted. "I have heard that before. Freedom is a foul word to kings and the barons." He chuckled. "Ah, well. I wish you God's blessings and all the good will in the world. When you are king, I shall visit you and demand equality."

Adrian grinned. "Very well. I shall share my wine and my home with you. Why do you wish to visit Greece?"

"I have learned that freedom is an old concept in that land. Perchance I will learn a few things and find some men who would ride back with me and help our cause."

Adrian nodded. "Rome. Greece. Palestine, if God wills. It sounds like a tour fit for a king. Perchance when I return, I shall be king. On such a day as this, I feel it is possible."

He laughed aloud and kicked Bret to an all-out run.

CHAPTER SEVENTEEN

When luck enters, give him a seat! Jewish Proverb

Tours, France, June 1201

Judith dismounted at the gate of the monastery and rang the bell, holding the reins in her left hand. She glanced back at the mule and smiled. "Don't look at me that way, Georges. I did not steal you. I shall take you back to Grandfather when I return." She rang the bell again. "If I return."

A black-robed monk approached, his hands in his long sleeves. "Yes? May I help you, young sir?"

She brushed her hair from her forehead and tried to make her voice lower than it normally was. "I have come to inquire after my master who was left here, very ill. Do you have word of him?"

"Come in. I shall take you to the hospital where the physician may inquire into your master's status. This way."

She led the mule inside and tied him at the rail. Then she followed the monk's broad back down a long outer hall—she remembered the cloister and the hall—up a series of stairs and to the office of the priest in charge of the hospital.

Several minutes later she returned to the mule with a letter written on parchment from Miguel. She did not read the message immediately, but fetched the mule and rode down the street of Tours, watching for the man Patrick so she might avoid him. She did not see him, nor did she see the man she truly hated, FitzRauf. His maroon and black men-at-arms were everywhere in town.

Just a short ways down the road, she drew aside under some low-hung oak trees, dismounted and ate her midday meal. Then she unrolled the parchment and read Miguel's spidery handwriting. "I do not think you will come to claim this, but just in case, I thought I should tell you my plans. I am heading north today for Orleans and hope to be in Troyes by the end of the week. If I find you not in that city, I shall travel on to Dijon. Please leave word at the Jewish synagogue wherever you are, and I shall try to find you. If I cannot find you, I shall return to Madrid. It was there that I had word of my father. *Au revoir, Miguel.*"

She mounted and, upon asking directions, found the Jewish synagogue on a low hill just above the city. Several old men with long ringlets down the sides of their faces sat in the sun beside the gate. A lump formed in her throat, for they reminded her so much of Grandfather.

After dismounting, she left the message: a note she had written on the back of Miguel's parchment. The men eyed her suspiciously, but said they would deliver it to him if he came.

She rode, then, unmolested from the city, and toward evening halted in a small hamlet. She knew Adrian and his company would not stay at the inn, but there was a camping spot by the river. She would wait there for them.

She paced nervously behind a fringe of bushes. What if they came and left? What if they rode on? Choosing a place protected by heavy bushes and two fir trees, where she could view the clearing by the river and also a patch of the road going south, she unsaddled the mule and spread her cloak on the ground.

Evening descended, and a family of husband and wife and two small children, poor people by all indications, camped downriver from her. The children splashed in the water while the father started a fire and the mother brought out the food. She watched them for some time, the sting of her loneliness sharp and bitter, like the taste of alum on the tongue.

The stars came out, one by one. A coyote called in the forest. The children were hushed into their bedrolls and mother and father talked low over the campfire. A fish jumped out in the water. Judith's eyes closed and her head nodded, but suddenly she was awake.

Someone rode in—several riders, in fact. They were quiet, speaking in low tones, moving about, setting a guard. She peered through the fir boughs and recognized Adrian first, then, yes, Leon and the deaf boy and the monk. They ate standing and did not light a fire. Leon was the first on guard.

Twice she started out to identify herself to them; twice she stopped. If she let them go from here, would she be able to keep up?

But would they not send her back? Her salvation lay in company with others, preferably men, and so she must join up with them.

She started out the third time, but stopped. Nay, she must wait and follow at a distance and pray to Yahweh that she could keep up.

The next two days were the hardest days of her life. She could not sleep, for she kept vigil over their campsite; she ate very little; she was tired, dirty and lonely. Riding the mule was no sport, either. If she beat him when he would not go, he would lie down, and only get up when he desired. At times he bolted into a dead run, and since she had no saddle, she often found herself in a briar patch or lying on the road.

Adrian and his friends traveled south, mainly at night, visiting the villages only in the early hours of the morning. On the second night they joined the Vienne River and followed it. On the third morning, just outside the city of Poitiers, Judith broke from her cover just as the men sat around a low fire, eating a meal. The smell of the food drew her like a magnet.

"Who goes there?" Leon strode forth from the trees, sword in hand. The others were on their feet before she could answer.

"Judith." Her voice carried across the meadow on the still morning air, thin and petulant like a child's. "Please let me come in. I am very ... " She broke down, weeping, and hurried the last few steps.

Leon gripped her shoulders, tilted her head up so he could gaze into her eyes. "Ah. So the thief comes in at last. I thought someone followed."

Adrian stepped forward, a frown creasing his brow. "Judith? You followed us from Tours? You little ... sneak. And you stole Grandfather's mule."

"I did not steal. I merely borrowed him. And will return him safe and sound." She looked defiantly into Adrian's cold blue eyes. He was like all the rest—knights and barons—who oppressed her people. She hated him.

"Hush. Can't you see the girl is nearly starved?" Louis pushed him aside and took Judith's arm. "Come, child. Sit. Here is a loaf and ale. We have fish, when it finishes cooking, and strips of beef. Or would you like to wash first?"

Judith sat on a rock and wiped her eyes. The monk's kindness was almost worse than Adrian's anger. "Thank you. I ... I am rather hungry. No, I shall wash when I am finished." She fell to eating as if she had never seen food. Above her head, she heard their conversation.

"So now what shall we do with her?" Leon said, sounding slightly amused. "I mean, once she has eaten and—"

"Send her back." Adrian's angry tone cut like a knife. "She was told to stay behind. To go with Grandfather. She is nothing but a common thief. Look at her! She is filthy and ragged. We cannot have the likes of such a one in our midst. How would we appear to the mighty lords in Rome? In the Levant? As a raggle-taggle band of misfits, for certes. Nay, she must go back."

Judith threw down the fish spine she had depleted of flesh, wiped her greasy hands on her tunic and stood. She spoke very precisely. "I see Grandfather was wrong in his assessment of you, Sir Adrian. He said you were kindhearted and wanted to serve your people when you had your fief. But you aren't like that. You are only a spoiled child. You are like all the others of your race, you think only of gold and fiefs and kingdoms. You care not for ... " Tears stung her eyes.

She turned to Leon who was trying to hide a smile. "I appeal to you, my lord. Can you see beyond these miserable rags and this dirty face? Can you see a maiden in need? I promise I can carry my weight in your party, and I will not make you appear a raggle-taggle band. I beseech you, sir. If there is any kindness, any scrap of—"

"There is, and we will." Leon lifted his hand. He switched his gaze to Adrian, who stood with his hands on his hips. "Adrian, you must apologize to the lady. She was raised gently, much like you. She has breeding and education. We cannot leave her, nor can we send her back."

Adrian spat. "Lady!" He shot a glance at Leon and stomped away.

Louis cleared his throat. "God has brought her to us and we must take her along. I should have some say in the matter, for I am paying the way. She shall come."

Leon nodded. "On the morrow, in Poitiers, we will buy her some clothes. For now, let us get our rest."

***

True to his word, Leon purchased clothes befitting a servant in a fine house: tunic, sash, cape, hose and sandals. Judith still had her cloak, which she stowed in her pack, along with a comb and a hand mirror from Grandfather. Adrian mumbled an apology when they broke their fast that morning, but she knew it was not genuine.

Still, it was better than nothing and she accepted it with a nod. "I forgive you, Adrian. Please disregard the harsh things I said about you. Grandfather said you are a man of worth."

He shot her a glance that pierced her heart, as if he resented the fact that she quoted Grandfather. "I care nothing of what you think of me. You are here and we shall go on. There is nothing else we can do. Quarreling amongst ourselves will only aid our enemies. We shall take you seriously in your offer to help."

She bowed. "Please do, my lord."

Clean and combed and in decent clothes, she rode beside them on Georges, who seemed content to trot along beside their fine horses. At times Samson John let her ride his mount, for he motioned that he did not mind the mule. Indeed, he seemed to have an inner mule affinity, for he had no trouble whatsoever, either with staying aboard or making him go.

One evening Adrian pulled rein and sat his horse, viewing the tops of tents in a small valley near the Chateau of Count de Brougalone. Tournaments had been generally outlawed by this time, as too many nobles and knights were killed in the sport. But the games continued, for the gentry loved them and it was good for the local economy.

Adrian remembered DeArmond instructing him of the game. In the beginning tournaments were team events—two teams met in an open field and fought in a grand melee. The winners pursued the losers into the forest and returned with their captives. The losers had to relinquish their armor, valuables and horses. But now, two knights faced off against each other in the joust, thundering down the lists, trying to unseat their opponent with a dull-pointed lances.

With Leon's help, Adrian procured an ancient suit of armor from the village blacksmith that evening and entered the tournament, for all that was required to enter was armor, a lance and a horse. He rode Bret and used Leon's colors of blue and gold. He chose another name, recalling a favored squire, Guillaume de Xavier.

Adrian won the first round and the second. The crowds began calling Guillaume de Xavier, and he found himself the *chevalier* of the tournament. He sought to keep his face covered, but when he accepted the prize, he was commanded to remove his helmet and face the raised and covered seat of the nobles.

There, in the stands, sat King John with his entourage. Adrian's knees fairly quaked. He allowed his hair to fall into his face and accepted the golden mitre on a velvet pillow with sweaty hands. But John did not recognize him, for no soldiers came to arrest him afterward.

They rode out of the valley that evening like cats whose tails had been set on fire.

"It is dangerous for Adrian to ride in the tournaments," Brother Louis said when they stopped at their camping place the next morning. "This one could have been his undoing, save for the mercy of our Lord. Promise me you will not ride in another, Adrian." He dismounted with a grunt and set about unsaddling.

Adrian went cold. "Why do you think it unsafe, Brother?"

Louis turned to him, his face a study in amusement and distress. He chuckled low and his words came softly. "I remember who you are, my lord, even though it was many years ago. You reminded me. I sewed you up when you were a child in the castle at Mordelias."

"Ah." Adrian expelled his breath.

"But I keep secrets very well. Do not fear, my prince. I only care for your well being."

Adrian loosed the cinch on Bret and removed the saddle. "I need gold. I need a lot of it, if I am to wrest the kingdom from John. I can earn it at these tournaments, for I am good. I know I am good. I feel it."

Brother Louis shook his head and went off to prepare the meal.

The next evening after only a few hours ride, Adrian spotted banners flying in a large clearing behind the chateau at La Villediend-du-Clain near Lusignan. He thought of his friend, Baron le Brun, and wondered if he was in residence.

They made camp beside a stream. Adrian ate standing, shoveling the food in his mouth. He glanced at Leon. "One more.

Surely the blessed Virgin Mother would smile upon me one more time, if I promise her the tithe of my winnings?"

Leon chuckled. "Perchance. But you will not please Brother Louis."

"Brother Louis can stay here and pray." Adrian mounted and with Leon at his side and Samson John running as his squire, he entered the game.

Set against inferior knights, he won the tournament and noticed none in the stands he recognized. The next morning he sold his prize and patted his purse. He turned to Louis as they mounted in the city square. "It grows, Brother. It grows. I shall give a tithe to the Church. Do you think the saints are pleased?"

Brother Louis shook his head. "I think peril hovers near. This had best be the last one, for I am in a fever to reach LaRochelle."

They camped the next evening beside the river. Adrian rolled into his blankets early, leaving Leon to the first watch. Their horses were tethered nearby, munching on grass. Brother Louis, Samson John and Judith washed out the trenchers at the river's edge, then returned to camp where they settled down in their bedrolls, exhausted from a long day's ride.

Someone shook Adrian's shoulder. It was Leon. He stared up at a sliver of a moon that hung over the trees. All was still. Too still.

"We have company," Leon whispered.

Adrian eased from the blanket, pulled on his boots and buckled on his sword. "Robbers?"

"I think not. They are soldiers, men at arms." Leon roused the others, hushing their startled exclamations. He instructed them to roll up their beds, gather their belongings and crawl to the horses.

The hoot of an owl broke the silence. It was a signal.

Leon nodded toward the river. Two shadowy forms emerged from cover, coming upstream. "I shall lead them away through the forest," he whispered to Adrian. "You take the monk and the others to the village for safety."

"Nay." Adrian crouched beside him near the horses which Louis and Samson John had saddled. "Let's run for it. I have no liking for a battle in the dark against soldiers, whoever they are."

"Can Louis and the others keep up?" Leon put a foot in the stirrup.

"They had better." Adrian mounted and noted that the others climbed onto their mounts. A limb cracked in the forest. A booted foot crunched gravel by the river. Chills chased one another across Adrian's back, his main concern the monk and the girl and Samson John. He slid his sword from its scabbard and saw the glint of Leon's weapon, the whisper of steel as he unsheathed it.

"Ride!" Adrian sunk his heels into Bret's sides.

A horn blasted and men ran from the forest. Dark shapes materialized from the shadows, soldiers wielding sword and ax and lance.

Adrian hacked at a shadowy shape, heard the man's cry, felt his sword slice through muscle and bone. The mule screamed and he wondered if a soldier wounded it. Leon fought beside him; they were aided only by the dim light of the moon.

More soldiers emerged. English men-at-arms—Adrian knew from the shape of the helmets—King John's men. He ground his teeth and lashed wildly with the sword. *I shall not be taken by John! Not again!*

"Go! Go! Go!" Leon yelled at the others.

Adrian saw them ride off into the forest through the opening he and Leon hacked out. The soldiers were driven back for an instant by their fierce defense. "Leon! Follow!" Bret leaped with alacrity through the opening and ran along the river as if a thousand demons pursued. Adrian glanced back and saw that Leon, too, had made a break. But the enemy was well horsed and a column of them followed not far behind.

Adrian and Leon joined with the others about a half mile down the river; their sudden appearance from behind startled Georges, the mule, so much that he leaped into the race, Samson John clinging to the saddle. Adrian breathed easier when he saw Judith riding the pony well—he had to admit she was a good rider, the best he had ever seen in a woman.

It was a wild ride through the night. Adrian pulled up beside a stream to let the horses breathe and to get a drink of water. It seemed their pursuers were occupied similarly, for there was no rush of hoof beats on the track.

Judith came last to the clearing and piled off. "Just where—"

"Hush!" Adrian held up his hand, listening. He relaxed. "Keep your mounts close to hand. All of us need a drink and a short rest. But do not fall asleep."

Leon sat on his heels and watched while his stallion sucked the water into his mouth around the bit. "We shall wait until morning," he said, wiping his brow. "Then we shall ride on, for I know they follow."

"They are English." Adrian dipped his hand in the water and splashed it on his face. "My old enemy, King John. I marvel that he has men so far south. I wonder what their orders were."

Brother Louis snorted. "To take prisoners, of course. One particular prisoner. You just thought no one recognized you."

Adrian shook his head. "Nay. He would not know me. He thinks me dead. There is some other reason." He leaned against a rock.

Leon crouched nearby. "If I am not mistaken, one of Lady Matilde's chateaux is close by, or at least one of her uncle's, Lord Gilbert de Montfort. The lady might be persuaded to shelter us for a time."

Adrian glanced up. "Lady Matilde! Just the one I wanted to see. We shall ride on the morrow and seek sanctuary there." He stood. "That is, if Leon can find the way."

"I can find the way on the darkest night where there is no trail." Leon punched Adrian. "If you do not believe that, my friend, I shall show you."

Leon was as good as his word. They avoided the English soldiers and arrived at the castle gate just as dawn approached the next morning. Adrian led the way as they clattered across the drawbridge and drew up with a word to the guard of the castle.

"Tell Lady Matilde that Sir Adrian D'Arcy and Sir Leon de Fitzgerald are at her gate, wishing to speak a word in her ear." When the guard returned, they entered the castle and dismounted in the upper bailey where a groom took their horses. A servant led them to a small room adjacent to the Great Hall and brought mead in chased silver cups.

Brother Louis nodded his thanks for the mead and glanced at Adrian. "I and my servant and Judith will remain here."

Judith raised her cup with a glitter in her dark eyes. "We don't want to make you appear a raggle-taggle band. Besides, what would a great lady have to do with the likes of me?"

Adrian's felt his temper rise. "You shall all come. The lady must meet those of my train. And if we are to find sanctuary in her court, I counsel you to keep a still tongue in your head and your wits about you. She is the great-granddaughter of King Richard, yet she is not full of pride, nor is she a dullard."

"Ah, a lady full of virtue and beauty, wealth and power, yet she has no pride. I must meet this one." Judith drained her cup.

Leon smiled. "The lady Judith is no dullard either, Adrian."

A servant appeared and led them into the Great Hall.

A throne of sorts was set upon the dais on the far wall. The usual bedlam of dogs, chickens, children and servants that greeted one in most French and English castles was absent in this one. The serenity of the Great Hall resembled that of a cathedral. Silent servants laid long trestle tables with white linen clothes and beautiful silver dishes and there were no dogs whatsoever among the rushes on the floor.

Adrian glanced at the tapestries of biblical scenes on the walls and the glint of gold from the cressets holding the torches caught his eye. But it was the woman on the dais that demanded his full attention. She was veiled, so he could not gauge her temper or expression. Did she know she harbored a fugitive? Did she desire to see him, someone who appeared so meanly before her that night at Renault?

Slowly, without any greeting, she stood and watched them approach.

"Lady Matilde, I thank you for your hospitality in my time of need." He bowed his head and sank to his knees. Leon knelt beside him. Louis, Samson John and Judith also sank to their knees.

No response.

A new fear smote Adrian. Had they walked into a trap? Was she loyal to John? Would she imprison them and turn them over to the him?

Suddenly her laughter echoed around the room. She drew off her veil and extended her hands. "Rise, all of you."

Adrian looked up into her face and his heart gave a great leap of joy. He kissed her hand, unaware of little else save the lady. "You have rescued my life. The king's soldiers pursued us all night. They would have captured us ere long. How can I ever repay my debt of gratitude?"

"You can't." Lady Matilde laughed again. "Now the scales are balanced. We are even, as they say. And who are these others, Sir Adrian? You must acquaint me with your party."

Adrian rose and, with a flourish, introduced Sir Leon, who bowed and kissed her hand; also Brother Louis and his servant; and then Judith, whom he introduced at Raphael, his squire.

"These others may go to the rooms I have assigned." She beckoned and a servant woman approached and led them away. "But I would like to speak with you two." She nodded and, with a rustle of her silken skirts, led the way to a fireplace set in the wall. She seated herself near it and indicated that they should be seated also. Stools were brought forward, and they pulled them close to the cheery blaze, for even though it was summer, the castle was drafty and cold.

Leon stretched his legs to the fire. "I am afraid we have brought John's soldiers to your door."

She gazed at them as if she had caught a fine kettle of fish, but her voice and manner was subdued. "King John will not trouble you here. I am pleased you sought refuge in my home. I attended a tournament ... let's see ... two days ago, and thought I recognized the chevalier when he removed his helmet to receive his prize. I desired a word with you then, Adrian, but could not arrange it." She smiled winsomely.

Adrian's heart leaped. Her turquoise blue gown heightened the color of her eyes. Dark brown curls peeped from underneath her wimple. But it was her eyes—wide set, twinkling with amusement, fringed with dark lashes—that held his vision and his heart.

Servants brought wine in tall silver cups. She lifted her cup and drank. "I must admit to one of my chief faults. It is my consuming curiosity. I could not get your face from my mind, Sir Adrian, and I am consumed with wonder as to why you were a valet at Renault. What were you doing there? Who are you?"

"I ... uh—"

"And you, Sir Leon de Fitzgerald. What do you have to say for yourself? Are you not far from your home in the countries north of Paris? Does your father know you are keeping company with the likes of this Adrian?"

Leon's gaze fell and his face colored. "You have found me out, my lady. I have to blame my young friend for all my troubles. It was he who coaxed me to join him in the affair at Renault. My father knows nothing of me. He has no son, he would say, by the name of Leon, for I left his house and have turned against the system that brought him fame and wealth." He stood. "Do I have your permission to retire?"

"Ah, I have wounded you." Lady Matilde laid her hand on his arm. "I have a sharp tongue, Sir Leon. It is another of my faults. We would have you stay, would we not, Adrian?"

"I would be disconsolate if you left us." Adrian lifted his brows. "Be seated, friend, and take not to heart the lady's words. She means nothing evil by them. Her heart is as pure as driven snow. Be seated."

Leon nodded. A smile flickered across his face. He resumed his seat. "Thank you, kind lady and good friend. For certes, I like your fire and your company. So, Adrian, tell the lady your story." He received the filling of his cup.

The fire crackled and spit. Silence descended upon the Great Hall. Lady Matilde looked upon Adrian with a quizzical smile. Never had he suffered from a lack of words, yet now he found none to do his bidding.

He cleared his throat. "You are right, my lady," he said, blurting it out like a naughty schoolboy confessing to a crime. "My name is not Adrian D'Arcy. I swear by the Holy Mother of God, my old self died and is buried. Aye, except for the interference of a man who risked his own life to save me from the pit of hell, I would surely be buried in the river at this moment. My uncle, the … " He had said enough, probably more than enough, for he saw the truth dawning in Matilde's eyes.

"Yes?" she said, lifting her skirts and resting her feet on a stool. "Pray continue."

Adrian gulped his wine. "I am the son of a nobleman and was condemned to die for a crime I did not commit. That much I will admit, but nothing beyond." He shifted and saw his comments did nothing to amend his earlier indiscretions. "After I was rescued, I was taken in by an old man. I call him Grandfather. He was captured in a raid on Montebank. I discovered that the raid was done under the orders of FitzRauf. I know not why they took my Grandfather, except that he is a kind and Christian man and they hate all kindness. I vowed to free him."

"This is where I come in," Leon said with a low chuckle.

"Yes. I enlisted the services of Sir Leon and his men. With some of the villagers, we penetrated the fortress and freed the prisoners. I was enlisted to spy out the upper chambers and so donned the clothes of a valet. Thus I came into your chambers, my lady." He proceeded to relate his adventures. "I am glad you took my warning to heart, *ma cherie,* for I have heard since that many were killed in the *coup.*"

She nodded gravely. "I am grateful for your kindness, Adrian," she said in a low voice. "What a beautiful story! I am sure a *trouvere* will sing it someday!" She lowered her voice even further. "I shall not speak of the first story you told me, but I can guess your true identity. My heart rejoices, for I have followed your adventures and secretly loved you from afar. Perchance if you linger in my court, we shall have time to discuss this matter further, for I am sure you would like to meet with some of your old friends. Will you stay?"

Adrian shook his head. "This night only. Our traveling companion, Brother Louis, is on an urgent mission to the Holy See in Rome and cannot tarry."

"This night only!" She cast a glance to Leon. "May we not implore this monk to stay a little longer? Sir Leon, you are good with words, it is said."

Leon bowed. "I shall do all that is in my power. I fear for your safety, for John's men will surely report to him and he may come upon you in force."

She tossed the warning aside as if it were a shawl. "Nay, I fear not John." She stood and spoke formally with one of her lightning shifts of mood. "I forget my duties as chatelaine, do I not? I wish to invite you to the hospitality of the Chateau de Fontelaine as my guests. If you cannot stay longer, at least you shall enjoy a fine meal tonight."

They rose and Adrian took her hand. "Thank you, my lady. Perchance we can persuade our brother monk to stay two nights."

"*Tres bein.*" She adjusted her veil. "Now. I have duties to attend to. You are free to explore the chateau and rest. I shall have a servant take you to your room."

That evening, Adrian and Leon donned their best clothes, shaken from their packs. Adrian nodded at his reflection in the bronze mirror, for he had a servant cut his hair and trim his beard. He smoothed the linen hose that showed off his long, slender legs to great advantage, and donned a beautiful suede jerkin.

When he entered the corridor and joined Judith, he noticed she had bathed and wore servant's clothes, yet her black eyes glimmered like stars and her slender body was captivating even in its drab clothing. Did she long for jewels and lovely silk robes and soft velvet slippers? If she did, she did not show it.

The Great Hall bustled with activity when they made their appearance. Servants finished last-minute preparations on the long tables. Silver goblets held red wine, and at each place lay the *mazer*, a thick slice of day-old bread that served as a plate for the roast meat and gravy. Platters in the center of the tables were heaped with roasted almonds, figs, and dates.

A manservant with a towel over his arm ushered Adrian and Leon to a seat on the dais and allowed them to wash with scented water in a silver laver. Brother Louis, Judith and Samson John found places in the lower hall, below the salt. Adrian felt a pang as he saw Judith sitting beside the deaf boy and wondered if she longed to be on the dais.

But the moment Lady Matilde entered with a bevy of her ladies, he forgot all about Judith. The guests, both those above the salt and those below, rose to their feet when she entered, and a sprinkling of applause filled the hall. She nodded to them and looked at Adrian. Her eyes were cobalt blue tonight, like the sky at summer solstice, sparkling like sapphires. Her cheeks glowed with a warm, rosy color, and her red lips were curved into a half-smile, half-pout.

He took her finger and led her to her seat, noting she had dressed exceedingly well for an ordinary dinner, in a gown of white damask that was held tight to her slender waist with a sash of crimson. Over the gown she wore a robe of bright red samite, and a cape lined with white fox fur. A circlet of gold rested on the dark curls that were coiled on her head and her white veil reached to her shoulders. On her feet were soft slippers of green, turned up at the toes and embroidered with gold thread.

An older man with a full beard and bushy eyebrows accompanied her. Lady Matilde introduced him as Lord Gilbert de Montfort. He said nothing during the meal, only grunting now and then to indicate his need of more wine.

"My lady," Adrian said as the guests were seated, "you are too beautiful for mortal eyes to behold."

"And you, Sir Adrian, are far too clever with words for your own good. But I thank you. Sir Leon, is he always so charming with the ladies?"

Leon dipped his head. "Aye, my lady. He casts one eye upon them and they fairly swoon with delight."

Adrian wished he could kick him under the table, but the lady's rippling laughter eased the moment. A bishop from the nearby abbey stood at a signal from Lady Matilde and offered a lengthy prayer. Then a long line of white-clad servants came bearing trays. The first was the pantler who brought bread and butter, then the butler who served wine. The next course was soup made from roasted quail and vegetables.

Two people shared the soup bowl and since Adrian sat at Matilde's right hand, he shared the bowl with her. He found it strange to serve her, for he had always been served as prince. Yet he cut the chunks of roasted quail with the knife he carried at his belt and fed her with great delight.

Throughout the meal, Adrian heard as from afar the rumble of noise around the great room: the sudden eruption of laughter from the knight's table; the spilling of wine and the loud, coarse talk from the farm hands; and closer, the droning voice of the bishop who engaged Leon in a lengthy theological debate. Yet his attention was fixed solely upon Lady Matilde's face and eyes. Her laughter, the light in her eyes, the movements of her delicate hands, her wit and intelligence bewitched his heart beyond anything he had ever encountered.

After the meal was finished, they lingered at the table. Matilde paused in her recital of an amusing story to lift her hea   d listen to the musicians. Adrian became aware that the hall wa   empty, for most of the castellan's servants had retired, and   had also excused themselves, including Judith and Louis.

Leon shifted restively. "May I retire, Lady Ma given me a less than desirable companion than thine

"But the evening is fairly just begun," she sai suppose you will take Sir Adrian with you?"

"Nay, my lady. He is yours for the evening. I in your gardens."

"*Sans doute.*" Lady Matilde and Adrian stood and bowed while Leon strode from the room.

Then she shoved back her chair. "What shall we do? Would you like to stroll, too? We could explore the upper bailey where there might be an early apple for the picking."

"I would be enchanted, if you would accompany me."

With her hand on his arm, they descended the steps from the Great Hall, strolled leisurely through the stone hallways and came at last to the upper bailey where a large grass enclosure held immaculately kept lawns, flower beds, fountains and a small orchard of fruit trees.

The next day, Adrian spent almost every waking moment with her; riding with her before breaking their fast in a small, private dining room, accompanying her on her rounds of housekeeping duties, looking in upon an ill child, showing off his skills in the lists against two of her knights, having a late lunch with her under the apple trees in the upper bailey.

As the sun sank behind purple hills and stars appeared on a velvet sky, they feasted again, much as they had the evening before, and afterward they paced the gardens, her arm linked in his.

"I wish you could stay longer, Adrian. I would like to contact the barons and have them meet you. I am sure they would welcome you home." She looked at him fully. "You *are* Prince Arthur, are you not? Speak plainly to me now, for I must not be deceived."

He stopped and returned her gaze. "Aye. There is no deception in my heart or on my lips. I am Prince Arthur. Old Bric, the man I call Grandfather, can verify my story if you doubt it. But what do you intend to do? Do the barons truly want Prince Arthur on the throne?"

She shook her head. "Why ever not? They hate King John and the En. our claim can be proven and you rally the barons and their ey will follow your lead."

lady." He shook his head and kissed her hand. "As for the throne, I know this is not the right time. As uld say, I must wait for it. I … I must go and find ass the money I need to raise an army. Then the lly. But not now, *ma cherie*. I will leave on the e my way to Palestine. They say there are great the taking in that land."

She touched his face with a tender hand while tears fell.

He drew her to his bosom and held her tightly. "Do not cry. I shall return, I promise you. Ah, if only I had the means to support you, I would wed you here and now, John or no John."

He dropped to one knee, gazing into her face. "This I pledge thee, my lady. I am thy knight, and I shall ride for thee and for thee only. One day I shall return with gold in my pockets and lands in my name, and I shall wed thee in the chapel on the green. This is my solemn pledge." He stood and enfolded her in his arms.

"Oh, Adrian! Do you not know that the king even now arranges my marriage according to his wishes? How could we ever convince King John that we should wed?"

"I care not, *ma cherie*," he said, lifting her chin. "I care not, for neither king nor baron shall part us! If you truly love me as I love you, then we shall find a way. What say you? Will you wait for me?"

She nodded slowly. Their eyes met and held in a long, steady gaze. "Aye, Sir Adrian D'Arcy," she said in a low tone. "I shall wait for thee until the end of my days. I defy even the king to wed me to someone else."

He kissed her forehead and then stepped away, for her maids approached. "Come, let us walk by the lake. It is a fair sight to see in the moon's glow."

***

Judith turned from the window and slammed the lattices shut, fastening them with shaking fingers. In the moonlight down below she had seen Adrian and Lady Matilde. It did not take much imagination to figure out what they said or the import the meeting held.

She had seen the way Adrian looked at the woman, the way she looked back. Anger tasted bitter in her mouth, but something else was in her heart—something she did not want to recognize. Jealousy. Every womanly instinct rose up, shouting in her head. *I am just as pretty as she and far more intelligent. My family was richer, oh yes, much richer. Why am I here and she is down there in his arms?*

"I don't care." She slammed a heavy book on the low table and stumbled against the leg, tears blurring her eyes. She was only Raphael, his squire. It didn't matter. Adrian was a heathen. A dirty heathen pig. One who killed with no thought, like those who killed her family.

But, no. He was not like that at all. She had seen tenderness in his eyes, his gentle touch on the horse's flank when it gashed its neck on an overhung branch, the quiet awe in his eyes when he lifted them to a sky full of stars. But he was proud—too proud to notice her.

A trickle of tears turned to a torrent and she flung herself on the couch, weeping into a satiny pillow. In the midst of the storm, a knock came gently on the door. She rose and dabbed at her face, stifling her sobs. "Who ... who is it?"

"Brother Louis. We need to talk."

The monk drew her to an alcove that overlooked a small lake. He pretended not to notice her stained cheeks and red eyes and held the candle low, setting it down carefully on the bench by the big windows. They sat almost knee to knee.

Louis sighed and turned to her. "You are unhappy, my child."

She did not want to discuss her private turmoil with a monk of the Roman Catholic Church. His lean face was highlighted in the flickering light with its high brow and wide set eyes. The cross he had stitched on the front of his robe repelled her, yet she noted that he had covered it. For her.

"Tell me, Lady Judith. That is what I am here for."

"Brother Louis, you cannot know how miserable I am. Or can you? Have you been forced into servitude you did not desire? Drug along on adventures you would rather not experience? Have such loneliness for your own kind that you could barely ... " She caught her breath, willed herself not to weep again. "I suppose not."

He smiled but did not touch her. "Judith, I admire you so much. You are brave and honest and kind. Your desire to find your father is beyond reproach. If I had a daughter, I would want her to be like you."

"Thank you, kind sir. You have been such a comfort to me, despite our differences in ... religion."

A tear made its way down his cheek. He did not wipe it away, but glanced at her with a rueful grin. "This is a night for weeping, no? Perchance we are all tired." He cleared his throat and seemed to gather his thoughts. "I am fearful that the lady will convince our young friend to stay in France for a time." He gestured to the lake where two small figures walked arm in arm.

"What will you do if he does?"

"I shall continue on. But I have a proposition to make to you. I know you are unhappy with us, with this journey, with your servitude. Would you like to go without us? I have the means to pay for a guard, dress you as a lady and send you to Palestine. Would you like that?"

Her heart leaped and she looked up, square into his eyes.

"Ah. I see you do. Well, what do you say?"

"I ... I hardly know. Yes, I would like to travel like ... a lady. But I would be loath to leave you and—"

"And Adrian. You can say it, *ma cherie*." He chuckled. "He tries our patience, but he gets past one's defenses, does he not?"

She laughed, wiping her eyes. "Aye, that he does, Brother. But how could I accept ... ?"

"You can accept whatever our good Father provides for you. Tell me in plain language aye or nay."

Her pulse quickened. She leaned forward to grasp the sleeve of his black robe. Her voice came as a low whisper. "Aye, good friend. Aye. But we shall promise to meet some place in Palestine, for I do not want to lose you. Do you promise?"

"Promise? Ah, that is difficult. If you would say try, then I shall agree. We will try to meet in Jerusalem. At the Church of the Holy Sepulcher. Agreed?" He held out his hand.

She gripped it as if holding onto a lifeline. "Agreed."

***

Chateau de Fontelaine, Anjou, September 1201

It was scarcely a fortnight after Adrian, Leon and Brother Louis departed that the Chateau de Fontelaine received a distinguished guest who arrived with a large party of lords and ladies, plus twenty knights, all of whom had a squire each and a multitude of servants and retainers.

When they were announced, the Lady Matilde took to her bedchamber, hoping to avoid a meeting with the principal guests.

But the party had no inclination to depart, and on the third day her uncle pressed Matilde to give them an audience.

"We cannot sustain this hospitality much longer," he said, "or we shall be rooting about in the forest for our livelihood. See them and dismiss them, if you must, but they must leave soon."

Lady Matilde bowed and, with a heavy heart and many prayers, she accepted Baron FitzRauf and his son Sir Frederick into her presence the next day in the Great Hall. She wore no veil, for she wanted to see Adrian's enemy face to face.

The baron was a distinguished-looking man, tall and broad of shoulder with a commanding air. Behind him four servants in maroon and black carried a chair upon which rested an invalid—a man with blond hair and steely gray eyes. The servants set the sedan upon the floor as FitzRauf approached.

She was surprised that he was not old, barely in his third decade. His fierce black eyes smoldered with contempt, desire and pride. She drew in her breath, for his sharp glance pierced her soul.

"Lady Matilde." He bowed low over her hand and kissed it. She nearly withdrew it, for his touch seemed hot and foul. "Let me introduce my son, Sir Frederick. I am sorry he cannot rise to bow before you. He is recovering from a serious wound he encountered while fighting for my safety and honor." He turned and with a flourish indicated the young man on the chair.

She bowed her head, hoping to hide the rise of fear and anger she felt when she saw this man who hated Adrian so much. "I am pleased to meet you, Sir Frederick. I am sorry for your wound. If there is anything we can do to help you ... "

FitzRauf dismissed her offer abruptly. "All of his needs are taken care of."

She nodded. "I wish to apologize for my illness when you first arrived. I trust you have been treated well and have enjoyed the hospitality of this house."

"We thank you for your hospitality. We are on our way to my chateau in the south, where the climate is conducive to a speedier recovery for my son." He passed a hand over his forehead. "I still see that evil night in my dreams. It is a miracle that we were not killed, for many were."

She nodded, but made no comment.

"She knows of it, Father, for she was there." It was the first Frederick had spoken and his words were sharp with bitterness. "But she escaped with her life and her body whole. How very fortunate when so many of our guests were killed."

She expelled her breath. *Let the games begin!* She met his hostile stare. "God was gracious and my life was spared. I am sorry that so many died."

"Aye." Baron FitzRauf nodded. "And this ... what was his name? Oh, yes, Adrian D'Arcy. He was the one they say who stirred the villeins to attack my castle. Do you know of whom I speak, Lady Matilde?"

"I know Adrian D'Arcy." She strove to keep her face smooth and terror from her eyes. "What would you have of him?"

"Ah." He smiled, and she thought of a snake about to strike. "I know you must not be aware that this D'Arcy is a criminal wanted by both the English and the French. He is one thing that unites the two nations who have fought for centuries." He barked a harsh laugh, his mouth twisting into a sneer and the sheen of hatred brightening his eyes.

Frederick took up the tale, leaning forward in his chair. "He is an outlaw of the worst type, mingling with discontented villeins and slaves who long to break the bonds of their masters. It is his kind who keeps the countryside in an uproar and causes untold damage to property and lives. It is because of this ... knave, this brigand, that I am as you see me now."

His father nodded. "I have given my life to track down this man and bring him to God's justice."

Matilde gripped the arms of her chair to keep them steady and prayed her face did not give her away. "Aye? And what would you have me do, my lord?" Her voice sounded stilted and distant to her ears.

FitzRauf did not seem to notice. He leaned forward, his face white and his eyes livid. "We need information, Lady Matilde. I know that he came to your chateau. Now I am willing to believe that you and your uncle did not know you harbored a fugitive. But there are penalties we could exact from you if you prove to be uncooperative ... "

Frederick spoke in a low voice. "I also know a secret about this man. It may prove much to my benefit both financially and politically to whisper it in the king's ear."

"I know not of what you speak, sir," she said, withdrawing against her chair, but her heart pounded and she felt a flush creep up her neck.

"I think you do," he said, lowering his voice. "I know who this D'Arcy is. I recognized him as we fought. He is a relative of yours. He is Prince Arthur."

She laughed, blessing the saints that she could. "For months there have been rumors of sightings of the prince. He is in Rouen, waving from the donjon of the king's castle. He has been spotted on his white stallion in the forest where Merlin dwelt." She shook her head. "Surely you cannot believe that he escaped from the castle at Rouen. King John could not let him live. Nay, Prince Arthur was murdered and is at rest now. I have seen D'Arcy and I assure you, he is not Prince Arthur. King John would not believe you, for certes, you would lose your head if you mentioned such a thing to His Majesty."

FitzRauf turned to his son and they held a furious whispered conference.

She walked a distance from them, gazing at the colored glass in the oriel window high on the wall. Then she whirled about. "If this is your great secret and you are threatening me with it, then I think our hospitality has reached an end. I must ask you to leave."

"Ah, my fair lady." The baron, suddenly contrite, bowed in his most courtly manner. "I would never threaten you or your uncle. I am merely asking for cooperation in my search for this renegade. You must forgive my son for thinking of Prince Arthur. It consumes him at times. Have mercy upon him, for he is not himself."

She nodded but kept her peace.

"I must ask you a question. Think carefully about your answer, for your future may rest upon it." He paused dramatically. "What do you know of D'Arcy and where is he now?"

She knew the question would be coming, but when it came, her breath left her body for a second and the room revolved in a slow circle. She was thankful her back was turned and she had a few seconds to recover. "I ... know not, my Lord FitzRauf." She turned to him. "He was in the barracks with my knights. His companion, Sir

262

Leon de Fitzgerald, mentioned something to one of my knights about traveling north to see his father."

"You did not speak directly with D'Arcy?"

"Yes, I did. It was during a dinner we held, and both he and Sir Leon sat with us. He spoke of his grandfather and of his desire to return to the northern part of Brittany. Other than that, I know not. I swear by all the saints in the heavens and on a Holy Bible, too, if we had one."

He stared at her and suddenly his face relaxed into a smile. "Thank you, gracious lady. I hope your hospitality will extend throughout the evening, for I and my son would also enjoy dining with you."

She bent her head. "For certes. You are invited to dinner tonight." She watched him depart and rang for her ladies. "I need to go to confession, Lady Cherithe!" she whispered.

"You better wait until tomorrow." Cherithe took her arm as she returned to her apartment. "You may have to tell more half-truths tonight."

"Half truths! By Saint Joseph! I wish it were only half-truths. The lies I told will cost me plenty, but I am willing to bear the cost."

Lady Matilde found she did not have to further damage her conscience that evening, for FitzRauf and his son were the best of guests and the evening passed without incident.

The next morning she and her uncle saw them off in the lower bailey.

FitzRauf took Matilde's hand and kissed it. "I received word that King John is considering giving you to my son as his bride, Matilde." He glanced over at his son.

She met Frederick's eyes and saw his hunger, as if he consumed her as he would a thick slab of meat. Her stomach churned, but she kept her face calm. FitzRauf led her to the invalid's chair and joined their hands. Her skin crawled at the touch.

Frederick kissed her hand. "I would count it a blessing from God, *ma cherie*, for I have petitioned the king for your hand with many gifts."

She steadied herself. "I thought you were to wed the duchess of Poitou, Lady Francine."

A scowl darkened his countenance. "She refuses my hand. No, that arrangement has been canceled indefinitely. But you ... you are kind and thoughtful. You can look beyond my invalid's chair."

She bowed and withdrew her hand. "I thank you, my lord, but I have been promised to another."

Baron FitzRauf raised his eyebrows. "Ah? The king has arranged this?"

"Nay, he has not. But we ... I ... cannot speak of it ... " She choked back tears and turned away. Her uncle took her place and as she moved away, she saw the two men conferring, saw the flush that rose in her uncle's face, and knew he would approve of such a match. A slow burning anger rose in her throat and threatened to choke her.

FitzRauf smiled to her when their talk was finished. "Fare thee well, my lady," he said as he mounted his destrier. "I trust I shall see you soon. Perchance I shall find the miscreant, Adrian D'Arcy. You shall witness his execution. Would you like that as a wedding gift, my son?"

"Oh, Father. I could ask for nothing better. Thank you!" Frederick raised himself up and clasped his father's hand. The party departed.

Lady Matilde retreated to her rooms to weep and pray.

BOOK THREE

THE ANSWER TO HATE

And man, proud man, drest in a little brief authority,
Most ignorant of what he's most assured,
His glassy essence like an angry ape
Play such fantastic tricks before high heaven
As make the angels weep.

William Shakespeare

CHAPTER EIGHTEEN

A small rock may hold back a great wave. Homer

Rome, January 1202

A cold wind lifted Adrian's hair as the ship drew near to the port city of Ostia Antiqua. He drew his robe closer to his body and glanced down the rail at Brother Louis and beside him, Samson John. Their faces were turned east, watching the dying sun tinge the clouds with red and gold. A range of low hills lay dark on the horizon. "It will not be long." He nudged the monk's side. "How do you feel, Brother Louis, now that you are so close to your holy city?"

"I ... I feel humble." Tears slid down Louis' face. Last night Leon shaved Louis' head, so now he appeared again a monk clad in his plain black robe with a red cross sewn to the front. "I only hope that I will be equal to the demands of Pope Innocent the Third. It is an awesome thing to have an audience with him. Not many in Christiandom do, you know."

Adrian smiled. It seemed as if Louis was appearing before the highest court of the land, before the most powerful king. But, of course, for a Roman Catholic, he was. "No, I don't suppose they do. My advice, brother, is that you strive to be yourself. You are clever and wise and full of kindness. Don't try to appear anything more than you are."

Louis shot him a quizzical look. "I shall take your advice to heart, sir. Now I must retire. Tomorrow will be a full day."

Adrian watched him pace to his cabin. What did Rome hold for them? A shiver coursed his body, a premonition of evil. Shaking it off, he found his bunk and slept soundly.

Their horses were unloaded before daybreak, and they ate at a small inn in the city of Ostia where the Decumanus Maximus met with the Via Aurelia which led all the way to the ancient city of

Rome. Golden stones glowed in the morning sun. Majestic columns lined the street of the Capitolium and the Forum, built by Rome over a thousand years ago.

"It makes our buildings in France seem new." Leon finished his ale and swallowed the last of the crusty loaf they had been served with olives, cheese and fish.

Louis said nothing as they mounted and rode towards Rome. His face was glistening with sweat, even though the sweet morning air was cool. Samson John, too, kept his eyes fixed to the east as if he watched for the return of the Messiah.

The cobbled street stretched straight ahead, dotted here and there with guard posts by the sides of the road. Traffic increased as they approached the city.

"Where do we go?" Adrian called to Louis, raising his voice above the noise of rumbling wheels, horses' hooves and the din of the throngs of people shouting at the tops of their voices in every language under the sun. He had to repeat himself before the monk took notice of what he was saying.

Louis, too, had to shout. "The Lateran Palace. I am told it is in the southeastern part of the city. We shall have to ask for directions." He reined his horse to a halt as they waited for a large party of nobles to pass. Louis drew closer to Adrian and lowered his voice. "But first I would like to visit the Basilica of St. Peter. Let's stop here and ask the way." He dismounted at a guard post and accosted the young man who stood ramrod straight to attention.

"St. Peter's Basilica?" Adrian glanced at Leon. "What is there?"

Leon shrugged. "The tomb of St. Peter, I suppose. Ah. It looks as if our good monk has some information."

Louis motioned north. "He said that just before the city walls at the Porta Aurelia, we turn left. That road will take us north to the Via Cornelia. Then we turn left again and the Basilica is very close, on the right hand side." He mounted. "Come."

Adrian sighed and reined Bret to follow Leon and Louis. This was all nonsense. Why couldn't Louis find the pope, whether it was where he dwelt or where he held audiences, do his business, get an inn and leave in the morning?

He spotted the creamy limestone building of the basilica before they arrived. It towered over the other buildings. A guard halted them at the gate, then nodded them on when he learned their business.

As they approached the church, Louis said, "I have learned this place was where Nero had his gardens and his circus. It is the place where he killed so many Christians during his reign, using them as human torches to light his gardens. It is said to be the place where they hanged St. Peter upside down. This is sacred ground, my friends. We should kiss the very stones beneath our feet."

The grounds around the basilica retained the feel of a garden with old fountains almost buried in the midst of bougainvillea bushes and tall, stately cypress and sycamore trees scattered over a gently rolling park.

Brother Louis led the way up the steps and they entered the cool interior of the old stone church. Adrian's eyes followed the lines of the walls and columns to the top—up, up, up—where in the far distance one could discern the frescoed ceiling. In the great echoing sanctuary, they trod down the long center aisle and paused where another walkway intersected it, forming a cross. There a throne-like chair sat under an elaborate canopy.

"The Bishop's Chair," Louis whispered.

Opposite the chair loomed the gigantic rectangular tomb of the Apostle Peter, its marble sides glossy, its top decorated with golden statues, symbols and flowering vines.

Louis fell to his knees, as did Samson John. Adrian bowed his head and waited. It seemed to take an eternity while Louis said his prayers.

When his prayers were ended, Louis led the way down the stairs and to their waiting horses. From the corner of his eye, Adrian saw a man in the shadows mount a horse. When they rode off the grounds with a nod to the guard, the horseman followed. He was a large man who wore a flat-topped hat and a black robe.

The man followed them across the Tiber at Pons Aelius, then down into the crowded and noisy streets of one of the busiest cities in the world. After a time, Adrian lost sight of him in the crowded streets.

***

"He is here." Giovanni removed his hat, brushed a hand through his hair and combed his luxuriant black beard with his fingers. The man he addressed sat at a large desk, surrounded by heaps of papers, scrolls and books. His bulk filled an oak chair and his multiple chins wabbled as he chewed on a nut.

"In Rome?" The man rose ponderously. Everything about him was slow, like a river of molasses. It was one of the many things that Giovanni despised about him.

"No. Jerusalem. Where do you think?"

"And you followed him? Is he alone?"

"He is in company with three others—one, a servant boy; the other two are French knights." He let his eyes rest on the man briefly, then looked out the window, down in the street. "The last I saw him, he was trying to get through a blocked street down near the Hippodrome. They will be here shortly."

"Tell me when he arrives."

Giovanni met the man's eyes. "You do not want me to ... distract them? Or kidnap the monk?"

"That is unnecessary and full of risks. All we desire is to prohibit the monk from seeing the pope. With my position at the Holy See, I don't think that should be too difficult. That will be all."

Giovanni nodded. "Yes, my lord." He left the stuffy apartment with quick steps and began his vigil near the plaza of the Lateran Palace.

***

The crowded streets of Rome neither interested nor invited Adrian who was jostled by a vendor selling sweetmeats and smashed against a stone wall as a dozen soldiers galloped past. Pushing away from the wall when they were gone, he stood on tiptoes to spot Louis' black robe and bald head in the mass of people ahead.

Louis had asked a dozen people for directions, but every one of them gave him only a shrug and a shake of the head, or false directions that led deeper into the maze of the old city, down narrow fetid streets, where they battled crowds and heat and confusion.

Near midday, they stopped and bought a loaf of bread, cheese and wine. They sat at a small table outside. Adrian was surprised and pleased that the wine was warm and full of rich flavor. Of course, it should be. This was Italy. They went on, following behind Louis and his shadow, Samson John.

Now they walked, leading their mounts, for the way was too crowded to ride. Adrian heard shouts ahead. The mass of people stopped altogether. He leaned against the warm brick wall and shook his head. Another noble passing by? A riot? Who knew? These Italian were crazy, for certes. The sooner he could leave this rat-invested hole, the better.

It was a riot, or a fight, he knew not which. Louis turned and mouthed something, but Adrian could hear nothing over the roar of the crowd. He tried to turn his horse, but bumped into a solid mass of bodies behind.

"Meet ... at the ... " Louis shouted, and motioned away to the south. "Meet ... "

The fight erupted all around, and Adrian was nearly knocked off his feet as bodies reeled into his. A man with a bruised eye swung a cudgel that hit the wall where Adrian's head had rested. Adrian swung his fist with all his might and hit the man in the stomach. Fending off other attacks, he backed into Bret, moving him back ... back ... Bret whinnied in terror. "Steady. Steady, boy." Adrian rubbed the side of Bret's head.

The street widened where another intersected it and formed a circle with a fountain in the center. Adrian was flung back against the fountain, blocking blows here and there, receiving others, landing punches now and then on a solid jaw.

Bret reared with another scream; the reins pulled through Adrian's hands, yet he hung onto them. The way suddenly cleared and he bolted down a side street, turned again and fled, Bret close behind. The horse was a good companion, for people saw his flying feet and hurried out of the way.

He came to another fountain. Sinking down on the ledge, breathing hard, he looked about—it was fairly peaceful, if a street in Rome could be called that. Bret shook his head and took advantage of the water. The horse lifted his head from the water, and Adrian patted his neck. "Well, old friend, we escaped with our hides intact, but I wonder where the others are. I wonder where we are."

Many people could have supplied him with directions to the Lateran Palace, if he knew how to say it. Too bad he hadn't studied

Latin more diligently instead of gazing out the window and dreaming of tournaments.

A ruined stone edifice stood to his right. Was it the Forum? Which direction was southeast? Louis must have been trying to tell him to meet at the Lateran Palace. But how could Adrian find it? He glanced at the sinking sun. Ah. East must be the other direction, and then south would be ... there. He started down a street, keeping southeast in mind.

An hour later he came to the wall, an ancient wall encircling the city. Louis said the palace was near the wall on a hill. He looked to the right and saw a small forested hill rising above the clutter of buildings. On top of it something rose into the sky. Was it a tower? An obelisk? Didn't Louis say that one of the popes, or was it an emperor, brought an obelisk from Egypt to the palace?

The traffic on the streets thinned now that evening approached. After riding a short time, he came to a piazza which fronted a huge building. In the center of the piazza was an obelisk, and in front of the obelisk was a statue of a man on a horse.

Adrian did not need to be told this was the Lateran Palace where the popes dwelt and did the business of the Church. He dismounted and led his horse past the obelisk, and discovered from the inscription it was the Obelisk of Thutmosis III of Egypt. The man on the horse was supposed to be Marcus Aurelius.

Leaving Bret at the rail, Adrian mounted the steps. Another inscription told him the palace had once been the residence of the Emperors of Rome, but Constantine gave it to the Church for the use of the holy fathers. Inside he stepped into the "Aula Corcilii", a magnificent hall where the various Councils of the Lateran met and discussed business. The hall contained many small side chambers, apses, each decorated with velvet hangings and soft carpets and golden utensils.

A priest in a white robe approached, his feet whispering on the marble floor. "May I help you, sir?"

"I am a knight of France who would see the palace. Is it open for visitors?"

The man bowed. "You came alone, sir?"

"Nay, I came with a party, a monk from France, and another knight and a servant. We have traveled far. The monk's name is Brother Louis from Mordelias, France. Have you any information of him? I understand that he has a conference with the holy father. We were separated just now on the city streets and he said to meet here."

The monk nodded. "Come this way, please." On silent feet he led Adrian down a hallway, then up marble stairs, through arches and past closed doors. He knocked on a massive oak door and opened it.

A priest sat at a large desk, but the size of the desk did not conceal the man's massive body, nor the rolls of fat enclosed in a black silk robe. He glanced up, his cold, blue eyes appraising Adrian from head to foot. He did not rise. "Ah. The knight. Where is Brother Louis?"

Adrian spread his hands and shrugged, surprised that the priest knew of his companion. "I do not know, Father. I came to find him. We were separated on the street."

The priest gestured with his hand. "Sit down, then. When the monk arrives, he will be brought here. Would you like some wine?"

"No." Adrian perched on a brocaded seat near the wall, but then he stood. "If you don't mind, Father, I would rather wait for him near the entrance." He moved to the door and turned the knob.

"I do not think you want to do that." The priest hefted his great weight out of the chair.

Adrian turned the knob and opened the door. In the hall stood at least a dozen soldiers, dressed in red and black. They stared at him with swords drawn. He froze; his right hand reached for his sword hilt, but he remembered he had to relinquish it at the door of the palace. Gently he closed the door and turned back to the priest. "What ... what is this all about? We are only pilgrims to the Holy See."

The priest sank down on the chair with a rustle of silk, his cold eyes glittering and his mouth twitching in what Adrian thought was an attempted smile. "You tell me, Sir Adrian. Yes, I know your name. I think you are much more than pilgrims. You tell me about Brother Louis, the humble monk who desires an audience with the pope. You tell me what he carries, for you have traveled with him. You should know." He popped a handful of cashews into his mouth. His jaws slowly crunched them.

Adrian stood stiff, his heart thumping in his ears, a dozen escape plans racing through his mind. He had faced evil on the battlefield, had fought it in the lists, had seen it on the faces of barons and serfs.

Yet to find it here, in the center of the religion he was taught to give his allegiance to, took his breath away.

The priest's mouth twitched again. "You cannot flee to warn him." He leaned back and poured himself wine from a decanter on the desk. "Since we will spend some time together, you should know my name. I am Father Dominic. Sit down and drink my wine and tell me your story. If you value your life." He raised a cup. "And the lives of your friends."

***

Acre, Kingdom of Jerusalem, December, 1201

Judith disembarked at Acre along with a score of other passengers, her traveling companion, Sister Theresa and her guard, Baldic. From the very first, she was struck by how the strange combination—she, a Jew, in company with a nun and a warrior of Bulgaria who wore Roman-style dress and spoke about as much as Georges, the mule.

The fortress of Acre was a formidable stone wall that fronted right onto the beach and the city lay tucked into the harbor behind it. Her heart came into her throat. Now what? She followed Baldic and the nun off the ship and into the crowds by the quay, confused by the myriad languages, the shouting, the smells, the vendors, the strange sights and sounds. Her thoughts jumbled like marbles in the pocket of a small boy as she walked the streets.

She must locate the Jewish quarter. Hadn't Father once said they had relatives in Acre? But the city sprawled like a mammoth spider as far as her eye could see to the south and west. She felt alone, separated from her family, from her people and from her friends.

"Where should we go, Lady Judith?" Baldic pulled her to a halt in front of a stall.

"I ... I do not know, Baldic. Where are you going, Sister?"

The nun held her skirts above the refuse thrown into the street. "St. John's Hospitium. I will work there. I shall abide in the nunnery."

"Do you know where this place is located?" Judith dodged a man with a tray on his head loaded with pastries. A small boy and a dog ran helter-skelter down the narrow street.

Sister shook her head. "We shall ask for directions."

"Do you speak the language?" Judith fended off the advances of a crippled man who begged for a coin.

"Nay. What language do they speak?"

Baldic pushed aside a fat priest. "Aramaic, for most part. But some here speak Arabic, or French, or German, or Latin. Pick which you want." He snapped his fingers.

Judith laughed, surprised he said so much, so eloquently. She looked up and realized she couldn't see Sister Theresa in the press of the crowd. Without a thought for Baldic, she dodged through the crowd like a hound on the track of a rabbit, praying he followed.

After awhile, she spotted the nun's black habit and accosted her, but the nun did not slacken her speed, striding away as if she wanted to put as much of Acre behind her as possible.

Baldic was panting when he caught up with the woman and persuaded her to stop. "Wait ... and stop here for a moment. We are not running ... a race. Don't you think we should find ... the place where we go before we run ... our legs off?"

Judith stared at him. "Can you speak Aramaic?"

He waved his hand. "Enough."

"Well, then, ask the way to St. John's Hospitium."

Baldic shrugged. "Why ask? Who knows? We may find it by just looking."

"We will also find sore feet."

As they continued through the crowded streets, Judith nudged Baldic several times to ask directions and almost pushed him into the path of a priest who was garbed in a black robe.

Baldic knew Latin better than he knew Aramaic and after a short conversation the priest motioned them to follow. He led them through a maze of narrow streets to the very brink of the sea where a wall was erected against storms and tiny hovels leaned together like old women with no teeth and vendors sold their wares.

Above smaller buildings towered a sturdy stone monastery, built like a castle. Sister Theresa rang the bell and they waited while a monk came unhurried from the cool dark depths of the building.

He bowed to them, then opened the gate and led them inside. "My name is Brother Titus. Please come in. This place used to be a castle, but was turned over to St. John's Hospitaliers, Knights of the King's Realm. We serve pilgrims and soldiers. Come this way, please. A sister will take the ladies to their rooms. You, sir, may come with me."

Judith was struck again that she found sanctuary in the church she hated. She was housed in the nun's cloister, in a small room that held a cot, a pitcher and a stand. On the wall was a crucifix. She took it from the wall, touching it with shrinking flesh, and laid it beneath her bed. Then she washed her hands and face and opened her pack. She appreciated the clothes Louis bought her—fine linen gowns, a silk robe, two pairs of leather sandals, a cape of damask, and enough sashes and scarves to please any woman's heart.

Why did he do it? He might never see her again. She wept a little when she remembered her parting from Louis...and from Adrian. Louis pressed her hands between his and murmured a prayer over her head and wept a tear or two. Adrian merely bowed and said he was pleased that she could travel to Palestine without delay. Had she seen envy in his eyes? A longing that he might accompany her?

She sighed. But that was all. She had not seen any approval of her new appearance, nor regret—indeed, he seemed pleased that she was no longer his concern. They promised to meet again, but she knew from the clipped way the words fell from his lips he had no intention of meeting her again in Palestine, or anywhere else.

Tres bein. She had other matters to attend to—she would let Adrian go his way. He was merely a heathen, after all. What did she care what he thought of her?

For two days Judith haunted the marketplace, the narrow streets, and the plazas of the Jewish quarter, asking questions and getting no replies in answer, only friendly conversation and polite rejections. She was glad she had studied Hebrew all those years with Grandfather.

On the third day she fell into a comfortable conversation with an old man who sat at the fountain near the center of the quarter. Before long, she shared her whole history with him. He listened with bright eyes, nodding and asking a question or two. When she was finished, Elihu patted her hand.

"I see you need help, my daughter. Come home with me. We will make room for you until you can find out about your father." He rose slowly. "Ah. My old bones complain. Come, child. You are one of us."

The house gleamed in the hot sun, made of white limestone, large and airy, like her home in France. She stepped through the open doorway into a tiled courtyard where a fountain sent a spray of water into the air and palm trees grew and flowers brightened the borders. She heard singing and followed the song that drifted into the main dining room. The room was filled with light, for a bank of high windows opened to the sun. A small table sat along the wall and cushions lined the floor. She stopped and spread out her arms, feeling as if she had come home.

Elihu took her elbow. "Come, meet my Deborah. She will take care of you like a mother hen." He steered her through an arch, into an open kitchen area.

The singer was a woman with gray hair caught behind her neck, with flour on her hands, and an ample waist bulging beneath her robe. She wiped a streak of flour from her cheek and stood, smiling.

Elihu said, "Deborah, this is a young lady I found by the fountain. She has no one—no family, no home. She has come to look for her father. Her name is Judith ... " He squinted at her.

"ben Itzchaki." Judith's voice was low and scratchy and her hands nervous and sweaty. "My father is Elias ben Itzchaki."

Deborah turned and raised her brows. "The family of ... "

"Yes. I am a descendant of the great Rashi. I was born in Troyes, France."

Deborah nodded and returned to her dough. "Elihu, take Judith to Rachel's room." She smiled again at Judith. "Do you have bags, dear?"

Judith nodded. "I shall go back for them. They are at St. John's Hospitium."

"But not before you share our midday meal. Here. Sit here. Then Elihu will go with you to the monastery and you shall stay with us. My daughter Rachel died ... " She averted her face and kneaded the dough with strong fingers. "She died last spring. I shall show you her grave."

Judith almost said *tres bein*, but then remembered her Hebrew. "I am sorry for your loss." She sat upon a cushion and accepted a silver cup from a servant. "You don't know how much your hospitality means to me." She looked around and almost wept for the sweet familiarity of a Jewish home, for hearing Hebrew, for knowing these people understood her.

That evening she settled into Elihu's home and slept that night with no troubled dreams. Elihu promised he would inquire after her father, but cautioned that the trail was cold and it was like looking for one particular grain of sand on the seashore.

The days turned into weeks, and Judith paced the courtyard, for she could not rid herself of the need to find her father soon. Perchance he was dying; perchance he called her name; in any event, she must hurry. Each evening Elihu told her the same story: many slaves passed through Acre, but no one remembered a Jew named Elias.

One day, nearly a fortnight later, Elihu returned from the marketplace with a strange look on his face. He asked for a cup of wine and motioned for Judith to sit beside him. She had been helping with the wash, but her heart began tripping madly in her ears when she saw his face. He had news at last.

"I cannot say whether for good or ill, or if it is truly of your father, or not." He sipped his wine. Judith felt she would explode if he tarried any longer in the slow way he had of speaking. "While I was sitting there in the sun, it was very warm today, was it not?, a boy came by with a bladder filled with water and kicked it—"

"Elihu." Deborah entered the room and lowered herself to a cushion near her husband. "Get to the point."

"*Oi.* As I said, I sat near the fountain, where we met, Judith. It is my favorite place because I can see so many who come and go. Deborah, you remember Josiah, the man who—"

She nudged him.

"Ah, yes. Well, while I sat there, a caravan came into town. There was a lot of excitement, I can tell you. Martha hobbled out from her house. You know her, Deborah, she broke her leg last spring, and—"

"Elihu!" Deborah rolled her eyes.

"*Oi.*" He shrugged, settled himself and took a long drink of his wine. "I talked with the caravan owner, Elijah ben Isaac. He remembers a shipment of slaves coming into port, maybe three years ago, or more. There were some Jewish men amongst them. He remembers it because they were French and he doesn't see many French slaves here."

Judith leaned forward, barely breathing."That would be about right, for it would have taken them some time to travel here. And?"

"He cannot be certain, but he knows where they were headed."

"Yes?" Judith held her breath.

"Damascus. The entire shipment was bound for Damascus, for a great caliph who lives there." He sipped his wine. "Of course, there is no proof that your father was in this group."

"Who is this great caliph?"

Elihu shrugged. "Elijah ben Isaac will know. But how can you free your father? Once the Arabs have a man, they use him up and toss him aside as if he were an animal. Worse than an animal, for they care for their horses better than their slaves, better even than their wives."

"That is not very comforting," Deborah said with a sniff.

Elihu shook his hoary head sorrowfully. "I am sorry to bring you bad news, Judith. You must resign yourself to his fate and think of what your life holds for you here. You are young and beautiful. You should marry. We shall act as your parents and see that you find —"

"No, Elihu." She stood, her hands gripped tightly at her sides, her face hot. "I thank you both. You have been very kind and helpful to me. But I must travel north to find my father. Is there ... do you know of any ... ?"

Elihu pulled himself to his feet and wagged his beard. "I was afraid you might insist on going. My brother's son, Jacob, travels to Damascus in a few days. He might be persuaded to let you journey with him."

"That is what I shall do, then. Will you ask your cousin for me, Elihu?" She laid her hand on his arm. "Please?"

Elihu nodded. "Tomorrow morning. But you must promise that if you do not find your father you will return here."

"I promise that I shall return, Elihu. If I can. I know not what the future holds." She straightened. "Will your brother's son require payment? If so, I have no—"

"It will be taken care of, as if you are my own daughter, Judith. No. Do not refuse the gift. They say that when one helps another, both are made strong. It is true. So take the gift and give glory to God."

Two weeks later Judith bade her friends fare well, mounted a sturdy-looking donkey that had her belongings packed in a bundle behind the saddle, and headed north along the Great Sea and then east through country held by the Muslim Sultans.

She was pleased that two women accompanied the men and she fell into an easy friendship with the younger of the two, a girl named Hadessah. She traveled to Damascus to wed the son of a business partner of her father's.

One evening as they camped in a meadow not far from Mt. Hermon, Hadessah cast a worried glance upon Judith. "What will you do once we arrive in Damascus? Father knows the Caliph of Damascus, Al Mu'azim Issa, and will be able to gain an audience with him, but how can you learn of your father? You cannot ask outright."

"I know not, Hadessah. I know only that I must go. Perchance I shall acquaint myself with the servants in the great house of the caliph. There will be a way." She found it hard to sleep that night, for the girl's question aroused doubts in her mind. She watched the stars wheeling in their vast circles and heard the hoot of an owl and the low speech of the men around the fire.

The next morning they rode past a huge fortress near the village of Panais. Judith kicked her donkey to ride close to Hadessah. "What is that?" She nodded to the fortress set upon a hill.

Hadessah frowned. "It is called Subebe in the Arab tongue. It was built by the crusaders. We call it Nimrod's Fortress."

"Do the Franks still control it?"

"Nay, they lost it to the Arabs about fifty years ago. Since then the sultans have lived and ruled their kingdom from there. They say it is impregnable. You should pray that your father is not there, for no one escapes Subebe."

Judith shivered, as if a cold hand skimmed over her skin. With relief she followed the train past the castle and around the southern slopes of Mt. Hermon.

That evening as she laid out her bedroll and crept into it, she heard a soft sound and lifted her head. A man approached on quiet feet. She knew him, had seen him often with the caravan. Saul, a merchant from Acre, a friend of Jacob's, journeyed with the party to attend his business in Damascus. Judith was uncomfortable around him, for he gawked at her in a bold fashion and made no attempt to conceal his desire for her, even though he had a wife and two sons in Acre.

Each evening he stole to her bedside and talked in a low voice—a monologue, indeed, for she would not answer. Last night she rose, rolled up her bed and moved closer to the tent where Hadessah and her women slept. Saul only chuckled and returned to his own bedroll.

But tonight as he lowered himself to the grass beside her bed, she sensed his evil intent. The camp slept, for all were weary.

"I know you try to avoid me, but it is no use." Saul reclined on an elbow and stroked her hair. She shrank away, smelling alcohol on his breath and the rancid smell of his unwashed body. "I have asked Jacob about you. He said you were not married, nor even betrothed. Yet you are more beautiful than any woman I have ever seen. I would have you."

She tried to sit up, but he pinned her down. Her words came in gasps as she struggled against him. "Nay. Why do you do ... this thing? It is not lawful ... nor decent. Saul, please. Have pity on me ... I have no one ... who is my protector." It was the wrong thing to say. He rolled over, so his weight held her down. She felt as if she were drowning.

"Jonathan said I could marry you, but for tonight, we shall be one. Then in Damascus I shall wed you in a legal fashion."

"But ... you have a wife."

"She is in Acre. You shall be in Damascus. Even Abraham had two wives, no? You should not mind. I shall take care of you and you shall bear my children."

He pulled at her gown. She pushed him away. He tore frantically at her clothes and she screamed. He covered her mouth with his hand and lowered himself onto her.

She brought her head up and slammed it into his mouth and nose. He reared back and yelled. Blood spurted from his nose. She kneed him in the groin, sending him rocking in soundless pain. Tying on her sandals, she grabbed her pack and fled.

Stumbling over rocks and down into a wadi, she splashed into a stream. She plunged her head in the water and after raising it, listened for footsteps. How far had she run? She could still see the twinkle of the campfire. A jackal yapped not too far away, and off in the distance, a lion roared.

Climbing up out of the wadi, she continued on her way, stumbling over rocks in the darkness, tearing her robe on thorn bushes, falling into narrow gullies and skinning her legs. Dawn touched the sky with reds and purples. She collapsed under a slender tamarisk tree and slept the sleep of the completely exhausted.

The next morning, she knew she was in trouble, for it was hot even before the sun was high. She left her pack behind last night, somewhere, in one of the ravines, for it was too heavy to carry. No water, no food. Her feet bled, for her sandals were in shreds. She knew not where she was.

Yet as the day grew, she saw Mt. Hermon to her left. The road should be below her, in the valley that was shrouded in an early morning mist. She descended into a wadi and found a stream where she washed her face and drank deeply. When she finished, she studied the terrain. If she followed the course of the valley, then headed north, she should reach Damascus. She hitched up her robe so she could walk freely and set out north and east, praying to find water.

For two days she walked. Each day she grew weaker. It was the heat that defeated her, an enemy sucking her life and sapping her strength as she struggled to put one foot ahead of the other. On the third day she stopped beneath a broom tree, her breath coming in gasps.

She struggled to her feet and plodded on ... and on ... but as the sun neared its zenith, something was wrong with her body. Her mind told it to hurry, but it refused. Her steps lagged slower and slower. She had not eaten for three days, yet it was thirst that drove her mad. Her tongue was swollen, her throat dry, her eyeballs gritty, her head swam dizzily, her feet burned and every muscle of her body cried out in agony. If only she had taken a flask. But now it was too late.

I must get to the road. Someone will help me there. With the last of her strength, she propelled herself onto the road and stood there, swaying, wondering if Jacob's party had passed already. Surely they had.

People passed on the road, but no one stopped to help her. She sank to the ground. Her heart drummed in her ears and sweat poured the last of her precious body fluid to the sand. This was the end. Trying to crawl into the shade, she almost laughed. What a stupid way to die.

A face loomed into her vision. Gran-abba. He was saying something. She leaned forward. You must complete the task I gave you to do. Remember the Sacred Scroll, the Secret. You must not fail me, Judith! This is a holy thing you must do for your people ... your people ....

She fell on her face and lay in the sand without knowing. Sometime later, she regained consciousness. Staggering to the shade of a large rock, every cell of her body crying for water, she prayed, "Oh Yahweh, great God of my fathers, help me now. I vow to Thee that I if I live, I shall avenge the death of my mother. I shall fulfill this thing about the Gran-abba's scroll. Please!"

Her mind seemed to rove wither it may, here and there and off over the hills. She saw herself sitting beside the rock, a woman she did not know, poor and thin, with dark hair and rags for clothes. She tasted death in her mouth, feared it, hated it, yet a sense of peace enveloped her. She seemed uninvolved in this poor woman's plight, and she wondered dully why the woman did not find a way to end it all.

Out of the bright haze of the sun and fear and pain, someone stopped. Kind words echoed in her mind—and the sound of water running. Someone lifted her head, poured water in her mouth. Oh, how sweet it tasted as it trickled down her throat. Someone lifted her and placed her on an animal. Someone mounted behind and held her upright.

The sun slanted across the brown hills as she came that evening, unknowing, to a hostel. A tinkling, plashing sound filled her ears. She wondered where she had heard that before; then it came to her—water in a fountain. Someone laid her on a bed in a cool room.

Darkness descended and she dreamt. She lay at the edge of a great desert. A man stood before her, clad in black with a long sword in his hand and a red bull on his shield and a cross on his chest. She hated the cross; she hated the man. Suddenly a sword appeared in her hand. She plunged it into his heart. He cried out, blood flowed over her and he fell. Blood. So much blood. She screamed.

A hand lifted her head, and a voice said softly in her own tongue, "Rise up, little one, and drink."

She opened her eyes and heard the tinkle of water. A man's face filled her vision and she shrank from him. Yet it was not a knight with the red cross. This man wore a simple white tunic, unadorned except for an emblem on his right shoulder of two snakes twisted together.

"You have called for water," he said. "Here is water. Let me help you drink." She allowed him to put the cup to her mouth.

She drank, then sank to the pillow. "How ... long... ?" Her voice was a mere thread.

"For many days." He set the cup down. "I thought at first you would die. Indeed, you lingered near death's door, but then you began to breathe easier and your fever abated." He seated himself, patted her coverlet and smiled. "I am very glad you are still with us."

She smiled tentatively, for the man's eyes were kind.

"Let's begin at the beginning." He sat back. "My name is Stefan and yours is Judith."

CHAPTER NINETEEN

Above all, never be afraid. The enemy who forces you to retreat is himself afraid of you that moment. Andre Mourois

Rome, Italy, January 1202

Louis collapsed on the pavement and wept. The riot in the street had separated him from all his friends—even from Samson John. He wept for the boy. How could he ever find him again? And how could Samson John ask for directions—for anything? They would throw stones at him and set dogs on him.

He surveyed the sky. Evening approached as the sun descended to the horizon. Hours had passed since the riot, since he searched the crowded streets in vain for his companions. Wearily he stood. It was time he tried to find the Palace of the Lateran. Perchance the others would find their way to the palace, too. Southeast, the man said. Near the wall. He glanced again at the fading sunset and set his course with a prayer on his lips. Before long, he stopped and drew in his breath. It was here, very near here, where the riot took place. He spotted the place where they ate.

Well, he might as well eat again. At the vendor's stall, he bought a pastry and was bringing it to his mouth when a hand clapped him on the shoulder. He whirled. Strong arms wrapped around his body.

"Ah! Brother Louis!" Leon released him and laughed. "Eating again? But we just ate, my friend."

"It was hours ago and I'm hungry. Have you seen Samson John? I'm worried half sick—"

"Right here, Brother. At your feet, if you had bothered to look down."

Samson John sat on an upturned barrel near the wall, his face turned to gaze down the street, tears streaking his muddy face. Louis touched the boy's shoulder. Samson John jumped, gave a strangled yell, leaped to his feet and embraced Louis.

"Ah, ha. So you found your way back here. Praise God!" Louis laughed, ruffled the boy's blond hair and gave him the rest of the pastry. He turned to Leon. "Now where is Adrian? Do you know what happened to him?"

Leon shook his head. "I looked for him, but he has disappeared. He was last in our line, if you remember. At least I didn't find his body, so we know he lives."

Louis bought another pastry for himself and one for Leon. "Perchance he went off to the palace. I tried to tell him to meet us there."

"Aye. He would do that." He stood and squinted up the street and down it. "Yet I wonder. It seems as if he would return here. Surely he would not stay there overnight?"

Louis shrugged. "Perchance he would, waiting for us to arrive. What are you thinking? We should find the palace before the sun goes down."

"I feel uneasy about things, Brother. I noted a strange man who followed us from St. Peter's and I am wondering if he did not instigate the riot. My suggestion is that we find an inn and stay there for the night. Then on the morrow, very early, I shall find the palace and reconnoiter."

Louis shook himself as if warding off an evil spirit. "I would like to see the pope as soon as I may and be out of this business. But I will follow you, Sir Leon. You know more of warfare and stealth than I should ever care to know. We shall find an inn for the night and pray for Adrian. Lead on."

***

"Am I a prisoner, then?" Adrian peered out the window. Dusk was settled over the city and he wondered about his friends. He had passed hours of grueling questions from Father Dominic and several others who came and went, yet there had been no sign of Brother Louis or Leon.

"A guest, Sir Adrian. Merely a guest." Father Dominic called a monk. "You shall be fed and housed adequately. On the morrow, if your friends arrive, you shall be free to go about your business."

"And if they do not arrive?"

Father Dominic raised his brows. "Then we shall see."

***

Leon left the inn just as the sun topped the ridge to the east, turning the yellowed stones to gold. The innkeeper had drawn him a crude map of the way to the Lateran Palace and so, on foot, he followed the winding streets south and southeast.

Few stirred in the piazza when he arrived. Servants swept the cobblestones and drew water from a well while a priest mounted the stair and entered the front door. He studied the palace for some time, noting who came and went, where the horses were stabled and the windows—which ones were thrown back, which ones were left shut. He moved to the back of the building. Service people, servants and food suppliers filed in and out of an arched doorway that led to an inner courtyard. Ivy grew up the back of the building, networking on trellises, relieving the old stones with patches of green and white.

He approached across the piazza and inquired directions to the stable. As he walked the center aisle in the stable, he found Bret stabled among the other horses. He patted the horse's rump, returned to the piazza and entered the Aula Concilii through the main door.

A monk met him with a bow and Leon asked to see the palace.

"Ah, but it is closed to visitors at this present time," the monk replied with another bow.

"When will it open again? I have come a long way."

The monk looked aside, as if taking a cue from an unseen source. "I do not know. Please return in a few days. I believe our difficulties will be arranged by then. Thank you for coming. Good day, sir."

Leon meandered to the back of the palace, following a narrow street that led off a main thoroughfare. A baker went before him, pushing a cart loaded with loaves of bread. He accosted the man. "I am a buyer for my lord, the Duke of Picardy. He arrived in the city and entertains a large party tonight. Can you tell me where I may buy bread, such as you have here?"

The baker's eyes brightened. "Come along, young man. I have to make this delivery, but then we shall talk at my shop."

Leon followed the man into the spacious courtyard, up the steps and through the archway that led into a foyer and a hallway. He helped the man trundle the cart down the hall. They emerged in a kitchen where a large staff bustled over hot ovens. While the baker was engaged in a heated debate with the chief cook, Leon drew a young serving girl aside. "May I have a private word with you, my lady?"

She giggled and patted her hair. "I can't talk to you for long, sir, or the cook will give me a beating. What do you want?"

"Come outside. Pretend you draw water." He ducked out a side door that led directly to the courtyard and she followed, a bucket in hand. "How would you like this?" He spun a gold piece into the air.

She gasped. "Ah, my lads and lassies! And how's would a girl likes me earn such a thing?" She glanced at him with awestruck eyes and then a knowing look came into them. "I'm not what's you thinks I is, sir. I don't do that sort a thing."

"Nay. I do not want to share your bed. I need information concerning a guest. I think he might be kept in a cell. A locked cell." She gasped again and he hushed her quickly. "Say nothing. This is a secret between you and me."

She nodded, but her face was flushed as she drew the full bucket from the well with all her strength.

"He must be fed and so someone must know of this man. If you can find him and lead me to his cell, then I shall give you this coin."

"Why do you comes to me? I knows nothing of what you say." She spoke pertly, but her eyes followed the course of the golden coin as it spun upwards in the sunshine. Grasping the bucket handle, she whispered, "What is his name?"

"Sir Adrian D'Arcy, inquiring after a monk named Brother Louis."

She laid a finger on her nose. "Meet me here when the sun is there." She indicated a spot in the sky, just behind a tall birch. "I will see what I'se can do for you."

Several hours later, hours that dragged by like the moving of a snail on a warm rock, she reappeared in the courtyard and beckoned to him. Following her inside, he saw that the morning meal was finished and the kitchen deserted save for the cook who sat by the fire and drank from a flask.

She beckoned again and Leon followed her through the corridors and down two flights of marble stairs, past hundreds of doors, into the depths of the palace. At the end of a passageway, she stopped abruptly and indicated a door.

"This here." She glanced up and down the hall. "I have the key. Here. The guards are gone for a few minutes. Hurry."

Leon turned the key in the lock and swung the door open.

Adrian lay on a cot but leaped to his feet. "Leon! I was just—"

"Hush. Come." Leon stepped inside while Adrian grabbed his cloak. Locking the door, Leon handed the key back to the girl. "I hope you do not fall into trouble for this. Here is your reward. If I were you, I would find a job somewhere else."

Her eyes, large and dark, glittered as she pocketed the coin. "I shall find something better than that, me lord." She reached up and pecked him on the cheek. "And if you evers needs a companion in your bed, look for me." With a giggle and a backward glance of her dark eyes, she led them to a small door and down a stairwell.

Several minutes later, they stood outside the palace. Adrian laid a hand on his arm. "So you saved my skin again. How did you manage it?"

Leon smiled. "Masculine charm and a little gold. Come, let's go. I suspect Brother Louis still wants his audience with the holy father before we leave the city. I don't know about you, but I am tiring of Rome."

"Aye. I tired of it before we were in it five minutes. But, wait. Do you think you could fetch my horse and sword? The sword is in a box just inside the main door and I imagine you know where my horse is."

Leon nodded. "Wait here."

Adrian followed him back to the edge of the piazza and in a few minutes, Leon appeared from the stable, leading Bret and carrying the sword.

As they made their way down the street, Adrian cast a glance at Leon and shook his head. "How do you propose to get Louis in to see the pope? Our good monk has some powerful and determined enemies."

Leon shrugged. "Perchance he himself will think of a way."

"At least I know my way about the palace now."

"Aye, and you know enough not to shout out your name and Brother Louis' name as soon as you enter." Leon laughed and clapped Adrian on the back. "Let's stop for some refreshment. I haven't broken my fast yet this morning and I wager your meal left a lot to be desired."

***

Adrian followed Leon's lead to the inn where Louis welcomed him with outspread arms and a shout of joy. Yet his face fell when Adrian told his story. They sat on two cots in the foul-smelling room and tried to think of a way to get beyond Father Dominic and see the pope.

"If we could only see him outside the palace," Adrian said. "I have a strong dislike for that place."

"If we had all our wishes, we would not be here." Leon rubbed the side of his head and strode to the latticed window, throwing it open to catch a breath of air.

A commotion arose in the street. Adrian joined Leon at the window."What is this, another riot?"

It was not a riot, but a procession.

He watched as pages, men at arms and servants preceded the nobles. It was a church affair, for the men who marched on foot were dressed as bishops and cardinals, carrying crosses on tall poles. In the midst of these, four men carried a chair. People lined the street, cheering. A rosy-cheeked young man in the chair waved to the crowds.

Pope Innocent III. Adrian was surprised the pope was so young. He looked as if he would rather walk, for at times he called a halt and descended into the crowd to bless a child.

Brother Louis crossed himself and sank to his knees.

"I wonder … "Adrian left the room and found the innkeeper, who was at the door, sweeping.

"Good sir. Does the pope pass this way every day?"

The man shook his head. "Only once in a while. They vary the route, you know." He brushed a hand across his eyes. "Please excuse the tears. It moves me to see him, you know."

Adrian nodded. "Where does he go?"

"To St. Peter's for morning mass. But he stops now and then to bless a church or meet with officials. This morning he will stop at St. Mary Marguerita's Church down the way here. They just received a gift from the Holy Lands—a relic, I believe. St. John's thumb bone."

"Aye. Thank you, good sir."

The others stood in the common room just behind Adrian.

After relaying the information he learned, he led the way down the street, Brother Louis close on his heels, clutching the box he had brought from Mont St. Michaels, followed by Samson John. Leon remained at the inn to watch their belongings.

"Adrian." Louis tugged on his sleeve, pulling him to a halt. "How do you propose to speak to His Holiness? Do you not know he is guarded closely? Common people like you and I cannot speak with him."

"He blessed a child on the way. He will give us an audience. Stay close." Wending his way through the thick traffic on the narrow street, Adrian followed in the wake of the procession, and arrived a short time later at a cathedral where the pope's entourage waited outside on the steps.

Adrian detoured around the press of people and found a side gate into the garden. From there, he entered the church through a small service door, mounted a series of stairs and emerged at a doorway leading into the nave of the church.

He peered inside. Pope Innocent III had just finished blessing the reliquary and was turning to speak to the assembled people. In a few moments he would begin his processional back to the street. Adrian felt Louis' breath on his neck as he watched with bated breath while the pope finished his prayers. Louis thrust the box into his hands.

He stepped inside the church, whispering to Louis, "Stay with me. You must speak to him, for I cannot."

"Nay. I ... I cannot, either. This is crazy. Come back." Louis pulled on his clothing, but he forged ahead. Now the pope raised his head and his arms in a general blessing of all the people.

Adrian pushed farther in, past the bent heads, past the bishops in their pointed hats, past the guards, to the front row of the church, to the very feet of the man who was God's representative on earth. He sank to his knees, for his legs lost all strength.

"Who is this?" A sharp voice rang out. The pope looked up, startled.

Adrian kept his eyes on the floor. "Holy Father," he heard himself saying in a squeaky, high voice, the voice of a child. "This Brother of France and I have brought you a gift." He laid the box Louis had carried through the streets on the carpeted floor near the pope's feet and glanced back. Louis prostrated himself on the floor and was weeping silently. "It is from St. Jacques and Mont Michaels monasteries in France."

The mention of the two monasteries caught Innocent's ear. He looked down, surprise flitting across his face and smiled, stretching out his hands. "Come forward, my sons. Do not mumble down there near the floor. Come forward."

Guards surged towards them, men with swords drawn and fierce faces.

Innocent held up his hands. "I am in no danger. These brothers present me with a gift and I want to bless them for it. Rise, brothers."

Adrian found strength in his legs to stand. He reached back and pulled Louis to his feet. A feeling such as he had never felt before swept through his body as the pope's hand rested on his head— euphoria, elation, love, joy—and he shuddered from the thrill of it. He kissed the ring on the pope's finger. Louis did the same.

The pope leaned closer, his voice a mere thread, a whisper. "I go to St. Peter's. Come with me and I shall meet thee alone after mass." He straightened and nodded to a page who came to take the box.

Adrian laid his hand on the box. "Your Majesty ... I mean, Holy Father, I have guarded this box all the way from France and I vowed I would let none touch it save you alone. I will carry the box." The pope inclined his head and Adrian saw a gleam in his eyes.

He knew.

Adrian clutched the box to his chest. A man with a black beard stood not far away—a man he had seen before—whose dark eyes flashed and who edged toward them. Adrian grasped Louis' arm and motioned to Samson John. When the boy was close, Adrian grabbed the boy's tunic. "Hang onto him!" he yelled in Louis' ear above the din of the crowd as the pope emerged from the church. "We must stay close to the pope or we shall lose the only chance we have to meet with him privately! Come on!"

Pope Innocent cast a glance in their direction and seemed to nod his head. Adrian did his best to keep close, finding a place to march in the midst of the bishops, feeling uncommonly out of place.

Louis seemed in a daze, but as they approached St. Peter's Basilica, he picked up his feet and stumped along with the pope's regalia as they entered the church and filed down the nave. Adrian found himself near the front and glancing around, he sighed with relief. He did not see the black-bearded man in the crowd.

Mass continued far longer than Adrian's patience, but at last it was over and he and Louis and the boy sat in an echoing hall awaiting their audience with the pope. A squad of armed men marched down the hall and stopped in front of them, surrounding them. In the midst was Father Dominic who glared at Adrian. "So you have come to see him yourself. It will not work. Give me the box and you can go free." He reached for the box.

Adrian clung to it with his left arm and drew sword with his right. "I am fairly good in the use of this weapon, my friend. I shall sell myself dearly, despite the number of armed men you bring against us."

A hush fell and the priest nodded to his men. The sound of steel hissing from scabbards filled the hall.

Adrian and Louis backed against the wall. He handed the box to Louis. "Take this and flee. I shall keep them busy for a time."

"Lay down your swords. This is a house of peace."

So silently had the walker approached, so intent was Adrian's attention focused on his enemies that he jumped at the first syllable and whirled, his sword still aloft.

Adrian lowered his sword. Pope Innocent III stood not ten feet away, his face crimson, his eyes flashing. The Ostiarii Guard, dressed in red and black, filed out to stand behind him. "Father Dominic, I do not understand your position here. Command these men away at once. I have conference with these brothers from France and I intend to hear all that they have to say to me. Go."

The priest cast a baleful glance at Adrian and, after making a respectful obeisance to the pope, turned and departed, followed by his men.

Innocent waved Adrian and Louis inside his private chambers, apologizing for the misunderstanding. He clapped his hands and servants in white tunics served wine in golden goblets, while he seated his guests on padded chairs. He himself stood and paced, as if he had too much energy to sit. "Now tell me, my good brothers, what it is you brought me."

Louis lifted the box and opened it. Inside a parcel was wrapped in leather, then wrapped in linen, then again in velvet. Gently he removed the wrappings and revealed two books, one from St. Jacques and one from Mont St. Michaels. Bowing, he laid them in the pope's hands. "My brothers and I have labored long and industriously for many years to present you with this gift."

The pope ran his slender hands over the cover of the books which were inlaid with silver and gold. "I shall send a message to the monasteries to thank them." He laid the books aside and pierced Louis with an intense gaze. "Is this all you were to deliver?"

"No, Holy Father." He turned the box over and released a secret spring. Inside was an oilskin packet. "I have come to deliver this." Again he bowed as he laid it in the pope's hands.

Innocent sat in a throne-like chair as he opened the packet and withdrew sheets of parchment. Silence filled the room as he scanned the contents. Adrian heard a bird outside the window and the voices of people in the square, still chanting prayers. He had wondered little about the contents of the secret letter as he traveled with the monk, but now his curiosity drove him nearly mad.

After a time, Innocent folded the sheets carefully and replaced them in the oilskin. He nodded to Louis. "Do you know anything of what these papers contain?"

"Only a little, Holy Father. I am a humble monk and I know very little of world affairs. The abbot at Mont St. Michaels told me it concerned the new crusade gathering at Venice."

Innocent nodded, absently rubbing the ring on his finger. "Aye. The crusade." He rose to pace again. "It has been my dream to free the Holy Lands from the control of the Muslims. It was on my instruction that this new crusade be launched, yet when Richard and Barabossa died, I despaired, for they were my chosen leaders and were known to be valiant warriors, men who would have followed my directives to the death. Now ... " His forehead wrinkled and his hands shook. "Now these papers confirm what ill thoughts I had concerning the direction of the crusade, especially since they have allied themselves with the doge of Venice who has little love or loyalty for me."

Adrian cleared his throat. "We know very little of these affairs, Holy Father."

Innocent smiled grimly and sat down. "And now we have Prince Alexius of Constantinople aiming to join the crusade. Where he will lead it does not take much imagination." He smiled sipped his wine. "Let me explain. Prince Alexius was deposed by his uncle, Alexius III, and has been in the court of Philip of Swabia for six years. Now both the prince and Philip are determined to use the manpower of the crusade for their own ends. Besides this, I am aware that the doge of Venice has a vendetta against the Greeks in Constantinople. I believe he does not intend to attack Alexandria or the Arabs in Palestine, but our Christian brothers in Constantinople. The prince will play into their hands for his own interests. And the prize? Gold, my friends, so much gold that it staggers the imagination. They say that one third of all the wealth in the world lays in Constantinople."

Adrian gasped. Gold. More gold than a man could dream of. He would have to go to Constantinople and see this wonder for himself.

Innocent stood and paced to a window. "I fear for our Christian brothers all along the Adriatic Sea coast, for there are many undefended cities that the crusaders may attack. I especially fear for Constantinople. It is a Christian city, Greek Orthodox, yes, but our differences are purely doctrinal, not warlike. It has never been taken, but the army they are raising is equal to none the world has ever seen." He wiped his face with shaking hands with a linen cloth.

"What would you have me do, my Father?" Louis left his chair to kneel in front of the Pope. "I am only a monk, but my life is given to serve you."

Innocent looked upon Louis as he would a small child and placed his hand on the monk's head. "Thank you, dear Brother Louis. I would have you take a letter to the leaders of the crusade who are meeting in Venice next summer. If they do not heed my words, then you must go on to the King of Jerusalem who abides in Acre. He will give you aid. Perchance he will send you on to Constantinople to warn the holy emperor, Alexius the Third. Whatever the case, you must try to convey the seriousness of the situation and halt the crusade from murdering Christian brothers who give their allegiance to the Holy Roman Catholic Church." Innocent lifted his eyes and met those of Adrian. "And you, friend knight? What would you do?"

Adrian fell to his knees beside Louis and bowed his head. "I am your vassal, Holy Father. Allow me to serve you and I shall do my best to see that these messages are delivered safely."

Innocent closed his eyes in silent prayer, then placed his hands on their heads and pronounced a blessing. When he was finished, Adrian rose and returned to his seat. The pope called for parchment and pen and was busy for some time. At last he rolled up the parchments, sealed them and looked up.

"There. This papal bull states that if the Crusaders attack Christian cities, including Constantinople, they shall be under anathema, they shall be excommunicated, their souls shall burn in hell forever. It is all I can do. May God go with you."

Louis bowed as he received the message, then tucked it in his robe.

Innocent paced to the door. "I can give you safe passage back to your inn, but beyond that, I am afraid I am powerless against those who oppose me. There are many like Father Dominic who have been bought. You must flee tonight, my friends. Go east across the mountains and hire a fishing sloop to take you to Venice. Here. Wait a moment." He scribbled something on a parchment and handed it to Adrian. "Stop by the bursar's office on your way out. They will reimburse you for traveling expenses. Please send me regular reports. I shall pray for good success and safety. God bless."

They bowed themselves from the apartment, found the bursar's office, received a purse of coins, then left through a side door that led into the street. Two of Innocent's guards accompanied them to the inn. There, they grabbed their belongings, saddled their horses and fled the city.

***

Damascus, January 1202

"Here, Judith. Swallow a little soup. You must gain some weight." The man in the white tunic spooned liquid into her mouth.

Judith raised her head. "How do you know my name?" Her voice was a whisper.

He smiled. "You have told it to me many times while you slept. You would say, Judith! My name is Judith! as if heaven and earth depended upon my knowing your name. I also know many other details of your life." He gave her more soup.

It tasted of chicken and herbs. She was surprised that it was so good. "What do you know of me?"

"You have told me your story while I sat beside your bed. I had others take notes, as well, so we could discover who you are and where you belong."

"I don't belong anywhere," she said, sadness and bitterness mingling in her tone. "You must have soon discovered that." She tried to sit up, suddenly alarmed. "They may come back for me—the party I was with from Acre! The man's name was Jacob...Jacob, I cannot recall his other name. Oh! Yeshaki. And there was a man who journeyed with us, his name was Saul. He tried to ... he attacked me and I ran. They may come here."

He smiled. "I know of no Jacob Yashaki, nor am I under his authority. I answer to our patron, Philip Nicholas Xavier, from Greece. I answer to the Caliph of Damascus. If we have trouble, I have soldiers ready. Rest assured, little one. He has no claim on you and cannot take you away from this hospice. You are safe enough for a time." He gathered up the utensils.

With a sigh she rolled over and fell into a deep sleep. In this, she dreamt no more of iron-clad knights with white robes and red crosses, or of blood on her hands, or of her mother's scream as she died. This sleep was as deep as the sea and as sweet as honeysuckle wine in the moonlight.

The next day she felt well enough to venture outside, for she longed for the sunshine. Yasmin, the dark-haired woman she had seen the day before, combed Judith's hair and held her arm as she tottered with queasy steps to the balcony. The woman tucked a blanket around her legs and brought her water and a scroll.

Judith leaned back and gazed at the sapphire sky, a sky seen only in the desert countries, so blue it defied description. Two date palms swayed in the breeze below in the courtyard. A gray-striped cat rubbed against her legs. She closed her eyes, strangely comforted, as if she had come home.

The next morning Stefan brought her an orange, plucked fresh that morning from the tree in the courtyard. "I am sorry I could not see you earlier." He sat beside her and peeled his own orange. "How are you this morning?" His smile belied the weariness behind his eyes.

"I am fine, thank you," she said, smelling the orange. "How wonderful it smells. I am very much in your debt for your kindness and your care. I am so used to ... other kinds of treatment. And this land is hard."

"We will not speak of debt. Let me peel it for you, little one. The skin is tough on these fresh ones. You do not like it here in your Holy Land?"

She relinquished her orange and shook her head. "It is a harsh land, what I have seen of it so far. I come from France, near the mountains. I love the smell of pines and firs. We even have snow once in a while. I was born in the city of Troyes. My ancestor was the great Israeli scholar, Rashi."

He nodded. "I have read Rashi. He truly was a great man."

"Yea. But alas, my father and grandfather decided to move to Dijon. My family was very wealthy, until ... until disaster struck. But you know all of that, don't you." She nibbled at one of the slices and allowed her eyes to slide sideways to him. "Why do the Christians hate us? We are content to let them live and raise their families. Why do they kill Jews as if stamping out a nest of rats?"

He looked down at his hands. "There are many reasons, jealousy, anger, pride. Yes, even greed. I do not know why people hate one another. Hatred is an evil that invades all who open up to it. It can only be conquered by love."

"Love!" Judith turned her face away. "I feel no love for the men who destroyed my family or those who enslaved me. I have no desire to love them, nor would they love me, if they got their hands on me."

"Ah, well." He patted the blanket and rose. "Take your ease and let your heart soak in the peace that is in this house. God will ease your burdens and give you love."

In the days that followed, she helped in the hospice wherever she could. Yasmin, an Arab woman from the village, helped in numerous ways. Galen, a young physician, assisted Stefan in the surgeries and was in charge of purchasing supplies and herbs. His wife, Petrina, took care of the children and ruled in the kitchen. A tiny woman with an enormous amount of energy and cheerfulness, she seemed to be everywhere at once.

One evening as they sat around the fountain in the front courtyard, while Petrina strummed her zipher and Galen recounted a funny episode that occurred in the marketplace of Damascus, a furious pounding of hooves and a cloud of dust approached the gate. The horses and riders were clad in armor. Five men dismounted hurriedly, some of them falling out of the saddle. One of the knights staggered into the courtyard, calling for help.

At the first sight of the iron-clad men with their white tunics and the bold red crosses, Judith stood and stared with widening eyes. As the leader approached, her heart climbed into her throat and she thought she would be sick. She did not see a man in need of help—she only saw the eyes in the narrow slit of his helmet and the blood on his sword. With a strangled cry, she turned and fled out into the desert, heedless of Stefan's call.

She ran until she could run no longer, then fell onto the warm sand. The sun disappeared and darkness enveloped the land with the suddenness of a dropped curtain. She heeded nothing save her memories, Mother's death and Nero's last cry and Father lost to her in the vastness of this strange land. She wept into her hands, wept until she had no more tears to weep. A lion roared not far away and a pack of hyenas jabbered in another direction.

Getting to her feet, she cast about for a light, but realized with sinking heart that she was lost. Sand dunes rose around her, a wind moaned, and the night was as black as a panther's coat. She took several steps, but the sand pulled her back, as if the desert clung to its prey. The lion roared again, closer. She gained the top of the dune and gazed into the darkness, the wind whipping her thin robe about her legs. She shivered.

Nothing! No light, no sound, no trace of life. She wondered what it would feel like to be eaten alive. The lion roared again, very close. Perhaps just over the dune. In a few moments she would see a tawny head appear, and then … then, the end would come. She lurched to her feet and ran, slogging uphill, sliding downhill.

She collapsed and lay still. The indigo sky was spangled with sparkling stars, so close she felt she could touch them. A soft wind stirred across the face of the dunes, moving the sand in small rivulets, cooling her brow. She heard music and sat up to hear it better. It was far away, faint and haunting, as if the desert sang to her. She stood. Yes, it came again on the wind like a harp being played by gentle hands.

A whisper of comfort entered her cold heart. God would heal her heart; the great Yahweh who created the stars and the desert and the lion who stalked it had a plan for her life. And then, above the wind, she heard a voice.

"Ju … dith! Ju … dith!"

The faint glow of a torch held aloft shone on the horizon. She called out and began running towards the light. A figure appeared and drew closer. Stefan! Soon she was sobbing in his arms. "I … I did not think you would come."

He smiled and took her hand. "Ah, child. I could not let one sheep go astray, could I? Stop weeping. You are safe. None of the knights will hurt you. Are you well? Do you want that I should carry you?"

"Nay, I shall walk if you lead the way. Thank you, Stefan."

***

Venice, Italy, July 1202

Venice stank like rotting eggs and the sty of a pig and rancid wine combined. Father Dominic pulled his rich robes closer to his enormous body and covered his nose. He hated water, hated to travel on it, hated to immerse himself in it, hated to see it. In Venice it was everywhere, lapping at one's heels like a rabid hound.

His only consolation was that he was numbered with the powerful and mighty at the conference. He sat in a narrow hall in an upper chamber of St. Mark's Cathedral on a hard wooden bench and looked around the room.

Count Louis of Blois just entered the arched doorway with his retainers, knights, vassals, lesser lords and servants, and was seated near the front. Already present was the tall distinguished baron, Lord Geoffrey de Villeharndoiun, Marshal of Champagne, with his entourage. Seated on the front bench was a small man with a dark beard, neatly trimmed, who looked more like a student than a count. Baldwin, count of Flanders, did not turn many heads, yet if one watched closely it would be noted that all, from great to small, looked to him for approval and counsel.

A little later, Boniface the Marquis of Montferrat arrived. The marquis would draw attention in any crowd with his shock of white hair, his high forehead, his dark and flashing eyes, and his muscular body. Dominic decided he must be prematurely gray, for his movements were those of a young man. This man was born to lead, Dominic decided, and lead he did with a strong hand and brilliant mind.

With him was a man Father Dominic did not know. He nudged Father Bernard, the abbot of Tours, who sat next to him. "Who is that with the marquis?"

"Do you not know? Baron FitzRauf of Poitou. It is said he is a close confidant to King John and he gains more ground each day."

"What is FitzRauf doing here?"

"He has promised a great deal of money for the crusade. Sh! They are about to begin."

Count Boniface moved to the podium and spoke in glowing terms of fighting the infidel Muslims and freeing the Holy Sepulcher from their hands, of going to Egypt first, as that seemed to be the Arab's base, of returning with gold and relics for the Church.

Father Dominic sighed and settled back for a nap. He'd heard this before.

"And here we are on this day, this good day of blessing and peace, to discuss our journey with the doge of Venice, who has promised the crusaders naves and usseriis and transports and galleys so we do not have to make the grueling journey over land. I confess that we have fallen short of the number of men who were to join us. Therefore, I am asking you, lords of the land, to contribute to our need. I pledged ninety-four thousand silver marks to the doge. We must not be embarrassed by lack of funds. I call upon all of you to raise what you may to send us on our way." He sat down.

A considerable pause fell while the nobles spoke amongst themselves. Suddenly, a voice sounded above the din. "My lord Boniface! I have a message from Pope Innocent III."

Dominic looked over his shoulder, staring as if a ghost entered the hall. It was the young knight, D'Arcy! But his men were supposed to have killed him. Beside him stood the insipid-looking monk, Brother Louis. How did they get here?

The men hushed. Boniface rose and stared down the hall. "Yes?"

The knight approached. His clothing was rumpled and dirty and it did not appear he had washed since he left Rome. He held forth a parchment. "Here is a letter to the leaders of the crusade. I assume I should deliver it to you, my Lord Boniface." He bowed and handed the parchment to the Marquis, who took it as if it contained a viper.

"Thank you." His lips a thin, white line, he broke the seal and unrolled the parchment, scanning its contents quickly. He glanced up, his face flushed, his eyes flashing dangerously. "This is very ... unexpected. I did not know the pope sent his messages in the hands of ... of unknown knights. Where ... ?" He looked down the hall, but the knight had vanished while he studied the parchment.

The room exploded into exclamations, shouts, and calls for the guards. Father Dominic rose ponderously to scan the hall, but the young knight and his companion were nowhere to be seen. Boniface called the meeting back to order and eased past the moment, handing the scroll to a servant.

Father Dominic exchanged meaningful glances with the abbot. "We shall speak of it later."

Abbot Bernard nodded.

Later that evening, Dominic met with Boniface, Baron FitzRauf and two or three others in a small tavern at the water's edge.

Boniface explained that the letter from the pope contained a directive from His Holiness against attacking Christian people. "But we shall continue on, for we have no intention of going to Constantinople, nor any other Christian city. Where does Innocent get his information from? That's what I would like to know." He bent his head back and emptied his mug of wine

"I met with this D'Arcy in Rome," Dominic said. "He found a way to get to the pope above my head. Yet this miscreant is bound for the Outreimer, to take the papal missives to the king of Jerusalem, Almaric II. Someone must get there ahead of him or we shall have the king of Jerusalem warring against the crusaders."

FitzRauf set his mug down carefully and smoothed his beard. "I shall do that, my lords. I have two reasons to travel to Palestine."

"Two?" Dominic shifted his weight and signaled to the maid for the refilling of his cup.

"Aye, two. The first is to settle my score with this D'Arcy. He nearly killed my son. The second is the matter of a Jewess, a slave I once owned. She ran away from my castle. I have word that she is now in Acre. I go to reclaim my property."

Father Dominic chuckled and patted the fat bottom of the serving girl who hastened by. "You go a far ways to reclaim it, my friend. For that cost, you could buy a dozen more."

"You have not seen the maiden." FitzRauf glared at the priest. "Your tastes may run to cheap bar maids, but—"

"We are off the subject." Boniface wiped his mouth with a linen napkin and glanced around the group. "Let FitzRauf alone, Dominic. If he wants to take care of personal business in Palestine, that is fine with me. Our concern is that he stops this ... this insidious lie before it spreads." He leaned closer to FitzRauf. "I have a contact you may wish to see in Palestine. He is a servant to the Muslim sultan. His name is..." He lowered his voice and whispered in the baron's ear.

Father Dominic finished off his drink and wiped his mouth.

Boniface straightened. "And now, my friends, I have another meeting to attend. Tomorrow we have our great convocation with Dandolo, the doge of Venice. May God go with you and give you peace." With a smile to each at the table, Boniface plunked down a silver coin and departed, his back straight and his stride full of purpose.

"I don't know about him," Father Dominic said as he left. "I don't know where his loyalties lie."

"With his purse, of course." FitzRauf laughed. "Good even, Father."

***

Acre, Kingdom of Jerusalem, July 1202

"What shall we say to le Brun this time?" Sage drew out his quill and smoothed the parchment.

"I don't know." Lord Montgomery slapped the dust from his dilapidated hat and replaced it on his head. Its proud feather hung limply in the heat. They sat in a small, low-roofed tavern near the waterfront. "I wonder where he is. If you hadn't insisted on dallying for supplies, we could have followed as he left Rome. I only surmise he came to the Levant. He could be in Egypt, for all we know."

"You want me to write that?" Sage held the feather adroitly in his hand, his eyes on his master.

"I do not want you to write that, ye jolthead! I was just talking ... to myself, it seems, since speaking to you is like talking to a dog."

Sage stiffened, anger rising red and dangerous before his eyes. But he hid it with a stretch and a yawn, wrapped his parchment and quill in soft cloth, and replaced them in his pack. "Very well, my lord. What shall we do now?"

"Do? We can do nothing, Sage." Montgomery gulped the last of his ale and swiped a hand across his sweaty face. "We can only do what we have done the past two weeks. Watch the port, walk the beaches and hope he is still alive."

"And for how long shall we do this?" Sage stood and shrugged his pack on his shoulder.

Montgomery winked at him. "Come now, Sage. Surely you would not think of abandoning our task? Not when our master pays us so well? *Eh bien.* We shall watch the boats. We shall ask our questions. Then I suppose we shall have to consider living a life in the Outreimer on our master's largess. What say you to that? Would you like a castle with a half dozen women waiting on you?" He laughed.

Sage followed his master into the sunshine and down to the quay where boats were tied and water lapped against the pilings.

Montgomery grew more expansive. "Ah, I can see it now. We shall be like the caliphs and have what they call a harem."

Sage nodded, unimpressed by his master's visions of grandeur. "And what of Baron le Brun?"

"He is far away in the cold realms of Brittany. And we are here. Put your worries aside, lackwit! We shall profit from this venture, or my name isn't Lord Beregund Montgomery!"

"But it is, my lord."

"Oh, my God! I am saddled with a fool."

Sage controlled his face, but his heart churned with hatred. How long must he bear his master's imbecility? He didn't mind being called a dog, but a fool was something else. He stared at Montgomery's retreating back and grimaced. *I am not the fool, Montgomery. You are.*

A month later, Sage burst into his master's room.

Lord Montgomery was already living the fine life he had described. Sage found him sprawled across a low divan, clad in an open, silken robe, revealing his hairy chest and skinny legs. Beside him lay a scantily clad woman.

"I saw him!" Sage closed the door. "Lord Montgomery, I have seen Prince … I mean, Sir Adrian in the city. In company with a monk of the church. I swear it."

Lord Montgomery merely grunted and popped an olive in his mouth.

Sage allowed his eyes to wander to the girl.

"Is that so." Montgomery tossed a blanket to the woman. "Cover yourself, woman. Now, then. What were you were saying? A lord, a prince of his people, travels with a shaven poll? And tell me, which ship did he arrive on, lackwit?"

"I know not, but it is he. For certes, I saw him myself. I shall write to our master."

Lord Montgomery hitched himself off the bed. "For certes, he says. What do you think of my page, Christina? His head is filled with Arabian fleas." He whirled to impale Sage with a drunken, bright leer. "How did he get here, Sir Sage of the Cribbed Hand? Perchance he came on a magic carpet." He laid his head back and roared with laughter. Wiping his eyes, he said, "Be off with you, jolthead! I am busy." He lowered himself to the divan and drew the woman toward him.

Sage closed the door carefully and that evening sought out the meanest tavern in all of Acre, a place filled with loud-mouthed men who drank ale and bragged of their sins, a place where heavily painted women beckoned to rooms above. He felt more than a little out of his depth, but he cornered an evil-smelling man and bought him ale. Sage told him what he wanted. A gold coin flashed in the lamplight and disappeared quickly into his new friend's pocket.

"Tonight, if you can." Sage said as they parted. "Morrow night I shall meet thee here and pay you the rest."

So it was that Lord Montgomery died in an untimely manner in the city of Acre. The new Lord Montgomery sent a message to Baron Hugh of Lusignan that Adrian D'Arcy had been sighted and they were following him inland.

Sage dismissed the young woman, collected his master's belongings which included a purse of gold coins, and sought lodging in a different inn. That evening in a better tavern, he ordered a mug of the best wine in the house, and a meal fit for a king. Before he finished, a group of hard-faced knights entered. They spoke French.

Sage watched them, suddenly alert. The knights were well dressed, well armed. From their conversation he learned that they had recently landed in Palestine. Then he heard a name that sent prickles down his spine. *D'Arcy.*

He stood, picked up his mug and approached their table. Wine had loosened their tongues and, in a short time, he was seated among them, telling them he also sought this outlaw from France. "What is your mission concerning this person?" He spoke with the accents he had heard from Lord Montgomery's lips for so long.

The leader of the group, a large dark-visaged man who wore the clothes of a lord, replied, "We will take him prisoner and ship him back to France." He winked and emptied his mug. "I wouldn't mind killing him here, but I have a wedding to attend. My son's marriage to a beautiful lady. We will skin him alive for their pleasure." The others roared their approval. He slammed his fist on the table and called for more wine.

Sage nodded. "I would join with you, then. It has been my business for the last year to keep track of this man. It is good news I give you, for I saw D'Arcy in the city just yestereve. I know not whether he has left the city, or stayed. But I am assured we may find him."

The lord leaned forward. "Where was he?"

Sage shrugged. "Not far from this very place."

The lord leaned back, a grin curving his mouth. "How fortunate that we should meet like this, on our first evening in this land. I am Baron Ahab FitzRauf. And your name?"

"Sa ... I mean, Lord Montgomery."

"Well, Lord Montgomery, who is this baron who employs you? What are the plans of this baron?" He impaled Sage with a hard, cold gaze.

"Baron Hugh of Lusignan. I know not his plans, my lord. Only that I am to watch D'Arcy and send back reports."

FitzRauf grunted. "I know Baron le Brun." He glanced around and lowered his voice. "I also know of a man who can tell us what we say in secret ... even in this very room. He is a servant to the Muslim chief who abides in a castle inland." He glanced at Sage. "Can you lead us to this man?"

"What is his name? I cannot find a man with no name."

"Ah. But this man is the vizier. His name is Christopher Ignatius III."

Sage nodded. "I have heard of him. I will do it for a price."

FitzRauf threw back his head and roared with laughter. "*Eh bein.* A hundred silver marks. We start on the morrow."

"It will take me time to get a horse and traveling gear. I will need three days."

FitzRauf grunted and exchanged looks with his four men, then nodded. "Two days. Here, in front of the tavern, or we go without you."

"Done." Sage gathered his cloak about his shoulders and bowed. "It was a pleasure."

***

Damascus, August 1202

It had been an unseasonably hot summer. Judith sat one morning on the balcony, enjoying the cool breeze from the west, the zephyr.

"Ah, here you are!" A soft rustle of cloth, the slap of sandeled feet on the flagstones, and the faint smell of herbs accompanied the words.

Judith glanced up as Stefan sat on the bench beside her. She marveled again at how singularly attractive the man was with his classic Grecian features—the deep-set and dark eyes, the crisply curling hair, the wide forehead, the prominent nose. His long, slender hands rested on his thighs. She thought of the times she had seen those sensitive and dexterous hands working over a bloodied child or a pregnant woman.

She smiled. "What news do you bring me, good friend?"

He shook his head. "You must not be alarmed, *agaphtos*, but I have had word from the king of Jerusalem, concerning your former master. It came to me through the Caliph of Damascus."

She gasped.

He laid a hand on her arm. "Do not be alarmed. Baron FitzRauf has made an appeal to the Caliph for your return and the Caliph sent me the message. He asked if we treated a young Jewish-French woman and gave the description."

"FitzRauf … here? In Palestine?" *Oh, God. My old enemy. Here!*

Stefan nodded. "He must have an army of spies to track you this far."

"What shall you answer?"

"I shall tell the truth and leave the result to God." Stefan enclosed one of her small hands in his. "I shall tell him that you were nearly dead and that we brought you here. If the man persists in his claim, I shall pay what is owed and you shall be a free person again."

"But … but can you … do you have the money? I am not worth a lot, but—"

"It is not your concern, Judith." When she did not respond, he said, "Are you well?" He held her hand tightly.

She nodded, sighing. "I thank you for your kindness. But I feel … as if I must move on. It is not that I am unhappy here, but I do not want to bring danger upon the hospice and your work. I must go find my father." She removed her hand from his and stood at the railing. "It has been over four years that I saw him last, yet I remember everything about him, his laugh, his eyes, how they twinkled when he smiled. He was … is very dear to me. I have tarried here too long. I must go."

He stood beside her. "Where would you go?"

She shrugged. "Damascus. That is where I last heard of him."

"It would be unwise for a maiden to venture out alone. I would send someone with you, but I can spare none at this time. If you will wait, we may find a family who would take you on as a servant to care for their children. There is no imminent danger and I shall delay the matter of answering the Caliph."

She nodded. "I will wait, if it pleases you. In the meantime, I shall work. It seems work is the best medicine for my heart."

"You have a good and tender heart, Judith. I … I do not wish for you to leave us. I would miss you very much."

Judith heard something in his voice. She raised her eyes in time to see tenderness—nay, something more than that—in his dark eyes. "Thank you, Stefan. Good even."

CHAPTER TWENTY

Hate, like a two-edged sword, cuts both ways. Thomas B. Costain

Acre, Kingdom of Jerusalem, September 1202

Louis opened the door to his cell and sat upon the bed, so exhausted that he wondered how he could finish his duties for the day. Samson John entered the room with a pitcher of water. What a blessing the boy had been this last fortnight! Boy? Louis gazed at the young man who unlaced his sandals and washed his feet in the basin. Nay, the boy had grown before Louis realized it and now was of marrying age. Or would be if he hadn't joined this mad mission across half the world.

Why had they come to Palestine? He couldn't remember. He rubbed his head and fuzzily brought to mind the great call of God on his life. But he had been detained—again, and now, mayhap, the mission had failed. *What is it in my life that thwarts me from doing Your will?* Was God judging him for impudence? Was it pride?

Suddenly the door burst open and a young man dressed in shabby clothes stepped inside. Louis squinted at him through waves of exhaustion. Who ... ? It took several seconds before he knew. Adrian! Louis stared at him as one would look upon a saint from the grave. He tried to rise but fell back on the cot with a thump, his knees buckling.

Yet was this truly Adrian? He seemed different ... changed. The filth of the streets clung to his once-spotless hose and tunic and cape. His frazzled beard obscured his chin and his yellow hair hung wild and uncombed down his back. He slumped into the room and stood looking about in a puzzled manner.

Louis reached for his arm. "Adrian! I canna believe my eyes. You are as an angel of God."

Adrian focused on Louis and fell to his knees, grasping Louis' shoulders, tears flooding his eyes and rolling down his cheeks. "Brother Louis! *Mon ami! Mon ami!* You live! I have searched the city from top to bottom for you and find you here—here at St. John's, where I should have looked first. What have you been doing these weeks?"

Louis shook his head, his voice a thin whisper. "I ... I have been to hell. This dreadful plague ... you cannot know ... " His chest heaved and he wept soundlessly into his hands. "You cannot know the horrors out there. When we were separated, I had no time to tell you I was bound for St. John's and once I arrived, they asked me to help. The plague was just beginning then. I have been busy every moment, day and night. But you said you searched the streets for me. Have you seen the dead and dying?"

Adrian nodded, lifting his eyes to Leon who entered quietly and stood beside the door. He, too, was mud-splattered and red-eyed.

Louis smiled. "Ah. Our noble knight. Come, sit." He pulled a stool from the wall. "Sit, friend, and we shall talk. Here is Samson John, helping me as always."

Adrian perched on a stool. "Leon and I have helped in the plague, too, in whatever way we could. In between those times, I searched for you. It seems strange that we are separated each time we seek an audience with pope or king. Do you suppose someone is behind it?"

Leon nodded, shifting his feet, as if impatient to be off. "I know someone is hindering us. I saw the black-bearded man here, the same one we saw in Rome and again in Venice." He glanced over his shoulder. "I wonder if they are in this very monastery."

Louis sighed. "Whether they are or not, I shall perish if I do not eat, and there is the bell. Let us go to the hall, friends. If you would help me ... "

Adrian was shocked to see that Brother Louis could hardly move. He and Samson John assisted the monk into the great hall, where they found places at a long board table, filled with monks. After the blessing, they ate in silence while a priest read from a passage of the Holy Writ. Adrian had to nudge Louis several times to keep him from falling asleep in his plate.

Back in Louis' cell, they held council.

Leon paced the small room. "We must flee Acre. If the plague does not kill us, the work will. And if the work fails, then our enemies will have ample time to plan our deaths."

"But we have not met with the king of Jerusalem." Louis removed his sandals and lay down on his cot. "We have not given him the pope's message."

Adrian glanced at Leon, then returned his gaze to the monk. "We have learned that he has fled to Damascus to avoid the plague. If we are to meet with him, we must go to that city. Besides, Brother Louis, you need a rest."

Louis groaned. "Riding to Damascus would be a rest? I am disinclined to ride, you know. I do not like horses." He looked up at the concerned faces above him. "Adrian, you must arrange it. I will say I must travel to Damascus to purchase supplies, for we are running low."

Adrian rose. "It would be better if you said nothing at all. We do not want to give our enemies an idea as to where we are, *hein*? We shall meet you at the stables tomorrow morning at dawn. Sleep well."

***

Damascus, September 1202

Restless, Judith tidied her room and paced to the courtyard where the fountain spewed water into the air, where the date palm rustled in the cool evening breeze, where a cat lay curled on the cushions on the bench. She stroked the cat that opened one eye and purred her acceptance of the caress and then curled up tighter and resumed her nap.

A moon rose over the low hills to the east. Judith wrapped a robe about her body, for she heard the jackals out in the desert, a lonely and wild sound. She loved the evenings here in the courtyard, but of late she had been longing for home. For Father. Her mind traveled over the vast distances to a curving river valley that smelled of pine and oak and moist, damp earth, to a bustling French city where Jews dwelt together in safety and peace, to home. Home. Ah, to be home!

She heard the scrap of a sandal on the paving stones and glanced up. A tall form stepped quietly to her side and sat down on the bench beside her. Stefan. Her heart warmed and a smile came easily to her lips as she adjusted her robe. Her knee touched his, but she did not move over. His presence was a comfort beyond words.

He leaned closer and she smelled his clean scent. "How did your day go, *agaphtos*? I hope you did not work too hard."

Judith raised her eyes to his. "Nay, good friend. I find joy in this work. Yet I ... "

She dropped her eyes and played with the tassel of her scarf. "I find it hard to tend to some ... to the Christian knights." She hated to say it, but she had often spoken to him of the hard lump in her heart that appeared whenever a knight came to the hostel for help.

He sighed. "It will take time, dear heart. Let God heal your heart. I noticed you do not veer away now. That is something."

"Yea. That is something. Yet I cannot rid myself of—"

"Hatred. Yes, I know." His tone was low as if he were comforting a child and his hand enfolded hers. It was not the first time he held her hand or put his arm about her shoulders. "It is like a glass of clear water. One drop of hatred can foul the water and bring death instead of life. God can heal you of this thing, Judith. I have prayed for you much."

He leaned closer and she thought for a moment he would kiss her. It startled her to realize she wanted his kiss. Was he ... ? No, it was unthinkable. But was she ... ? No! A thousand times no! How could she love a heathen? A Greek! Yet she had to admit he had become dear to her, very dear.

A lion roared off in the distance. Stefan lifted his head. She wanted to brush the dark hair from his forehead, to sweep away the weariness that dwelt in his body, to ease the cares of so many people from his mind.

She touched his face. "Do you remember ... ?"

"Of course." He kissed her hand but stood abruptly and paced to the fountain. "I ... I came to tell you news."

She gasped and half-rose, then sank back down on the bench. "Is it about my former master, FitzRauf? Will he come for me? Must I go with him?"

Stefan gazed upon her, the tenderness in his eyes unmistakable. "He has no claim on you anymore, Judith. I sent a purse of gold for your payment. Yet it is unsafe for you."

"I know! I must leave." She stood and took a step toward him, gripping the edge of her scarf. "I must not endanger you any longer. Tell me what I should do." She swayed as if she would fall and in an instant he was beside her, his arms around her.

His lips brushed her forehead. "I have heard from a friend who knows an elderly Jew in Damascus. He is a goldsmith. He is looking for someone to help in his shop. I mentioned your name. You are to visit him."

She sighed and leaned into him. It felt so safe, so comfortable in his arms, close to his soft, rough tunic. She gazed into his dark eyes, eyes so full of tenderness and longing that her heart broke. She stifled a sob. "I do not know, Stefan. It is so hard. Please pray for me."

"I shall, *agaphtos*."

She pushed away from him, her voice practical. "Now I must go and prepare for my journey. Good even, friend."

As she made her way to her room, her heart beat triple time for he had called her *agaphtos*. *Beloved*. It was not the first time he had used that term but tonight he had spoken it with such tenderness that she did not doubt his meaning.

But whatever they shared could never be. She would leave and he would fade from her life. A tear found its way down her cheek as she pulled her bags from under the bed. Was this the way it would always be? Torn from those she loved? Denied a secure and happy life? Always on the move, always without a home? She threw her meager belongings into a pack, smoothed the bed and glanced around the room.

A gentle knock sounded on her door. She opened it to find Stefan.

"I am sorry to bother you at such a late hour, but we have had visitors and it concerns you."

She sucked in her breath and a shiver descended her spine. "Who ... is it... ?"

"FitzRauf. He and his party wanted a room but I said we were full. He was not pleased and would have forced his way in, yet I had the presence of mind to call several of my guards before I answered the bell. I told him we were protected by the Caliph in Damascus. That seemed to hold some weight with him, for he did not want a fight. He said he would return in the morning."

"But what of the payment, the gold you sent?"

Stefan shook his head and rubbed his forehead. Weariness seemed to emanate from his pores. "He refused to acknowledge he received any payment for you."

"I will leave. Now." She collected her pack. "I am ready, Stefan. But you said guests. Who else arrived that concerns me?"

He stepped back and allowed a large, burly shape to fill her doorway.

"Baldic!" She wanted to embrace him, but he stood stoically with his arms folded. His only show of emotion was the twinkle in his eyes.

He bowed stiffly. "I found you at last. You do not tell me where you go."

"How did you find me, Baldic?" Judith almost laughed for he seemed so comically dressed in his tall boots, short skirt and leathern joskin.

"I overheard the baron say he was looking for you and I joined his party. Of course he did not know I came to aid you in escaping from him."

Judith grasped the door jam, for her knees had given way. "Jehovah be praised, my good friend. I must leave tonight and you will come with me."

Baldic bowed and said he would fetch the horses.

Stefan led the way to the front courtyard and there they faced each other, fingers entwined. Judith looked around the courtyard, a lump heavy in her throat, tears stinging her eyes. It was here ... not long ago that she came as a fugitive, a waif, and would have died had it not been for Stefan's kindness. How could she ever repay him?

She looked up at him and saw mirrored in his eyes the pain she felt in her heart.

"If you truly do not want to leave, there is a way ... " He dipped his head and kissed her cheek. She did not pull away but only sighed deeply. His low words touched her heart. "I love you, Judith. Surely you have known it for a long time. I want you to be my wife, to stay here by my side always. But I do not know ... "

"How I feel about you?" She lifted her head. His lips were very near, tears stood in his eyes.

"Will you give me an answer?"

She pushed away from him and held herself stiffly, clutching her robe. His words awakened in her heart what she had suspected—she loved this man. She loved him more than she could have dreamed possible. But it could not be. She felt torn; the few feet between them widened to an unimaginable gulf. She heard her voice, a strangled, bleating like a wounded lamb. "How can love cause such pain?"

He did not answer, but stood gazing at her.

Her resolve was melting. She wanted him—wanted his love, the security he offered. It would not be a bad life, this life at the hospital. And she could look for her ... She pulled herself up sharply and shook her head. "No. No. Never!" She gasped, for he jerked back as if she had stabbed him.

His voice was formal, distant. "Do you refuse me... because I am a Gentile?"

She shook her head again. "It cannot be. It would not work."

Taking a deep breath, he seemed to summon strength from an unseen source. "I received word from my patron. He wants me to return to Greece. Now that you are leaving, I shall accept his offer. I shall leave and you shall go to Damascus."

"And will you never return?" She stepped to his side, tears stinging her eyes, trickling down her cheeks. She knew nothing save the nearness of his lips, the love that had shone from his eyes.

He drew his breath in sharply. "No, I shall return. Then if we are still friends, you will visit us here and I will teach you about my God. Then we shall be one in our faith."

"Your God?"

He nodded, his face hidden in the shadows. "I have never told you before, and it is a great fault, for you should have known. I serve and love the One you hate the most." He stepped closer and looked upon her with such love and agony and tenderness that she would remember it forever. "My God is Jesus Christ."

She gasped and stared, stricken. "But you are a Greek!"

He bent his head. "And a Christian. Not all those who follow Jesus are evil. I pray that when I return you will have learned to let go of your hatred. Hatred will kill you, Judith. You must let God heal your heart."

"*Which God*, Stefan?" She was unable to restrain the bitterness swelling inside her heart like a wave of the sea. Who was he to lecture her on what she should do? "The one who allowed my father to be taken? Who killed my mother? Who allowed me to be taken as a slave? To be attacked like a woman of the street? Is this your God? The God who allows my people to be killed in his foul name?"

"Judith!"He took a step toward her, his arms outstretched, but she cringed away from him. He coaxed her as he would a wild animal. "I am still the person you have known. Please reconsider. I am not evil. You know that."

She froze, her heart a lump of ice, tears streaming down her cheeks unheeded. Time seemed to stand still as he stood before her, pain and love and despair on his face. She could not move, could not take that first step to him.

He dropped his arms and walked to the arched doorway leading into the hospice. But he hesitated and turned back to gaze at her as if to store her face in his memory. "Fare you well, Judith. I shall pray for you."

She could not answer, for bile rose in her throat and threatened to gag her. She held her veil to her mouth and shook her head.

He strode from the courtyard, stumbling once, reaching for the doorpost as if blind, then disappeared.

She gathered her robe about her, grasped her pack, and joined Baldic who stood outside the courtyard with his horse.

***

On the road to Damascus, September 1202

As always, it was the heat that defeated Adrian. Its merciless glare beat upon his head, and even though he had it covered with a broad-rimmed felt hat, still he felt its hot breath as a dragon's fire, as the blast from the smelting oven. He reined to a copse of tamarisk trees growing beside a tricklet of water and shoved back his hat. "This is supposed to be the Holy Land, yet I feel as if I were in hell." He reached for his flask and drank a little of the warm water.

"Holy Land or no, I prefer the cool mountain passes of France." Leon reached for his flask, too.

Louis pulled up beside them. "Ah, France. To think I used to complain about the heat there." His face was flushed and his eyes looked puffy and red, as if he had been weeping.

Adrian stoppered the flask and kicked Bret into the sunshine. How far was it to Damascus? It seemed to be taking an eon. Hearing a noise behind, a grunt and a soft thud, he looked back. Louis lay face down on the hot sand.

Adrian dismounted and felt his pulse while Samson John leaped from his mule. Untying his flask from his saddle, Adrian bathed the monk's face. "He was overcome by the heat. Samson John, get some more water. Leon, help me carry him back to the shade of that tree."

Thankfully, a small stream flowed not far away across a rocky field. Samson John ran to fetch water while they laid Louis in the shade and tried to make him comfortable.

Leon wiped the sweat from his face. "He was so exhausted when we left Acre. I hope it isn't the plague."

They froze, exchanging frightened glances, then hurried about, caring for Louis as best as they knew, as if activity in itself would ward off the fearful sickness.

Adrian was worried. Even though Louis was overheated, his face was pasty gray and his breath came in gasps and his hands were cold. Adrian straightened. "This is not a bad place to camp. We have firewood and water and cover from the elements. What castle did we pass back there?"

"Subebe." Leon furnished the answer as he laid a fire and retrieved his flint from his pack. "It was once a Christian fortress but now it belongs to the Arabs."

"I wish it were ours still," Adrian replied. "We could find help there. Damascus is another two day's ride."

They had been on the road for five days. In thinking back, Adrian knew the monk had been fading, but he wanted to reach the city before he collapsed. Now what would they do?

That night Adrian was awakened from a light slumber by a shake; Samson John motioned to Louis' prone figure. Adrian leaped to his feet and checked the monk. Louis moaned, thrashing about as if in pain. His body burned with fever. Adrian woke Leon and they bathed his body and gave him as much water as they could.

As dawn crept over the low hills to the east, castings beams of light into a turquoise sky, Adrian returned to his bed and closed his eyes. The monk slept fitfully and it seemed his fever abated.

Later that afternoon, Leon returned from the village nearby where he had gone to buy more food. "I inquired in Panais and discovered that a medicine woman lives there. I visited her and she said to bring Louis to her. I am afraid we must move him."

"I am thankful you know Arabic," Adrian murmured as they turned to Louis.

They built a stretcher of sorts that slid behind Louis' horse, yet it was a long five miles over a rough path. Louis' condition worsened as the sun beat upon his flushed face. Adrian brushed the flies away at one of their frequent stops, gave the monk a drink and said a prayer, wondering if they would arrive at the village only to find him dead.

The villagers stared at their strange procession as they marched past the well and continued down the main street, past rows of ramshackle homes, the huge stone structure of the mosque, past the market and more wealthy homes. At the end of a long and narrow street, Leon stopped at a thatched home made of mud bricks.

An elderly woman with a veil over her face met them and beckoned them inside. Her home was humble, yet cool, and she began work to immediately on Louis, calling for water.

That evening Louis seemed to be resting easier. She had found some medicine in Louis' pack and gave it to him. Adrian and Louis bought a few supplies in the market and had a meager supper over a campfire in the woman's back courtyard, sitting on a stone bench that lined the wall.

Adrian poked the fire with a stick. "How long will it take, do you suppose?"

Leon shrugged. "She said it may be a few days. Or it may take many weeks."

"In that case, I say we should take the message to Damascus and try to get an audience with the king."

Leon nodded, glancing up as the woman's son, a man in his late thirties, approached. He rose and they spoke for some time. When he returned to the fire he said, "He works in the castle and has just returned home. We can find lodging in the inn down the street but we may also roll out here on the ground if we want."

Adrian added a log to the fire. "I would like to stay here, near Louis. We will wait a day and if he doesn't improve, we shall ride."

Leon smiled, the old flashing smile Adrian remembered. "*Eh, bein, mon ami.* The sooner we can finish our mission and be on our way, the better."

"And where will you go when our task is finished?"

"To Greece. Remember? Greece, the ancient land of freedom. My heart broke when we sailed so close to it and could not stop."

Adrian laughed and slapped him on the back. "*Mais oui.* And perchance you would meet a fair Greek maiden there. No?"

"I might meet one, my friend, but it would do her no good."

The next day they left a few coins with the woman, made sure Louis was well tended and saddled their horses, anxious to find the king of Jerusalem, deliver the letter and return.

Samson John saw them off at the woman's front gate, his face streaked with tears.

The weather was fine, and they made good progress, stopping only briefly for a lunch and to water the horses at midday. As evening stole over the hills, Adrian began looking for a place to camp. They approached a dense thicket of tangled bougainvillea bushes and short palms edging a small stream and a clearing. "This might be a good ... " Suddenly, from the side of the road, a horde of dark faces sprang from behind a cluster of hot rocks.

Arabs! It seemed hundreds of them brandished bared scimitars and emitted high, ear-splitting shrieks like the whirling dervishes Adrian heard in the hills behind Panais.

He yelled and kicked Bret, glancing to the side to see Leon's sword spring to his hand in one fluid motion.

Bret leaped almost straight up; Adrian clung to the saddle and swung his sword downward as the horse descended, meeting flesh and bone and the shriek of his enemy as a head rolled to the ground. But a dozen filled the man's place. Bret leaped again, whirling in one spot. A score of dark men scattered like flies.

Adrian slashed and slashed again, yet the blows of his enemies fell like rain and dust stung his eyes and he was cut in a dozen places and his arm ached and he wondered what had happened to Leon.

At last they overpowered him. He was surprised they did not kill his horse. He found himself face down on the ground, seeing only their booted feet and hearing their excited chatter as his arms were lashed. He struggled against the bonds. Someone kicked him in the ribs. Someone else hauled him to his feet and lifted him to Bret's back.

Then, with another wild yell, they were riding away. Adrian glanced back. A still form lay on the ground. Leon! *No ... oh, God, not Leon!* Yet he knew if his friend lived, they would have taken him. He bent his head but tears would not come.

He gritted his teeth and yelled his grief. He would revenge the death of his friend. *Leon. You were much better than I. Why couldn't I have died ... and you lived?*

As dawn tainted the sky with fierce red the next morning, Subebe loomed into sight. Lashed to his horse, Adrian had ridden through the night with only a short pause to water the horses. The castle on the hilltop seemed a jumble of rocks from the distance, but as they approached, he saw it was of no mean proportions. Huge curtain walls encircled it, rising and falling with the uneven terrain. Gigantic gates stood like legendary monolithic sentinels, dozens of them spaced along the wall, bristling with battlements along the top.

Through a haze of pain and grief, Adrian appreciated the defenses of this castle and wondered how it could be taken—indeed, how one could escape. Since he was a captive, the troop entered through a gate on the eastern side leading directly to the stables. Dismounting, his captors hauled him roughly off his horse, removed the packs, stripped him, and led him down dank hallways and curving steps into the bowels of the castle. There, in the dungeons, the slaves were kept, brought out to the light of day only for their work projects.

Adrian was untied and given a dirty tunic to don. An overseer approached, a great bear of a man, who looked him over, jabbed him here and there, then told him to proceed down the hall. Adrian followed the direction of the man's finger, for he could understand only a little Arabic. At the end of the hall, a gang of men had just finished their morning meal in a large room filled with coarse wooden tables and benches. He ate what was left—a piece of dry bread, some gruel in a dirty bowl, and drank a swallow of tainted water.

Then he joined the crew for the day's work, following behind two score men, all of them tanned almost black. About a mile from the castle they halted where a rock quarry spewed boulders, some large and some small, into a cupped depression of land. Like the others, Adrian hefted a large wooden box and an overseer tied it around his back. This was then loaded with stones and the gang was whipped back up the hill to the building site.

As he labored in the hot sun, his muscles screaming, his wounds oozing blood, his heart breaking with grief, he remembered the Dagda, the ugly god of the ring that he had been given in France by Mother D'Engle. Why not pray to that god? The ring was long gone, but the memory of Dagda was as fresh as the day he prayed to him in the cottage in the wood.

Besides, what had his Catholic faith done for him? When had the sallow and impotent Mother Mary helped him? He pledged his life to serve the pope and the church and this was what he got in return. No, he needed a stronger god.

He thought briefly of the God grandfather taught him and shook his head, sending a spray of sweat into the air. No, Jesus was for old men and young children. He needed Dagda. Silently, fervently, he prayed to the old god, begging for his help, pledging his life to him, promising him whatever he wanted, if only he would help escape this suffering.

The sky remained brassy, the sun beat down, sweat poured from his body in stinging riverlets, and there was no answer—not from Dagda, not from Jesus, nor from Mother Mary. He was abandoned, without hope—and now he came to the end.

That night he was given a crust of bread and thin soup in which floated the eyes of a fish, was led to a crowded and fetid cell, and chained to the wall. He would not saw through the bars of the window high above his head.

The cell that had been made for ten or fifteen men held twice that number, and the smell of unwashed bodies, filth and urine was almost more than he could bear. He propped himself in the corner and fell asleep, only to waken by being jabbed in the ribs. He had fallen onto a man. Everyone shifted, and he found a spare six inches of floor where he could sleep.

Six days went by in this manner, yet to Adrian it seemed a lifetime. On the sixth night, his pains were so acute and his soul so tortured that he lay upon the cold stone and prayed, *Eh, mon Dieu, eh, mon Dieu.*

The small, wiry man chained next to him stirred. "Are you French?"

Adrian was surprised. They were not allowed to speak to one another, but the man's mouth was near his ear. "*Oiu.* Are you?"

"*Oiu, monsieur.* But I am mostly Jewish. Where are you from?"

321

"I was born in Mordelias. Near Rennes, in Brittany. Where are you from?"

"Troyes. Then Dijon. I had a family; my business was prosperous. Then the party I was with was attacked and I was taken as a slave."

"How long have you been here?"

"Four years I have been a slave—three of them here. But … we must hush. The guards come by about this time."

Adrian closed his eyes. His body and heart still throbbed with pain, but he was strangely comforted. The little Jew next to him brought memories of France, of riding the pine-needled paths, of his mother's castle, of his beautiful horse.

Yet something in the man's story tickled his memory—something about Troyes, about Dijon. He shook his head. No, it would not come. Sighing, he adjusted himself and drifted off to an uneasy sleep.

Every night he scratched a mark on the wall and prayed for release, yet he had little hope his prayers meant anything at all. Prayers and faith were a luxury for those who were free. For the slaves of Subebe, there was only work, exhaustion, dreamless sleep for a few hours and then work again. Plans to regain his throne in Brittany receded into something like a hazy dream, a misty cloud, a willow-o-the-wisp fantasy.

His only hope was to live to see another sunrise, and then that, too receded, and the longing for death took its place.

***

On the road to Damascus, October 1202

It was a night of inky darkness. Evil seemed to lurk in every bush and tree along the winding way. Judith patted her mare's neck for reassurance and watched Baldic's broad back ahead. Surely if anything came out of the darkness, Baldic would take care of it. Surely.

Yet she was not comforted. Her heart seemed as cold as the snow she'd seen on top of the mountains in France. She sniffed. A putrid smell like something long dead wafted on the wind. There— beside the road—a lump came into view. It was something dead. A man? A beast? She turned her head and tried to calm her nerves.

If only the moon would shine, but it had gone behind the clouds. She wanted to call out to Baldic, "Let's turn back. I want to return and make it right with Stefan. I can't leave him like this." But she did not.

A mist gathered in the low places along the road like ghostly shrouds. Out in the desert a pack of hyenas laughed and jabbered, probably one of the wildest and most ferocious sounds Judith had ever heard. A cold wind tugged at her cloak—the east wind from the desert, the *sirocco.*

She glanced into the dark shadows that seemed to creep with eager fingers toward the road, and she listened with cocked ears for the slightest sound in the dead of the night. Perhaps FitzRauf had not gone to Damascus. Perhaps he waited in that copse of trees ahead, in the black of the shade.

She could not stop the trembling that overcame her. *Oh, God. What have I done? Why couldn't I return his love? What is this monster inside me? This gaping wound? Why can I not rid myself of it?* No answer came to her, only the whir of a bat's wings, the jabber of jackals, the heavy tread of horse's hooves, and the faint jingle of the bridle.

Baldic said a few words at the gate of Damascus. Judith heard the clink of coins exchanging hands. The small gate set low in the wall opened and they led their horses through.

"Where did you get the money, my friend?" She glanced up at him as they remounted.

He smiled. "Your benefactor at the hospice, Stefan, gave me money for this. But I have money of my own. I did a bit of guarding while I was in Acre and met some wealthy Greeks. They hired my services." He patted his sword.

"I see you have learned to speak French better."

He grinned and led the way confidently to an inn, paid for their room and stabled the horses. She was surprised that she was given a room to herself and that Baldic slept in the common room. When she remonstrated with him, he merely shrugged and said he was far more capable of defending himself than she. And Stefan wanted it this way.

Stefan. Again. How long would she be indebted to him? She undressed with shaking hands, washed her face in the small basin and fell upon the bed, asleep before her head hit the cushions.

The next morning, long before the sun rose, Judith awoke. She dressed, washed her face, packed her bag and appeared in the common room while the innkeeper was still stoking the fire for the morning's bread. She shook Baldic awake and waited while he used the privy and washed his face. By then the innkeeper served ale and cold bread, cheese and figs on the rough wooden board.

With Baldic faithfully dogging her steps and with help from several people along the way, Judith found the shop of the Jewish goldsmith, Jonas ben Phineas. He was tending his shop, and when she saw him, her heart almost stopped, for she thought it was Gran-abba. He had the same long, white beard, the same bald head, the same stoop to his shoulders.

"Jonas ben Phineas?" She bent her head. "I am Judith, daughter of Elias Itzchaki, from the hospice. Stefan said I would find you here. I am applying for a job. They said you were looking for someone to help. My father was a merchant, too, and I helped him often. I think you would find me useful." She bowed deeply.

When she looked up, the old man had come around the counter and was holding open his arms to her. "Ah. Yahweh Himself has blessed my day! Come. Come into my arms, child. You look so much like my daughter when she was your age."

Judith allowed herself to be hugged, made over and invited behind the shop for a cup of tea. Baldic preferred to stay on the street, stoic and watchful. Jonas heated water, sprinkled leaves into it, and poured it out into small cups. They talked while they drank the fragrant brew. Judith found herself telling the old man her story and he listened intently, nodding his wise old head, his eyes moist.

"It is a story, to be sure. I am sorry I cannot help you locate your father. But I will ask my friends in the city." He straightened and pierced her with an intent look. "Where are you staying, my daughter?"

"At … at an inn, for now. I know not where I shall stay, sir. First I thought to speak with you and see if you could employ me. Then I will look for a permanent place to stay. Do you know someone, perhaps in the Jewish quarter, who would let me live with them?"

He nodded, his white beard wagging. She saw now that he did not look like Gran-abba, but kindness dwelt in his heart and shone in his eyes. "I do. I know of an excellent place. You shall live with me, my daughter. My home is large and I pad around in it very lonely and sad. You will bring me joy. Ah. Do not fear. I have two daughters to keep you company and many servants. But first I shall show you my business. Then when the sun falls, I shall take you home. Does your ... friend, the man outside, does he come with you?"

"For as long as he is needed, Gran-abba. I am sure he will be useful to you and to your household."

The day fled on swift feet. Judith looked up in surprise when Jonas said it was time to fold up shop and go home. She rode with him in a litter born by four muscular slaves, all black. She felt like a princess when she entered his beautiful home atop a small hill, met the household and was shown her rooms. Jonas even assigned several of the maids to be her personal attendants.

A young girl named Elizabeth seemed apt and friendly, eager, and yet not too talkative or curious. Judith knew they would be friends.

That evening Jonas shared his evening meal with Judith and then led her to the rear courtyard. They spoke in low, desultory tones while a servant played the zipher and the palms whispered in the breeze.

Judith stretched and leaned down to buckle her sandals. She noticed Jonas' eyes on her neck and realized she had allowed the capsule to appear outside her gown. Tucking it inside, she yawned and asked to be excused.

But he leaned forward, his eyes shrewd and alive. "May I ask what it is you wear around your neck?"

She was stunned to silence. He sat and waited patiently, his eyes never straying from her face. At last she said, "I ... I wear an amulet my Gran-abba gave me as he died. It is a family heirloom."

"All these years and through all your days you have worn it and protected it?"

"Aye." Where these questions were going, she had no idea. She stood and began to walk across the flagstones. "I am so tired, sir. I must seek my bed."

"Stay."

She stopped.

He hefted himself from the bench and came to stand just in front of her. "What is it, child?"

She lifted her chin and enclosed the small capsule with her hand. "I have never told anyone. I was sworn to secrecy. Gran-abba told me … " Tears misted her eyes. "That I should keep it always and someday I should find out what it means."

He listened without moving, almost without breath. "Come with me."

She followed him into the house where he lit a candle from a small lamp, through the atrium and down narrow steps to a sunken room. Inside he set the candle in a holder. After brushing back a tapestry, he unlocked a little door set in the wall and withdrew a small box.

Inside the box, another container was wrapped with soft material. This held a small golden vial, a cylinder similar in size to hers. Gently he unscrewed the lid and tapped something into his hand.

She stared. It was a scroll.

"Is this something like what you carry in that wooden cylinder around your neck?" His eyes glimmered in the faint light cast by the candle.

She gasped, frozen. "It is, Jonas. Gran-abba said there were others who had the other parts of the secret. I cannot believe I have found you."

"Nor can I believe I have found you," he said, very low. "But the moment I saw the cylinder you carried, I knew. Have you read it? Do you know what it says?" He leaned forward, eagerness in every line of his body.

She shook her head. "I cannot read the ancient writing. I have always thought someday I would find a scholar who may read it for me. But even then what can I do?"

He nodded and carefully replaced the scroll and the box in the wall opening, then locked the door. "I have had several scholars read the scroll for me."

He turned to look at her in the flickering light.

She would never forget the dank smell of the tiny room, the reflecting light of the candle in his eyes, the sense of wonder and awe that made them whisper. "What is it?"

He spoke each word precisely. "The Secret of the Ages. Taken together, they reveal where our most sacred relics lie, hidden since

Jeremias! Do you understand, Judith? The Ark ... the treasures of the temple. They exist, child."

Judith's world tumbled about as if a windstorm entered her mind and rearranged all the pieces. Her heart pounded loudly in her ears; her knees threatened to give way. "I knew they were hidden, but I thought it a myth. What does it mean, Jonas?" She grasped his hand.

He clasped her hand with his gnarled ones. "Now that I have found you, our destiny is clear. We shall find the other scrolls and then we shall find It. You know our wise men say that when the Ark is found, our Messias will come. We shall embark upon a great adventure, Judith." His eyes glittered like dark jewels, alive, compelling. "What say you?"

Her heart gave a great leap. *Yes! We shall find the Secret Treasure, and Messiah shall come. With His mighty sword He will drive the Christian knights and the dreadful red cross from our land.*

In that one blinding moment, she forgot Stefan, the hospice, FitzRauf, her search for father. This ... this was her saving grace! This would become her life.

The flame of the candle flickered. He waited with bated breath. Time stood still.

She exhaled. "Yea, Jonas. I shall go with thee."

It took Jonas a fortnight to prepare for the journey but at last the morning dawned when the servants saddled and bridled the horses, the bags were packed in a wagon, and the guards waited at the gate.

Judith climbed up on the wagon, pulled the lap robe over her knees and grinned at Elizabeth who perched beside her on the padded seat. Jonas mounted a sturdy roan and waved to the guards. A servant, a young man named David, sat on the seat of the wagon and snapped a whip to the horse.

The party wound its way off the hill, through the beautiful city gates of Damascus and down the road south on the King's Highway. As the sun rose over the mountains to the east and a fresh breeze whipped her veil, Judith could not keep a smile from her face or calm her wildly beating heart.

They planned to visit Tiberias where they would consult translators, and have them read the ancient scrolls. She touched the golden capsule Jonas gave her that replaced the plain wooden one she had worn for so many years. *I am on my way at last, Gran-abba. I will find the secret of this thing you have given me to do.*

Jonas was a careful man; he knew of the dangers on the road. A guard of four soldiers, including Baldic, accompanied the party.

Mt. Hermon loomed on the horizon the next day—a long, high mountain marking marked the northern boundary of Palestine. That evening they camped near the village of Panais where sycamore trees cast dark shadows. Jonas told her the village was named for the Greek god, Pan, and that the Greeks made the god a temple in a cave not far from the village.

The following morning the guards broke camp and saddled the horses. Jonas sat on a log while Judith packed the food. He began to say something, but the words stayed frozen in his mouth, for strange men exploded from the nearby trees riding small, agile horses, swinging scimitars that glittered in dawn's new light.

The guards drew their swords, but they were too slow. The Arab riders attacked with inhuman screams, slashing with deadly accuracy. She rose, stunned, her hand to her mouth, hearing the clash of steel on steel, the grunts of men, the neigh of horses. The guards died one by one, their blood staining the grass, their screams echoing in the glade. Judith bolted, a wild dash of panic and fear. Blood and gore, disembodied heads, the dead and dying lay strewn in the grass ... and the killing continued.

The scene became a blur in her mind—evil faces, the flanks of glossy-coated horses, the flash of steel in the sunlight. She dashed toward Jonas, but time stood still and it felt as if she raced in mud. Elizabeth scrambled for the cover of the trees, but a rider swooped down and snatched her up on his saddle.

Jonas stood in frozen terror, calling her name. A horse thundered behind; Judith screamed, then hands grabbed her, lifted her like a sack of wheat, deposited her in front of a rider. Her last view of Jonas was his face, upheld, his eyes pleading, hands outstretched. Behind him rode an Arab on horseback with an uplifted sword.

It seemed a lifetime, but it was only a matter of moments. The rider, a young man with a dark, ferocious face, held Judith tightly in front of the saddle. She did not squirm to get away.

Stunned, she could not think. Her life lay shattered beside the crippled wagon and the lifeless body of Jonas.

CHAPTER TWENTY-ONE

If you devote your life to seeking revenge, first dig two graves.
Confucius, 551-478

Panais, Palestine, Sunday October 16, 1202

Samson John sat outside the medicine woman's home on a crude wooden bench and played a game of stones with two young boys of the village. In his world of perpetual silence, he was pleased with small pleasures: the light of joy on his new friend's face when he hit his target; the sun on his back; the feeling of comfort to know his master, who was his life and light, was improving each day and could now sit up and take his meals and speak.

A man stumbled down the street. He was cut in a dozen places, his black hair and beard were matted with twigs and dirt, his clothes hung in tatters and he seemed unable to see, dazed, feeling his way. The boys called out names, approaching the man and jeering. Samson John knew what they said, for he read their lips and had picked up a smattering of Arabic. Soon they would push against the man and he would fall. Then perchance they would throw stones at him or try to steal his purse.

He sprinted to the boys, pulling on their tunics, shaking his head, shielding the man from their taunts, for he recognized him— the man was the guard his master employed in France to go with the girl with the black hair and the snapping eyes. Samson John did not stop to wonder why or how this man was in Palestine. He only knew he must get him to the woman's home so he could be made well.

The man resisted efforts to pull him into the woman's home, but at last Samson John succeeded in getting him into the house where they collapsed on the dirt floor.

Louis, who had been asleep on a cot near the back of the house, raised up. "Who did you bring in, Samson John? A beggar … ? Look at his clothes … why…"

Samson John motioned, made guttural sounds in his throat. Louis hauled himself from the bed and with uneven steps approached Baldic. Samson John watched as he turned the man's body over and studied his face. "Baldic! But how? Never mind. I must treat him. Samson, get my pack, will you?"

Hurriedly, Samson John retrieved the pack. He helped fetch water, lift Baldic to the bed, took his clothes to the fire outside, and ran to the market for lye.

Samson stayed by Baldic's bed, alert and unwavering, while his master returned to his own bed and sank down upon it. He made several trips to check on Louis during the next two hours, but discovered the monk was merely exhausted by his efforts to save Baldic.

When Baldic awoke, his gaze flickered across the mud walls, to the woman who bent over a table, to Samson John and at last to Louis. He tried to raise himself from the bed, but dropped back.

Samson John shook his master awake and went to sit on the floor, watching. He read the man's lips when he spoke to Louis.

"I know you. You are the monk. From France." He lay back, tired from his effort to speak. "Wait. Let me think. It is coming back. Yes. You hired me to guard the Lady Judith. Judith!" He sat upright, then fell back heavily, as if he fainted.

Samson John was beside him in an instant, dabbing a cool cloth on his head.

Louis stepped to the man's side. Samson saw concern etched in the lean face and he trembled. "What do you know of Judith? Where is she?"

"I failed. She went to Damascus and was injured, so she stayed at a hospice. I found her. We went to stay with a man who employed her ... A Jew ... he took her home, made her like his grand-daughter. They were journeying to ... Tiberias. I know not why. We were set upon just south of this village. Arabs. They killed the man and took Judith. I heard them say something about Subebe."

"When did this happen?" Louis bent closer.

"I know not. Two days ago, I think. Yes. I walked for two days and nights."

"Subebe!" Louis glanced at Samson John, saying it again so the boy could read his lips.

Samson John nodded. He knew they spoke of the girl with the black hair, knew his master was alarmed and fearful. The name of the castle on the hill above Panais filled him with unspeakable dread as if a monster of nightmare proportions breathed fire upon him.

There was much more talk, but he knew only a little of it. Once his master turned to him and said, "We must free the girl from the castle." Samson John spread his hands and shrugged his shoulders.

Louis shook his head. "I don't know how we shall accomplish it, either. They say no one escapes Subebe. But we must pray and think and try."

Baldic grunted low in his throat. The sound was lost on the boy, but he saw the look on the man's face—he wanted revenge.

That night Samson John curled up on his bedroll on the floor and prayed as he always did that no snakes would crawl in with him. He hated snakes. But the memory of the girl would not go from his mind, for she had been kind to him. He thought about the monstrous castle on the hill and what her life would be like inside it. Would they eat her alive, like a lion devouring its prey? Would they enslave her? Put her in a *hareem*? It was a new word he had just learned and he marveled over its concept, yet it was nothing new. Did not the kings of France have women, many women?

The next day, Samson John indicated to the boys he met in the marketplace that he would like to see the castle. They took him to a place where they could see the massive front gates. They showed him the side gates. They followed the curtain wall around the fortress, clambering over rocks and down into dry wadis, past stunted juniper trees, to a point where the canyon sheered off below them.

Samson John shared out a lunch he brought, along with a flask of ale and a denarius to both of the boys. Their eyes widened when they saw the coin, and they ate their food in companionable silence in the shade of a tamarisk tree.

The older of the boys stood. "Would you like to see a cave? It leads into the castle. Come on. But you must keep it secret. Do you promise?"

Samson John nodded solemnly.

They set off, following the eastern wall and after an hour's search, they found it—a small opening behind a bush and a jumble of rocks. "Here it is!"

He crawled in behind them and was surprised to see an opening large enough to stand. The ceiling remained high for some ways back, farther than he could see in the dark.

The boys tugged at his sleeve. "It goes on back there. Then there are steps." They pretended climbing. "We have never gone up them. They lead to a door. Sometimes, it is said, the door is unlocked and you may go into the castle. But this is secret."

He put his finger to his lips.

After they explored the cave, they emerged outside and continued around the castle. Suddenly one of the boys pulled him down behind a bush. Not too soon, for a column of slaves came marching past, a guard at the head and a guard at the end. The slaves each carried a load on their backs. Samson John did not know what it was they carried, but it must have been very heavy, for each man's body dripped with sweat and their backs were bent cruelly under the load.

He felt sorry for them and noted each man's face. A young man with matted blond hair and a blond beard appeared on the path. Samson noted him yellow hair. The slave looked down just as he passed the bush. They both gasped. Samson John knew that man. He was the man who helped his master in France.

Soon all the slaves and their guards passed up the hill to the castle. The boys waited for a few minutes, then tore down the hill toward the village. Samson John came after, pulling his robe up to his waist, his head full of news for his master.

It was the young man they met in France. He was here—a slave in the castle! He thought Adrian and the other tall one had gone to the great city up north.

Running through the low ground cover, not heeding sharp thorns or rocks, Samson John fled to Panais and arrived at the widow's house. Bursting in, he dashed to Louis' side. His master slept, but awoke at once when Samson John jostled his arm.

***

On the road to Subebe, Monday evening, Oct. 17, 1202

Judith moaned. It had been only a day since their capture but it seemed a lifetime. Her hands and feet bled from the chains that bound them. The chain looped around a thick palm tree, securing her so she could not escape. Judith knew Elizabeth suffered in a like manner.

Their Arab captors were careful and vigilant, but not cruel, and they brought food that evening. Elizabeth nibbled at her share, but Judith's stomach turned at the smell of the food. *I will not eat while I am in captivity. I shall starve myself before I serve another master as a slave.*

The camp settled down, silence filling the air as stars appeared one by one. She lay back against the tree and groaned, her desire to die so strong that she lay where they dropped her, inert, lifeless, only her mind alive and her heart beating. Yet she lay awake—awake and horribly alive.

Through the long hours of darkness she struggled with her fate. Madness and despair shook her body as with the ague, horror crawled up her throat and gagged her. A whirlpool of melancholy sucked her into its hellish depths. Time and again death hovered near, whispering its seductive taunts. She cried out to Yahweh to let her perish under the cold, brittle stars.

Just as dawn touched the sky with a band of pink, Judith sat up and looked around, surprised. It was like the dawning of the first day of earth. She heard the dry grass rustle. Joy touched her heart. Tears sprang to her eyes. God walked beside her in the grass. She smelled the sweetness of His breath on the soft morning breeze, saw a flower bend to His touch near her hand. She felt enveloped by strong arms of love, and heard His voice whispering in her mind. *I love you.* A gentle breeze brushed her cheeks.

Her heart replied, *Who are You, Yahweh, that You would take notice of me? I do not know You, yet You know my name and touch me and make me strong with Your love.*

Someone wept. Elizabeth. Judith turned and patted the girl's head, for she could not reach her arms to hold her. The girl stopped sobbing.

"I prayed I would die," Elizabeth said, wiping her face, "but then I knew Yahweh would not allow it. Did you sleep well, mistress?"

"I slept very little, Elizabeth. I wrestled with the angel of death all night. Even as our father Jacob did. Perchance it was very near here that he dreamed of a stairway to heaven."

Elizabeth leaned closer. "There may be hope, mistress. I do not believe Baldic was dead. His eyes were open. He saw us leave."

Judith's heart leaped, but then reality struck. If he lived, he would need help and time to heal before he could come to their rescue. There would no help coming from Baldric. Yet she must keep a cheerful face for Elizabeth. "Yea, my friend. We must hope and prepare ourselves for whatever lies ahead."

***

Panias, Monday afternoon

Now that his fever abated, Louis rested easily, and thought often of Adrian and Leon, wondering if they had accomplished their purpose in meeting with the king of Jerusalem. Louis could not believe how quickly Baldic recovered from his ordeal. He prowled the cottage, sharpened his sword, and explored the village.

That day, Louis dreamed of France—the pine forests, the damp mossy places under the waterfalls, the misty mountains with their snowy tops. And then he was a child again, kneeling in damp earth on the edge of the meadow. He clenched his fist, and watched his mother bolt from the knight who pursued her—she stumbled and fell. He heard her grunt, heard the knight yell his triumph as he descended upon her.

But she rolled at the last moment, and as she did, she tripped the man and they sprawled together on the green turf. Then, as agile as a cat, she sprang to her feet and ran back to fetch her mattock. The other man dismounted and caught her in his arms. Louis heard them scuffling, saw the other knight rise, and walk slowly forward with a malicious grin on his bearded face, saw the sword poised ...

Someone shook him. He opened his eyes, and sat up, rigid with fear. Yet it was only Samson John's face looking into his. Something was wrong. The boy was trembling, his face sweaty and red as if he had been running. "What is it, my son? What is wrong?"

Samson John shook his head, motioning wildly. Louis sat up on the cot and calmed him, for he could make no sense of what he was trying to say in his agitated state. When at last he did understand, he turned to Baldic.

"Baldic, have you followed this? Come here. This is important."

Baldic set aside his sword and stumped into the room, kneeling beside Louis. "The boy says he went to Subebe with some friends. They showed him a cave, a secret cave that leads up into the castle. Am I right, Samson John?"

The boy nodded, his eyes glowing with excitement.

Louis glanced at Baldic. "You know, he might have something here." They spoke in hurried tones of possible ways to use this information when Louis felt the boy tug his sleeve again. He looked down. In the dirt he had drawn the figure of a man. The man wore a crown on his head, but even as Louis looked, the boy rubbed out the crown. Then he drew a chain on the man, bent his back with a load, and extended the chain to the castle.

It took both Louis and Baldic some time to decipher this news. "Adrian? You saw Adrian, lad?" Louis could scarcely believe that Samson John knew he was Prince Arthur.

Samson John nodded and pointed at the picture.

"But what is Adrian doing in Subebe?" Baldic studied the drawing. "And as a slave?"

Louis shook his head. "That is not too hard to understand. The Arabs attack many travelers in these parts. The woman's son told me this. He may even have tipped off the Arabs in Subebe. Leon and Adrian never made it to Damascus."

Baldic considered this. Then he fetched his sword and fastened it on his waist. "We must rescue them. When Adrian is freed, he will be able to aid us in rescuing Judith. Now, I have an idea. Tell me if you think it bears weight or not." He leaned closer to Louis and spoke in French.

When he finished, Louis nodded. "I think it will work. But I think that we must move from this house. There are too many prying eyes. We must move from here."

"In my roving about the village," Baldic said, "I noticed an abandoned Catholic church. In the rear we may find shelter and privacy. What do you think?

"I think it is a fine idea. Let us do it tonight."

***

Subebe, Monday evening

"It was strange, I tell you," Adrian whispered in the ear of Elias the Jew that night. "As we were coming back to the castle, a bush moved as I passed, and I saw a face."

Elias cocked his head the way he did when a thought struck him. "Do you have friends on the outside?"

"Aye. A monk and a deaf boy. The monk was sick nigh unto death when I left him. Yet, it could have been the deaf boy. I thought I saw some tracks in the dust. What shall I do?"

Elias shrugged. "Wait and see. They may try to contact you. We shall keep our eyes alert on the morrow when we go to the quarry. Silence, now, friend, or we shall be put where no man will find us!"

Adrian worried about the Jew, for in the last few days, his strength lagged—even his desire for food waned. Once a man's strength was depleted, he began a swift downhill journey to death. Perhaps their captors sensed their failing strength, and worked them harder; perhaps there was only so much a human body could endure.

The next morning Adrian was gratified to see Elias eat his share of the gruel they passed down the board. That day the sun seemed to bore a hole in Adrian's back, and the rocks seemed to weigh more than the earth itself as he scanned the barren hillside, gazing intently at the whispering bush as he passed it each trip.

As the sun began its westward journey to the horizon and a cool breeze sprang up, Adrian picked up his last load of the evening. He stood near a densely packed clump of scrub juniper bushes. Once or twice he heard a rustle in the branches and a scratch as of small feet in the dirt. He edged closer. Looking back down the line, he saw the guard tipping his flask to his mouth while the other guard laughed.

Suddenly, a brown hand reached from the bottom of the bush. As if he were picking up a stone, he leaned over and grasped it. The feel of the boy's hand on his sent a quiver down his back. Something was pressed into his hand. He straightened. The guards had taken no note. A bit of parchment rested in his palm. He shoved it inside his dirty tunic and chanced a glance at Elias, whose brows lifted and a glint shone from his eyes.

They marched back to the castle. Once back in the cell, Adrian retrieved the parchment—carefully, carefully. Elias' body stiffened. It was not quite dark in the cell, for the last of the evening light found its way through the high window.

The message was brief. *Tomorrow when sun is high, we will cause a diversion. Go to the bottom of the gully. S.J. will be there. L.* Adrian let out his breath and whispered to Elias the contents of the letter.

Elias expelled his breath. "It is well. If you are a religious man, I would pray to whatever god you know. Many things can go wrong." Silence fell while they listened to the guard's heavy boots echoing down the hall. "I hope this deaf boy knows his way about."

"If he does not, we shall find our way." Adrian smiled in the dark. "Do not worry. We shall both be free by tomorrow this time."

But the following morning, Adrian felt less certain of the outcome. How could a sick monk and a deaf boy create a diversion? He had seen other times when something occurred, two riders who appeared one morning, or an earthquake that shook the land, and the first thing the guards did was to encircle the slaves and tie them together. Then they would deal with whatever threatened.

As the sun reached its zenith, perspiration rolled from his body more than usual, and he fought the urge to look up and around, a sure sign to the guards that something was boding. It was after high noon before the guards allowed them to stop for their midday meal and water. Adrian watched the sun in its run across the vast circle of the brazen sky, watched the guards and watched himself lest he stumble or delay the line.

The air was heavy as if a storm brewed and a low cloud covered the heights of Mt. Hermon. Flies flew up his nostrils and settled on his skin. His insides felt as if they were on fire and his breath came in raspy gasps. He sneaked a peek around the countryside as he waited in line to be loaded. A crow cawed from above as it circled, and the guards barked at the slaves and snapped their whips. The sky was a dirty yellow.

I cannot endure the waiting. Oh, God. Jesus Christ, Lord Of All, I beseech Thee .... He sucked in his breath, surprised that he prayed to Old Bric's God. *Look down upon me now, I pray, grant me Thy mercy and—*

A thunderous explosion filled the air, shook the earth and sent a shower of stones upon the men standing in the quarry. Adrian fell to the ground, then glanced up, thinking it was thunder.

There was no time to wonder—this was the diversion. The guards brushed themselves off, and began to encircle the slaves who sprawled in terror among the boulders.

Elias grasped Adrian's shoulder. "Come!"

They ducked behind a huge rock, even as another blast shuddered the air and cascaded a shower of rocks upon them. Elias' grip remained strong, and as he led off in a sprinting, crouching, dodging run, Adrian wondered that the man who seemed so close to death a few days ago now was agile and strong and quick.

In the gully, a small figure emerged from behind a rock—Samson John. The boy motioned for them to follow. At the very bottom of the gully where the creek bed sank below the level of the bushes, they could escape detection. Shouts echoed off the cliff walls, footsteps approached. They had to crouch and run. It was not easy, but Adrian scurried away like a fox with the hounds on its tail, leaving behind not so much as a whisper or the rattle of disturbed pebbles.

Samson John disappeared behind some bushes. They trailed behind and found themselves in the opening of a cave. Once inside, Samson John turned to them, putting his finger to his lips. *"Sh."*

They waited. After what seemed an eternity, Samson John peeked outside and motioned them to follow. The sun had disappeared and night approached.

Panais, sleepy little village that it was, lay quiet in the shades of night when they passed silently down the narrow streets and came at last to the abandoned Catholic church. Weeds grew in the courtyard and the fountain was dry. The hinges squeaked painfully from rust, and no light brightened the interior of the church. Indeed, it was a shell, for long ago it had been stripped of anything valuable.

Samson John led them to the back where they found a broken-down stable. From the dark interior emerged the tall and slightly stooped form of Brother Louis who enveloped Adrian in his arms.

Louis released him. "Samson John has proved his worth this day, for certes." He patted the boy on his shoulder and received a smudged grin in return. "It was he who discovered the secret cave and tunnel into the fortress. It was he who recognized you when you toiled up the hill with stones on your back."

Adrian turned and bowed to the boy. "I thank you, my friend, and I shall be forever in your debt." He was struck with the improbability of the moment. Who would have thought the prince of Brittany would bow to a deaf mute servant boy?

Samson John beamed.

Louis glanced behind Adrian. "Where is Baldic?"

"Baldic?"

"Aye. The guard who came with Judith. I shall tell you the whole story later. But it was he who arranged the diversion." He smiled. "Was it grand?"

"Grand? It was incredible! What was it? It sounded like the wrath of God descending upon us." Adrian laughed.

"He met some high-ranking Greeks in Acre. They boasted of a strange kind of fire and gave him some of the powder. I know not what they call it, but it is very powerful. Baldic said it came originally from Cathay. The Greeks in Constantinople have used this strange fire for centuries in defending the city."

Adrian lowered himself painfully to a stump, so utterly exhausted he did not know if he could rise again. "Whatever it was, it certainly worked. Praise be to God." He stopped, remembering he had just uttered a prayer to Grandfather's God when the strange fire fell. Coincidence? Nay. Perchance there was something to faith in this God after all.

Louis stirred the fire. "Who is this with you, Adrian?"

"This is a friend I found in the slave quarters. He has been there for three years—far too long for any man to endure. His name is Elias."

They greeted Elias. Louis showed them a tub of hot water he had prepared for them. Adrian luxuriated in the water briefly, then Elias also enjoyed the bath, the first he had taken for over four years. They feasted on the food that was prepared—strips of lamb, roasted over the fire, figs, cheese and bread from the *souk* Louis had bought that day. Plain food by any standard, yet it seemed a feast of the finest delicacies to Adrian.

Afterward, they sat around the fire and talked.

But Elias seemed ill at ease, eating his food with his fingers while standing in the shadows. When he finished, he pulled Adrian aside. "I thank you for your hospitality, but I feel as if I should leave. Tonight. Now."

"But, why? Surely you need rest."

Elias shook his head. "I want to find my family."

Adrian tried to dissuade him, but saw his arguments were useless. He put together a pack of food. Louis gave him money to purchase a horse and new clothes. When he was ready to leave, Adrian saw him to the gate. "Are you going back to France?"

Elias glanced up and down the street. "I shall go to Jerusalem first, our Holy City. It would please me to have you come with me, but the monk said something of a girl who is held prisoner in the castle."

Adrian nodded. "Aye. We must find a way to free her."

"When you finish what it is you must do, come to Jerusalem and look for me. Fare ye well, my friend. Go with Yahweh."

"Go with God," Adrian managed to say, tears stinging his eyes. He watched the slight figure slip down the darkened street, then turned back to the stable.

***

Subebe, Wednesday afternoon

"How is our little treasure, the last of our brides doing, Mohammed?" Ignatius set down his jeweled drinking cup and gazed up at a tall black man.

Mohammed smiled, showing a crescent of white teeth in a black face. "She is quiet and submissive, my lord. That is all I ask from the women at this stage. She will not be any trouble."

"Is she eating enough?"

"Yes. The little mistress and her maid keep to themselves, but they eat what we serve them." He stood to attention while his master perused a parchment.

Ignatius glanced up. "Thank you, Mohammed. You can go now."

As soon as the door closed behind him, a rustle of silk curtains from the back of the apartment parted and a French lord emerged. He stalked to the desk and leaned on it. "I am charmed she is eating. How am I supposed to get her if she is the bride of the Sultan?"

Ignatius held up his hand. "Do not be hasty. All things will arrange themselves, *monsieur*."

A servant burst unannounced into the apartment. Ignatius rose from his desk while motioning to the French lord. The lord decamped again to the rear of the apartment. "Yes? What is the meaning of this unseemly intrusion on my privacy?"

"Lord, my master." The servant, a skimpy man with a bald pate, fell to his knees and lowered his face to the floor. "There was a disturbance. The slaves ... there was a loud sound and they fled. Some of them escaped."

"Some of them?" Ignatius came from behind his desk, his tone deepening.

The servant cowered on the floor. "Two, my lord. The one called Adrian, the other a Jew who was taken years ago."

"Adrian!" The French lord burst from the back and stomped forward, his face brick red, his eyes bulging from their sockets. "What is this? I thought this place is ... "

"Hush!" Ignatius whirled on his French guest. "You will speak only when spoken to. Now leave me!"

When the lord disappeared, Ignatius turned back to the servant who was still kneeling. "When did this happen?"

"Just now, my lord. The guards came and told me. Shall I send for them?"

"That can wait." He paced the room and returned to the desk, stroking a black cat that leaped to his desk. "I still have the upper hand, for I have the girl. He will come for the girl, and now he has been weakened for the kill. I have no fear that he has gone far. No, indeed. Aybu, get off the floor. Send two spies to the village. Tell them to search for the two slaves who disappeared. Then report back to me."

The servant left.

Ignatius smiled, a smile that grew to a snicker and then to a roar of laughter.

The French lord appeared by his desk, a worried frown on his florid face.

Ignatius wiped his eyes. "I shall have him back. Yes, my impatient and odious French friend, you shall have your fun with him. It will be a pleasure to see this through to the end. A pleasure indeed."

***

Panias, Wednesday evening

Adrian drank the last of his ale and rubbed his head, for the stable in the old Catholic church had grown fuzzy and swirled in a crazy manner. Heavy footsteps thudded in the dirt. He looked up as a burly form filled the darkened doorway. *Baldic!* The man was covered from head to toe with dirt, his clothes were torn, he was bloodied in various places, yet he wore a huge grin on his darkened face.

Adrian rose and extended his hand. "Ah. Baldic. The man who won the day today. It is good to see you, my friend. I thank you with all my heart."

Baldic took Adrian's hand, and wrung it thoroughly before sitting down beside the fire on his haunches. "It was nothing. Is there food? I am nearly famished."

Brother Louis laughed, and brought the remainder of the meal to him. As Baldic ate, they caught up on their news. When Adrian told of the Arab attack, and that Leon was most probably dead, Louis crossed himself and said a prayer for Leon. Silence fell while the fire crackled, and Baldic finished his meal.

He told Adrian of Judith and the killing of her guardian. "I have avowed myself to rescue the lady, and I shall." Baldic set down his mug, and glared into the fire.

Louis nodded. "Aye. But what can we do?"

"Brother Louis, you and I shall go see the castle." Adrian straightened, fighting the weariness that sucked the life from him. "I saw only the lower regions."

"Aye. The medicine woman's son works there. Perchance he could get us in."

Adrian strove to keep his mind focused. "It is worth a try." He slumped down by the wall of the stable where Louis covered him with a blanket. "Wake me early."

The next morning, clad in new clothes Louis purchased at the *souk*, they found Hashi, the son of the medicine woman, at home.

Adrian put on his best smile. "We were gone on business for a time, Hashi, but now we return. We desire to see Subebe, where your glorious Sultan dwells. Is it true that pilgrims may visit the awesome citadel of the sultans?"

Hashi nodded vigorously. "It is possible, although I do not know if you could enter the castle now. We have great excitement. Fifty beautiful women from all over the land are being prepared for the arrival of the Sultan Al Aziz of Egypt. They are a gift from our sultan, may he live forever."

"Yet we still desire to see it and cannot wait. Can you inquire for us?" Adrian drew out a coin and let it lay on his open palm.

Hashi nodded. "Yes. I can do this for you. We are proud of our castle and I invite you to come." He held his hand eagerly for the coin, but Adrian tucked it away again.

"When may we go with you? Today?"

The Arab thought for a while, then came to a decision. "Come with me and I shall speak with the head steward. Meet me here at midday. No weapons."

"You shall receive your coin then." Adrian bowed.

As they walked the street back to the church, Adrian halted. "Why are we doing this? Would Judith truly be unhappy as the wife of a ... " He knew the answer. He saw her as clearly as if she stood before him, her eyes blazing, her chin raised, her profile clear and clean in the last rays of the evening light. Nay, she would die in confinement, more so as one of fifty brides in the harem.

Judith. Her memory stirred his heart—the way her lips turned down in a smile, her slim body, her slender neck, her eyes—ah, eyes that captivated a man's soul. "She is very beautiful." They entered into the courtyard of the church.

Louis smiled. "But she hates Christians."

"Why should she hate Christians?" Adrian led the way into stable and found Samson John building the fire.

"She is a Jew," Louis replied as if that was enough. When Adrian made no remark, he continued. "Have you not heard her story? It will make your blood curdle. Her family moved from Troyes to Dijon and, while there, Christian knights broke into her home and killed her mother before her eyes. They carried FitzRauf's banner. The same man you hate so thoroughly." Louis gazed at him steadily. "Can you not see how she would hate all who wear the cross?"

Adrian nodded. "But the father. What of her father?" He suddenly recalled the way she held her head when she puzzled over a problem. His mind snapped open. *Troyes, Dijon. A missing father. A missing daughter.* He paced the small enclosure, once, twice, his heart thumping nearly out of his chest. "Her father, Louis! Did you hear his name?"

Louis turned his eyes to the sky and hummed low under his breath. "I believe I did, but it escapes me. If I heard it again … "

"Elias? Was it Elias?"

Something in Adrian's tone caused the monk to stare. "Why, yes. I think that's it."

Adrian erupted into a wild dance, capering about as if on stilts, waving his arms in the air.

Louis attempted to grab his tunic. "Adrian! Are you mad?"

Adrian stopped spinning and gripped Louis' robe to pull him close. "Her father is Elias! The Jew who was here, whom I met in Subebe! It is he, Louis. For certes, it is he. He told me of a wife and a daughter … he said a beautiful daughter. It is she—Judith!" He released Louis and collapsed on the stool. "I tell you truly, good friend. Their stories agree. Now I must fly to find him. He could not have gotten far—"

"But we must stay and rescue Judith from the castle. Only after she is freed can we find her father and bring about their reunion. Surely you see that." Louis straightened his robe. "We must get her out of there before the wedding and it is too late for her."

"Yea, I see it, you lean old monk." Adrian sighed. "So close. So very, very close."

The next day when the sun was high, Adrian steeled himself for the visit to Subebe, even allowing Louis to pray over his head. Hashi led them to the great fortress on the hill, a steep climb from the valley below. The view commanded the Hula valley to the south and, on the far horizon, the lower Galilean hills. A circuitous trail led up the hill to the fortress, the last part of it directly under the curtain wall and the battlements. Adrian was familiar with this arrangement, for it was used in most castles and afforded the best possible defense against an invading army.

The great defenses of the castle drew a low whistle from his lips. The castle boasted no moat, but two great gates formed the entrance through the curtain wall. The gates were made of iron and were guarded on each side by towers that bristled with arrow slits, and could only be lifted by massive wheels from inside the towers. Adrian and Louis followed a servant who led them through a small door built into the right tower and through which all foot traffic flowed.

Adrian's heart sank when they were stopped and searched. He could not penetrate this fortress the way he did the Castle Renault. Inside the gates they were ushered to a small room, motioned to cushioned benches, and given wine in tall cups made of glass with molten silver on the rims. They did not speak.

In a short time a servant in a silken robe of yellow appeared in the doorway and motioned them to follow. He led them from the outer bailey through an immense arch built of ancient yellowed stone. "Nimrod's Arch," the man said in flawless French.

The inner bailey was not level, due to the natural terrain of the hillside, but the owners of the castle had utilized the terrain to build steps and small courtyards and fountains and tiled walkways.

A tall, square keep dominated the center of the inner bailey. Soldiers emerged from it and Adrian surmised it was the barracks and officer's quarters. Off to the left, steps descended to the blacksmith shop, kitchens, pens for animals, and the other stalls necessary for the upkeep of the thousands of people in the fortress. It was on the lower level that he had lived and died inches at a time—he knew that area well enough.

He was bewildered by the maze of corridors, arches, courtyards with fountains, and vaulted halls. They followed the servant through another guarded arch that led the way up a wide marble stairway. At the top there was another hall, and then they walked through tall oaken doors into the citadel itself.

The sultan's palace was built on the northern edge of the fortress, overlooking the valley below with sheer rock walls forming the foundation. They did not stop to inspect the larger-than-life inscriptions that were carved into the stone walls, the beautiful mosaics on the floors of the courtyards, the tinted windows made of colored glass, or the tapestries of vivid beauty.

The servant did not pass the women's quarters, or if he did, he made no mention of it. Adrian shook his head. *Oh Lord in Heaven, how shall we find Judith? How shall we help her escape from this prison?* His quest to free Old Bric from Renault seemed child's play compared to this.

At last they stopped at a massive door. The servant knocked and another opened it. They bowed to one another and the second servant motioned them all to enter. It was quiet in the apartment. Oriental carpets hushed their footsteps. Adrian heard the soft plucking of strings on a harp and the gentle splash of water in a fountain. Birds twittered from their cages along a wall where light from high windows reached them.

The servant motioned them to sit on silken cushions on the floor and served them hot drinks in golden cups. "It is tea," Louis informed Adrian in a whisper.

On every side were precious ornaments: large vases from Cathay made of an unusual translucent glass unlike any Adrian had ever seen; beautiful tapestries; strange silver implements for eating, he supposed, for they were set at a table; mirrors of real glass with golden frames; a golden hourglass set upon a bronze stand.

Hearing a silken rustle, he glanced up as a tall man entered and stood before them. Adrian sank to his knees and heard Louis fall to the carpet beside him.

The man chuckled. "Rise and be welcomed," he said in Greek.

In utter surprise, Adrian rose and stared at the man. Though fair of skin, he possessed a long black beard that was elaborately curled, dark eyes snapping with intelligence, a strange cap made of silken blue material from which hung golden bells, and a long blue robe heavily decorated with gold and silver thread. The robe was open to reveal his bare chest, a pair of loose silk trousers, and a silver belt made of interwoven chain links. He wore a golden chain from which dangled a ruby set in diamonds. The lush blue of sapphires sparkled on his fingers.

"Please be seated," the man said.

Adrian sank down on the cushion and tried to keep his mouth shut.

The man seated himself a low stool, took a handful of nuts from a silver bowl and popped them in his mouth. After crunching them, he said, "I am Christopher Alexander Ignatius the Third, a humble servant of the great Sultan Al Issa, may he live forever, the son of Saladin Yusef Ibu Ayyubm. As you have surmised, I am Greek. I come from Athens and I served under the Emperor of the Byzantine Empire, Isaac Angelus in Constantinople."

"And you serve here ... under the ... Muslims?" Louis kept his eyes lowered.

"Yes. I left Constantinople two years ago. I came to Antioch and converted to the Muslim faith. Because of my great learning and grasp of many languages ... do you prefer Latin? French?"

"French would be more suitable for me," Adrian said.

"Very well. French it shall be." He smiled, but it was more a twitch of his mouth than a real smile. "Because of my great learning, the sultan in Jerusalem found my services of value. I was then encouraged to travel to Subebe to assist the sultan here with his many guests and his financial affairs. He has found me … irreplaceable." He attempted his crooked smile again. His long fingers embraced the stem of a crystal goblet from which he sipped red wine. "And you? What are you about and why do you travel to Subebe?" He nodded to Adrian.

"I am Sir Adrian D'Arcy, and I travel to the Holy Lands to serve God and my king. I came with this brother of the true church on a mission for the holy father, Pope Innocent III. I can say nothing of that mission, save that we are in a great hurry to reach Damascus." He shifted and hoped his voice carried conviction. "Our purpose is one of curiosity to see your wonderful fortress. Upon learning that visitors are allowed, we thought to have a look."

The steward nodded and then switched his bright gaze to Louis.

"I am Brother Louis of St. Jacques Monastery in Mordelias, Brittany. I am a pilgrim, my lord. I came to the holy land to serve God and my king. Sir Adrian has taken me into his service for my care and keep."

The steward waited, looking at them with a question in his eyes as if he expected more explanations. When none came, he nodded. "Very well. Come. I shall show you parts of Subebe that are open for guests. When we enter the court of the sultan, you are expected to remove your shoes and kneel with your faces to the floor. I will indicate when it is time to leave. I will not introduce you to His Highness. Come."

Adrian glanced at Louis with raised brows as they followed him from the apartment.

Ignatius gave a running commentary as they strode along. Then he opened a gigantic door and led them into the Great Hall.

Adrian had never seen such a display of wealth. It seemed everything from the cressets on the wall that held the flaming torches to the spittoons on the floor near the throne was made of gold. But gold was only a part of the great wealth in the room. He saw carpets and tapestries, tables covered by white linen cloths groaning with food, silken garments on the slaves who waved long feathered fans above the sultan's head, jewels that sparkled from every corner and on every hand, a large heap of jewels in a basket near the sultan's couch.

The sultan sat like an overweight caterpillar on a large throne high on the dais, surrounded by scores of slaves, servants, old men and young men, who seemed to function as counselors. Adrian was interested to note the differences of this court as compared to the English court of his uncle, King Richard, or the French court. In comparison, the best of Europe and England seemed barbaric and poor.

Adrian and Louis had only a few seconds to gaze about, then they were compelled to kneel with their faces to the floor. After a few moments, they were tapped on the shoulder and ushered out. Adrian saw Louis shaking his head as if he bemoaned the waste of all that wealth. The monk, no doubt, was thinking the gold in that room would feed the poor in Acre for years.

The vizier accompanied them to the outer courtyard. Just before leaving, Ignatius embraced Adrian, pressing something into his hand. Adrian led the way down the hill and back toward the village, his mind in a whirl.

"It is an impossible task we have set before ourselves," Louis said. "I am sure you realize that. Have you any thoughts about it? I was so confused with all the strange sights and sounds that I could not think beyond putting one foot in front of the other."

Adrian chuckled. "I had a few, but let us see what the esteemed Vizier of the Sultans, Christopher Ignatius the Third has to say."

Louis glanced up in surprise as Adrian showed him the small piece of paper that Ignatius had pressed into his hand. It was the first paper Adrian had ever handled. He looked at it curiously before he unrolled it. The characters were in Latin, so he passed it to Louis.

Louis read, "Meet me at the Greek temple above the village tonight when the moon is high."

CHAPTER TWENTY-TWO

Cry havoc! And let slip the dogs of war! William Shakespeare

Panias, Thursday evening

Louis settled himself on the dirt floor near the low table where they ate flat fried bread, hard cheese, curdled milk, figs, and stale wine. Baldic and Adrian sprawled on old hay nearby. When they finished, they sat in the courtyard, gazing at the great pile of rocks known as Subebe. The light of the westering sun gilded the stones gold.

Louis sighed. "It is a strange request. Meet him in the pagan temple area by the cliffs? Alone? Can we trust this man, Adrian?"

"It may be a trap, of course." Adrian stood to pace. "He knows more of our affairs than he was willing to say. Is he for us or against us? Who would suppose that a great man such as he, and a Muslim as well, would conspire with us?"

Louis tossed a stick on the fire. "I know not, but we must devise some plan to rescue Judith and her maid soon, or she will be forever gone. Do you have a plan?"

"Nay, I do not. It is so much more difficult than I ever dreamed. How may we penetrate the fortress, find the women's quarters, subdue the guards, find Judith, and escape? I have a feeling that we would not even get past the first guards before we were taken. There are too many of them and the fortress is ... well, what it is meant to be, fortified and strong." He sighed. "I fear there is little hope."

"But God can do things we cannot," Louis said gently.

"Aye. That I know. Well, let us proceed, whether we fall into a clever trap, or no. Perchance this man is the angel of God."

Adrian led the way through the village and up the hill. A full moon appeared now and again from behind gray scudding clouds blown on the east wind. Oaks and olive trees in the grove rattled their dry branches, and small animals scurried through the scattered leaves. A rock wall loomed above, and where they walked a stream gurgled, gathered in pools, then cascaded down a waterfall.

It was a night for ghosts and demons and the cackle of evil women.

The remains of Roman and Greek temples protruded from the face of the rock wall. Some were ancient and some newer. The temple to the Greek god Pan sat at the far end of the cliff in a cave.

It seemed to Adrian that he walked into a wall of darkness as he led the way up the wide stairs. Evil voices whispered in the air, his legs felt like pieces of wood, and his heart too large for his chest. His breath came in gasps as if he had run a steep course. He paused and glanced back at Louis.

The monk covered his head with his cowl and was muttering under his breath. With every step he crossed himself.

"It is ... evil here, is it not?" Adrian whispered as they paused under a scrub oak. There were signs of the worship of Pan—a bloodied spot on the stone near the cave where a goat had been sacrificed. "I wonder where he is."

A strong voice answered from inside the temple to Nemesis. "I am here!" A cloaked figure appeared in the narrow doorway. "Do not fear. Come inside and we shall talk."

Adrian glanced at Louis, then stepped into the ruins, feeling as if he was entering a spider's web. The ceiling had long since fallen in, but a bench, built of stone, sat along the wall. The walls of the temple were narrow and at the far end he saw an indentation where the goddess once resided.

Christopher Ignatius chuckled. "She is not here, and my man guards the footpath. Come, sit." He spoke as they perched cautiously on the bench. "Did you know they still worship Pan over there? Did you see the blood on the stones? They say that if blood emerges into the pool below, it means the god has accepted their sacrifice. It is a pleasant place, it is not?" He grinned, showing his teeth.

Adrian thought of a wolf about to spring on its prey. "What do you want with us? I find this meeting strange, to say the least."

"To say the least!" Ignatius responded with a sharp cackle of laughter. "How about saying the most! What do you say, Brother Louis of Mordelias? World traveler, friend of the holy father? How goes your mission with that august personage? Ah, not too well. I am sorry for you."

Louis' head jerked up. "You ... know?"

Ignatius nodded. "I know many things, for I have a legion of spies at my command. I am like the Old Man of the Mountain. I make it my business to find out about all who pass by, but I knew you long before you came to my door. We expected you to pay us a visit. I must say, you are a very interesting person. Not like a monk at all."

Louis could only stare.

"And you, Sir Adrian D'Arcy," Christopher said, turning his leonine head to him. "You are a displaced person, are you not? How is your family in Brittany? I hear King John is more interested in his child bride than in running the country. He is having troubles with his barons, is he not?"

Adrian found it difficult to breathe. "I ... know aught of King John."

The man cackled. "And so we come to the fair Jewess, Judith."

Adrian gasped—he could not help it. Louis murmured something too low to hear.

"Ah. I surprise you again. I have known of this lady for some time. She was a slave, owned by Baron FitzRauf of France. She escaped from her master and came to Damascus where she worked for a Greek in a hospice. One of my spies saw her and thought she would make a lovely completion to our search for fifty beautiful women. They do not know she is a Jew. Do not be troubled. I shall not disclose her secret unless it profits me."

"I suppose profit is all that matters to you." Adrian stared at the man, willing him to show his true colors.

But Ignatius leaned back and knit his fingers together. "And now you show up and ask to see Subebe. I am paid to gather information and I ask myself, 'Why do these men come? What is their true mission? Why do they watch Subebe?'"

Adrian did not know what to think, but he knew he could not fool this man. "We came to rescue the maiden. If you know this, you also know that I was held here as a slave for a fortnight, and that important papers were taken from me, papers that should be seen only by the king of Jerusalem or the Holy Roman Emperor of Constantinople."

Ignatius leaned forward. "You speak plainly. Aye, I know of these things. Go on."

"If you would turn us in to your master, then let it be, but we are going to try to free Judith from Subebe. She shall die otherwise."

"Why is it so important that she live? Do not all die?"

Louis shifted and spoke with great passion. "It is important that all live and breathe and serve their Creator. Besides the fact that I value all human life as God's creation, I feel she has a special mission to accomplish. She must be free."

Ignatius leaned closer. "Do you know what this mission is that she must do?"

"Nay, my lord. I know not. It is only a feeling, a premonition."

Silence descended while the man studied them intently, his face hidden in the shadows. Adrian knew that Louis was sorry he had mentioned Judith's secret mission to this man, for the monk closed his eyes and his lips moved in a silent prayer.

Ignatius straightened and pierced Adrian with a gaze so strong he felt it pinning him to the wall. "What you attempt is impossible. I would take no interest in it, save that I am wearied to death of my master's service. Books, figures, reports, words, numbers ... all of this fills pages upon pages in my apartment. There is this, as well—I am truly not a Muslim. I took this position for my own gain. I secretly loathe them and would do anything to thwart their plans as long as I am undetected." He glanced sharply at them. "You are aware that you have set yourselves on a course of suicide?"

Louis nodded. "We know, my lord, but nothing will stop us, not even you."

"I knew you were not as other monks!" Ignatius chuckled. "And what do you say, Sir Adrian D'Arcy? Would you continue this and lose your chance for the hand of a fair lady in France?"

Adrian jolted upright and faced him squarely. "I know not what I will lose or gain, my lord. I am set on this course and I agree with Brother Louis. I shall seek to rescue Judith until I have no life in my body. Yet if I live, then I shall travel to Damascus and as far as Constantinople if need arises, for I am not freed from our service to His Holiness. I will say this, however. If you are hoping for gold as payment for your services, you will be disappointed, for we cannot pay you. God will have to reward you."

"Ah!" Ignatius' cackling laughter echoed off the walls. "Very well spoken." He leaned forward again, and Adrian knew the real business of the evening was at hand. "I will give you aid, as far as I am able. I have devised a plan. Of course, a million things may go wrong and you may have to change the plan as you go. You know the general layout of the castle, Adrian, but I shall give you the floor plans for the upper levels. Brother Louis, you shall position yourself at a portal I shall show you and be ready there with mounts."

Hope blazed into Adrian's heart as he listened.

Ignatius pulled a tightly rolled parchment from his robe and handed it to Adrian. "Study this, then burn it. The sultan's caravan has already arrived. The wedding will take place tomorrow at sunset. Adrian, very early in the morning you will appear in the village square. We need many hands to help with the final preparations and so I shall send out servants to hire those who would work. This way you shall come unhindered into the fortress."

"But my lord, I do not have black hair, as you can see." Adrian removed his head covering. "Nor dark skin. Surely they will notice."

"As to that, I have brought you this." He reached into a pocket and pulled out a jar. "Anoint your hair, your face and hands and legs with this ointment." He turned to Louis. "Wait outside at the Horse Gate with the highly esteemed Sir Baldic and your mounts. Yes, I know of this man and his passion to avenge himself. He may have the occasion to find himself thus occupied. Study the map. The portal where you will wait is marked. The plans for the escape are written on the parchment." He stood. "I believe … "

A servant appeared in the doorway. "Master! They come!"

Ignatius nodded. "Very well, Mustaphe." Unhurried, he turned back to Adrian. "I believe I have covered everything. Good even, sirs. " He bowed to them and disappeared.

Adrian stepped out to see where he had gone, but there was no trace of him and no sound of his passing. He tucked the parchment inside his tunic and motioned to Louis. Carefully he stepped down the stairs, past the pools, but there! Torches winked in the darkness below. Men filed up the stairs. Louis would have bolted, but Adrian pressed him back. They knelt behind a massive rock.

It was as Adrian suspected. The men came to worship at the place. He waited until they passed, hearing only the slap of sandaled feet on the stones; the hissing of torches; and a low, moaning song, like wind straining to be free. At last they filed into the mouth of the cave, and Adrian motioned for Louis to follow him.

"We have much to do, Brother," he said as they approached the church. "And very little time."

"Aye. It will be a long night."

By candlelight they poured over the layout of the castle. Baldic schooled Adrian on them, getting him to draw them out from memory. Invariably he would get something wrong, but Baldic was patient and they would try again. Samson John studied the drawings, too, and reproduced them with startling clarity.

At one point Adrian threw down the parchment he had been studying. "I see a thousand flaws in his plan. What does he think I am? A fool? Here. Look. It says as the brides proceed forth from their quarters, the last bride shall be Judith and she shall wear a green gown. But how many others will wear green? They will all be veiled. Will Judith know about the rescue? And how am I to get into the citadel?"

Louis looked over the plans. "Here. It says you will be given the garb of the personal servants to the sultan, which will gain you entrance unhindered into the citadel." He shrugged. "As for Judith, I would assume he would let her know the part she must play."

"There's nothing in this about Judith. The instructions are to follow along the line of the women as they file out into the inner courtyard, locate Judith, and bump her or cause her to stumble. When she falls, then the two of us will roll several times down a stairwell. Then I am to grab her and run."

Baldic grunted. "It does not sound feasible, Adrian. How far shall you get if there are guards and servants about?"

Adrian stopped pacing. He met Baldic's eyes. "I hope he is not setting us up for a very disastrous end for his own amusement."

A heavy silence fell.

Again they went back to their studies.

With a sigh, Adrian rolled up the parchments, extinguished the lamp and fell onto his pallet. Dawn streaked the sky with light, but they managed two hours of sleep before they broke their fast. With a quick glance at the plans one final time, Adrian cast them into the fire.

Baldic anointed Adrian's hair, face, arms, and hands with the brown sticky stuff in the jar while Louis went to the *souk* to buy the attire of a servant—loose fitting pantaloons, sandals, and a jerkin.

Before they parted, Louis laid his hand on Adrian's arm. "I shall pray for thee every moment."

Adrian nodded and looked into the monk's brown eyes. "Thank you, Brother, for your help and kindness. You remind me sometimes of my grandfather. That is the highest compliment I can pay any man, for he truly is a man of God."

Louis bowed his head. "I thank you. Now let us pray and commit our way to God."

"Make it speedy, my friend, time is running out."

***

Subebe, Friday morning

Something stirred in the women's quarters. Judith felt it in the tepid air, a moving of hands to tuck away a stray hair, a smoothing of silken garments, a straightening of postures.

She had been surprised when they were taken not to the slave's quarters in the depths of the castle, but into the citadel in the center of the fortress, up many stairs and down many corridors to the harem. It was then that she understood—she would not be a slave in the common sense, but a concubine to an Arab sultan. The thought froze her blood.

The harem was divided into two compartments, one for the wives of the Sultan Issa and their children, and one for the women who were part of the gift to be given to the Sultan Al Aziz upon his arrival—fifty virgins gathered from all parts of the kingdom.

Upon their arrival, Judith and Elizabeth enjoyed a bath and were given loose-fitting pantaloons gathered at their ankles and waist, a tunic that slipped over their heads and held tight with a sash, and soft slippers for their feet. Everything was made of silk and, despite Judith's fear and desperation, she enjoyed the feel of the cool material on her skin. When she undressed, she held the small capsule tightly in a fist to avoid it being seen.

They talked little and kept to themselves. Every day she attended classes where a bald-headed eunuch taught the women proper etiquette for behavior in the sultan's bed. Since the man spoke in Arabic, and Judith understood that language only a little, she gave herself up to dreams of her past life.

Today all the women were ushered into a large courtyard that separated the two living arrangements. She glanced up as the heavy oaken doors were thrown open and two tall, bare-chested slaves entered. They lifted trumpets to their mouths and rent the air with two shrill blasts. The slaves stepped aside for a man who wore a white and gold cape and blue silk pantaloons. Someone of great importance. This man stood in the doorway with a parchment unrolled in his hands. He read it in three languages—Arabic, Armenian and Greek. She was grateful Stefan taught her Greek.

The proclamation, when it came to bare facts, said the great Sultan Al h Ad-din Aziz Ayyub of Egypt would arrive the following day. The wedding would take place at sunset. The trumpets blew again and they left.

The doors clanged shut. Judith looked at Elizabeth. "It seems I shall be married soon," she said in a low voice. "Perchance we should tell them we are ... " she mouthed the word *Jews*. "Surely the great sultan would not wish to marry one of our race."

Elizabeth shook her head and took her mistress's hand. "Nay! We shall keep the secret. Our deliverance may be nearer than we think."

"Hush!" Judith whispered, for in that moment, a large woman approached and ordered them to back to their apartment in the virgin's quarters. Meekly they went, but Judith's heart was heavy. Once she was married to the sultan, there would be no rescue and no hope.

***

Panias, Friday noon

Louis shifted from one foot to another and looked at Subebe until his eyes ached. *Ah, Lord God, how I long to be inside helping Adrian!* He paced to a large rock, then back again, his fingers toying with the tassels on his scarf. He turned to Baldic, who stood surveying the fortress with a serene expression. "How can you remain so calm?"

The Bulgarian seemed unmoved by uncertainty and waited patiently. "God will bring your enemy into our reach. You must wait."

Louis wiped the sweat from his face. "I am waiting, but I dread the moment when it arrives. Oh, my God! How I long for this to be finished." He climbed off the rock, and leading the way through a low scrub of brush and juniper trees, he said, "Do you suppose we should rally forces outside the castle in case there is fighting?"

Baldic, always slow with his thinking processes, considered the idea for a time, then shook his head. "We cannot not fight the sultan's men. If we did, we would draw attention to ourselves. Nay, we must do all we can to aid them when they come out."

"That is just what I am worried about. If we are pursued, how will we flee without a back guard?" They arrived at the Catholic church and hurried to the stables.

"I shall be the back guard." Baldic sat on a stool and drew his sword. It shone in the sunshine. He felt the blade. "It longs to taste Arab blood."

"But you will not survive, my friend. There will be hundreds, nay, thousands, who come out. You will be killed outright."

Baldic's eyes shone as he looked up with an eager smile. "I care not, Brother. I care not. I have lived well, and if I die, I die. I shall count it an honor to give my life for the lady."

Louis shook his head and turned to prepare their midday meal. Only a few more hours. This time tomorrow it would be over. *Oh, God!*

***

Subebe, Friday 2:11 p.m.

Adrian placed his shoulders under a wooden yoke and lifted. A pail of water hung on each side. Careful to avoid a spill, he carried it up the stone stairway into the castle. In the courtyard, he lowered the pails, set them on the ground, unhooked them, then turned and returned. Back and forth. His back ached, his legs screamed in pain, the sun burned his head. Sweat ran in rivulets and he worried it would wash off the brown paste. It was as if he slaved again for the sultans and he wondered if it was worth it.

As the sun began its descent and a Muslim horn sounded the ending of the day, a servant presented him with a bundle wrapped in plain cloth. He opened it in secret and found a pair of blue silk pantaloons, a white silk shirt with the sultan's emblem embroidered on the sleeve and an embroidered vest. A gold-colored silk sash completed the outfit.

Retreating to a quiet courtyard, he donned the clothes and thought again of the plan. He groaned. *No! No! A child ... a fool could think of a better plan.* It was too simple, and it depended upon a man who lived in

356

the realm of lies and duplicity. A cold sweat beaded his brow as he wrestled with his options. There were no other options—he needed Christopher Ignatius.

He rested beside a fountain in a secluded courtyard and chided himself. What was he doing here? Was this forwarding his own plans? Why rescue this Jew? Ignatius' words came back to him like a tempter's whisper. "Do not all die?"

All the emotions he had carefully dammed behind a thick wall of careful resolve rushed over his mind. His knights—*oh, dear God*—John starved them to death. He thought of his mother. Once upon a time he made a vow to avenge her, to bring God's justice to his uncle's door. He thought of his sister, his friends, his people. All lost, all gone. And here he sat, doing what? He could slip away, even now, and forget Judith. Her plight seemed small.

But he shook his head. Something fine and noble sprang up in his heart. *She must not die.*

The sun slanted long rays across the castle and a stiff wind whipped the sultan's banner. The wedding would take place soon. Adrian bowed his head. *I have given my vow. I must rescue Judith and if anything is left of me when I finish, I will kill King John.*

***

Subebe, Friday, 3:06 p.m.

A young maid swept the curtains aside from the apartment where Judith and Elizabeth rested and motioned for Judith to come to a low stool where they would comb her hair and apply cosmetics.

Judith rose, her mouth dry and her heart pounding like a heavy drum in her ears. She cast a quick glance at Elizabeth, whose little face was as white as the silk tunics of the servants. Judith had slept none at all during the rest time. Her mind followed a dozen paths of escape, but they vanished like smoke in the wind.

Now it was time. She would be bathed, perfumed, combed, and given final instructions before she began that long walk down the stone corridors to the Great Hall where the sultans and all the mighty of the land waited. The maid, whose name was Zena, coaxed her to eat a few bites of honey cake and drink a few swallows of wine. As Judith ate, an idea full blown, ready to be executed, sprang to mind.

While Zena bathed her in a private room, she said, "We are much of the same height and build, Zena. Look. Your long, black hair is very much like mine."

Zena giggled. "Oh, no, mistress. You are much more beautiful than I."

357

"But if one did not look directly in your face, if you wore a veil, it might be difficult to tell us apart, am I not right?"

"Come." Zena held out the towel. "Put on your gown and I will do your face. The gong will sound, and you must be ready, or my head will roll."

As Judith stepped from the bath, she wrapped the towel around her body, but she did not don the beautiful green silken gown that was laid out for her. Instead, she grasped the maid's arm and pulled her close, so that she gazed directly into her eyes. "Would you like to be the wife of the sultan, Zena? And be waited on every day, and have delicate things to eat? Would you?" Her grip tightened when the girl tried to shake her off. "You know how sad I have been. I shall tell you a secret, Zena. I am a Jew. I was taken against my will and my friends were murdered. I do not wish to be ..."

"Mistress!" The girl tried to pull away with a frightened scream. "You are hurting me! We shall be late! I beg of you, get into your robe and let me comb your hair."

"No!" Judith grasped a scarf and flung it around the girl's neck and pulled it tight. "We shall change places! When I release you, put on my robe. With the veil, no one will know. At least not for a while." Slowly Judith released her.

Elizabeth had been watching with open mouth and now she assisted Judith into the maid's clothes, dressed the hysterical girl in the green robe, and adjusted the veil over her head.

"Now, Elizabeth. Go out in the main room and pretend to be very frightened. Ask one of the other maids to come. Quickly. We have little time. Chose someone very small."

Judith made Zena lie on the floor with her face down. When the other maid came in, she screamed and bent over. Judith quickly used her scarf on the neck of the second girl and forced her to change clothes with her maid. They had barely arranged themselves when the first gong sounded. Quickly gathering the jars of ointments and creams, Judith left the small room. She motioned Elizabeth to follow.

They fell into the last of the line, and Judith averted her face from the keen gaze of the eunuch. This would be the real test, for the man knew her and liked her. But he was busy and preoccupied. His eyes flitted over them without recognition.

Judith tried to still her shaking hands, her pounding heart. Surely he can hear it. *Oh, Yahweh, grant me mercy.*

***

Friday, 3:31 p.m.

Louis packed the saddlebags and rolled up the beds. He, Samson John, and Baldic ate a bit of dried cheese and some figs they had plucked that morning from a tree near the Greek temples. They washed this down with warm wine.

"What consumes your thoughts, Brother?" Baldic asked as they waited.

Louis looked up from his rosary and shook his head. "I fear ... something has gone wrong, very wrong." He stood, noted the position of the sun. Soon they would leave for Subebe.

"I feel it, too," Baldic said. "What shall we do about it?"

"I have prayed earnestly for direction, and I feel we should not attempt either the Horse Gate, nor the small gate on the western flank. I do not trust the sultan's vizier."

"What of the secret tunnel into Subebe? Samson John can show us where it is."

Louis nodded. "Aye. We shall hide there. But we will need someone inside to tell them where we are. Will you go in?"

"Nay, Brother. Not I. I would be spotted in a short time and killed. But we could use some of this brown paste on your face and hands and dress you like a wealthy Arab."

Louis ground his teeth and swallowed. He did not want to go inside the fortress. People went in there and never came out again—alive. But he nodded and led the way to the *souk*. He would have to buy a robe befitting a wealthy Arab, jewelry, and probably a sword too. Baldic could show him the rudiments of swordplay. But they had little time--very little time.

***

Friday, 4:05 p.m.

As the castle readied itself for the wedding, Adrian made his way unchallenged to the higher apartments, to the door of the women's quarters in the citadel. Dozens of servants crowded the hallways, and every six feet or so, two guards stood with feet spread, eyeing all who came and went, hands on their scimitars and broad-axes.

Adrian found the door of the women's apartments but did not hesitate there. He hurried by with a bent head and a distracted air. Just down the hall he found an embrasure in the wall where there was a seat and a colored-glass window. In the palace of the sultan, servants were expected to stand and wait for orders. And so he stood, like so many others, with arms folded across his chest, feet spread apart, eyes on the oaken door.

The moments sifted away like sand in the wind and time seemed to stand still. Waiting was torture, but he reminded himself that, above all, he must keep a calm demeanor. Servants came and went through the massive door, and each time it was opened, he heard the women's excited chatter and the tinkling of children's laughter. The scent of perfume and incense floated out to him.

His throat was dry. He consciously relaxed his knotted muscles, taking deep breaths to still the rising terror in his mind.

A gong sounded, reverberating up and down the stone hall like a call from hell. The hallway was cleared and the doors opened. The maiden servants who assisted the young women in the quarter came out first, holding their pots of ointments in little cloth bags, veils covering their faces, heads bowed demurely.

Adrian marveled at how young they appeared. They filed by silently; only the slap of their sandals could be heard. The last one in line tripped on her gown just as she passed him. The one before her turned and aided her; they went on down the hall.

Another gong sounded and three male slaves with a tambourine, a flute, and a drum emerged. To the beat of the music, the women formed an orderly line and, without so much as a whisper, filed by. Adrian resisted the urge to wipe the sweat from his forehead.

It was almost time. His hand went to his sword hilt. No sword. He licked his lips. Other servants lined the halls, waiting in attendance upon the ladies, watching the procession silently. Adrian's back prickled, as if someone ran their fingers lightly up and down it.

The gong sounded again, and an expectant hush preceded the opening of the doors. Three more slaves appeared with musical instruments. He heard the sound of whispered sandals on stone, the waft of perfume, the silent sigh from fifty throats as the women of the virgin's court began their processional down the hall.

Adrian's heart threatened to beat its way out of his chest as he watched the first of the maidens approach. To his horror he saw that the very first woman wore green. She was tall, slender, and carried herself with a stately air. He tried to peer past her veil, but unlike the wives' veils, these covered the whole face. Only one was to wear green.

He waited and counted three more of the women in green. None of them appeared to be Judith, but he did not know … could not tell for sure. At the end of the line there came a slight maiden who glanced about, stumbled, and seemed unsure. She wore green and was trailed by another smaller girl who trembled visibly. He fell alongside, for now the brides had all emerged and the door was shut. The other servants grouped behind and alongside the brides. The guards closed in the rear.

Adrian approached the place where he was to make his move, where the hallway branched and a stairway descended to the left. Sending a silent plea to God for help, he stumbled and fell heavily into the slight maiden ... rolled, tangled in her gown ... heard cries, shouts, screams ... grabbed the maiden ... and bolted down the stairs.

The maiden's veil was torn off. Adrian stared into a stranger's face. She screamed—he released her. But the guards pinned him to the ground and shackled his wrists.

"Bring him to my apartments, if you please," a precise voice said from above.

Adrian looked up. At the top of the stairs, Christopher Ignatius stood with folded arms and a smile on his thin lips. The guards wrestled Adrian up the stairs.

"Gently," Ignatius said. "We do not want him damaged. He is a prince in his own land." He looked at the others who had gathered in the hall. "Continue. Everything is under control." The maid in green was restored her veil and the procession resumed.

***

5:03 p.m.

Louis and Baldic followed the slim figure of Samson John along a dim trail that wound through scrub oaks, prickly bushes and rocks. Louis had donned his Arab clothes: a tunic to his calves, a long robe, a *kuffiyeh*, and heavy jewelry around his neck. The brown paste lent a dark shade to his skin, yet he felt obvious, unconcealed.

He anxiously watched the sun's descent to the horizon, for he wanted to be inside the castle before the wedding began. But there was no hurrying Samson John. The boy glanced back now and then, cautioning them with his hand to silence. They crossed a small stream, then ascended toward the glowering, massive wall of ancient stones.

At last they arrived at the cave mouth. Louis took and deep breath and turned to Baldic. "Say a prayer or two for me, will you? If you know how to pray."

Baldic snorted. "I knows how to pray, Brother. I pray that my sword will taste blood."

Louis shook his head. "I can never understand you, so I will not attempt it. Fare well, Baldic." He turned the boy's face to his. "Fare well, Samson. Do what Baldic tells you. I shall see you in a few hours. If I do not return by ... the time the moon rises over the hills, then run to the village. Someone may come with a message."

***

5:17 p.m.

At the first turn of the corridor where a recessed cupboard was protected by a sheer curtain, Judith stepped out of line and pulled Elizabeth with her. She waited with bated breath for the sound of an alarm, for calls, for hurried feet, searching for them. But there was only silence and the far-off sounds of the procession, receding farther and farther away. "We must get off this main corridor." She peered out from the curtain, but ducked back in, for another procession was coming, led by the eunuch.

It seemed to take forever, but at last the wives passed, and then the virgins came. She could not resist a peek when the last of the line filed by. The two girls on the end seemed about to faint from fright. Servants and guards by the score followed the line of women. They turned a corner and their footfalls faded away.

From down the corridor a scream echoed. Judith gripped Elizabeth's arm in fear. What was happening? Men shouted. Something shattered like an earthen pot being smashed. This was what she had been waiting for. She peered out again. Despite the uproar, the hall here remained silent and empty.

She gripped Elizabeth's hand and fled down the opposite way from the commotion, bolting like cats in front of a dog, their flimsy slippers slapping against the tiles—past the doors leading into the women's quarters, around another corner, down a curving stair, through a courtyard, down another hall.

Judith stopped, panting hard. The servants on this floor moved about their tasks serenely. No one ran in the palace of the sultan. She glanced about and found two jugs sitting beside a doorway. Lifting one to her head, she indicated that Elizabeth should carry the other.

Thus they continued down the hall and arrived at another stair. Following this, they entered a large outer courtyard. Judith stopped and gazed about, realizing they were still deep within the citadel. She was lost. Lowering the jug to the floor, she said, "I know not where to go. What do you think?"

Elizabeth shrugged, very close to tears. "I know not, mistress." She pointed to narrow stairs leading to the top of the wall. "Why don't you look out and see where we are?"

Judith nodded and mounted the stairs. The sun flung brilliant golds and yellows into the sky, and down below servants lit thousands of torches along the corridors and in the courtyards. She saw to her chagrin that they were still within the citadel, that there were walls within walls, that no way led directly to the main gates. The builders must have planned it that way to guard against intruders. It was also an effective way to keep prisoners. She sighed and rejoined Elizabeth.

Far away she heard music, trumpets blared, voices were raised. The wedding. How long did she have before they were missed? How could they get out? Surely they could not just stroll out of the gates.

"You!" A heavy voice boomed across the courtyard. She knew enough Arabic to understand the words. "Why do you sit and dream?"

The burly shape of a large woman descended the stair, bearing upon them as a storm cloud over the horizon. Judith's heart sank. What should she do? Run? Give up? If she ran, would the alarm be raised? If she went along, would they be trapped with guards watching their every move?

She glanced at Elizabeth's stricken face, gripped her hand, and fled.

***

5:33 p.m.

"Do you believe in God?" Ignatius looked down his nose at Adrian as if he were an insect.

Adrian lifted his chin. He stood in Ignatius' apartments unshackled, but guards stood at the door. "I do."

"And did your God answer your prayers this day? I assume you prayed."

Adrian did not reply.

Ignatius gave a short, cackling laugh. "Ah. I see He did not. And tell me, Sir Adrian, how did you suppose that you would get away by rolling the girl from the line of brides?"

"That was your idea. I thought you planned a diversion."

Again that barking laugh. "With a dozen guards standing around? Do you not know that each of the ladies has her own personal guard? Did you not suppose that, my friend?"

"I did not know, but I assumed you knew these things. Why did you not take this into account? It was your plan." The man was playing with him as a cat plays with a mouse—as long as Adrian provided enough amusement for him, he supposed Ignatius would let him live. He thought bitterly that he had believed everything the man said.

"Ah, you Europeans are … what is the phrase you use … lackwits! My bird friends are more intelligent than you!"

Adrian straightened and his eyes blazed, his Plantagenet spirit rising. "We may be dullards in Europe, sir, but we fight with honesty. We do not torment, lie, or deceive. I am a knight and we live by a code. You know nothing of such things, I see!"

Ignatius gazed at him steadily, his steely black eyes glittering. "And where has your code gotten you, young man?" A red flush of anger rose on his face, then he turned aside and drank from his cup. "Yet I cannot waste time on you. I am needed."

"Where is the girl?" Adrian took a step forward.

"Ah. The girl. But you are not the one to ask questions. It is I. Never fear for the girl. She is well taken care of. I have something else planned for you. Do you recognize this?" He lifted a sword from his desk, proffered it hilt forward.

"My sword."

"Come. Take it, for you will need it."

Adrian received the sword and bowed. "I thank you. Now—"

"Not so fast, *mon chevalier*. There is someone who wants to see you. A *compatriot*."

Compatriot! Leon! But, no, Leon was dead. Who, then?

That moment a furious pounding sounded on the door. Ignatius flung it open. Two guards entered, dragging a girl between them. Behind came two more with a second girl.

"Judith!"

Judith looked up, staring at Adrian, puzzled, bewildered, until recognition swept her face and she smiled. The smile quickly disappeared. "So. We meet again after so long a time. How strange that—"

"Hush!" Ignatius closed the door behind them and turned to Adrian. "So now you know where the girl is. She is safe ... with me." He nodded to the four guards. They dropped the arms of their captives, bowed, and left the apartment.

Judith and Elizabeth stood together, entwined in each other's arms. Judith was dressed in the garb of a servant: white pantaloons, blue tunic, tied with a gold sash. Adrian could not help noticing how slender and comely she appeared.

Ignatius opened the door. "We must proceed to the open courtyard. Come." Six tall guards who had been in attendance along the walls of the apartment filed in behind Adrian.

He gripped his sword and followed down the hall, through Nimrod's Arch, and into the bright sunshine of a courtyard with a fountain in its center. He glanced around the enclosure, but there was no escape, no chance to bolt, for the guards closed in behind him.

The sword felt good in his hand, yet he knew himself weakened, far out of practice and in a confused state of mind. Grandfather taught him that more than half the victory of a sword fight was in your mind. Two guards stood at the arch which led down a flight of stairs. The others were excused.

Ignatius waved a hand, and from the arch stepped a man.

Adrian blinked, for the sun was making its furious descent to the horizon and shone directly in his eyes. A man approached, but his face was blurred. Something familiar about him teased Adrian's mind. Where had he seen ....

"Here he is, my lord," Ignatius said to the man. He rubbed his hands together and nodded to Adrian. "You must fight this lord of France, my friend. And the prize? Ah. Our lovely maiden, Judith. Now that I see her, I would almost fight for her myself." He laid back his head and roared with laughter.

Adrian pulled himself up. "You are a cur, sir. But I will fight this man and I will win."

Ignatius did not respond. He drew from his robe a packet wrapped in oilskin. "Another prize. A letter from His Holiness, Pope Innocent the Third. The person who delivers this will find favor with the Emperor of Constantinople, and may be rewarded with riches and fame. I would like to be the one who delivers it." He set the packet down on the edge of the fountain, then stepped back. "I will superintend the duel for a few moments, so I hope one of you kills the other quickly. I want to see blood before I leave." He bent his head. "You may begin."

"*En garde!*" The man opposite Adrian lifted his sword, took the stance. "As you can see, sprink, I wear no armor, save my leathern jerkin. This is to make the duel more interesting."

Adrian drew his sword and managed to put the sun at his back. At last he knew the identity of the man. FitzRauf. He heard a gasp and glanced at Judith. Her face was as white as new-fallen snow. She slumped to the flagstones.

He gritted his teeth. FitzRauf was a master of the sword, taller, and heavier than he, had a longer reach and years of practice. Stories of his prowess flitted through his mind, but he shoved them aside and lifted his sword.

"I wounded your son ... and by the grace of God I shall not wound you, I shall kill you. *Prepare to die!*"

CHAPTER TWENTY-THREE

The mill of God grinds slow but exceedingly fine.
English Proverb

Subebe, Friday, Oct. 21, 5:55 p.m.

The door was not locked at the top of the stair. Louis peered out, saw no one, and slipped into the corridor. His first impression of the castle was moldy stones, for he came in at the lowest level. There was very little to see save rooms for storage, water cisterns and cells for the prisoners. He hastened past the cells, hoping the prisoners would not see him and cry out. The smell from the dungeons was overpowering, putrefying human flesh along with sewage, rotting garbage, rats, and sour water.

He found another stair and followed it to the top. From studying the map, he knew he was under the stables and outer courtyards. He supposed Adrian would be near the stables since he would escape through the Horse Gate. Another flight of stairs led him to a wide arch that gave way into an enormous courtyard.

The courtyard was empty, save for a servant who scurried through with an uplifted tray. Far away he heard the sound of revelry, the voices of thousands who ate and drank the sultan's bounty. How long did he have? Had the wedding begun? Evidently they had started the feast, but when would the actual ceremony commence?

Each of the four walls held arched doorways. Which one led to the stables? He ducked behind a potted palm while a contingent of soldiers marched past, filed through the widest arch, climbed a stair, and disappeared.

Casting about for a possible clue, Louis started down two hallways, but returned to the courtyard. His nose led him at last to o ne that smelled of the stables. At the end of it, he emerged into a large courtyard and crept down a wide ramp. Silently flitting from embrasure to embrasure in the wall, he came at last to the stables where hundreds of fine Arabian horses pricked their small ears over the stall doors. Guards stood at intervals, whips in hand, shouting orders to the slaves. Louis kept in the shadows and watched but did not see Adrian.

He left and walked through vast archways, passed beautiful courtyards. He thought that Judith, and therefore Adrian, must be in the citadel. From his study of the maps, he knew where it was located, but finding the right way there was another matter. More by instinct than knowledge, he followed a hallway and mounted a stair, the same way the soldiers had gone a few moments before. Yes. This was it.

He approached the broad stair leading into the citadel, but two large Arabs with drawn scimitars guarded it.

The blast of trumpets and the sound of many voices echoed down the stairs. His heart dropped—the wedding had begun. Was he too late? Should he go back? Nay. Judith needed his help. He lifted his head in a haughty manner and glided from his hiding place toward the stair. Any moment he expected to be stopped and searched, but the two guards merely pierced him with a glare and let him proceed.

Another contingent of soldiers emerged from the top and began their descent. Louis kept his eyes averted. One of the men called out, "Halt! Who are you and why do you go into the citadel?"

"My name is Sheik Abdul Sha'alah," Louis said in Arabic, hoping his tone was proud enough. "I have come for the wedding of the Sultan Al Aziz."

The captain bent to peer into Louis' face.

Louis brushed past him and took another step.

"I said halt!" The captain nodded to his men. They surrounded Louis. "You do not have the look of an Arab. I swear you are a stinking Frank. I ask you again, what is your name and your business in the home of the sultan?"

He held himself stiffly, his mind racing, calculating his chances, his risks. The men muttered and glared at him and pricked him with their scimitars, circling like a pack of hyenas. They disdained him, thought him to be foolish and stupid and inept. They lusted for his blood.

Something he had never felt before rose up inside, blinding him in its intensity. He would not be captured, tortured, and killed by these heathens. With a smooth motion, he shed his outer robe and drew his sword. But at the same moment, he kicked out and connected with the chin of the captain. The captain fell, but there were four others. He tossed down his weapon, for he could fight better without it. Thank the mercy of the sweet Virgin Mother for the training he had received at Rennes!

They howled like demons and came at him without formation or thought, their blades slashing the air where his body stood a split second before. The two guards from the gate sprang up the steps. Louis flung out his robe in a sweep and caught the swords of three of them in it. At the same moment he kicked one of the guards, catching him in the solar plexus. The guard fell back and plowed into his comrade. They tangled together as they fell and landed in a heap at the bottom.

Another man rushed at him with bared teeth and extended scimitar. Louis spun away, leaping up the flight of steps, gaining the top. He was panting but not winded. He grabbed a lance that lay on the stair and stabbed the guard between the eyes. The man fell, his weapon clanging on the stone steps. Two more came up the stairs, yet now they came cautiously.

Louis danced on the top step, beckoning with his hands. But before they could regroup, he turned and fled through the arch, down the hall and up a flight of stairs. Behind him sounded shouts and pounding boots on the floor, yet he ran like a soul escaping hell. Ducking into another hall, he found a closet and, upon entering it, pressed himself against the back wall, breathing as lightly as he could. The noise of the soldiers passed by.

For now he was safe. But they knew he was near and would be looking for him. What could he do to help Adrian if he could not emerge from hiding? He laid his head on his hands and closed his eyes while tears of relief and frustration found their way down his cheeks. *Oh, Lord God, help me now, I pray.* Deep in his soul he knew it would be a miracle if he was able to emerge from Subebe alive. And what of Adrian and Judith? Where were they?

***

6:06 p.m.

Ignatius found a seat in the corner. "Hurry. I want to see one of you die."

Adrian glanced at him. "You piece of scum. You planned the deaths of many innocent people just so you could see me die."

Ignatius' lips twisted into a smile and he nodded. "I also brought Judith to Subebe for that same reason."

"Here! I am here, fool!" FitzRauf shouted. "As I live and breathe, your blood will stain these stones in payment for what you did to my son. And then I shall have my way with the woman before I kill her."

Ignatius clapped. "Hear ye! Hear ye! And if you do not kill him, FitzRauf, my men will. He will not live to deliver his message, for barons and bishops alike want to see his dead body."

The baron attacked, murmuring, "Ye whelp! Ye jolthead! By the Rood, I have lived only to kill you." Hatred like a sharp bright blade flashed from his eyes and fueled his arm.

Adrian struggled to defend himself, blocking the slashes with the clash of steel on steel, yet he was outclassed, and Tate or Gabriel or Leon were not there to back him. And he had no protection save his pride and his spirit. He called deep within himself and found a towering rage, a flame consuming everything. He screamed, a deep and savage cry. It was with such a cry King Richard slaughtered hundreds of the Saracens outside Tyre and saved the day for the Franks.

Yet Adrian was not Richard. He had not the strength of arm, nor the height, nor the monstrous passion to kill. Yet one thing the vizier had not accounted for was the strength in his arms and back and legs from lifting and hauling stones.

Adrian fought like one obsessed and knew nothing save the dance back and forth upon the marble stones, matching stroke for stroke. FitzRauf's sword pierced his guard, slashed through cloth and drew blood on his arm. And again, on the other arm. He paid his wounds no mind, yet he was losing blood and could not keep the pace forever.

Ignatius cheered when he saw the first blood, but then arose. "I see you are more evenly matched than I thought. There will be no quick solution. I must leave you to your fate. When I return, I hope I shall feast my eyes on two dead bodies."

Adrian redoubled his efforts, knowing naught but the face and eyes of his enemy, the distant splash of water upon water, his own grunts and yells.

FitzRauf was tiring. Sweat streamed down his face and darkened the tunic beneath his jerkin.

Adrian pushed his advantage and slashed viciously, catching FitzRauf's shoulder and arm in a long, rending slice. The baron screamed. Judith clapped and yelled encouragement to Adrian.

Sweat poured into his eyes as he warded off the blows that fell like the crash of the gods. The conviction came again. *I cannot keep this up ... I cannot ...* He danced back.

"You little fool. You cannot avoid my blade. Who do you think you are ..." FitzRauf lunged.

Adrian saw an opening and plunged his sword into the man's belly below his jerkin. Surprise and pain flitted across the baron's face, but he was not finished. He retaliated swiftly, more swiftly than Adrian thought possible, pierced his guard, and sank his blade into Adrian's side.

Adrian grunted and leaped back, passing a hand over his eyes, for his opponent's face wavered. Was it the sun? What was happening? He blinked to bring things back into focus. Yet the blink cost him another slash to his right arm. He stepped back and bumped into the fountain.

FitzRauf closed in with a bellow. "Ye fleeching cagmag! I would kill you in front of Lady Matilde. Frederick weds her before the year is out. But I would rather kill you now."

Through mists of pain, Adrian heard the words. Lady Matilde. His lady. *This man's son ... Frederick ...would wed his lady?* A fresh wave of hatred and anger swept over him. "I don't think so. Come! Let us ... finish this ... thou slayer of women and children. We will ... let God Himself ... be your judge."

FitzRauf's fatigue vanished, and his blade flashed with increasing fury. It nicked Adrian's arm, brushed his face.

Watch his eyes! Don't be afraid of him! Grandfather's words echoed in Adrian's mind. He parried the blows, but knew with sinking heart that his arm was tiring beyond help. Blood streamed down his arm, his side. Pain such as he had never felt before sent shock waves through his system. *Try something different. Surprise him.* He leaped on the low wall circling the fountain, and from his elevated position, rained stroke and stroke upon the baron.

FitzRauf seemed startled when his foe no longer fought below him. It took him several seconds to adjust.

Adrian did not give him those seconds, but leaped again and landed smoothly on a bench a few feet away. This time FitzRauf followed, but he was not ready when Adrian executed a back flip and landed behind him. His back was exposed. Adrian sank his blade deep, his sword cutting through the leather like through cheese.

FitzRauf screamed. Adrian withdrew the blade and sank it again.

The baron fell forward, gurgling in his blood, then lay still. Adrian staggered to the fountain and dipped his hand in the water, but Judith screamed, "Behind you!" He whirled.

Two guards descended upon him, their scimitars flashing, grins splitting their dark faces.

Adrian lifted his sword.

"This is not equitable."

He thought he was dreaming. From the corner of his eye, he saw a man enter the courtyard—a tall, well-built man clad as a guard. The man bounded to his side and even though his face was dark, his words were French and he spoke like one that Adrian knew. Yet he could not place him.

"Leon!" Judith gasped and rose to her feet, her hand at her mouth.

Adrian almost dropped his sword. "*Leon?* I thought ... ?"

Leon smiled. "To the task, my friend."

They fought shoulder to shoulder, and even though Adrian's strength dwindled with each stroke and his wounds bled, they killed their opponents and stood facing each other, panting like two thirsty dogs.

"I thought you were dead." Adrian sagged against him.

"Nay, I am not dead. At times I wish I were. But let us leave this place ere the vizier comes back. We have only a few moments reprieve. Our explanations can wait. Come, Lady Judith. We are very near the stables."

***

6:11 p.m.

Louis peered past the linen curtain on the closet. A broad hall led to the kitchens, for there was a line of servants clad in white tunics and gold scarves carrying trays laden with delicious smelling food. His robe was white. If he shed the jewelry, he could fall into their line and appear as a servant.

The ruse worked. A few moments later, he slipped off toward a doorway and found himself in a darkened hall, little used. Steps led down. He followed them. They ended in a small courtyard. One narrow corridor led away from it. Carefully, sensing a dead end, he made his way down the hall and found to his surprise that it ended in the courtyard where he had entered the citadel. Before him towered the same arch he entered by, Nimrod's Arch, and a flight of marble stairs descended to the outer castle gates.

He joined a group of Arab lords who strode to the arch. They descended the stairs, nodded to the guards, and headed for the apartments where the guests stayed overnight. He veered off as soon as he was out, and made his way towards the stables.

As he crept down a hallway, he heard a commotion. It was getting louder. Shouts. Screams. He hurried toward the sounds and entered a large open area where a melee of dim shapes fought. The dust was so bad he choked on it and then drew his scarf over his nostrils. At the center of the fighting stood a large form adorned with a bristling black beard, who wielded a sword like an ax. *Baldic!* Baldic here, fighting them off like flies.

A body lay at Louis' feet. He picked up the scimitar and entered the fight, for it seemed Baldic was in need of help. His first man was surprised by his rear attack and Louis killed him with one stroke. The next man was more than he bargained for, and now he was in trouble. The man's blade slashed close, tearing his robe, but not his body. But soon ... very soon it would slice through his neck.

Oh, dear Father in Heaven and blessed Mother Mary ... receive my soul.

***

6:21 p.m.

Adrian allowed Leon to bind his wounds with strips of cloth torn from his shirt.

Then he led the way from the courtyard, picking up the packet Ignatius had left near the fountain and tucking it under his tunic. Judith and her maid followed.

A commotion stirred the depths of the castle like a nest of bees disturbed. Shouts and screams and the clash of sword on sword reverberated from the stables, but when they flew down the ramp and entered the courtyard where horses were unsaddled and led to their stalls, Adrian stopped dead in his tracks.

An Arab man, bloody sword in hand, faced off with one of the sultan's guards. The guard had the advantage, pressing the strange-looking Arab back against the stone wall. The tall Arab would soon die. He shrugged and was about to turn to the fight when he stopped. *Wait.* Two Arabs who fought? He looked again. The face of the smaller man—he was not Arab, he was Brother Louis.

Adrian flew to the fight and dispatched the guard with two strokes, but was quickly engaged by more soldiers on every side— hundreds of them, it seemed. From the corner of his eye he saw Judith standing back, her hand at her mouth.

At one point Adrian looked up to see a large Arab holding a jug above the monk's head. Louis was concerned at the time with his own fight and did not see the jug descending.

Adrian leaped, crashed into the solid body of the man, the jug smashed on the stone floor, he fell, rolled, entangled in the man's robe. The man hit his side. Ah! Pain ricocheted through his body. The Arab straddled him; strong hands at Adrian's throat, strangling him.

A crash exploded. Pottery flew, and the man holding him fell. Another jug smashed into his head. Adrian leaped to his feet. The Arab lay dead at his feet. But who ... he turned. Judith held another jug, ready to throw, her face as white as her tunic. *She!* An Arab guard came at him with scimitar whining through the air. Adrian dodged, slashed with his sword, the scimitar stirred his hair, he stabbed, connected, spun, swiped sideways, found his mark. The guard fell.

But there were too many. The small space near the stables seemed to be full of the sultan's guards. Judith screamed. Adrian swung around to see a guard grab for her, but she stabbed outwards with a knife, the man turned away.

Where did she get a knife?

Another figure fought silently in the gloom—a burly black-haired man who growled under his breath, whose sword flashed in the dim light of the torches, felling guards left and right.

Baldic! How did he ... ? But there was no time to wonder, no time even to think. Dark faces were all around. Adrian slashed and whirled and slashed again, a macabre dance. All about slain bodies lay; the floor was slick from the blood; maddened horses thumped against their stalls, reared and screamed.

A sudden silence fell upon the stables. The Arabs retreated, regrouped. A peal of trumpets in the outer courtyard and shouts from a thousand Arab throats resounded down the hall. Adrian called his friends together. "Flee ... with Louis. Baldic and I will guard your backs. Go!"

Louis led the way with Judith and Elizabeth following. Last of all ran Adrian and Baldic; Adrian had to pull the warrior along, so full of the fight was he.

"We must go back ... through the lower tunnels. They will ... follow," Baldic said. "We feared the instructions from Ignatius to meet you at the Horse Gate. So we found another entrance, an unguarded cave entrance. Here. We must go down, sire."

Adrian turned and saw three flights of stairs descending into the bowels of the castle. Glancing back, he noticed that Baldic was right -- the Arabs had seen their escape route and followed, their steps echoing against the stone walls.

"We need to stop them." Baldic pulled out a pouch from his belt. "Here. Take this. Pour some of the black powder on the landing, then throw a torch upon it. But we must be away when you do. I will keep them off."

Adrian received the pouch and carefully poured some of the black grains on the landing. It must be some of the strange fire Baldic used earlier. He grasped one of the torches from the wall cressets.

Baldic held off the soldiers for as long as he could, then ran back. "*Now!*"

They descended six steps. The soldiers were almost to the landing. Adrian threw the torch up the steps. "Run!" He cleared ten steps in great, desperate leaps before an explosion rocked the stairwell. The tremor shook his footing and he fell headfirst, grabbed for a post, and pulled himself back from the abyss. Vaulting down the remaining steps, he looked back. A gap the size of the widow's house yawned where he had just stood.

The Arabs who were nearest had fallen to the depths below. The others cried out and strove to gain a footing on the crumbling stones. No one would use that stairway for a long time.

A few moments later, Adrian and Baldic arrived at the cave mouth where Louis held a torch. Adrian took a deep breath and lifted his hands. "We are all here." He noted each one: Judith and her maid, Louis, Samson John and Baldic. No. Not everyone. *Where is Leon?* He shook his head. That man appeared and disappeared like a genie. No matter, they must be away.

Louis slapped his back. "Well done, Adrian."

Adrian winced. "Go easy there, friend. FitzRauf's blade bit deep. And we are not out of danger yet." He tried to make eye contact with Judith, but she kept her eyes lowered and her face covered with a scarf. Was she not glad to see him? Thankful to be free?

He lifted his voice. "We must flee. Louis, douse the light. Follow Samson John and go quietly. We are near the walls. They will hear a footfall on a night like this." He took up a position at the rear and watched as they filed out of the cave and into the night.

Silent as wraiths, they drifted down the hill, following the gully, the walls of the fortress hovering over them. The lights on the battlements pricked the darkness and the occasional mutter of a guard drifted down like softly falling leaves.

Adrian winced over every snapped twig, every grunt and groan, every clattering rock their feet dislodged. But there was no outcry from the fortress, no pursuit.

Judith slipped and fell, for the slippers she wore were not suitable for the rocky ground. Baldic took her on his back and Adrian carried the maid, Elizabeth, even though his wounds sent shrieking pains throughout his body.

They reached the church where the horses stood at the rail in the courtyard, four of them, saddled, packed and ready to go. Louis bound Adrian's wounds again, and Adrian changed his clothing, for his garb from the fortress was soaked in blood. He mounted the Arabian gelding Louis had purchased, sorry he had had to leave Bret at Subebe.

A storm brewed in the dark sky as clouds flitted across the face of the moon. They made their silent way across the courtyard. Adrian dismounted and closed the gate, then turned at the sound of hooves on the hard street.

A man on a tall bay approached.

"Hold up," Adrian said in a hoarse whisper down the line. He wanted to tell them to flee but something looked familiar about the dark rider and the horse. The moon suddenly showed the rider's face. Adrian expelled his breath. "Leon. And you ride my horse."

Leon laughed quietly, pulling back his hood. "Aye, *mon ami*. He was alone in the sultan's stables and no one was about, so I thought to ride him to freedom. Whither are you going, my friend? Do you want to ride your own horse?"

"Nay, he seems to favor you. We are heading south, toward Jerusalem. There is a monastery, Louis tells me, near the Sea of Galilee, at the ancient village of Capernaum. We may stop there. But … you are coming, aren't you? I would like to hear your story since I left you lying dead on the road."

"That is a matter we will take up later. I do not like being left dead on the road. Proceed, my friend. I shall catch up with you. I want to do some scouting in the rear." He reined around and galloped into the blackness.

Adrian moved forward in the line and told them what Leon said. He nodded to Louis. "Lead off, Brother. I would like to shake the dust of this place forever."

***

Saturday, 4:03 a.m.

Judith caught herself on the verge of falling from the horse several times throughout the long night. She knew Elizabeth fared no better, for she arrested her descent several times, as well. Would Adrian never stop? Surely they were beyond danger now. Surely they were out of the sultan's reach.

She smelled moist earth and heard the music of running water. She was so thirsty she thought she would die. Twice she almost called out; twice she stilled her voice. She pressed her lips into a thin line and pinched her arm when she grew sleepy. If the men could ride like this … forever and ever into the mouldering darkness … then so could she.

Mist lay in pockets of the low-lying ground as light grew steadily to the east, casting long, black shadows on the lumpy ground ahead. As the light grew, Judith saw the lumps were bushes. Again she heard the babble of a river. She swung her head to get her bearings.

They had left the outlying skirts of Mt. Hermon and were descending into the Hula Valley where the newly born Jordan River flowed in a deep rift to their left.

She glared at the man's back who led them, Adrian D'Arcy. He had rescued her, yes. But he had also left her in France, would have abandoned her on the road, took no heed of her, and paid her no mind until ... Why had he come back to Subebe? She shook her head. It mattered not. He was a despicable Christian knight. Her hatred flamed fresh and hot. Why did he bother with her affairs? She wished herself free of him—of all who were of the Catholic faith.

At last Adrian pulled back his mount. He waited until they had gathered around. "We must find a place to camp. We are all very tired."

The monk nodded. "Aye. Where would be a safe—"

From the side of the road burst a dozen or more Arab riders, screeching a battle cry. Adrian yelled and kicked his mare into a dead run. Judith screamed.

The nightmare was not over. Her horse needed no prodding; she merely clung to the saddle and prayed that Elizabeth would stay put. The girl's arms were wrapped around her so tightly she thought she would suffocate.

They were in an all-out race for their lives. Adrian glanced back and so did Judith. The riders gained. Up ahead she saw a forking of the way—one way led up into the low hills on the right, the other descended into the dense growth along the riverbed to the left.

Judith found her voice. No one would capture her again—not ever! "Yahweh! Hear me now! Save me, I pray!"

***

Adrian kicked his gelding and appreciated the burst of speed from the Arabian. Reaching Louis' mount, he called out, "Go to the right!" Next to Baldic, he called out, "Take the left!" He dropped back and caught Judith's eye. Her face was pale and her veil had blown away, yet she rode the white Arabian horse like a native.

Elizabeth clung to her as a dying man clings to the prayers of a priest.

"Where are we going?" Judith shouted against the wind and the flying mane.

"Follow me! We have to separate!" He did not look back to see if they heard. As the road dipped into a ring of trees, he reined sharply to the left, dropped into a wadi, the horse leaped the bottom of it and climbed the other side with a clatter of rolling stones. Judith's mount did the same, then he led to a clump of trees where large rocks gave protection. He pulled up, surprised that Samson rode behind the girls. He must not have heard the instructions, or seen Louis riding up into the hills.

He rode back to the boy and explained as well as he could what happened. Samson reined around and was about to kick his mount when Adrian caught the reins. "Nay. You must stay with me." The boy grunted and groaned, but Adrian would not budge. "If you go out there now, you will be killed. Your master will find his way to us. Stay close."

He peered out from behind the rocks, gratified to see that the riders did not follow. Off to the right, near the cliffs that ringed the valley to the west, spurts of dust erupted where they pursued Louis. He prayed the monk would be able to elude them.

But they had to keep moving. When the Arabs discovered they followed only two horses, some of them would return to the road and follow their tracks.

He slid to the ground. "We have to walk."

Judith nodded, and the two girls dismounted. Her shoulders slumped and she walked with a shuffle, leaning on her maid. Adrian felt sorry for her, but there was no other way.

He chose a route leading into a valley where a stream flowed. They drank and allowed their horses to slake their thirst. Judith made no comments, only a word now and then to her maid. Adrian led them on at a slow, crouching gait. He watched the road to the left and kept sheltered by bushes and rocks.

"I can go no farther." Judith slumped down behind a bush. "I ... I am sorry."

Adrian gave her a drink from his flask and dug some bread and figs from his pack. "Here. Eat these. Can you ride a little farther? I see a green place ahead. We will camp there."

She nodded and swallowed a few bites of the bread. "Yes. I can make it that far."

***

Saturday, 6:01 p.m.

That evening, Adrian roused Judith. The girls had slept a little over four hours—he slept none at all. She woke and stretched and shook Elizabeth awake.

"Are we safe yet?" Elizabeth arranged her torn gown.

Judith shook her head. "I don't think so. Hurry."

Samson helped Adrian saddle the horses and they mounted up. Just before they left, Adrian saw a man—two men—on horseback approaching from the road. He pulled back into the shadows and drew Judith with him.

That horse … the man …

He cast his hands in the air. "It is Leon, by St. Jacques!" He dismounted. Leon stepped down and Baldic tumbled from the horse, more dead than alive.

Leon seemed at the end of his strength. "I found him down by the river. No horse. He fought them off, it appeared, for there were bloody spots on the grass. I imagine they took their dead. I gave him some water but he will need to rest."

Adrian led them to the camping place.

Baldic rested for a short time, then drank again and ate. He told his story. "They came like demons, but they did not know my sword." He patted it lovingly. "We killed plenty of them and they tired of the fight. They realized they had the wrong person." His blistered face broke into a grin. "So, hadn't we better ride?"

Adrian swallowed hard, amazed at the man's resilience. "As soon as you feel up to it."

"I feel up to it. I surely don't want to meet them again."

"What about Louis?" Judith gathered her robe and put her foot in the stirrup. "Are we just going to leave him?"

Leon mounted. "I shall go find him. Where did you send him, Adrian?" He was dust- covered and burned by the sun.

"Up in the hills." Adrian motioned to the west. "Meet us at the monastery." He glanced at Baldic. "Take Samson's horse and he can ride behind me." He tightened the cinch on his gelding. "This

Arabian isn't as big as Bret but he has a great stride and will go until he drops. Come along, my son."

The next evening they came to the ancient ruins of the city of Capernaum on the Sea of Galilee. Adrian rang the bell at the gate of a monastery. A black-clad monk answered the bell and opened the gate. One look at the weary, wounded travelers was all they needed to offer medicine, water, food, and lodging.

"Are you all right?" Adrian asked Judith after they had eaten and the brothers came to show them to their rooms. He longed to see a glimmer of good will in her beautiful eyes, but there was nothing but hatred. He touched her arm, but she shrugged away from it.

"Leave me alone," her eyes said.

He felt a prickling on his back, anger rising to the fore. At least she could thank him for saving her from Subebe. Suddenly he remembered something he should tell her. "Judith, I—"

She turned on her heel and left without a backward glance.

Adrian clenched his fists, forgetting what he was about to say. *Let it go. She is not worth the trouble. She is a merely a Jew, after all.*

CHAPTER TWENTY-FOUR

Happiness often sneaks in through a door you didn't know you left open. John Barrymore

Jordan Valley, October 22, Saturday 5:03 a.m.

Fleeing the Arab soldiers who came like a pack of mad hyenas on his tail, Louis rode up into the hills above the Jordan valley and hid behind an outcropping of rocks. He rode and stopped and listened and rode again.

Late in the afternoon he dismounted at a small driblet of water and allowed the horse to drink. It was a mistake, for the Arabs found him. Out of the gully they came, screeching and wailing. He left the horse and fled into the hills, hiding behind rocks, waiting, running, hiding, praying. It seemed an eternity of hot rocks and blistering sand.

Dropping exhausted behind a clump of bushes, he listened. No Arabs sprang from the rocks, no hoof beats, no screeching voices. Every muscle screamed with pain, his wounds bled, his mouth was dry, his tongue swollen. Sitting beside a large rock, he bound up his cuts as well as he could with the filthy ends of his old black robe, then leaned back and closed his eyes.

Delirious with heat, the loss of blood, fatigue, and thirst, his mind wandered in a haze. He saw visions of battles, of bloodshed, of swords piercing the heart of a man. And his familiar nightmare returned.

Mama! He squeezed the one word from his dry throat. The earth was damp, moisture seeped up through his hose, the sun a pale orb that disappeared behind a green hill. He caught at a twig and leaned forward, but horror kept his throat closed over the words that surely would have been his doom.

She was held in the arms of a burly knight. The other knight approached with a smile of victory and lust upon his face and a sword in his hand. She kicked and screamed oaths that would have burned the ears of a sailor. A backward thrust of her elbow found its mark in his crotch. He released her with a howl of pain.

The other man advanced quickly, thrusting his blade toward her, but she eluded the sword and ran for her mattock she had dropped on the road. With that in hand, she twirled and hit her enemy's head with a solid thud. He dropped like a stone in water, but the first knight recovered and came at her.

This time he knocked her flat with a blow to her chin and held her on the ground. Louis closed his eyes, heard the man's laughter and after a bit, the sound of horses' hooves on the hard-baked road. He ran with all his strength to where she lay. She was not dead, but a gaping wound in her chest gushed blood. She opened her eyes and at first did not know him. He knelt beside her and gathered her head into his lap, weeping.

"It is you, Son." Blood seeped from her mouth. She fumbled in her cape, inside where a pocket was and drew out a purse. "Take this, Son. It be yours. I ... I found a hidden cache of jewels ... yea, it be true. I sold them ... but these men ... they wanted more, they wanted me." She paused, and he thought she was gone. Then she roused. "It ... it be getting dark. I would not ... give them what they wanted. I am sorry ... " She moaned and touched his face. "Give your life to God, Son. He will ..."

Her hand dropped and her eyes closed. He laid his head on her breast and cried until he thought he could cry no more. The burgher of the village found them and carried mother to the house. She never opened her eyes or spoke more words.

The next morning she died.

Louis awoke. He lifted his head and heard the song of a bird nearby and the sound of water. *Water!* Slowly and stiffly he rose and found the creek flowing from the hills above. He washed his face and his body, tended to his wounds, and sat down on the sand under a tree.

He remembered the dream, yet he knew it was no dream. Now he knew how his mother died. And why. He understood the mystery of the jewel he had given the abbey. Laying his head in his hands, he wept.

The memory had been so painful that he had buried it deep, and only his ordeal in the desert had brought it back. He sighed and lifted his hands to the heavens. "Go with God, mother," he whispered, crossing himself, hoping that she had.

He rose and trudged to the road below. Arabs or no Arabs, he was going to find his friends and make his way back to France.

Hearing hoof beats, he tensed, ready to flee. But the man who stopped beside him was tall and lean and carried himself like a lord. Louis was gathered like a child in strong arms ... and knew no more.

***

Monday evening, October 24, 1202

Adrian and Samson sat in the courtyard of the monastery and nursed a fire. It seemed the boy had adopted him, but Adrian minded it not, for the boy was good company. They had spent the morning resting. Adrian allowed the monks to tend to his wounds. He watched for Leon and Louis, but neither came, and now the sun sank behind the low western mountains, casting long, bright rays into the sky.

He turned his face so Samson could see. "They will come. You must have faith."

The boy shook his head and stared at the fire.

Judith and her maid approached, finding a place to sit on a low bench near the fire. Baldic stood and stirred the fire. "Now, Adrian, I must hear of your adventures in the fortress."

"There is nothing to boast of. I followed the plan that Ignatius laid out for us, up until the time when the virgins made their procession down the hall. I intercepted the last maid in line, knocked her down, and we rolled down a stairway. But it was not Judith." He glanced at Judith with raised brows.

She did not look at him, but spoke to Baldic. "I changed places with the maid who did our hair. I feel badly, for she was probably punished. It was the only thing I could think to do. Elizabeth and I found our way to the marble stair, but they captured us and took us to that man's apartment. We were there when Adrian fought and killed Baron FitzRauf."

"FitzRauf? Here?" Baldic straightened, cast a startled glance at Adrian. "And you killed him? I heard he was the best swordsman in all of France."

Adrian nodded. "Aye. By the grace of God."

Judith gazed at Adrian for the first time and nodded. "For killing him, I shall be forever in your debt, Sir Adrian."

"I did it for myself as much as for you. Yet I am glad that justice was done. He was an evil man and everything he touched turned to evil."

Baldic held his hands to the fire. "When did Leon come in?"

"In the courtyard where I fought with the baron. Ignatius offered me Judith as bait. If I won, she was mine. But after FitzRauf was killed—"

Someone banged on the gate. Adrian rose, but before he could take one step down the tiled walkway, Samson uttered a cry and leaped to his feet, darting down the lane as fast as a startled deer, yet he could not see who shook the gate or hear the sound.

At the gate stood two men—one held up the other; both seemed at the end of their strength. Behind them stood a horse—a great, beautiful horse—but he, too, hung his head and seemed about to topple over.

Leon and Louis.

Adrian nodded to the gatekeeper who opened the gate and allowed them entrance. Louis slid to the ground and lay still. He was covered with dirt and sand caked his face and hair. Samson fell upon him, weeping aloud.

Adrian knelt beside him. "Louis! *Eh, mon Dieu!* Louis." He tried to brush the sand from the monk's face. He glanced up. "Leon. Look at you. You are as bad as he. Come in and ... " He could say nothing more, for tears choked his throat and blinded his eyes. At last he recovered his voice. "Judith! It is Louis and Leon! Bring some water! Hurry!"

The next morning, Adrian entered the courtyard where the others had gathered. He glanced at Brother Louis who lay on a cot. The monk wore a black robe and cowl, one that the brothers in the monastery gave him. Samson sat on the tiles, his eyes never straying far from his master's face. Every time Louis moved, the boy leaped to his aid.

"We must hear your story, Brother Louis," Adrian said as he seated himself on a low stone wall. "I trust you are well enough now to tell us."

Louis nodded. He was still weak, his hands were bandaged, and his face was burned and bruised, but his eyes shone with joy as he gazed upon the group. "I … can hardly believe that we all escaped." He brushed tears from his cheeks and told them his story. "And so Leon rescued me. He was as an angel of God, for I could not have gotten more than a mile down that road on my own."

"Another miracle," Adrian said in a low tone. "It seems God and the blessed Virgin Mother have been busy." He turned to Leon. "Now we must hear your story, for you have wandered in and out like the proverbial genie."

Leon laughed. "I felt like a genie, for certes. I do not think I shall ever recover from your abandonment of me on the road that day, Adrian."

Adrian lifted his head, frowning. "I was a prisoner, if you must be reminded."

"I know. I was only jesting." He laughed again. "Well, after they left me, I revived somewhat and a man came along who gave me aid. A Greek physician. Said his name was Stefan. He was on his way to Acre."

Judith gasped. "Stefan! But I know … I knew him. He saved my life. I lived and worked in his hospital near Damascus. He is one of the finest surgeons I have ever known."

Leon nodded. "I found that out. He took me to an inn and there he treated my wounds for many days … perchance a week, I know not, for I was unconscious for much of it. Then he bade me fare well and left. A few days after that, I made my way to Panais, for I heard them say something of Subebe and I guessed that is where they took Adrian."

"I shall be glad never to see that place again," Adrian muttered under his breath.

"I stayed in an inn and saw Samson John in the street one day outside the home of the medicine woman. I did not want to identify myself, for I felt that I could do my work best alone. And so I came to Subebe and hired myself to the vizier as a guard. I think he knew something was up, for he is very clever. He may have been playing along just for the fun of it."

Louis nodded. "Who can fool Christopher Ignatius the Third?"

Leon tossed a stick into the fire. "By that time, Adrian had escaped, and I discovered that Judith was held there against her will. I stayed on, waiting for my chance to help her. That I did on the day Adrian fought with Baron FitzRauf. I knew something was afoot, but

I could not find Ignatius. When I arrived at the courtyard, it was almost too late. The guards would have made diced chicken out of my friend in few moments."

Adrian frowned. "I think not, sir. Yet I was never so glad to hear a human voice as yours that day. I shall be forever in your debt." He held out his hand and Leon took it in a firm handshake. The others around the circle murmured their thanks. "And now I think—"

A loud clanging at the front gate erupted. Adrian looked down the tiled walkway toward the outside gate. "Now what?"

Louis lifted his head. "It is the signal for help. Someone threatens the monastery."

Templar guards dashed toward the gate. Adrian and Leon joined them. A young European man, dressed in gaudy silks and velvets, wearing a jaunty felt hat, stood at the gate. Two Arabs dressed in the white and gold of the sultan's service, accompanied him. It was these two that caused the uproar.

"I would speak to Adrian D'Arcy," the young man said.

Adrian nodded. "I am he. Leave the two Arabs outside and we shall talk."

The Templar knight opened the gate.

Adrian stopped a short ways down the walkway and faced the young man, speaking in clipped tones. "Who are you and what do you want?"

"I was told to deliver this to your hands." The young man reached inside his tunic and withdrew a rolled parchment.

Adrian broke the sultan's seal and read aloud the message, which was written in French. "So you won and killed my nice French lord. I see you took the missal and the girl and killed many of the Sultan's servants. He will forgive you their deaths but he will not forgive you for stealing the bride. We were one short and he was shamed. The girl's name was read in the ceremony, so she is legally the bride of the sultan. He wants her back. If she is not delivered to Subebe in three days time, he shall send a thousand warriors to your doorstep. You may be able to hold off that many for a few days, but not forever. I would not be cocky if I were in your shoes. It is not a light matter to bring the wrath of two powerful sultans upon one's head. Faithfully Yours, Christopher Ignatius III. Post Script: Do not touch the girl. The penalty for touching one of the sultan's brides is death."

Leon leaned over Adrian's shoulder. He let out his breath when Adrian rolled the parchment..

Adrian turned to the young man. "You may tell your master that I care not what the sultan thinks of Judith. She is a free French woman and we are under the authority of the king of Jerusalem. We will no more turn her over to him than fly to the sun. Tell him that."

The young man bowed. "I will tell him, but he is not my master. I am from France, as you are. My master is one you know and love."

Adrian stiffened. "Who is that?"

"Baron Hugh of Lusignan, he who is called le Brun. I am Lord Montgomery, and I have been following you ever since you were freed from Rouen."

"For what purpose?"

Montgomery shrugged. "To keep track of you. I send back reports. He pays the bills." He shifted uneasily. "My guess is that he wants you back in France to upset King John. But that is only my guess."

"I see." Adrian glanced at Leon. "I have business here in Palestine to perform for the holy father, Pope Innocent III. When I have completed that mission, I shall write to the baron myself. You can go now."

Montgomery did not look happy at being dismissed, but he bowed and left.

"It seems your dreams are coming true." Leon flung an arm around Adrian's shoulders as they walked back to the others. "After all."

Adrian laughed. "After all, I may not want his offer. But, come. We must talk with the others and decide what we should do."

Back in the courtyard he read the letter from Ignatius. Then he addressed the group. "Have we escaped Subebe only to have Judith taken again? They may stop us at the gates of Jerusalem, for the Arabs rule all this country. What shall we do? Where will Judith be safe?"

"I bring trouble upon all my friends," Judith said bitterly. "Why don't you leave me out on the road? They will find me ... and I shall not be a burden to you any longer." She turned her face away.

"I have a solution to the problem, but ..." Louis sat up. "But I fear it will not be ... acceptable to the lady, or to you, Adrian. But I must say it, for it seems the only way." Silence greeted his words.

He took a deep breath. "The only safety for Judith from the Sultan lies in proof of her marriage to another man."

Judith gasped.

Adrian cleared his throat and glanced at the girl. "Are you are suggesting that she marry one of us?"

"No. I cannot. This is why I fled from Subebe." Judith's face was ashen. She stood. "I could not marry the sultan. Now must I marry another heathen?" She turned to face them as wisps of her dark hair escaped her long braid and floated free in the breeze off the sea. Hatred and despair stirred the depths of her dark eyes. She held her slender body as taut as a drawn bowstring. She spoke each word distinctly. "Let them come. Kill me where I stand. But I will not wed this dog ... this Christian knight."

Adrian strode to her. A red haze filled his vision and he clenched his hands at his side. His words were low, yet they carried to every corner of the courtyard. "I have never hurt a hair on your head, Judith Itzchaki, yet you hate me. All of us here risked our lives to rescue you from Subebe, yet you hate us. I shelter you from harm, I protect you, I care for you as tenderly as a mother, yet hate is my only reward. Is there never an end to your hatred, woman?" He took a deep breath and paced to the low wall, then back again.

Leon made a motion as if to stem the rising tide of emotion. "Adrian—"

"Why must I bear this thing as if I, and I alone, hurt you? Do you think that no one else in this world has suffered wrong? What if I were to tell you that I lost my mother, sister, lands, titles, knights— all to the greed of my uncle? You have nothing in this world save your friends who are gathered here. We who could have died in Subebe."

She averted her face as if he slapped her.

"Look at us! Do we deserve your hatred? Why would I desire to wed a Jew? I would do it only because it is my duty. I would do it to protect you, not to consume you with lust or greed. We would be wed in name only. This I vow to you, Judith, for I am pledged to Lady Matilde. This I swear." He marched away.

***

388

Judith fled to her room, flung herself on the pallet, and wept bitter tears. Elizabeth tried to comfort her, but she pushed her away. "Go away, please go away. I must be alone."

When the tears were finished, she sat up. Tears alone would not cleanse or heal. What, then? The only other source for help was her faith in God. Was there healing of this sort from Yahweh? Would He answer her prayer?

Sighing, she knelt. "Yahweh, Lord God of my fathers, I pray that Thou wouldst take notice of Thine handmaid. I cannot heal my heart. Heal me. Oh, God! Heal me." She wept again and balled the blanket with both fists. "I don't want this thing ... this hatred. Take it away. Touch me with Thy Spirit. Help me to see the Light. Give me love. Please. Please. I beg of Thee."

She waited, silent, expectant. There came a stirring in the room, like the stirring of leaves blown upon the wind. A Presence descended, and a hand reached into her cold heart.

Quiet, joyful tears washed her cheeks. The Presence lingered a moment, then was gone, but a glow remained in her heart as if she had been dipped into the waters of the Jordan, as had Naaman. Truly, she was healed of leprosy of the heart.

A little later she returned to the courtyard. "I ... have something to say to all of you." She glanced at Adrian, but he sat on the wall with his back to her and kept his eyes averted.

"Say it then and be finished." Adrian's voice cut through the air like a knife.

She moved to him and laid her hand on his shoulder. It was a light touch that she allowed to continue for a few moments. "To you most of all, Adrian. I have been consumed with hatred for all Christians. You know that. A few weeks ago, I wounded a man who was far better than I in every way, a man who saved my life. I pushed him away because of my hatred." Tears choked her words.

"Stefan." Leon whispered the name, but Judith paid him no mind.

"I do not want to continue this way for the rest of my life. I thank you, Adrian, for your speech." She took a deep, ragged breath. "Please forgive me if I seem ungrateful. I know you risked your lives to save mine. I can never repay you for what you have done for a person you hardly knew, yet you loved and gave of yourselves. I have asked Yahweh to cleanse me of my wicked ways. I am willing to wed you, Adrian … if you would have me. Please be patient with me, for I have learned a wrong way of thinking and feeling. It may take time to accept you fully." She bowed.

Adrian held himself stiff and unresponsive.

Leon stood. "We are in a place of peace and quiet. The wedding should be done quickly, before the sultan's men arrive. I shall go and call the priest. Is there … anything you wish, Judith? I am sorry we cannot provide you with a Jewish wedding."

She shook her head. "It matters not. I will clean up a little." She bowed and went to her room.

***

Adrian bolted to the sea and paced along the shore in shock. While he had spoken bold words to Judith, he was filled with doubts and fears. What of his kingdom? He knew how important marriage was to royalty, the binding two nations, adding strength to each. He must not marry a Jew if he had any hope of sitting on the throne.

Yet there was something that gnawed at his soul like a dog with a bone. Now he faced it. Hatred. He had spoken to Judith about letting go of her anger and bitterness even as a small voice told him he harbored greater hatred than she.

He gazed out over the waves. His feet trod the place where Jesus called His disciples—a solemn place, a quiet place. A cool breeze from the sea brushed his hair and cooled his hot brow.

Yet he balled his fists and shook his head. He had a right to his hatred. It was his right to sit on the throne. It was his duty to revenge this wrong. For certes, he would make a better king than John. He fell on his knees and lifted his face to the sky. *Oh, God. I made a vow. I must fulfill it.*

A vision of the old god appeared before his mind. What was his name … Dagda? As Adrian thought of the Celtic god, his passion flared and hatred seared his mind as surely as if he had entered a furnace. He shrank back. *No. I do not want the old god.*

A voice whispered, "I can help you revenge your loss. I can help you kill—"

"Nay! I do not want you!" The face disappeared. He shuddered, his heart suddenly heavy, a sense of despondency overwhelming his spirit.

"What shall I do?" He groaned, grasping handfuls of sand. The sand sifted from his fingers. He looked at it. Just like his kingdom. His family. His love. Gone forever.

Closing his eyes, he saw a throne room where courtiers, barons, women and great people knelt before him. A crown rested on his head—a crown of gold and jewels. Gems glittered on his fingers and gold and silver shone in the candlelight. Power, fame, glory and honor were heaped upon his head.

Grandfather stood in the corner and sorrow filled his eyes. "You must give it up, son." The voice was gentle, but it was as if a sword pierced his heart.

"But how shall I give it up?" Slowly he unclenched his fists and opened his hands heavenward as all the dreams and ambitions of his life were poured out on the sand.

Grandfather. In his mind's eyes he saw the old man bending over a crippled child, his voice pleading with the Lord of All, tears streaming down his cheeks. Adrian heard Grandfather's voice, "My God and King, Jesus Christ, has made something of me. By His grace I live to honor and please Him."

He wept into his hands for his losses. Grandfather showed him the way of grace. He must forgive, not seek vengeance. He must sacrifice … what was it Grandfather said once? "To be a good king, you must rule with love and you must be willing to sacrifice your own life."

He raised his eyes to the gray clouds that covered the sun. "How can I give it up? How?" He bowed his head.

In the sand he saw two bare feet. They were scarred with nail prints. *Jesus!* The truth dawned on him: someone Else lost a kingdom, someone Else walked a long, humble road, someone Else suffered beyond words to describe. Sobs shook his body. He crumpled on his face.

"It is Thine, Lord," he whispered. "I give it to Thee. I give Thee my life. Please forgive my sins. Grandfather taught me to ask Thee for that. Forgive me for pride and hatred. Forgive me for the joy of killing. May I be gentle and kind, as Thou were when Thou walked this earth. I thank Thee, my God and Father. I thank Thee for hearing my prayer."

He stood. A bird sang from the row of tangled bushes near the shore. A ray of sunshine touched the clouds and turned them gold.

He looked about with wonder. Was this the same place? Why did everything seem to dance in lambent light? Where was the old hatred that sucked the life from his soul? Why did he feel … ten pounds lighter? From whence came this joy?

Adrian brushed the sand from his knees and returned to the monastery.

Another thought struck him. *What of Lady Matilde?* Would she wait through the years for him to return, only to discover he had married another? How could he break his pledge to her? But a sense of peace settled on his heart and he heard a voice whisper, "The Lady Matilde will find her way, and her salvation in Me. Leave her to My care."

***

The sun was starting its arc to the western mountains and a mourning dove cooed in the bougainvillea bushes. Adrian found Leon, who sat apart, perched on a rock, elegant and graceful even in his simple, travel-worn clothes. "Why is it not you who weds the beautiful woman? Indeed, you are a better man than I."

Leon chuckled low. "We will leave that judgment to God above, *mon ami*. As to marrying, I must inform you that I am married already."

Adrian looked up to see if he jested. But, no. He was serious, yet amusement twinkled in his dark eyes.

"It is true. She was taken from me by my father when I left for … life on the other side of the road."

"I did not know. I am truly sorry."

"Do not be, Adrian. It is part of the pain I carry. It makes me a better man."

Baldic joined them, and Adrian turned to him. "Well, Baldic, you old soldier. What do you think of the events that have transpired?"

Baldic smiled. "You are a fortunate man, sir. She is a lovely woman, Jew or no. I give you my blessing, and I pray you have a peaceful marriage."

So it was that Adrian, surrounded by Brother Louis, Samson John, Leon, Baldic and Elizabeth, was wed that day to a Jewess named Judith. As they joined hands and repeated the vows the priest intoned, he was stirred by her beauty, by her sweetness, by her trust.

She smiled slightly as she took of the bread and the cup, listened intently to the Latin words with a slight frown, and said, "Aye."

Adrian crushed the cup beneath his foot and spoke the Hebrew words she had written out for him. He bowed to her, and they signed a parchment. He noted the date. The 25th day of the month of October, Anno Domini 1202. Leon and Baldic and the priest signed in turn. The parchment was rolled, sealed and put away in Adrian's bags.

The brothers of the monastery invited them to a meal prepared in their honor, drawn deeply from their stores. They served their best pomegranate wine served in silver goblets for the bride and groom. Roasted chickens nestled beside freshly made bread, a dish of lentils was served with sweet cakes, cheese, pomegranates, figs, olives and oranges.

After the meal, Judith allowed Elizabeth to go to her rest while she sat before a warm fire that crackled in the courtyard, wrapped in her cloak. Beside her, very near, sat her new husband, and across the fire her good friend, Brother Louis. Baldic and Leon had ridden to Jerusalem on business of their own.

The night came down softly as the waves of the sea kissed the sand and the stars appeared in sparkling clusters. The *sirocco* gusted across the courtyard, stirring the coals of the fire. Palm branches whispered in the night like silly children at play. A palm stood in her home in Troyes, and also in Dijon. She lifted her head to the tree and smiled, peace filling her heart.

"The east wind blew like this the night my mother died." Louis sighed and pulled his robe closer.

Judith lifted her head. "Louis, I am sorry for you. Tell us the story, my friend, for an evil wind blew the night of my mother's death, too."

They listened in rapt silence as Louis told the story with many tears. "It was as if God was telling me it was not my fault. That she died because of greedy men, but not for the will of God. I can rest in that knowledge."

Judith touched his shoulder and met his eyes. "We have all suffered losses, my friend. I was wrong to think only I had lost loved ones. I wonder what transpires in France. I miss it. And you, Adrian. You still have family—." She put her hand to her mouth. "I am sorry to remind you, my husband."

Adrian cleared his throat. His voice was low. "Do not apologize, Judith. It matters not to me now, for you see, I found an answer to my problems today. I longed to regain my kingdom that was stolen from me, but I met another king just now down by the sea. The King of Kings." His voice dropped to a whisper. "I saw His feet. They were scarred by the nails."

Judith pulled her robe closer as the wind blew on the fire as if trying to put it out.

Adrian cleared his throat. "I yielded my quest, and pledged my troth to Jesus."

Judith lifted her face to his. "I would learn of this Jesus." She turned the word over in her mind, surprised she could say it without the sharp stab of hatred she had often felt. "I once hated Him, yet now I see ... I see something different in you. Would you teach me, Adrian?"

He nodded, tears stinging his eyes. This was far more than he expected. "Aye. It will be my pleasure, Judith." He looked into her eyes and dawning in them was the love for which he had longed all his life.

Louis cleared his throat. "Forgive me for asking, Lady Judith, but were you on some sort of pilgrimage ... a quest when your guardian, Jonas, was killed by the Arabs?"

Judith stared into the fire and Adrian noticed she fingered two capsules on a golden chain on her neck. "Yes. Yes, I was. And perchance one day I shall continue it." She lifted her eyes and smiled. "I want to tell you, now that we are married, about the secret I carry."

"Only if you desire it, *ma cherie*." He grasped her hand and kissed it. She did not wince or draw it back.

With her other hand, she drew out the two capsules. "My Gran-abba gave one of these to me when he died. Jonas gave me the other. Inside are scrolls, very ancient scrolls, on which is written a secret. There are two other families who have carried this secret down through the ages. When the four scrolls are together, the words reveal where the ... " She struggled to continue. "Where our ... temple treasures lie. They have been buried since the days of Jeremiah, and we believe that when they are found, the Messiah will return. I must find two more." She replaced the capsules.

"I see." Adrian leaned back, let the air go from his lungs. "I promise that when you feel the time is right, I will help you all I can. For now we will let it lie."

She looked up, her eyes shining with gratitude. She squeezed his hand. "Thank you."

There was a pause, then Louis said, "What are your plans, Adrian? I would like to travel on to Jerusalem, to worship at the Church of the Holy Sepulcher."

Judith gripped his arm. "I would also like to travel to Jerusalem. Perchance I may find some of my relatives there."

"Oh. Oh!" Adrian straightened.

"What's the matter, Adrian? Are you in pain?" Louis leaned forward.

"I just remembered something. Judith, my dear wife." He knelt before her on the pavement and took her two small hands in his. "Please forgive me, for I forgot to tell you that I found someone."

"Whom did you find?" Judith smiled, her eyes alight. "Is it good news?"

"Very good news. I could not give you a gift for our wedding, but perchance this story will please you. You see, when I was enslaved in Subebe, I met a man. A Jew."

Her eyes widened. "Yes?"

"We were not allowed to speak, yet at times we did speak, and we became friends. I admired him, for he was very strong. He did not seem strong; he was so thin. He had endured terrible torment and punishment for four years. We escaped and came to Panias. He left that night and walked to Jerusalem to find his family. He said he wanted to visit the Holy City, and then journey back to France, for he was French. He is in Jerusalem now."

She did not breathe. Her face drained of all color and her eyes were huge and dark, sparkling with a light of their own.

"Judith, his name is Elias ben Itzchaki."

She did not respond.

He began to repeat it, thinking she had not heard. "His name is—"

Suddenly she rose from her chair with uplifted arms and screamed. She would have fallen, but he gathered her close and held her while she wept and cried and laughed. "My father? Tell me all … how he fared … what he said. You say he is in Jerusalem. Well, then. We will depart on the morrow. This is the greatest gift I have ever received. You do not know ... cannot know ..." Again she wept and Adrian held her until her body stopped shaking.

"We may leave on the morrow, yes," he said, wiping tears from his eyes. She laughed and gave him a kiss on his cheek. They sat again on the bench.

Adrian related everything he could remember of her father and tried to answer her questions. The bell tolled from the monastery— two tolls.

They stood, and Judith laid her hand on Adrian's sleeve. Her face shone. "Now I have a husband and I have found my father who was lost. Thank you, Adrian D'Arcy, for you have given me my life when I despaired of it." The smile she granted him was as a burst of the sun's rays from behind a cloud, as stars falling from the heavens on a velvety night sky, as the sparkle of sunlight on the waves of the sea.

He bowed to her as she left, then resumed his seat beside the fire, unable to speak.

Louis was the first to break the silence. They talked of many things while the stars spun on their predetermined course. The bell from the chapel tolled thrice.

Adrian lifted his head. "Ah. We must get our rest. The monks will be up and about in a short time." He rose. "Well, what do you think of the day's events, you lean old monk? Do you suppose God is pleased with my actions?"

Louis laughed. "I know not what God thinks. And yet ..."

"Yet? Yet what?"

Louis drew himself up, beckoning to Samson who lent him his shoulder to lean on. His face became solemn, lightened by a twinkle in his eyes. "Yet I think you have made a very good choice indeed." He chuckled, grasping Samson's arm, pacing to his room.

Adrian gazed up at the star-studded sky. He remembered the stars from his mother's castle, how he watched them on a soft summer's night, and wondered where his star would lead. He remembered the stars as he studied them outside a small hut in France, and the gentle words of his teacher, giving glory to God.

And now, he was free. He stood and strode the length of the courtyard. Grandfather spoke of freedom. Leon spoke of freedom. Now he knew what freedom truly meant. He was free of his mother's spite and avarice and control. He was free of greed and passion for power. He was free of the evil that lurked in the courts of the powerful and mighty.

He raised his hands. "Oh, God, I thank Thee. You have set my feet on the solid rock and have given me a wife—Judith the Jewess." He stopped in utter amazement. Who would have thought he would wed a Jew? But was there ever a woman as beautiful and gracious as his lady?

A sense of responsibility fell upon his shoulders. "My God and King, I give Thee my life and pledge Thee my troth. Help me to become the kind of man Grandfather saw in me, for I know it is only by Thy grace and mercy."

Smiling, he found his pallet and stared at the ceiling, thinking not of Matilde, but of Judith—the love in her eyes, the promise in her kiss.

***

If you enjoyed *Sirocco Wind from the East*, purchase the sequel, *Mistral Wind from the North*, available on most online venues, from the author, and also as an ebook on all outlets. Watch for *Zephyr Wind from the West*, coming soon.

About the Author: Virginia Ann Work lives and works in Chewelah, Washington. Her husband, Dan, is the pastor of the Chewelah Evangelical Free Church. She has three grown children and five grand-children (and one on the way!), whom she adores. Her hobbies include painting, chalk art, hiking, reading, and having fun with her family.

A note from the Author: Writing Sirocco Wind from the East was pure joy. From the very first, I wanted to incorporate the story of Prince Arthur of Brittany (a real-life character) and found much fodder for the grist mill in Thomas Costain's book, *The Conquering Family*. Most of the characters surrounding Prince Arthur are from the pages of history, and some of the events in the story truly occurred. Judith's great ancestor, Rashi, was a scholar and law giver among the Jews and is revered by them. The situation in Palestine is drawn from history, with the conflict between the Arabs, the Jews, and the Christians continuing to this day. I was carried away with this story and when it was completed, found myself back in America in 2008, a little sad that it was finished. But I soon began the sequel, *Mistral Wind from the North*, and found myself once again back in medieval days with Judith, Brother Louis, and Adrian. Thank you for buying this book. For comments or discussion topics, see my website or search Virginia Ann Work:
http://www.virginiaawork.com

Glossary of Unfamiliar Terms

Al Andulas—Spain

Anjou—A province in central France, ruled for a time by the English (Angevin) kings

Aquitaine—A province in southern France that Queen Eleanor brought to her union with King Henry II; a rich English duchy for many centuries.

Bailiff—the underlord of the baron; the bailiff lived in the manor house and ran the daily affairs of the manor or fief, in later times, it became synonymous with sheriff

Bailey—a courtyard of a castle, enclosed by the curtain walls

Barbican Gate—steel mesh or linked iron gates that fell downward above the front gate after one crossed the drawbridge

Below the Salt—the salt cellar (large and usually chased) that sat upon the table of nobles and marked the dividing line between noble and serf. Nobility sat above the salt, commoners sat below it

Boon—a special gift or grant of land, money or position

Castellan—another name for lord or baron; one who owns castles

Chased—metal engravings on objects such as cups or flagons.

Corsairs—pirates

Cressets—brackets in the walls that held torches or large candles

Croft—a narrow strip of land behind the house of a commoner (see Toft)

Fief—an area of land under control by a baron

Franks—a general term used by those in Palestine from Europe and England; those who stayed in Palestine after the Crusade and lived there. The Franco-German Empire was a huge conglomeration from France to the Northern Sea. Later on the term *Latin* was also used to designate Christian armies from Italy.

For Certes -- For sure or certainly

Hallmote—local court of law held by the baron to settle arguments, assign punishment, and hear grievances. There were no courts of appeal and two sets of law governed the people under Norman law—one for the nobles and one for the commoner

Keep—a tower in the center of the castle complex; the last stronghold, usually where the baron and his family lived

400

Kirtle—a garment worn by women of the blouse family, drawn tightly at the waist. The tightness at the waist may have given rise to the later term *girdle*.

Largess—the master's benevolence or gratuity

Missal—religious portion of Scripture, later known as a letter

Necessarie—(or *garderobe*) the bathroom facilities

Outreimer—the coastal strip of Palestine from Joppa to Antioch that the Crusaders held until 1291 when the last fortress, Acre, fell to the Turks. Also called the *Levant*.

Pantler—a servant who brings the first course, the bread and butter.

Pledge your troth—pledge allegiance to a higher power and become his vassal

Postern gate—a rear or side gate for the use of the servants

Saracen—one of the many names for the enemies in Palestine and the Middle East. Others were: *Seljuk Turks, Arabs, Muslim, heathen*, or *paynim*. The common denominator of these was their faith, which was Muslim.

Saxon—from northern Germany

Seamster—a man who sewed garments for a living

Scimitar—a long, curved sword used by the Turks and Arabs

Scrip—a purse pilgrims carried to the Holy Land

Shaven Poll—a derogatory name for monks because they shaved the tops of their heads

Souq—(*suq*) Middle Eastern market place

Trenchers—a stale piece of bread used as a plate for meat and gravy, in later times it was an oblong wooden bowl

Toft—a narrow strip of land in front of a commoner's house (see croft)

Trailbastions--outlaws who lived in the forest with a gang of men, much like the legendary Robin Hood

Trouvere—French word for *troubadour, bard* or the German *minnesanger*

Vassal—a servant or slave; knights who pledged themselves to the king or baron

Villein—lower class of people in the feudal system, also called *serf*. Villeins were above slave, but below land owners and freed men. They were bound to the land and to the baron, and required to work so many days a year for him. They could not relocate. They received a small yearly compensation, a house, a strip of land they could work for their own table. Most had a few animals. They were not usually skilled or educated beyond farm work and menial tasks.

Virgate—a small portion of land allotted to the villeins to work for their sustenance; in some case they owned this strip of land. If so, they were called *virgaters* and they moved up a notch in the feudal system. Most serfs would rather own land than be free.

Wadi—a narrow gully where a river flowed in the rainy season in the Middle East

Wattle and Daub—a method of using mud and straw to build the walls of the houses of the commoners. These houses were flimsy affairs, and could be broken into very easily. No wonder the wolf in the Three Pigs story could huff and blow their house in!

<u>Reference books used to write this story:</u>

History of the Crusades, Vol. 1,2,3 by Steven Runicman
Historical Geography of Asia Minor by Ramsey, Vol.2
The Crusades by T. John
A Book of the Medieval Knight by S. Turnball
Pilgrims and Crusades by G. Evans
Deus lo Volt! Chronicle of the Crusades by Evan S. Connell
The Conquering Family by Thomas B. Costain
Life in a Medieval Castle by Joseph and Frances Gies
Life in a Medieval Village by Frances and Joseph Gies
Life in a Medieval City by Joseph and Frances Gies
The Knight in History by Frances Gies
English Through the Ages by William Brohaugh
The Lost Ark and the Last Days by Randall Price
France from the Air—by G.A. Rossi and J.L. Houdebine
Reader's *Diguest Illustrated Great World Atlas*
Medieval England by Brian Williams
What Life Was Like in the Age of Chivalry by the Editors of Time-Life Books
A Chronicle of History of Knights by Andrea Hopkins
Chronicles of the Crusades—edited by Elizabeth Hallam

Made in the USA
Middletown, DE
28 December 2020